MW01532120

CHALLENGE

JOHN J. NOONE, ED.D.

Noble House
Baltimore, Maryland

CHALLENGE

Library of Congress
Cataloging in Publication Data
ISBN 1-56167-421-4

Library of Congress Card Catalog Number:
98-86523

Published by

Noble House

8019 Belair Road, Suite 10
Baltimore, Maryland 21236

Manufactured in the United States of America

DEDICATED
TO
Persons with Handicaps
and to
My Colleagues Who Helped
and
Set Examples
Over the Years

Foreword

The setting for this story is in the early 1970s in La Plata, a small, quiet city in southern Maryland. It was beginning to feel an increase in population as city dwellers in the nation's Capital began to emigrate, seeking more open space for their families, yet close enough for a daily commute.

With expansion, some of the urban social ills began to appear. A survey of the population to determine the number of persons with handicaps, proposed by religious leaders, was the starting point for a range of activities well beyond the original purpose. As a result of young professional leadership in various disciplines, the community marshaled its resources and encouraged cooperation between agencies. The hospital and college joined hands, the school board and the newspaper recognized joint responsibilities, the state police became active locally, and the Carmelite Monastery opened its doors for a successful retreat for women, to cite just a few programs.

The focus of this story is on two young people who strive to meet the challenges set before them by family, friends, and the culture. But in a larger sense, it is the community which is awakened to the stereotypes surrounding the person with a handicap, the need for prevention for many of society's social handicaps, the training of young people for the professions, and the problems faced by the families of individuals who are unable to participate fully in society because of a disabling condition.

La Plata is but a symbol of what can happen, and in many instances does happen when the needs are exposed.

Chapter I

"Doctor, can I see my baby?"

"Here he is, Mother," the physician said as he placed the red faced infant on her breast. Anne McCoy squeezed her twenty-four years into a short plump body with black hair, smooth features and a strong body. She had just made it to the hospital the previous evening when her contractions began to increase. Now it was all over.

"He's so cute. I see a little of his father in his nose and mouth even at this early stage." She was exhausted by the trauma of labor pains, and the ride from the ward to the delivery room, but was now relieved with the birth of her first born, a son.

It had been a frightening experience for her, more because of the unknown, and she had wondered if she would survive the ordeal. Her small stature was accentuated by the bigness of the baby in her womb, but she was a solid woman. The doctor who had examined her said he could foresee no problems and all she had to do was rest and relax.

"Tell Al he got his boy, and I'm all right." In a few minutes she handed her little bundle of love to the nurse for the usual examination and the preventive medications.

Alvin and Anne McCoy had been married for four years when they decided to begin their family. She knew that Al wanted a son, but he had no preference, and he'd cherish a boy, a girl, or twins—whatever.

Along with the other expectant father in the waiting room, Al had paced the floor, read a page of a *Life* magazine, lit a cigarette, put it out after a few puffs, then repeated the process. This was his first child, and he was a worried young man. He suspected that Anne was having a hard time, and he really should be praying for her, but he found it hard to concentrate on anything.

Suddenly the double door swung open, and from the corridor came Dr. Patrick Bolton. He spotted Al near the window and moved toward him to announce in his gruff voice, "Mr. McCoy, your wife is resting comfortably after presenting to you and the world a son. Congratulations!"

"AAHH, thank God! Is he all right? How did it go? Can I see her?"

"You can go in for a few minutes, but don't stay too long. She's a bit tuckered out, and needs to rest."

"Thanks, for all you've done."

"No, not me. She's the one who gets the nod. I was present only to see that everything came out all right. The staff is examining your son and he appears to be a fine boy. Before you go in, the nurse will give you a gown for protective purposes."

Draped in the rumpled white gown, Al leaned over the side of the bed, put a hand on Anne's tousled hair and kissed her on the cheek. He was relieved and happy it was all over. Anne was pale and exhausted, yet pleased for both of them.

Dr. Bolton returned to the Neonatal care room, looked at baby McCoy and wrinkled his brow. Turning to the nurse, he said, "Nurse, have Dr. Jenkins paged and ask him to come here. Thanks."

Five minutes later, Dr. George Jenkins walked in, long white coat flapping, and a stethoscope hanging around his neck. George and Pat had been friends for a long time.

"Hi Pat, what's up?"

"Thanks for coming so soon, George. I think we've got a problem with this McCoy baby."

As Pat talked, George bent down to look closely at the infant. He counted up the telltale signs, some of which were not too apparent, but trained in neurology, he could spot the diagnostic indications: epicanthus folds on the eyes, apace between thumb and forefinger, short neck and thick tongue.

"Pat, ol' buddy, it looks to me as though we have a baby boy with Down Syndrome."

"For Chrissakes, I suspected he was Mongoloid, but wanted your confirmation. This is a mess. The family will flip when I tell them."

"Sorry, Pat. This does happen when we least expect it."

A young nurse in her twenties shook her head sadly while looking at the infant, for she had seen many with birth defects, and knew the heartaches the parents would suffer.

Later, over coffee in the lounge, Pat and George were talking about the forthcoming preseason Redskins-Colts football game. They had played college football for their respective alma maters, and enjoyed the game and followed the pros avidly.

When Pat became quiet, George asked "Deep thoughts, pal?"

"No, I'm just thinking about how to break the news of his son to Mr. McCoy tomorrow when I see him."

"I'm sure you've done this before, and I realize it's not easy to tell parents they've brought another problem to the world." George replied.

"It's what I'm going to tell them to do that worries me. I hate it, but it's got to be done."

"Care to share it?"

"Simply, they've got to put this kid in an institution, right now. They can't bring him home and make life miserable for themselves. They're young and need to plan their lives around a family. This kid will give them nothing but grief."

George was incredulous. "We're playing God these days?"

"Knock it off, George. It's my case, and my decision. I want these people to have a better crack at life than hauling around an idiot."

"You've been out of Columbia Medical School two years now," George said quietly. "Did you pick this decision making up by yourself, or did they teach you that in New York?"

"You know better than to put me on like that, George. Columbia, like most medical schools, can show you how to diagnose, but there is no real treatment for Down Syndrome. You know that!" Pat was getting upset with his friend and he didn't like it at all.

"Cool down, ol' buddy. How about another cup of coffee?" As he rose, he saw Tom Shane saunter into the lounge at the far end of the room and head for the urn. He called out, "Father, bring your coffee over here and join us if you have a moment or two."

As the tall priest approached, red hair and ruddy complexion around a wide grin, George greeted him. "Hello, Father. Welcome. Pat, you know Father Tom Shane, our new chaplain here."

"Hi Padre!" Pat rose to exchange greetings and shake hands.

"Gentlemen. Thanks for the invitation to join you. What's up?"

"Not much. We're on a break," George said.

The priest sat down and with the cup at his lips and scanned the large room with brightly colored chairs grouped around tables. At the far end adjacent to the table with the coffee urn, cups, and saucers was a cabinet with current magazines and periodicals. Between the open windows with draperies flapping in the breeze was a leather sofa, and nearby a radio put forth soft classical music.

Placing the cup on the table, he said, "I hope I'm not intruding. As I entered, you two looked as though you were in deep discussion, like you had a tiger by the tail, and it's about to take you," he finished with a smile.

"Oh yeah, we were . . ."

Before George could finish, Pat broke in casually. "What's new with you, Father?"

"Not much. I'm on my rounds of the parish, and I heard that one of my flock, Mrs. McCoy, was admitted yesterday for a delivery. I came by to see her."

"Have you been up to her room?" George asked.

"I peeked in the door but she was asleep. I'll come back later to see her and the McCoy son, the nurse just told me about her delivery ."

"That tiger you just mentioned, Father, is for real, and his name is baby McCoy," George said. "Dr. Bolton and I were talking about him when you arrived. As his parish priest, you should know what this is all about."

The priest was a perceptive judge of human nature and his eyes simultaneously enveloped the two physicians. George with his broad face, mustache, and paunchiness belied a keen intellect, which contrasted sharply with handsome urbane Pat, concerned with self-importance and knowledgeable in a superficial way. The tall one was affable, caring and warm, while his short partner was calculating, cold, and egocentric.

Sensing the ominous, Father Tom leaned forward, his flush rising and a voice heavy with annoyance he said, "Well, come on, man, out with it."

"The baby was born late this morning, and after we examined him, our diagnosis is that the infant is defective—Down Syndrome." Pat dropped his voice and continued.

"I've got to tell the baby's father to take his Mongoloid son and put him away in an institution as soon as possible. He should not take him home at all. The father and I will tell the mother that complications arose, and the baby died suddenly."

"Holy Mother!" Father Tom exploded, for he was shaken to the core. It was incredible what this doctor was about to do, and he churned inside. In a quiet voice he asked, "Was the delivery all right? Any bruises on the body? No strangulation by the cord?" The questions rolled out from him.

"None at all," Pat answered. "The mother had a rough time in delivery, following nine hours of labor, but she came through it all right. Then I noticed the signs of mongolism, and called George to confirm it."

"What is the treatment for that?" Father Shane asked.

"Medically, none," George replied. "Children with this condition are no different than those born normally, and may lead a long life. It used to be that they would die young, but no longer."

Pat chimed in. "My concern is with the parents. I don't want them to age before their time, caring for their handicapped son. I don't feel it's right to saddle them with a lifelong burden." He was stubborn and anger was rising within him, as he noticed the priest's reaction.

"Do you mean to take it upon yourself to decide what is right for the McCoy family?"

"Yes, Father, and later they'll thank me for it."

"To tell the mother that her baby died, then put it away in an institution is an outright lie. It's unconscionable!"

"It's everything we have to do. Can't you see?"

"No, I don't see, Dr. Bolton. You are putting this family in an untenable position. I can't believe what I'm hearing! You plan to ask the father to join you in a terrible lie to the mother about the baby? You place him in an awful dilemma."

"He's strong, and I'm sure he'll handle it. Everyone will be satisfied."

"I certainly won't!" Father Tom shot back. Then he added, "What are the medical ethics of this?"

"I don't think there are any."

"To lie about a death when none has occurred does not come under the rubric of the medical profession? I'm amazed!"

"Father Shane, I am the physician to this woman, and I'm doing what I think is proper for her and the family."

"You have no right to make such a decision for others in such a serious matter. If God blessed this couple with a baby who happens to be handicapped, he has a purpose in mind and will provide sufficient strength for the parents to meet the obstacles ahead."

"My responsibility as a physician tells me that I have the right to advise my patients as I see the need. I'll not see this family annihilated. They have rights too, and I want to protect them."

"Are we forgetting about the rights of this child who is a member of the family and needs the protection of everyone? What of the rights of the family to make their own decisions?"

"I have a duty to perform, and I'm going to see it through."

"You also have a responsibility to be truthful!"

Dr. Jenkins raised a hand. "Gentlemen, time out. We're getting nowhere. Pat, we're late for a staff meeting. Let's take no action for a few days. See you around, Father." He took Pat by the arm and they left a shaken priest.

Chapter II

David R. Sargent, M.D., was the soul of Powell Hospital, La Plata, Maryland. He was Chief of Staff, President of the Board, and undisputed leader of the medical community. A commanding figure, he was tall, straight as a ramrod, with silver hair adorning classic features, and he bore a military posture gained during his years as a surgeon in the Navy Medical Corps.

As the seat of Charles County, La Plata was close to the nation's capital and to Baltimore, where he had taken his training at Johns Hopkins Medical School. Following his residency, Dr. Sargent returned to the home turf to start a small clinic, which grew as the town expanded, and later he was able to break ground for the hospital.

This was home to the Sargent family for generations, for the ancestral tree was planted back in colonial times. The family records show that Mary Doughtie had a regular medical practice in 1659, a strong woman who did not hesitate to haul into court colonists who failed to pay their medical bills. Another forbearer, Thomas Ware, had read medicine under Dr. James Craik, a physician appointed to the Revolutionary Army by General George Washington. Following the Revolution, Ware set up practice in La Plata and was available to care for the soldiers on the peninsula during the War of 1812. The family had strong medical roots.

As he passed the open door of the lounge, D. R. waved to his new chaplain, Reverend Thomas Shane, who was nursing a cup of coffee, and murmured to himself, "I sure hope he's better than the last one we had."

After lunch, Father Shane went to the second floor, where he chatted and laughed with Tim Murphy, recovering from a broken leg. They swapped Irish tales and he heard Tim's confession. Next was Mrs. Olsen, not doing well in cardiac recovery. He stayed a bit, reassured her that everything would be all right, and promised to see her in the morning. He made several other calls, then went to the elevator en route to the Emergency Room. He jabbed the button and stood back to wait for the slow cage to appear. Footsteps down the hall caused him to look in that direction. There he saw a woman approaching with her arms full of records. He stepped forward with a smile to say, "Can I give you a hand?"

"Oh yes. You're a lifesaver," she said smiling.

"Comes with the territory," he replied filling his long arms.

"Thanks, Father. I just over loaded myself."

He looked down at this well dressed woman in her early thirties, with brownish hair and a pleasant face. He smiled and said, "I'm Father Shane, new chaplain here. Where do these go?"

"Social Services on the first floor. I'm pleased to meet you, Father. I'm Rita Evans, new as of a week ago, and a member of your parish."

"Great Babes in the woods! This could be fun!"

Before their conversation could continue, the elevator bell rang, the door opened and out bustled a blur of white, dark hair and a round face, a big woman in a big hurry. The chief nurse spotted Rita then the priest.

"Rita, I was about to have you paged. Hi Father! You two have met? Good."

"Father Shane came to my rescue, otherwise you'd have tripped over these folders on the floor." Rita said.

"All in a day's work, Mrs. O'Bryan," the priest added.

The chief nurse drew herself up. "A simple problem solved. We've got a bigger one now. A new mother who is going to be in distress shortly. Rita, I need to talk with you. Got a minute? OK. I'll be in your office in five minutes. Father Shane, this concerns one of your parishioners . . ."

"A Mrs. McCoy?" he finished for her.

"Yes. For a newcomer, you get around fast."

"I've already had a start on this affair. I went into the lounge for a quiet cup of coffee, and before I knew it, Doctors Bolton and Jenkins let me in on the news. Dr. Bolton and I were going at it hot and heavy when Dr. Jenkins blew the whistle on us. Time out. They had to attend a staff meeting. Yes, I'd like to sit in on your discussion."

In the Social Services office, he called the rectory while Rita put away some folders and straightened her desk. Peg O'Bryan knocked, came in, closed the door and sat down as she said, "I'm glad you two have met. Sorry I didn't get a chance to introduce you properly."

The neophytes nodded and smiled at one another.

"Our Mrs. McCoy delivered a darling boy who has Down Syndrome, but she and her husband don't know it yet, as the doctors wanted to complete the examination. I have just learned that the diagnosis is confirmed, and Dr. Bolton is going to tell her, then her husband. I'm afraid that this will be tough on the new mother, for this doctor's bedside manner is less than reassuring."

As Peg paused, Father Shane spoke up. "He's a miserable wretch. He plans to lay that news on her like a ton, and then he'll tell her to put the 'idiot'—his term—away in the state institution. Or, he may come up with the suggestion to her husband, alone, that they tell her the baby died so she won't have to care for it. I could blast him."

At this announcement, both women were shocked.

Rita could hardly believe her ears and uttered a cry which sounded like, "What? He was going to do that? It's incredible"

"Where did you hear that crap?" was Peg's earthy question.

"From his very own lips over an hour ago. They were talking when I went into the lounge."

"As her physician," Peg said, "Dr. Bolton has every right to tell Mrs. McCoy the diagnosis, but there is a delicate way to do it. I doubt that he has that finesse. In addition, the plots are outrageous."

"Both are unethical, the latter one criminal," said Father Tom.

"Much as we decry the statements of the physician, we cannot lose sight of the central figure in this drama, and that is baby McCoy," Rita said. "His welfare must be our prime consideration, and this means both mother and father must be part of the decision that is reached. We are dealing with three humans, and we may not be dishonest in our approach to helping them make plans for their future with their son."

"We need to get both parents together and explain what the diagnosis means," Peg said.

"Most of all, it is important that we are here to help them in every way," Father Tom added.

"The big thing is how the message is given to them," Rita added. "It will make all the difference in the world to their reaction."

"Dr. Bolton does have first crack at telling them the diagnosis," Peg said. "That is his right as her physician."

"Also, he can handle whatever medical care and

treatment is indicated over and above the primary diagnosis," Rita added.

"In the event that there are medical problems, our job then, is to provide support and encouragement to the parents," Peg added. "We'll treat this like any normal family situation; no major decisions to be made. It's too early for that anyhow."

"Agreed. The parents need to know the baby, to love, nurture, and care for him at home as with any normal infant," Rita said.

"The less we blow this out of proportion, the better off we'll all be," Father Shane added.

"Rita, can you join me tomorrow morning, and we'll drop in to see Mrs. McCoy? I'll bring the baby in from the nursery for our chat."

" I guess that about does it for the day, ladies. I'm off and running back to the rectory. If you need me in the morning, I'll be available. "

"That's one fine man," the nurse said as the priest limped out. "He's been absolutely wonderful and a joy to all our patients."

"I'm sure our family will like him at St. Dunstan's, where we'll see him every Sunday," Rita concluded.

When the day was over, Rita steered her black Rambler north on Route 301, recalling the events of the day as they tumbled in her mind. She was delighted with the stand Father Shane took; concerned for the McCoy family, shocked at Dr. Bolton's position, and pleased with her relationship with Peg O'Bryan. A friend once described her as "gentle as a warm breeze, but have your facts ready in any argument with her."

The car turned left onto a road. She slowed down for students emerging from the community college and noted the broad green campus in front of the red brick buildings.

Three blocks away, she nestled her car next to Joe's Pontiac convertible in the car port and entered the four bedroom ranch house by the side entrance.

"Am I ever glad to be home!"

Joe Evans leaned down from his six foot height to give her a smooch and greeting, "Hi, love! How goes it?"

"What a day, bad enough to be settling into a new job, but late this afternoon, we had hell."

"I've got just the tranquilizer you need. Get freshened up, and I'll have the drinks and cheese ready in a few minutes."

"Good man, Joe, I'll need your medicine."

Over drinks, they relaxed and chatted about their mutual activities of the day, and both enjoyed this time they could share with one another.

"I met our pastor, Father Thomas Shane, today, Joe. He is also the chaplain at the hospital, and he rescued me when I had both arms overflowing with folders. I think you'll enjoy talking with him."

"Sure thing, pet. Maybe we could have him over for dinner soon."

Rita, paused, smiled to herself and said, "I was just thinking how much we've accomplished in our ten years of married life."

"We sure crammed a lot of living into that decade," he conceded.

"You didn't know it, but when I first saw you on the Catholic University campus, when we were in graduate school, you were a 'goner,' and I've never let go."

"Huh! I noticed, and just slowed down enough to let you catch up, and purposely stumbled so you could put the snatch on me"

"Anyway, it's been great, and somehow we've combined careers and a family to create a good life. I am pleased with this new job at the hospital, and it's a relief from the hassles of my other social work assignments in the District of Columbia."

"I feel the same way, love. Going for the Ph.D. was one of the best things I've done, and it has opened up so many doors for professional advancement. Of course, the Kennedy administration in the early sixties gave all of us in the field of mental retardation a tremendous boost with millions appropriated for research, staff training, improvement of programs and community development."

"Yes and you psychologists managed to get on the bandwagon early in the game, because there was loads of money to court that 'ugly duckling.' But I must say that it has paid off handsomely for you and the field."

"In many ways that was the impetus for a revolution in how we treat the entire range of handicapped people, going from prenatal care, to special education classes and vocational training, to employment of the severely disabled. It has been remarkable what money and motivation can do."

Joe unrolled his tall lean body from the chair, brushed his dark hair with long fingers and went to the kitchen." Coming back he asked, "What about our kids?"

"I passed Roger delivering his papers down the street, Beth should be coming home soon from her ballet school, and Joseph is probably up in a tree nearby surveying his world. They'll all come in about the same time ravenously hungry, and put life into this quiet house."

"Our planning resulted in a nice family, and they sure add spice around here."

"For us, adoption was the only way, and we got the best kids. Think of it. Roger was only eleven days old when we picked him up, Beth came in at full term nine months, and Joseph was just shy of a year when he made his appearance. I still don't know how we managed, but we did, and it's been fun."

"Now they are growing like the proverbial weeds, and speaking of same, here they come up the driveway."

When they came in, Rita reminded them of their chores. "Roger, please take the trash out to the barrel. Beth, help me set the table. And Joseph, pick up your clothes in the bathroom. Thanks. Dinner will be ready in ten minutes. Come clean and hungry."

Joe watched his young troops disperse, then turning to Rita he said, "We are interested in your tale of Dr. Bolton and how he plans to dispose of the McCoy infant. Does the hospital have what we call a crisis intervention team?"

"Sure, we have a team, but it is for medical emergencies only."

"Like cardiac arrest or multiple operations for a person."

"Yes. Those are necessary, but in addition, I'd love to see a multidisciplinary team of professionals to handle situations like the one we had today.

"Would you have any opposition from the staff?"

"Sure, some people would object, but I think Peg O'Bryan would go for it, and some of the younger staff."

"You've got the patriarch, Dr. Sargent, to deal with. He may buck on that one," Joe offered.

"Peg and Dr. Sargent are close. They run the place, and I think she could talk him into it, assuming she would go along. Perhaps it's too soon for me to make waves. I'll just have to wait and see."

"Powell is large enough to have most of the medical specialties on board or as consultants. You also may call upon some of our staff at the Mental Health Institute as well as the medical schools in the District of Columbia."

"I don't think we'll have any trouble getting a variety of professionals to serve. The main problem is the establishment of the concept."

"My money's on you, girl. Right now, the man of the house is hungry!"

They were seated around the table in the area adjacent to the kitchen, Rita at the end closest to the range, Joe at the other end. Beth was at her mother's right to assist, while Roger and Joseph flanked their father. His hands were scrubbed clean and hair combed, although Joseph's arms still showed signs of dirt from where he had been playing with his father, remembering his own childhood.

"Beth, will you say grace, please? Joe asked.

Chapter III

The Rambler was parked and locked, and as Rita walked to the side entrance she had a queasiness in her stomach, a foreboding feeling that something was wrong. It was there when she awakened, showered and dressed, and had her black coffee with just a drop of milk in it. Joe was usually up first, and while the coffee percolated, he showered and shaved. Then he gave her the first cup and the *Washington Post* in bed. What luxury.

At 9:00 a.m. sharp, Peg O'Bryan, with a long face, appeared in the doorway and blurted out, "Guess what?"

"I'm all ears, shoot," was Rita's quick rejoinder.

"Our friend, Dr. Bolton, did it up last night in spades. He told Al McCoy that the baby was defective and he felt it would be best for Anne and Al to let him put the baby in an institution."

"Oh, no. He can't do that!" Her mood quickly changed from shock to anger.

"Wait a minute, Rita. Al was shaken to his boots, but he had the good sense to stop Dr. Bolton so that he did not say this to Anne. He asked a number of questions about the baby, the nature of Down's Syndrome and treatment required."

"Then what?"

"Well, he suggested to Dr. Bolton that they both go to Anne's room and tell her the news. Dr. Bolton would give her the diagnosis, while Al would be present to lend support and help. Nothing would be said about transferring the baby to an institution. Al wanted to see his son, and when the nurse brought bring him in, he and Anne could see the baby together."

"Ah, there's a good man. What happened then?"

"When they entered Anne's room, she could see in her husband's face that something was wrong. She cried when the doctor told her the diagnosis and was so stunned she hardly heard his words. Al took her in his arms, and they both sobbed. It was heart wrenching and the doctor left them alone."

"How is Mrs. McCoy this morning? I'd like to see her."

"Right after I came on duty, I saw her. She's still a bit in shock, and will be for another day or so. Al is such a fine person, strong, and he'll be a big help. Yes, you should go up to see her later this morning after rounds."

Rita could hardly wait for the appointed time. As she approached the room, a resident was just closing the door. "Dr. Mackey, I'm Rita Evans of Social Services, and I'm about to visit Mrs. McCoy. How is she?"

"Oh, hello, Mrs. Evans. Good to see you." He was a recent graduate of Rochester Medical School, taller than Rita, with reddish hair and an open face that included a faint mustache just sprouting forth. "Mrs. McCoy is fine physically, but I'm concerned over her emotional state. She's taking the diagnosis of her baby pretty hard. I'm glad you're here. Go right in. She should be almost finished nursing her son by now. I was afraid that Dr. Bolton would not let her nurse the baby, but I felt she should."

With tears in her eyes, Anne McCoy looked down at her baby nursing so contentedly at her breast.

"Hello, Mrs. McCoy. I'm Rita Evans of Social Services, and I wanted to come in to see that new son of yours."

"Hello. Do come in. Mrs. O'Bryan said you'd be around, and I've expected you. How do you like our son? He's a fat rascal." She dabbed at her eyes then continued. "We're almost finished, then we can talk."

"He's a beautiful baby, Mrs. McCoy, and he looks so peaceful. Have you decided on a name for him?"

"Well, we had a name all picked out for a boy, but now, I don't know. We'll have to talk it over more."

When the nurse had taken the baby away, Mrs. McCoy had another cry, then wiping her eyes and regaining control she said, "What are we going to do? Al is such a dear and has been so good. I feel terrible about giving him a less than perfect baby. What will our families think?"

"Right now, your concern must be for your baby and your husband. Some family members may want to step in and make decisions for you, but only you and your husband can decide what are the next steps. Don't let anyone else intrude on this matter."

"I overheard a nurse saying that the new baby would probably be sent to an institution. Could Dr. Bolton do that to my baby?"

Rita was tempted to reply, "Over my dead body," but she held her tongue. "Absolutely not! You have the right and duty to care for your children. No one can take that away from you. Baby McCoy is now your responsibility."

"If he's not normal and needs treatment, how can we manage him? I've heard terrible stories about the care these children get in the state hospitals."

"Not many of us are completely normal, Mrs. McCoy. Our staff will tell you what needs to be done, including Father Shane, the chaplain, who'll give you lots of support. He is my parish priest, too."

"You know him?"

"Yes. We met yesterday and discovered that we're both new and have much to learn about La Plata. Perhaps you can help me to find the library, knit shop, children's stores, etc."

The new mother gazed off into space, then said, "He is so tiny and helpless. I'm afraid I'll mess it all up."

Rita paused to let Anne think, then said, "I don't think you will at all. How you hold him, nurse him, and talk to him will give him a sense of being wanted and loved. He was warm and secure while you carried him for nine months, and now that he has made his appearance, you are his major support system."

"How do I act like this? I might do something to hurt him."

"If there was nothing wrong, how would you respond and act? Do the same with your son. He is a person now, and despite what people might say, he has worth, dignity, a soul, and deserves an opportunity to live a full life. You and your husband have a lot of strength and can see this through."

Anne seemed more relaxed and not as tense as when Rita first came in to talk with her. She smiled and nodded as Rita continued her counseling.

"There will be times when you'll be angry, frustrated, and feeling sorry for the baby, your husband and yourself. You'll want to lash out, to hurt, and to cry. These are normal reactions, and it's better to express these feelings than to bottle them up inside. I'm sure your husband will know and understand. It will be a team effort on both your parts."

"Yes. Al is very understanding and knows how I feel about things."

"Speaking of the men folk, remember that your husband needs your attention, too. There may be a temptation to devote all your time to the baby. You do need some time for yourself and your husband, a time when you can sit and talk over the activities of the day."

Mrs. McCoy replied, "We've been so busy working that we haven't taken time to talk like you said, but I think we should."

Rita looked at her watch and rose to leave. "This has been good, and now I must be off. When your husband comes in, tell him that I'll be happy to talk with you both at our mutual convenience. The more we can respond to your questions, the easier this whole program will be. I'll not try to smooth over the tough times coming up, but if I can help you to get ready for them, it won't be too difficult to handle them."

🍎 🍎 🍎

At two o'clock, the staff had its regular meeting. This was her first appearance, for she had arrived the week before when the meeting had been cancelled. Rita looked around the large room, found Father Shane's eyes, nodded and smiled. This was a first for him, too. She swept the room and recognized a few familiar faces.

"I am pleased to introduce our two new staff members," Dr. Sargent said in opening the meeting. "Mrs. Rita Evans is our Chief of Social Services, and the Reverend Thomas Shane is our chaplain and the pastor of St. Dunstan's Church. I am happy to welcome them to Powell Hospital."

Both stood to be greeted with smiles and a round of applause.

Among the announcements was a county wide conference scheduled for October to be held at the community college; Dr. Sargent would be a participant.

At lunch, Peg O'Bryan had told her that the staff meetings were usually long and boring. Rita had confided to her and

Olivia Bowen, a dark skinned physical therapist, her conversation with Joe about a team for emergencies. Both approved the idea and thought it worthy of presentation to the staff.

As the meeting drew to a close and Dr. Sargent asked for additional items under new business, Rita raised her hand and stood up.

"I wonder if any consideration has been given to the establishment of a team of professionals who would be available in the event of an emergency."

"We do have an emergency team now, Mrs. Evans," the chairman reminded her gently.

"I am aware of that, Dr. Sargent, but it calls upon the medical specialists only for medical emergencies. We have need for the other disciplines in physical therapy, occupational therapy, the chaplain, the nurse, pharmacist and others," she said.

"In this hospital, major decisions are made by the physicians regarding the care and medical treatment of patients."

Rita was aware of this mild reproof, but was not chagrined and stood her around. "I believe our role is to look out for the welfare of the whole person, with primary emphasis on the medical and physical aspects of the patient. As each discipline plays its part in the total treatment process, we are serving the person and the community well.

"You're trying to say something, and I'm not getting the message. Please explain further, Mrs. Evans."

"This example should clarify what I am driving at. Yesterday, a woman delivered a baby diagnosed as having Down Syndrome, and the physician was going to suggest to the father that they tell the mother the baby died, and he would then arrange to transfer the infant to the state institution for the retarded."

A perceptible murmur ran through the room.

Dr. Bolton rose to his feet. "I am the physician who made the delivery, and as soon as the diagnosis was confirmed by the neurologist, I made the suggestion just outlined to the father. In my judgement, this would be the best thing for all concerned, and the family would not have to face a lifelong burden of caring for a mongoloid child."

"That is not good professional practice, Dr. Bolton," Rita retorted. "You have no right to impose your own standards on patients. Parents have rights and should make the decisions regarding their children, but they need professional help and information to guide them."

Father Shane, flushed, rose to state, "The parents of this baby are my parishioners, and are completely devastated by their son's impairment. Fortunately, the father kept the doctor's suggestion to himself."

Rita broke in, "The nurses were aware of it and the mother overheard their conversation in the hall, and assumed it was about her son."

"My plan is valid, and I'll do it again," Dr. Bolton said heatedly.

"Your plan is an outright lie and incredible!" Rita answered.

Dr. Sargent rapped for order. "Wait, let's not get hysterical. Mrs. Evans how would your crisis intervention team help in such a situation?

Calmed a little, Rita replied, "Upon confirming a birth defect diagnosis, the physician would call the nurse and social worker together to review the situation and how it would impact on the total family structure. The worker would then discuss this with the parents and with them begin to develop a plan to meet the needs of the patient and the family. The decisions would be that of the parents, based on all the available information. Other disciplines may be invited to join the team to add their skills and knowledge for a resolution of the case."

"The physician doesn't make decisions?" Dr. Bolton asked. "I find that a hard one to buy."

"His decisions are vital to the medical regimen of the patients, and all other disciplines must back him up. They are supportive, and as experts in their own fields, they must be recognized as such," Rita said.

"Thank you for the suggestion, Mrs. Evans. You did a good job of presenting this idea to the staff, and making this a most interesting meeting. I'll ask Dr. Jenkins to head up a committee to explore further the concept of a Crisis Intervention Team. It may have possibilities. Dr. Bolton, I want to see you in my office when we adjourn."

Later in the corridor, Rita was greeted with the comments: "That was wonderful!" "Gutsy way you crossed swords with Dr. Bolton." "We've disagreed before with him, but not in public." "Heroine!"

Father Shane shook her hand and said, "Right on!"

The consensus was that C.I.T. was an idea whose time had come.

Dr. Sargent wasted no time on the preliminaries as he faced Dr. Bolton in his office. "I am outraged that you would have the nerve to even think of arranging a transfer of an impaired baby to the state institution without my knowledge. For your information, Dr. Bolton, I am the one who is in charge here, and it's my responsibility to . . ."

The office door closed on his words, as his secretary insured the privacy both men needed. They were still arguing when she locked her desk and departed.

Joe saw Rita driving up to the carport, and noticed her harried face as she came through the door.

"Hi love! Have a nice quiet day?"

She burned him with a look, then pecked his cheek.

"Huh! I'm drained. A quiet day? Lord, what a bummer."

Chapter IV

"Father Thomas Shane?" The telephone jolted him for a moment on a quiet Tuesday morning and interrupted his thought for a sermon.

"Speaking. What can I do for you?"

"I am your neighbor, Reverend Albert Burns, pastor of the Lutheran Church down the street. I heard you had been appointed to St. Dunstan's, and I wanted to introduce myself and welcome you to this area."

"This is a surprise and a pleasure. Thanks. It's nice of you to call, Reverend Burns, and I hope we can meet soon to exchange greetings. This is a fine community, and many have extended a warm welcome."

"Another reason I called," Reverend Burns continued, "is to invite you to our monthly ministerium to meet our brothers in Christ. I am the host for the next one scheduled a week from today at our house."

Father Shane checked the calendar. "I'm free, and I'd be honored to attend," the priest replied. He knew that his predecessor did not belong, but he was interested, and wanted to be a part of the total community. Pope John had opened up the window, and Father Tom was an active ecumenicist.

He had no difficulty finding the house, a modest

He had no difficulty finding the house, a modest dwelling adjacent to the Lutheran Church less than a mile from St. Dunstan's.

"Glad you could be with us, Father Shane," Reverend Burns greeted him at the door and took his hat. "Do come in. The others are in my study. Today we number five, usually there are nine or ten, and our full membership is twelve."

"Hope I didn't scare anyone off," the priest said facetiously.

"These fellows don't scare easily. In fact, they are looking forward to meeting you, and they are aware of your visits to some of their parishioners who are patients at the hospital."

"Nothing to it. I just stop by long enough to say hello while making my regular rounds."

"That's just the point. You care and want to help even in the brief visits. Here we are."

They entered the study, a small room with desk, comfortable chairs and a large table strewn with books. The clergymen stood as they came in the door.

The host made the introductions. "Father Shane, let me present the Reverend James Wilson, pastor of the Methodist Church, Reverend Robert Steele of the Unitarian Church, and Reverend Jake St. John, pastor at the Episcopal Church. We're pretty informal around here, and use Jim, Bob, Jake, and I'm Al."

Father Tom shook hands with each man, accepted an invitation to a crab feast from Jim, was pleased to learn of Mr. Donaldson's reaction to his bedside visit in the hospital from Bob, and received a gracious welcome from tall stately Jake.

Al Burns started the meeting with a short prayer, then launched into a discussion of common interests like the upkeep of buildings and grounds, staff salaries, young people's activities, church music, service to the community, etc. Tom Shane found it interesting and made note of several items for use at St. Dunstan's.

He was grateful when Mrs. Burns entered the study bearing a tray of coffee and a mound of homemade Danish. She was a tall, beautiful blonde, the daughter of a minister. She had met Al when they were in college together. Martha Burns greeted the new member warmly and made him feel at home. She reminded him of his younger sister in age, size, hair, and beauty.

"We'll have lunch in about two hours," she announced. "Come hungry."

At noon, the group went into the dining room where they continued their discussions. Father Shane found the group to be informative, congenial, and knew he'd enjoy these monthly sessions.

As they finished lunch, a five-year-old boy was dropped off by the bus and came in the back door calling out, "Mom, I'm home from school!" By the time he finished talking, he was at the dining room door looking at his mother.

Martha Burns balanced the dessert tray, looked at her husband and said, "Al, will you do the honors?"

"Tommy, I'd like you to meet Father Shane of St. Dunstan's Church. This is his first visit here, and he's also the chaplain at the hospital."

The little stubby hand was lost in Father Tom's, and he looked into the priest's eyes unafraid. "I'm pleased to meet you, Father. One of my classmates goes to your church."

"I'm happy to meet you, Tommy. We'll have to get better acquainted, since we both have the same name."

The little boy's round face, slanting eyelids, thick tongue, and mannerisms all said "Down Syndrome."

A quick shake of the hand, and he was out to the kitchen ready for his lunch.

"That's quite a boy you have there, Al," Tom said when the others had left.

"When we learned that Tommy was handicapped, it was a terrific blow to me, but the staff at Powell was great. It took a while for us to get over the initial hurt and anger, but we survived, and now we love him deeply."

Martha Burns came into the room with a cup of coffee to join them briefly. "Father Shane, I heard that one of your parishioners has just delivered a handicapped baby, just like our Tommy. I do hope that Dr. Bolton hasn't been making his 'noble suggestion.'"

"As a matter of fact, you are right on both counts. The birth of the baby has these young people in a tizzy. Fortunately, our new Chief of Social Services is helping out and she is a marvel. Thank God the husband dissuaded Dr. Bolton from making a decision about institutionalization."

"When Tommy was born, our doctor did the same thing to me, and like a damn fool, I persuaded Martha to let us put him into the institution," Al blurted out.

"I was just as much at fault, and equally to blame," his wife added. She brushed a tear from her eye and a strand of blonde hair over her left ear, then looked at her husband ardently. "Al was a tower of strength during the period Tommy was away. I know how hard it must have been for him, but for me as mother, to have put away my baby, the pain of the separation was almost too much for me to bear."

"Before the end of that month, we couldn't stand it any longer and called the director of the place to have Tommy ready for us to take home," Al said.

"I can't tell you how happy we were, Father Shane, to pick up that little boy and reunite him with us. He is an absolute joy, and has made our lives meaningful," Martha added.

"I'm sure the good Lord had a purpose in sending Tommy

to us, and although he is handicapped, he is not a burden to us. Rather his simplicity and loving ways enrich all of us," the father concluded.

"Our experience with Tommy during those first few days was terrible, and I know what that new mother and father are going through. Do you think I could help in any way? Sometimes it helps when a parent who has gone through the experience is able to share with a new parent and help her over the rough spots."

"Your offer to help is generous, and I'll convey this to Mrs. Evans the social worker, and to the parents. Thank you Al, for inviting me to the ministerium, and to you Mrs. Burns for an excellent lunch and your offer to help. We'll be in touch. Good-bye."

That evening, Father Tom called Rita at home to tell her of his conversation with the Burns family and their son Tommy.

"Do you mean that Mrs. Burns would be willing to talk with Anne? Yes, by all means, if both McCoys agree," she said.

Two days later, Father Shane brought Martha Burns to the hospital, where he introduced her to Rita, and then left to make his rounds.

Rita started off. "I'm pleased with your offer to talk with Mrs. McCoy. She is a dear person and a bit shattered, but I think she and her husband have started to come up from the bottom of the pit. They are on the move."

"Having been through such an experience, I can appreciate their feelings, and turmoil. My husband's faith and goodness has been a real help in getting us over these hurdles, and it takes a strong mother to face up to something so difficult."

"Shall we go to her room and talk? She is expecting us," Rita said.

Both women had hit it off immediately, and talked all the way up to where Anne McCoy lay staring out the window.

Rita knocked on the door. "Mrs. McCoy, may we come in? I've brought Mrs. Burns, the lady I told you about, and I believe Father Shane had mentioned to you his meeting with her son Tommy."

"Hello, Mrs. McCoy. I'm Martha Burns, Tommy's mother. I think we have some common interests."

"It's so good of you to come. Please call me Anne. Sit down and be comfortable."

"Tell me, how is the little fellow getting along?" Martha inquired.

"So far, just fine. The doctors and nurses see no medical problems, and Mrs. Evans has been such a great help. When she told me you are the mother of a boy like our son, I was pleased with your offer to talk. There are so many things I want to ask," Anne said.

"Yes. I know exactly what you're thinking. It's a terrible period to go through, and if I can answer your questions, I'll be happy to. When this happened to us, I just wish there had been someone around to talk to, someone who had gone through the same trauma."

"Where do I start? It all seems so hard and difficult. If he had a birth defect I could see and could care for him . . ." Anne's voice trailed off. There was a trace of bitterness, and a tear in her eyes.

"It's really not difficult. Since he has no medical problems, act as though he has none. Most new mothers are scared stiff, but they soon get over it and take the baby in stride. Before you know it, you'll be an old hand at caring for him. Just love him and then watch the response you get."

"Dr. Bolton gives the impression that he'll ruin our lives, and we shouldn't be stuck with this burden."

"Take it from one who accepted a similar verdict and

put the baby away in the state institution. My husband and I couldn't live with the thought that our son was being cared for by someone else, and in less than a month, we had Tommy back with us. I couldn't wish this on anyone, and I would murder any doctor who would put parents through such anguish. My dear clergyman husband would read me out of the church if he could hear me now." Martha's anger soon turned into a gentle laugh.

Rita remained quiet while the two mothers talked.

"Among other things, Anne," Martha said, "keep your man happy. Devote some time for him, for men may be more aggrieved and keep it all inside. Encourage him to talk about it if you feel he is saddened."

"Martha, how did you announce to your families that Tommy was handicapped? This worries me," Anne asked.

"At first I lied to mine, that our Tommy was ill, and never said a thing about the institution. Then we both told our families flat out what had happened, and our son was home with us. My mother was on the next plane, and fell in love with her grandson. Al's parents were upset at first, but now they enjoy having Tommy with them on the farm in Vermont each summer. We sure miss him when he's away."

"What about your neighbors?"

"They have been wonderful and supportive. Tommy plays with all the kids his age and goes to the Day Care Center with several of the other children every day. You'll find the county basic in its school system for the handicapped as well as for the normal child."

"I'm happy to hear that," Rita said. "I need to know more about the facilities and resources here in the county. Perhaps you can give me some leads and information."

"Sure, anytime."

The two mothers had struck a resonant chord and talked constantly for over an hour. Anne's questions were answered truthfully, and Martha did not pull any punches. "It's not an easy job to care for a handicapped child, but it can be done, and there are many willing hands available to help you."

That evening, when Al came to her room, Anne's spirits were up as she related her conversation with Martha and Rita. "You'll like her. She's very down to earth and straightforward. They must be a devoted couple and have other children, too."

They exchanged activities of the day, and when the baby was brought in for his nursing time, Al just sat there watching with tenderness. Before he left he said, "I think we should arrange for Father Shane to baptize our son as soon as the doctors let us go home. I'm tired of this place."

"Me too," Anne replied. "I'm anxious to leave and get settled at home once again. Rita Evans and Martha Burns have helped so much, I feel better now, and not so much alone. I think we can handle this lad, with some help, of course. How do you feel, Al? I mean about our son?"

"I've still got some questions, and I'm a little worried, but nothing major that would cause me to leave the McCoy son and heir either here or in the state institution. We have enough friends now to help us if the going gets rough, and I guess it will at times."

"OK. Let's go home when they spring us loose. Also, we'll need to think of a name for our boy."

"By all means. You seem so much better, tonight, Anne, and you've given me a lift. Tonight, I'm going to celebrate and let off some steam."

"Good night, dear. Have one for me."

The following Sunday afternoon, Father Shane baptized the baby in St. Dunstan's Church before his parents, godparents, and friends. James A. McCoy was brought spiritually into the house of the Lord, and physically, with much love, into the house of McCoy. The Evans and Burns families were special guests and rejoiced in the decision Al and Anne had made.

The reception was lavish. Al McCoy went all out to celebrate the birth of his son and the arrival home of mother and baby. It was a warm September day, so the neighbors and family could drift out into the yard. On the porch, a buffet was laid out and the table groaned with food.

The two clergymen were under the shade of a maple tree enjoying their meal. "It's too bad the Catholics dropped Latin from the liturgy, Tom. I felt that it added something special to the Mass. In high school and college, I took quite a bit of Latin, and considered myself a scholar."

"With a twinkle in his eyes," Tom responded, "Me too. I could even dream in Latin, and this was long before Pope John changed to the vernacular."

"Ol' Pappa Giovanni was quite a guy. Too bad he didn't hang around longer. I had great admiration for the man."

"If he had, he probably would have reconverted the Lutherans!"

The two men were on an intimate first name basis and enjoyed their repartee. Tom had won the hearts of the Burns family when he accepted their Tommy so freely.

"I've been thinking," Al started to say.

"That's dangerous!" Tom shot back.

"No, seriously, Tom. We know we have two handicapped kids just in the Burns and McCoy families. I wonder how many other children are handicapped in one way or another. What have we done for their spiritual lives? Our Tommy can sit in church with his mother and listen to me preach, but that's over his head. We need something down to earth for these children."

"If the churches are doing nothing in this area, perhaps our ministerium should explore ways and means to fill this void. Let's bring it up at the next meeting and see what the others think about it."

"Apparently this is a neglected segment of the population, and we know what Christ said, 'Suffer the little children to come unto me.'" Al continued, "There are others who need our assistance, and I'm concerned with adults who are handicapped in wheelchairs, on crutches, and those unable to go up or down steps. How do these people ever get to a church, if at all?"

"I make home visits, hear confessions and bring them the Eucharist during the week. I suppose some haven't been to Mass in a long time. I've just arrived and know only a couple of people so disabled. There may be a lot more."

"Friend Tom, we have some work to do among our clerical brethren, and we need to compare notes as to who is doing what for the handicapped."

✄ ✄ ✄

Jake St. John was the rector of St. Agnes Episcopal Church, and as host for the meeting, was pleased to introduce his quest, Rabbi Halpern whose congregation was in Bethesda, Maryland. They had been friends for many years.

Al Burns broached the topic of reaching out to meet the spiritual needs of handicapped children and adults in the county. The idea met with instant approval, for none of the clergymen had done much beyond making home visits or going to the hospital.

Rabbi Halpern spoke up. "I've been involved for several years in pastoral counseling for the handicapped, and I'd be happy to share some information with you. This is a vitally needed area for all concerned. First, you need to know your population at risk, and this involves the degree of disability, age range, mental/emotional illness, church affiliation of the family, behavioral problems, etc."

"Once we gather this information, we can begin to plan to serve them," Al said.

"This is a mighty big job, and it won't so easy," Bob Steele offered.

"Whoever said that the job of a clergyman is easy," Jake said. "I'm all for it. Let's get going."

Al Burns was asked to chair the committee to set in motion plans to survey the handicapped population of the county. Tom Shane and Jake St. John were members, with Rabbi David Halpern to serve as a consultant. An initial form would be drafted and sent to all the other members of the ministerium for additions, deletions and comments. A final form would be given to the church membership for completion. The local media would be asked to donate public service time to cover those who wouldn't get the information via the church. The ministers had taken on a large order.

Chapter V

Rita was on her way to the Community College to attend the conference Dr. Sargent had mentioned in the staff meeting that awful day when she blew up. Dr. Bolton had been cool to her ever since, and she had a good idea what had transpired when Dr. Sargent confronted him behind closed doors. Her own perceptions had been reinforced by talking with Peg O'Bryan later. Not much escaped those eagle eyes!

Dr. Jenkins asked her to serve on the committee to explore the concept of a crisis intervention team, and she gladly accepted. They were making progress and hoped to present a complete protocol at the next staff meeting.

Several new buildings attested to the evolvement of the college from a stepchild to a full blown facility providing academic and vocational skills in the two year curriculum leading to the AA degree.

As Rita waited for the elevator, she noticed the section devoted to Human Services and made a note to inquire what this involved.

The conference was concerned with the interrelationships of community agencies, and she learned about the social and civic groups from one end of the county to the other. By the time it was finished she had made numerous notes about people and programs which she would use advantageously later. While the conferees were people in her own age range, she enjoyed being on the campus and liked the idea of being with the young people she saw there. Rita felt that students were open-minded and inquisitive in their approach, not hardened in cement as many of her peers were.

A few days later, she had finished talking on the telephone with Anne McCoy who was doing quite well with her son James, along with the assistance of Martha Burns, when Dr. Sargent appeared in her doorway.

"Got a minute or three?" he asked.

"Why yes, Dr. Sargent. Do come in."

The director came forward to sit by her desk, wearing a wan smile and a perfectly fitted tan sports jacket and brown slacks. "I'm here to ask if you would be so kind as to substitute for me at the college next Wednesday. Dean Keyes asked me to talk with the students in the Human Services sequence on the handicapped child. This conflicts with a meeting I have at the State Health Department, and I wonder if you are free?"

"Yes, I am free and will be happy to substitute."

"Thanks, Rita. Call Dean Keyes and get the details. I'll get back to him to confirm these arrangements. You'll enjoy the students there and the faculty. The college is a credit to this community, and I'm happy we can cooperate with them."

After he left Rita glowed, knowing it was the first time he had called her by her first name. He had been gracious to her ever since the staff meeting and admired her forthright stand on an issue.

❧ ❧ ❧

She strolled leisurely across the campus, passing students engrossed in thought or gabbing, and was ushered into the office of the dean. He was of medium height, middle age, and balding fast. Clasping Rita's hand, he brought her over to a woman seated near his desk to say, "Let me introduce you to Dr. Claire Cohen, Chief of our Psychology/Sociology Division. While I was the one to invite Dr. Sargent, it is Dr. Cohen who is in charge of the meeting on Wednesday, and with whom you will be working.

Dr. Cohen rose, extended her hand in welcome, and flashed very white teeth in a large round face. "I'm pleased that you can be with us, Mrs. Evans, to join our group of faculty and students. Many of our staff are involved with the handicapped in one way or another, and we felt that it would be helpful to have someone from the hospital speak to us."

Dean Keyes added, "We want our students in the Human Services Sequence to get a picture of the total individual who has been injured which may or may not pose as a handicap. Dr. Sargent has told me of your background in Social Work, and of your counseling with patients at the hospital."

"I'm happy to hear you refer to the disabled as a person first, then the condition which may delimit his/her capacity. This has real meaning for the families of the persons who have a disability and focuses more on their identity as an individual," Rita responded.

"It would be most helpful if you would bring this into your presentation, Mrs. Evans," Dr. Cohen said. "Professionals often deal with the patient and neglect the other members of the family in the program."

"I'll include that point in my talk," Rita said, "and at the end I hope to leave room for questions and discussion. I'm looking forward to the program."

"You ladies seem to have this well in hand, so I shall

leave. Good to have you with us, Mrs. Evans," Dean Keyes said as he departed.

"Do you have the time for me to show you around our campus?" Dr. Cohen inquired. "We're rather proud of our buildings, but even more so with the caliber of the faculty."

"Why yes, I'd be delighted."

As they roamed down the main corridor Rita noticed the soft colors on the walls and the paintings and said, "I'm interested in the Human Services Sequence you offer."

"The student spends four semesters in class with emphasis on the basics—English, history, math or a science, physical education, public speaking and electives. Depending on the interest shown, specialties are available in areas such as nursing assistant, social work, behavior modification, teacher's aide, etc. The student goes out on agency visits the first year, and in the second year he/she is assigned a block of time to work in an agency under supervision doing a practicum. We are always looking for projects for them, so keep us in mind if you will."

"That sounds interesting, Dr. Cohen, and I'll be happy to think of your program, and how we may collaborate."

En route home, she stopped at the store for some gourmet items, for she was careful of the diet she provided her husband and children. She believed in basic meals, not heavy on the calories. Salads were a big favorite, along with fish and chicken for the evening meal.

She was the first to arrive home, and by the time Joe's car came into the driveway, she had the ice cubes in the glasses already.

"The makings are all out, dear," as she reached up to kiss him. "Dinner is in the oven, so we don't have to rush."

She thought he looked pooped out as he nibbled on cheese and crackers.

"Any mail today, Rita?"

"A few bills, the usual junk mail and a nice letter from mother."

"What's up with that ol' rascal?" He was fond of his mother-in-law, and Rita knew that she had a soft spot for him.

"She wants to come down next week for a visit, so you'd better not be away on a trip. She'll be disappointed if you're not at the airport to escort her home here."

"When she calls confirm her reservations and arrival time, tell her to bring that big black bag with all the money in it. Bet she's loaded!"

"No way is she loaded!" Rita retorted. "You know right well that after Daddy died in '68, she's run the farm and practically supported those characters up there. The woman has more brains than all of them put together. She just needs a rest from the arguing and fighting that goes on there at the farm. That brother of mine I could shoot!"

"Well, Esther is no slouch in an argument, and she can start one, too."

"Don't get me started on that crew! Better fill your mouth with cheese and crackers before you say something about my family. Dinner will be ready at six sharp."

Rita had taken his mind off the day's work and told him about the meeting at the community college and her presentation on Wednesday.

Later that evening after the kitchen was tidied up, Rita organized her notes, sought help from Joe, and began mentally to cover the major points of her speech. They worked well as a team, supplementing one another.

The lecture hall was filled with students and faculty when Dean Keys introduced her on Wednesday the fifteenth. Rita was calm and assured as she gazed at the two hundred faces arranged on sloping tiers.

"Good afternoon. I am honored to be here to share some

thoughts about working with persons who have disabilities. The Total Person is what I choose to call this talk, and I plan to leave room at the end so that we can engage in a question and answer period.

"To begin with, no matter how mild or severe the injury or disablement, the person has a self which must be protected. We are all aware of the kinds of insults to the physical body of the person, but the insult to the inner being, the attack on the self identity can be equally or even more damaging.

"Let me give a few examples of what transpires. There are now too many persons in institutions for the mentally retarded who are unable to leave because parents don't want them at home, or they have no families, or society doesn't want them in group homes and too often refuses to recognize them as independent individuals. These persons with mild or moderate handicaps are fully aware of these insults, yet they are stigmatized by being in the institution and prevented from enjoying full citizenship.

"There is the person with cerebral palsy who has normal intelligence but whose erratic physical movements becloud the fact that he can function in a job, yet employers will not hire him. Given the opportunity, he can be an asset to a company, but the refusal dampens enthusiasm for going out to challenge the world.

"As for the family, the impact can be quite severe. When the newly born infant is diagnosed as having a handicap, the parents are faced with decisions regarding care and treatment, or even institutionalization. At home, the mother is the one who usually bears the full brunt of caring and nurturing. Fathers may want to help, but frequently are unsure of what they can do. In one instance fathers were invited to attend Saturday morning sessions in which they brought their handicapped children for play and training in how to cope with their activities. It has been a complete success.

"Brothers and sisters of the handicapped may rebel at being left out or not know just how to interact. I am aware that one parent association formed a subsidiary group of siblings of handicapped children, which has proved to be beneficial.

"These are but a few of the examples of how the handicap affects the individual and his family. Each family situation is unique."

Hardly glancing at her notes, Rita had a quiet audience for over forty minutes. Suddenly, she realized that she had run over her time and stopped to take questions. An hour later, she had finished, and was sorry the time had run out.

After dinner Friday evening, Joe, Rita, and daughter Beth drove into Washington to pick up Grandma at National Airport. The two sons stayed home to watch TV.

"Your mother is one of my favorite people," Joe said as they drove along Route 301. "She's pretty sharp and considerate to time her arrival after our working hours, and on a flight where she could enjoy her drink and dinner."

"Mother is a business woman, and runs a pretty efficient farm up there. She keeps those men on the job and maintains a quality and quantity operation, otherwise the New York State milk inspectors would close her down."

"I sure have to hand it to her the way she took over when your dad passed away. I've seen her in operation, and she is sharp when it comes to buying, contracting for services, selling, and overseeing her two hundred acre farm operation."

"At her age, she should be taking it easy. If my lazy brother had more gumption, he could be running the farm, but he's not, and she does it all."

"Look, your mother loves doing it. She'd die on the vine if she didn't have her hand in it all the way up to her elbows. She's the queen bee there and thrives on the work. Keeps her young."

The car threaded its way through traffic, past the Jefferson Memorial, and other national monuments to the crowded airport. "I always get a thrill when I see all these buildings with the flag flowing at the mast above them. It's such a beautiful city," Rita said.

"The best," Joe replied.

The 7:45 PM Capital Airlines flight was late as usual, and the airport was in a confused state when she arrived.

Esther Emmet was pert and perky as she walked slowly up the ramp, and her small mouth broadened into a wide smile when she saw Rita and Joe. Beth ran forward to greet her and carry the black bag she always took on her trips.

"Mother, you look wonderful! I like the suit, and your hair—a new hair dresser? It's very becoming."

"Hi, babe!" Joe leaned down to give her a kiss. "Pretty snazzy these days, and looking very prosperous."

"It's good to see you both again. Beth is getting so big, I almost didn't recognize her. I'm glad to be off the plane. It was nice, and those girls, the stewardesses, were so good to me." She was sparkling, with her gray hair curled, red lips to match her finger nails, and wrapped in a light blue suit. "My bags will be in soon, and then let's get going. I'm anxious to see the new house."

Joe looked at Beth struggling with the black bag. "Here, let me carry that, Beth. It looks heavy."

She surrendered it, and when Joe heaved it, he turned to Esther and said, "Feels as though you have a hunk of Fort Knox here. You're loaded, Grandma. I'm glad you came."

She returned the banter. "Yep Joe. I loaded it with pet rocks, just for you. Be careful with it!"

"Mother, how are things at the farm?"

"Oh, everything is coming along great. I got a good price for the corn, the potatoes are ready to be harvested, and the apple orchard is in the best shape ever. I had some plumbing repaired and the barns painted."

"Harold and the family?"

"Your brother Harold just returned from the hospital, ulcers again, but he's all right. Kate and the children are well. They seem to be doing well in school. Tell me, how are Henry and Joe Jr.?"

Beth spoke up. "They're nice brothers until they tease me, but I can take care of myself all right."

Chapter VI

When Rita was interviewed for the job as Director of Social Services, the hospital was looking for a mature person with experience and a master's degree from a recognized school of social service. The staff consisted of a young black woman in her final year of part-time studies at Howard University. Anita King was a small, frail, married woman in her mid-twenties with drive and an outgoing personality.

The other member of the department was Alex Snyder, single, touching his third decade, and a recent graduate of the University of Maryland's School of Social Work. As soon as he completed his B.A. at The University of Virginia, he was drafted into the Army, and discharged two years later with shattered legs and in a wheel chair. To escape a hovering mother and sister during his convalescence, he embarked on a career in social services, and upon graduation started work at Powell Hospital. There were few places he could not get to in the hospital, and he was the delight of both staff and patients.

Within a short time, Rita had developed a smooth working relationship with her staff, although she had to confess to a special feeling for Alex as he had a charming air and infectious humor. She held individual weekly conferences, delegated responsibilities, and did not hesitate to assign herself cases as the demands of the hospital required.

Another important staff member was Billie Jean Akers, a five year employee, who knew everything that was to be known about the office and the hospital. She was willowy, with dark hair and dark eyes obscured by very thick glasses, without which she was as blind as the proverbial bat. In effect she was the office manager, courteous on the telephone, and a whiz on the typewriter. The four members made a good team.

It was three weeks after her talk at the college and the feedback was favorable. Dean Keyes had called Dr. Sargent and followed it up with a letter indicating how much the faculty and students had enjoyed her talk and their pleasure in having her as a speaker.

Billie Jean buzzed Rita on the intercom. "Rita, pick up on number two."

"Hello," she said.

"Rita, this is Al Burns at the Lutheran Church. Something has come up and I wonder if you could give us a hand."

"Be happy to help, Al. What's the problem?"

"Our ministerium has come up with the idea of surveying the handicapped in our area, possibly covering the entire county if we can swing it. We hope to do it under the auspices of the churches around here."

"Sounds like a great idea."

"Our group is enthusiastic about it, but we need more information on the numbers of people who are disabled, by age, extent of disability, those in wheelchairs, those on crutches, etc."

"Yes, I know what you're talking about. Father Shane mentioned it in church last Sunday, but didn't go into any detail. I think this would be valuable information to all of us in the community."

"Our problem is that we need someone to help draft a survey form, simple and nonthreatening. None of us have any background in this. Do you have any suggestions?"

"I'm no good at that, Al. Let me check with the staff here and with my husband, and I'll get back to you."

"Great, I'd appreciate it. Thanks, Rita."

The next day at the end of her conference with Alex, she inquired casually of his background in statistics and research.

"I used to ate that stuff up in graduate school. It's a challenge, and I enjoy messing around with figures."

She had him. Then she told him briefly about the proposed survey of the ministerium.

"What! Get mixed up with those Holy Rollers? No way, woman!"

"Slow down, Alex. This is not a religious function. It is merely a way of identifying people who may need assistance due to a disability. We just don't know how many are affected in the county."

He relaxed in his chair, lit a cigarette and listened while she told him about the ministerium, and their concern for people who could not attend services. He could empathize, for there were still many places which were denied him because of inaccessibility.

She concluded by saying, "Have a chat with Father Shane or Al Burns.

"Either one can fill you in on the details."

The next day, Alex found Father Shane emerging from a patient's room and called out, "Hi, Father. How goes the battle?"

The priest responded, "Hello, Alex. I'm doing OK. What's with you?"

Rita had told Father Shane about her talk with Alex, the timing was right.

"The usual." Alex replied. "Time for lunch. How about

you? I'm buying."

"I'll flip you for it."

Over coffee in the cafeteria, the priest said, "Alex, it's good to see you bustling around, and you certainly give your patients a good dose of cheer. From what I've heard, you had a rough time."

"The roughest was in 'Nam after they shot me down. Then when I came home, the family damn near made a baby out of me all over again. I had to leave, but I had it all figured out what I wanted to do with my life, and here I am. It's great here. I love it."

"It sure is. I had wondered how I'd fit in as chaplain, but the staff made it so easy, and the patients are wonderful. Many are from my parish, but I see everyone who requests a visit, and sometimes those who don't. I feel they need a little bucking up."

"You have your brand of good cheer, Padre. Those folks need it. By the way, how come they ordained you with a limp? I didn't think that the church went for that."

"Years ago, those men with a disability were prevented from studying for the priesthood, but no longer. It's a whole new ball game now."

"You had the lame leg before you went in to be a clergyman?"

"That? A gift from one of our Korean friends during that little exercise some years ago."

"You were in Korea? A.G.I.?"

"Yep. The same. Many of our guys didn't make it and I'm a lucky one. It wasn't too bad, but enough to put me on a hospital ship and home."

"Well well. Two of us veterans. We'll have to swap some war stories. I've got some beauts!"

"Bet I can top some of yours."

They had found common ground, and the distance

narrowed between them.

"I hear you and the Reverend Burns are hot on the trail of the handicapped in the area. I've done some survey work before, and know a bit about research and statistics. If you need help, give me a call.

"Thanks Alex. We might just do that. I'll be seeing Al Burns this evening, and tell him of your availability."

Three days later, Tom brought Al to Alex's office where they discussed the content for the survey form and how it would be passed out to the members of the churches .

Alex said, "There will still be many people you won't cover through the survey. How about a house-to-house count?"

"We don't have the manpower to do that. Maybe we'll ask the local media to announce it on the radio and in the newspapers." Al said.

"We'll just have to do the best we can, and hope that people will pass the word along," Tom Shane offered.

Rita came into the office. "I heard the last part of your conversation and would like to offer a suggestion."

"We're open to anything. Let's have it," Al said.

"Dr. Cohen at the Community College told me recently that she was looking for projects for her students in Human Services. Maybe this is an area she'd be interested in having the students participate."

Alex spoke up. "Rita, give Dr. Cohen a call and explore this idea with her. She may want the students to do a sample nose count, knocking on doors, and this will help us to iron out the wrinkles in the form before it goes to the churches."

"An added benefit," Rita added, "would be for the students to help in tabulating the results and in the preparation of the report. This project could serve more than several good purposes."

The next day Rita called Alex with good news.

"Dr. Cohen and I were in the check out line at the food market last evening, and since it was a long line, we had ample opportunity to talk. Briefly, she was delighted to learn of the project, and I gave her as much information as I could. She thought this would be an excellent project for the students, and would like you to call her today."

"Thanks, Rita. I'll get on the horn right away."

When Alex called the college, Dr. Cohen told him that she'd be happy to talk with him about the project, and a meeting was planned for the following day.

The college had parking for the handicapped, ramps for wheelchairs, and hand rails along the corridors. Alex had no problems at all in finding Dr. Cohen's office on the first floor.

"Come in, Mr. Snyder. I'm delighted to meet you. Mrs. Evans has some pleasant things to say about your willingness to take on this project."

"Well, she had a nice visit here recently, and told us how gracious you were to her."

"It was our pleasure, and her talk was most informative."

Alex was fascinated by this short, fair-faced woman with sparkling eyes and light blonde hair. She was dressed in a deep red suit. She was poised, spoke in clear tones, and gave evidence of her ability to be the head of the department.

"From what I already know, the project to survey the handicapped in this area poses a challenge, and I hope our students will be involved in several phases of the activity."

For the next hour, Alex talked and showed her the draft of the survey form. Dr. Cohen had a few suggestions to make, and together they made a revision. Then they discussed just how the students would be able to help in the sampling of some of the homes and in the tabulation of the results.

When they parted, they had a complete package, including the names of students who would be census takers, the areas to be covered, and social agencies to be called upon to provide information on handicapped clients.

On the following Sunday, the clergymen spoke about the projects from their pulpits, and asked for the cooperation of their parishioners in completing the form for a family member who is disabled, and to welcome the students who might be visiting for a follow-up visit where indicated. They were also asked to take home a form to pass along to a family where there is a disabled person, and who might not obtain one in a church.

After his sermon at St. Dunstan's, Father Shane was outside greeting people when he saw Joe and Rita. "Thanks for your help. Alex has taken over very well. He amazes me. Inside of a week, he's got it all firmed up. Dr. Cohen has given him all kinds of support. Our forms are in all the churches this Sunday."

"Great sermon today, Padre." Joe said. "It's about time we opened up the churches to the disabled. Good luck in the campaign."

Driving home from Mass, he said to Rita, "That's a neat trick getting the college students involved to identify the handicapped, tabulate the results and assist in writing the report. What a break for them. Were you aware of all this?"

"Oh, just a little. Alex is only coordinating the project. It'll be good for him in many ways."

From the back seat, Beth piped up. "Daddy, don't forget the bakery. I get to pick the Danish today." It was standard practice for the Evans family to stop for bakery goodies after Mass for their big Sunday breakfast.

❧ ❧ ❧

At the next staff meeting, Dr. Sargent asked Dr. Jenkins if he was ready to report on the progress of his committee.

"Yes, sir, and I'm happy to report that the Committee

on the Crisis Intervention Team has talked with most of the hospital staff and selected persons in the community and the results are positive. We recommend that as a matter of policy there should be appointed a core team to deal with crises affecting a patient. This will consist of a physician, a nurse, social worker, and the business manager. The team will be called into action immediately to discuss a particular situation, exclusive of a medical emergency. A core member will appoint a substitute to serve in his/her absence.

"We recommend a team of other professionals to assist in problems requiring their expertise, such as the chaplain, a lawyer, pharmacist, etc. In this way, major decisions affecting the lives of the patient and his family will be made for the good of all concerned. As the need arises, we can call for assistance from community agencies, as well as the medical centers in Washington and the universities there. We recommend approval."

Dr. Sargent thanked the committee, and asked for comments, all of which were favorable. A unanimous vote indicated all were in favor of the C.I.T. becoming part of the policy of the hospital.

Rita wondered why Dr. Bolton remained silent and offered no comment, and if his previous behavior was symptomatic of other problems. It would surface in due time, she was sure.

That evening, Joe was quiet, and she knew that something was troubling him. She raised the question and he replied.

"I was at the state hospital today on a site visit from our institute, and the place is a mess. Those poor bastards don't have a decent crack at treatment. They're better off dead, or at least not in that hell-hole."

"I'm with you, roll it out," she encouraged.

"These patients are like zombies, drugged up to their

ears, and no physicians around. The nurses do the best they can, but they're stuck in their cubicles making out reports and charting medications that don't do a damn bit of good. The nursing assistants can only bathe, feed, toilet and sleep the patients in those big sterile wards. It's plain custodial care in a warehouse. I'd like to put a match to the place and burn it down."

Joe was furious. He'd been in enough hospitals for the mentally ill and the mentally retarded to know that some programs are possible and that these patients can be helped.

"What can be done, Joe? Is the institute in a position to recommend positive changes?" Rita had worked in a state hospital for the mentally ill and knew that staff and programs could be effective in changing the behavior of seriously disturbed patients.

"The change has to come from the state level first, and then the director of the hospital, if he is committed to meaningful programs. Right now this guy's so frustrated that he takes off to lecture at the medical school and to consult. That's a cop out and he's neglecting his patients and staff."

"It concerns me that the public isn't aware of what's going on."

"Unless one isn't affected by having a family member as a patient, those conditions mean nothing. Occasionally a reporter writes a searing article on the state hospital, an investigation ensues, promises are made and the storm blows over until the next time. Nothing really changes.

"What we really need is more of a sense of accountability on all levels. When we broach that, professionals are hurt, for they think they do not have to answer for how they function. Then the unions get into the act, and their role is to protect their membership. The accountability thing is a washout."

"Any solutions coming down the pike?"

"Yes, I think there are. We are aware of a movement to mandate that every patient must have an individualized program that is reviewed regularly every six months or so. It will be developed by a team of many disciplines, based upon a complete diagnosis and evaluation. Goals will be established and objectives to attain these goals will be spelled out and placed in the patient's chart on the ward. Whoever 'lays on hands' must note it in the chart, date and sign it. The idea will be to identify who does what to the patient and insure that the activity follows the prescribed objectives outlined by the team.

"We should see some progress if this idea becomes a reality. We'll also hear the screams and yells of the professionals when the paraprofessionals have access to the charts and make entries in them.

"Is this lack of treatment what your Dr. Bolton wanted when he recommended transfer of the infant McCoy to the state hospital? He should go there for a week as a patient and find out what it's really like!"

"Time out to refill the drinks. I'll do the honors," Rita said.

"We went into the section of the hospital where there are about one hundred patients with mental retardation, and there was absolutely nothing going on. The TV was blaring in all the wards, and the nursing assistants were trying to keep clothes on the patients. What a waste!

"I feel sorry for the young children who are condemned to stay there most of their lives. Most of them should be at home and enrolled in a community program. It's remarkable what a trained staff can accomplish with a multidisciplinary approach. Elsewhere, I've seen severely disabled persons feed themselves and take care of their own personal needs through behavior modification programs."

Rita returned with the glasses. "What we need is a

revolution in emphasis from a medical model to a more functional mode of care and treatment. I have no quarrel with the medical model if it treats the whole person, and has good supervised activities based on individual needs. The problem, I believe, is we expect physicians to be 'all things to all men' and that just doesn't work. There are too few doctors and we saddle them with paper work and administrative duties. I question the wisdom of hiring physicians who cannot practice legally in the community because of licensure standards, yet they are allowed to practice in state hospitals. Some of these physicians come from cultures so vastly different from our own that it is hard for them to adjust. A monumental barrier is communicating between doctor, patient, and the staff. As if the difficulty of language is not enough, there is also the attitude of many of these foreigners towards the patients that is downright disdainful!

"At the other end are the direct care staff who are with the patients most of the time, but they don't have the tools to work with. It's the old story of not enough staff who are overworked and underpaid. In between these two levels are the various disciplines and technical support staff, but there is little coordination of effort. Now, your C.I.T. is a good vehicle to provide this level of coordination among all aspects of care."

"The bureaucracy of the state system is so entrenched by the time the buck gets passed up and down the line, the consumer can wither on the vine, or quite simply be forgotten," Rita commented. "Many of the patients should not be there in the first place, or be in there for a short period of time for intensive treatment.

"What we need is a good preventive program in the community, and quality control of patients committed to the state institution."

"The idea of quality control is good, but we'll be long gone before that is a reality," Joe said.

"Time to eat, love," Rita said, rising to go to the kitchen.

Chapter VII

It was a cold, blustery, and rainy day. The trees were bare, the wind whistled through the branches, and the clouds were lowering and growing more ominous. The temperature had fallen rapidly, and hovered in the low thirties. It wouldn't take much for the freezing rain to turn to snow.

This was the middle of November, and as Rita pulled into the parking lot, Alex Snyder was just getting out of his car. For a moment she watched as he put the wheelchair on the ground, moved his body into it, placed a brief case on his lap, locked and closed the car door then started towards the entrance.

She came alongside him. "Hi Alex! How goes it? How about a push?"

"Morning Rita. Yes, I'd appreciate a push in this weather. Here, put your things in my lap, and we'll get there quicker. What a miserable day!"

"Glad I won't have to go out again until I leave this afternoon."

Alex Snyder was a big man in the shoulders and trunk, black hair in a mod style down to his collar, over his ears and meeting an unusually dark beard which he kept nicely trimmed. It was becoming on him. Strong facial features would break into an infectious smile, and his laugh was a booming one. Rita liked this man.

Once inside, she shook the rain off her coat, retrieved her materials and said, "I hear you're quite a buddy of Father Shane and Al Burns. How come? Did they mesmerize you?"

"You get around, don't you?"

"I knew once you talked with them, you'd like both men. How is the survey coming along?"

"For clergy, they're OK, and those two guys are swell. I never knew the Romans and the Lutherans could get along so well. They have many commonalities. You should hear the stories they rip off, all clean, too. I'll tell you about the survey during our conference today, or is it tomorrow? Briefly, I'm happy with the results so far."

At one o'clock that afternoon, Alex rolled in for a meeting with Rita, who looked upon these sessions as consultations with peers. She was not one to take on the role of superior, but rather preferred putting the staff member right at ease. A tape recording would reveal a wealth of information being exchanged. The careful listener would become aware of how easily Rita provided direction to her workers.

Once the intra-office matters were completed, they turned to the survey of the handicapped.

"For the last several weeks, I've been ambivalent between love and hate for you for sneaking me into this project." Alex began.

"Sneaking? Why Alex, I just mentioned . . ."

"Yeah, I know your 'mention' bit, but don't get me wrong. I love it."

"Well, at least you're impartial, and I get both the good and the bad. Let's have the bad news first."

"You've disturbed my routine of a quiet evening reading and watching TV occasionally, and on weekends I've deserted the house to be out there with the students. I've even gone to several different churches on Sundays just to see if I could get the wheelchair in and out."

"That's a load of pleasant 'bad' news. Bet it did you some good to get out of that apartment you're in. I hope the proximity to the churches did you some good. Now for the good news."

"This is a real exciting project, and I'm knee deep into it. As I said this morning, Tom and Al are great to work with. They've been to my place where all the data is kept, and we've had some good sessions on the information we've gleaned so far. When we finish, we usually have a drink.

"The students at the college are very cooperative, eager and inquisitive. I enjoy working right along with them, supervising their interviews and data collection."

"Any significant trends at this early stage?"

"Let me give you the broad brush first. Our county population stands about 58,000 and growing rapidly. In this area, covering about a five mile radius, there are approximately 22,500 persons with rapidly increasing residents, enough for the college and this hospital to consider expansion in their physical plants. The results are encouraging, but no trends are showing up at present. It's a bit early for that. We'll continue to accept responses to the survey, and as of this time, we have a remarkable return. Next week we'll start to tabulate results. The local media have provided space and time, and the ministers give it a 'hard' sell from the pulpit, so I feel we have saturated the area with information about our survey."

"What about figures?"

"We have just over 6,000 forms completed, and of these 5,000 have an emotional dysfunction including alcoholism, drug abuse, and about 1,000 reflect a wide range of physical handicaps. I'm sure that we'll get many with both a physical and mental handicap, as well as sensory defects. Keep in mind that these are approximate figures."

"It appears to me, Alex, that you have quite a large population at risk, even with these results. The clergy must be pleased, and I'm sure our local social agencies will be impressed with the data."

Alex sat back, fished out a cigarette and lit up. He was happy to share the survey results with Rita, who had been responsible for getting him involved, and he was totally immersed in the project.

As they finished up the conference, she said "We're having a few friends over to the house a week from Saturday, and we'd be happy to have you join us at 7 o'clock. Joe will be interested in some of your preliminary findings, and I think you will enjoy talking with him. The house is ranch style, all on one floor, so you'll have no trouble getting around. You'll know some of the guests, Father Shane, Al Burns, and our physical therapist, Olivia Powers and her husband. Let me know in a day or two."

"Sure, Rita. Thanks. Sounds like an interesting gathering."

Two days after her talk with Alex, Rita was near the outpatient department and noticed Dr. Donnell, Chief of Pediatrics, and Dr. Rick Jones huddled in a corner. As she passed by, Dr. Donnell called to her. "Rita, can you join us for a minute? Rick was just telling me about a little girl with cerebral palsy who is giving her mother a tough time. She seems such a sweet child, but we know she has a terrible temper, and gets upset frequently."

"I'm on my way to a staff meeting, but I can hold it off for a bit. What's the family name?"

"Donatti, the girl's Andrea and the mother Rosa. They're here every three weeks for treatment," Dr. Donnell informed her.

"Yes, I know the family. Olivia Powers, our physical

therapist, told me about the case, and one of our workers, Anita King, has been to the house."

Dr. Jones added "We're at the point now where we're going to change the program, and Mrs. Donatti will have to carry out some of the exercises at home. Continuity of this treatment will give Andrea better flexibility in her arm and leg muscles. The trouble is that mother and daughter are in conflict. They fight and Andrea refuses to obey her mother. Rosa is a perfectionist, neat, clean and proper, and will do things rather then let the child do them for herself. I grant that this does take her a long time since she is uncoordinated and awkward in her movements."

"Did you have anything specific for social services to do— some miracle you wanted performed?" Rita inquired with a twinkle in her eyes.

With a straight face, Joe Donnell shot back, "Could you get Peg O'Bryan to sit on Rosa, and let the child be?"

She smiled. "That would do it! Seriously, I'll check this out with our staff, and get back to you real soon."

When she talked with the physical therapist later, Olivia said, "Andrea needs a strict regimen of muscle exercises for at least two hours a day, one in the morning, and again in the afternoon. Her mother is just not one to follow this routine."

After a few moments of silence, Rita turned to Olivia. "How long would it take to train a person to help Andrea with these exercises?"

"With the right person, about two weeks. What do you have in mind?"

"Possibly a student at the college, one who is in a physical education program, gymnastics, occupational therapy or physical therapy."

"Anyone of those would be fine."

"Billy Jean, will you get me Dr. Cohen at the college?"

Later Dr. Cohen returned her call.

"This is Rita Evans to inquire if you would consider another project for a student."

"You did such a good job involving our students with Mr. Snyder on the survey. They are thriving on it, and learning a great deal. What do you have in mind now?"

"This would be an individual project. We have a nine-year-old girl who has cerebral palsy, and the staff here is ready to accelerate a treatment program involving exercises of her arms and legs. To obtain maximum benefit, these exercises must be carried out at home on a daily basis. Our problem is with the girl's mother has neither the stamina or the patience to carry out the program."

"You are inquiring if we have a student who could take this on as part of her practicum?"

"Yes. If this is possible, our physical therapist could train the student in about two weeks, and our social worker could help in working through with the mother."

"Sounds OK to me. I'll check it out and get back to you."

A few days later, Dr. Cohen called to say that she had discussed the request with the head of the Physical Education Department, and asked that Rita call her to provide more information.

Mrs. Heywood, in a subsequent meeting, listened to Rita describe the need for the request. Olivia Powers explained the types of exercises needed to flex and strengthen the muscles, and Anita King told how she would work with the mother. Mrs. Heywood was also a ballet instructor, and was aware of the function of muscles and felt that a student under supervision could carry out the assignment readily.

Mrs. Heywood was of medium height, and carried a supple body. She was an avid sports enthusiast, and on one occasion, she noticed how the football players were awkward and stumbled over their own feet. When she suggested to the coach that she'd be willing to help, he demurred at first, but then felt the boys needed to be quicker on their feet. The result of a few lessons in ballet produced a faster team, and a winning season. The boys enjoyed the classes, and the coach offered her a job, but she refused.

She readily agreed to participate in the hospital project and selected a slim twenty-year-old dark-haired girl.

"Tina, may I see you after class?"

Showered and sparkling, her long hair in a ponytail, Tina Federov appeared in the office of her instructor.

"Here I am, Mrs. Heywood. What's up?" She was an engaging young woman, with an outgoing personality and was a leader among her friends in the college. Cynthia was fond of her and enjoyed having her in class.

They sat in a small cluttered office just off the gymnasium and close to the locker and shower facilities for the girls. Cynthia was a perfectionist in her work, but this did not apply to her desk, which was a mass of papers and books.

"Tina, do you have a project lined up for the term?"

"Not yet, Mrs. Heywood. Do you have some ideas for me?"

"We do have a request for a student to work with a handicapped little girl at home."

"What would this involve?"

"Essentially the kinds of things we have been stressing in our dance classes and gymnastics, the use of muscles, exercises, etc." She then laid out the details of working with Andrea, the difficulties faced by those with cerebral palsy, the need for strict training and adherence to a schedule.

This took Tina off guard, and she said she needed to think about it and discuss the project with her mother. Cerebral palsy was a new term for her, and she had little knowledge of what it entailed.

That night her mother told her, "I think you'll be happy working with people because you enjoy being with them.

The project sounds interesting, and since you'll be supervised by the hospital therapist, you won't hurt the little girl. Give it a try, and see how you like it. This may open up a new field for you to pursue."

"Mother, I know absolutely nothing about cerebral palsy, and I'd hate to muff the whole thing up."

"Tomorrow, I'll bring home a book from the library and we'll go over it together." She was a librarian at the county level and had access to the books out front as well as those in the stacks.

Tina's father, a language specialist at the U.S. State Department, also encouraged her to give it a try. She had two younger sisters, one in junior high, the other in the eighth grade, and while both teased her, they told her to go ahead.

Tina decided to take on the project for her practicum, and drove her red Mustang convertible, a gift from her parents, by the Donatti house out of curiosity. It was five blocks from her house, located in a nice area, a red brick, one story dwelling with a wooded lot in the rear.

There were no signs of life, yet she had hoped to see the little girl out in the yard.

At a meeting later at the hospital, the social worker told Tina, "We all know that Andrea can do these things, and you can help her to meet the challenge. Her mother may be difficult, for she's possessive, domineering, insecure, and defensive about her daughter. She still believes that she may have done something during her pregnancy to cause these injuries, so there is an overlay of guilt. We'll help you with the mother so she doesn't interfere, and perhaps we can eventually get her to the point where she'll help rather than throw roadblocks in the way."

Andrea had no answers to the many questions which tumbled through her mind. As she looked out the window, she could see other children at play, walking, running, riding bicycles, going to school and having fun. She knew she was different, but could not verbalize this.

It seemed so many years ago when her father went off on a trip somewhere and never returned. He loved her and used to take her on his lap and tell her funny stories. Then he was gone, and she never knew why he disappeared. Her mother always made her mad and she knew that she could torment her by not doing what she wanted. She could scream and she knew that this upset her mother. Andrea's brother was tall and attractive, but he was away at school most of the time, and came home for the holidays and in the summer.

Heavy braces had been on her legs for all of her nine years, and she hated them. Her small body weighed less than fifty-three pounds, with a small wasted trunk, a narrow chest and thin shoulders from which sprang two narrow branches with tiny twigs which had little coordination to do the things she wanted them to do. Her face was emaciated, careworn beyond her years, although her complexion was smooth, and her brown hair was frequently matted for she rebelled when her mother tried to comb it.

Mrs. Donatti at first did not like the idea of someone coming into her house to work with Andrea, but relented when the social worker told her the doctors felt it was necessary if Andrea was to improve. In addition, she knew that she could not cope with her child's tantrums, and this would relieve her of the somewhat distasteful exercise routines.

Andrea had seen Olivia and Tina get out of their cars in the driveway and come to the front door.

"Hello Mrs. Powers, do come in."

"Mrs. Donatti, I'd like you to meet Tina Federov."

"How do you do, Tina. I'm happy to know you."

"How do you do, Mrs. Donatti," Tina replied.

Andrea was sitting in a large wooden tilt-back chair on

rollers in the recreation room when her mother brought in the therapist and Tina. She had been told of the visit and that Mrs. Powers would bring in a student from the college to work with her. She smiled when Olivia said, "It's good to see you again, Andrea. How are you today?"

A slow smile crossed her face as she sized up her visitor, and she responded with a quiet "Hi."

"This is the student I told you about, and her name is Tina."

Tina came forward and stretched out her hand in greeting. "Hi, Andrea. I'm happy to meet you, and I'm sure we'll get along well together." She smiled at the little girl who kept swirling her head and darting critical looks at the young woman.

Rosa excused herself to return to the kitchen to attend a boiling pot.

Olivia lifted Andrea out of the chair, and placed her on the large exercise mat on the floor. There she was able to point out to Tina the stiffness of the girl's arms and legs, and the proper type of exercises to be performed. All this time, Andrea continued to look at Tina without much expression on her face.

"Something must be bothering her today, Tina. Usually she is talkative and pleasant. Do you have any questions now as to what needs to be done and how to go about the program?"

"No, Mrs. Powers. I have a good grasp of the activity, and I think we'll get along just fine. Andrea may be a bit apprehensive with a new person around, but we'll get over that. If it is all right with you and Mrs. Donatti, I'm free this afternoon and would like to stay and get acquainted with Andrea before we start the program."

"I have no objections, and, in fact, that's a good idea. Check with her mother to insure that she has no plans for

Andrea. I do have other calls to make, so I'll leave. Let's meet here day after tomorrow at 3:00 PM to get started."

Mrs. Donatti returned to the room, gave her permission for Tina to stay, and walked Olivia to the door.

Andrea was still lying on the mat, her dark eyes boring into Tina. Her hair was flayed out, and Tina thought it needed attention. She sat close to the little girl and said, "I think we'll have some fun together once we get acquainted." She reached out to touch the girl's hair. "You have such pretty hair. Would you like me to brush it for you?"

Andrea nodded and came out with a subdued "Yes."

Tina looked around, got up and found the brush she had noticed on a table. As she knelt to pick up Andrea, the little girl let out a yell that could be heard for blocks. So much noise from such a child!

"Anything wrong?" she asked, and the reply was a louder yell.

For a few moments Tina did nothing, and thought that her mother would come to find out what all the yelling was about. Then she remembered that Olivia and Anita had said Andrea could put on quite an act, especially for a new face.

Tina looked at Andrea and said nothing, but observed that there were no tears and the eyes opened once then closed while the yells bounced off the walls. Tina turned her back to Andrea, got up off the mat, went to the table, picked up a magazine and sauntered to the window overlooking the driveway.

She waited a discreet two minutes and when the room was quiet, she returned to the mat and looked at the little girl flushed with her exertions and said, "Where were we? Oh yes, I was about to brush your hair. Ready?"

"Yes."

Tina knelt down, raised Andrea up, and slid in back of her, placing the girl between her outstretched legs, both facing the window. This gave Andrea some back support, and would prevent the child from falling forward or to the side. She brushed the hair slowly, untangled each knot and soon had the dark locks glistening.

At one point, Andrea leaned forward and suddenly came back hitting Tina in the chest. Both fell backward. She had the feeling that Andrea was about to test her again with a scream, but she forestalled that by saying, "That was fun, let's do it again." Soon they were on their backs once more, laughing together. They rolled over on their stomachs, hair askew, having a great time. "Now I'll have to do your hair all over again, and mine, too."

It was an afternoon well spent. Tina got to know her little charge as a spoiled brat, but that would change. Tina was not fazed by the outbursts, and she knew she would be able to help the little girl.

"When you come back?" Andrea asked haltingly, as Tina prepared to go home.

"Do you want me to return?"

A nodded yes was the answer.

Once "broken in" to one another, they both enjoyed the exercises. Olivia Powers came several times to insure that Tina was familiar with and could perform the exercises regarding the posturing of the arms and legs.

On one occasion, Tina asked the therapist if she could make up games for the exercises, and demonstrated what she had in mind.

"That's wonderful, Tina. I can see that Andrea likes it, and she'll be more inclined to participate in the therapy. They will pose as a challenge to her."

Andrea was starting to make progress in mobility, and Tina made it a point to encourage her in a positive way. When the little girl became obstreperous and had an outburst, Tina just remained calm and let it blow over. Her classes in psychology and behavior modification were valuable as she dealt with the girl. She was putting theory to practice, and was amazed to find that it worked.

Tina enjoyed her studies at the college, where she was learning to become a laboratory technician. Now, however, due to her work with Andrea and the close association with the hospital staff in social work and physical therapy, she began to wonder if she should change direction and pursue a career working with people. Perhaps her mother was right, that she'd be happier with a human services responsibility. This would mean more education than she had planned on, but she was confident that she could handle it.

"Social Work is a fascinating field," Anita King told her one day. "In addition to your work as a therapist, you are able to see the interaction between a spoiled handicapped child and her rigid mother who won't let go. We must work not only with the client, but also with other members of the family, because they all relate to one another. We can't solve all the problems, but if we can help people to understand one another and to see themselves in a better light, they may be able to help themselves and solve their own difficulties."

"Then yours is a helping profession, providing information so they can sort of clear things up," Tina replied.

"That's right, Tina. We also have to look beyond the obvious physical condition, and see what's going on inside the person. Take Andrea for example. Despite her physical handicaps, she has average intelligence and recognizes that she is not like other children, who can romp and play. This damages her self image. In the effort to gain attention, she is demanding and impetuous, yet she responds to those who are strict to her. You found that out when you didn't rise to the bait of her outcry that first day you met her. Andrea needs the challenge of doing things for herself."

"She's starting to reach for a glass of milk or her brush

now, and I let her. She's pleased when she does, and smiles at me. Maybe it's because I'm close to her in age, and we work together that I find her more open now, and emerging as a 'normal' little girl. She does respond to love and attention."

"What have you found out about her father and her brother?"

"She vaguely remembers her father, whose airplane was lost at sea returning from a business trip to Europe. Her only brother, Tomas, is a student at the University of Virginia, and she adores him. He writes frequently to her, and when he's home, they play and talk a lot. In a way, Tomas is like a father to her."

"What you're saying, Tina, is that he provides the parental support she needs, in contrast to her mother who feels as though she has to do everything for her daughter. In effect, Rosa's world begins and ends with Andrea. She feels sorry for herself and this has caused her to become introverted. Since you have come into the house, I've noticed a lessening of tensions between them and you are the catalyst in effecting changes in their behavior. You bring a spark to the Donatti family."

One morning Tina arrived early and over coffee Rosa said, "Tomas is in a play at the university next weekend. His letter came in the mail yesterday, and he is pleased with the progress his sister is making. I had written to him earlier, and he wants me to thank you for doing so much for us."

"Would you like to go there and see your son in the play?" Tina asked.

"No. I couldn't even think of it." Rosa replied.

All that day she did think of Tomas and the play, but she also was concerned with Andrea and who would take care of her at night.

Tina had told Rosa before leaving that she was free for the

weekend and could easily stay in the house to care for Andrea.

Rosa spent a sleepless night and finally realized that she had a reliable person in Tina, and that she owed it to her son to visit him. In the morning she announced to Andrea and Tina, "Time for me to go to Charlottesville, and see my son in his play. Thank you, Tina, for the offer to stay here and look out for Andrea. I know you'll both get along well."

The little girl smiled and clapped her hands in approval.

❦ ❦ ❦

Tomas broke off from a group in front of his fraternity brothers when the Cadillac Coupe deVille arrived, and he ran to open the door and give his mother a kiss. "Hi Mom! You're looking great. Sure is good to have you here."

"I just decided to accept your invitation and get away for a bit. Tina has everything under control."

"Sounds as though she has done wonders with Andrea. Is she OK?"

"She's doing many things by herself now, and Tina doesn't put up with any of her nonsense. What a relief to have her around."

Chapter VIII

"I must have rocks in my head, Roger," Joe said to his son.

"You said it, not me," was the quick rejoinder.

"When your mother and I planned this party for the Thanksgiving Weekend, I had completely forgotten about the Army-Navy football game. What a boo-boo! Good thing we don't have tickets to go to Philly!" _

Rita and Beth were just as happy. Every fall, from September to mid-January, it was football for the men in the family. College games were on Saturdays, the professional teams played on Sundays, and now there was talk of a "Pro" game on Monday evenings.

"Now, love, you should be happy that you know where I am on weekends, and you can go out and do your own thing," Joe would say to her.

Joe, Roger, and Joe Jr. had to make the best of it and pitch in to help get ready for the party. They wrapped up the chores before the kickoff time, and if they had to move away from the TV, Roger's transistor would keep them in touch with the game.

Everything was in order when the first guests arrived shortly after 6:00 PM. Alex was the first to wheel in from the carport, followed by Peg and Phil O'Bryan, the Powers, Joe and Mabel Edwards and their daughter Donna, from Joe's office, Al and Martha Burns and Dr. Clare Cohen.

Father Shane had confessions at St. Dunstan's, while Rabbi Halpern had a service underway, and both would be along shortly. Some of these guests came early and would leave early, while others would be late and stay later.

"This is just to inaugurate the Holiday season," Joe and Rita said in toasting their guests.

"What a way to go!" Alex Snyder exclaimed, a scotch and water in hand. He was talking with Dr. Whitlow, Joe's boss at the Mental Health Institute, and they were discussing the recently concluded survey of the handicapped in the area. Joe brought a martini for Dr. Whitlow and one for himself as he joined the two men.

"This is a most interesting project," Dr. Whitlow said. "I'm impressed."

Alex gave credit to the clergymen. "They are the ones who get the credit for the idea, and their help in pushing it along. I'm having a ball with the data and the students who are doing the leg work."

Dr. Cohen, a whiskey sour in hand, joined in. "You've given our students an opportunity to work on a real problem, and their experiences in interviewing, cross checking information, and assembling data have been valuable to all of us at the college."

"I see this as another demonstration of the college's responsibility to provide viable skills to the students, and at the same time assist the community in working through a difficult problem," Dr. Whitlow added.

"What I like about it is that it was done so quickly and rather effortlessly," Al said from the back of the group.

They were standing near the bar, set up in the recreation room, and Rita had emerged from the kitchen to speak to Joe. Hearing the last remark from Al Burns she said, "If you bureaucrats at the institute had the project, it would still be in the discussion stage, committees would massage that survey form to death, the policy polemics would rage for ages, the final form would be five pages long, and maybe two years from now, we'd have the final results!" With that parting shot, she left forgetting what she had meant to ask Joe, and before he could reply in defense.

The director of the institute, Dr. Whitlow, agreed with his hostess. "Mrs. Evans is so right. There are so many turfs to protect, and everyone wants to get into the act. Sometimes I wonder how we ever get anything accomplished. My hat's off to the private sector."

"We do it cheaper, too," Alex added. "This will come in under one hundred dollars."

"Does the raw data provide significant results?" Joe asked.

"So far, yes. It looks promising,"' Alex replied.

Dr. Cohen added, "There is a high correlation between the results on the survey and the personal interviews on the sampling by the students. We expect a few straggling forms yet to come in, but they shouldn't affect our basic figures."

For the benefit of those in the group, Al Burns gave a brief review of how the survey came about, the need of the clergymen to know how many handicapped are in the area, and the role of the hospital staff in helping to develop the survey form, and the assistance provided by Dr. Cohen and her students at the college.

"It pleases me to know of this interaction between the college and the community, and how it will aid both parties," Dr. Whitlow said.

"We have another project underway," Dr. Cohen replied. "This is on an individual basis. One of our students is doing an outreach program in the home to assist in the training of a little nine-year-old girl who has cerebral palsy. The hospital's physical therapist and social worker have been providing direction for the student, and we can see great progress in the girl's physical and emotional life."

Joe turned to his director to say, "This type of activity needs to be publicized among some of our hospitals throughout the country to let them know the resources available in the community colleges."

"I agree, Joe, but the students do need competent staff to provide the training, if the kids are to do the job. Let's explore this further next week."

Father Tom Shane arrived, gave his coat and hat to Joe Jr. and joined the group. "I've been getting fragments of information about child abuse and wife beating. Do we have any data that reflect this?"

Alex replied, "No, and I doubt that this will show up on the survey. Most people don't regard this as a handicap, but it surely is a serious problem. It is the type of thing that stays within the four walls of the house. Children are too scared, and wives too embarrassed to talk about it."

At this point, Rita came out of the kitchen to announce, "Dinner will be ready in ten minutes, so drink up. The buffet will be in the dining room and there is ample room in the living and recreation rooms and the porch. Come hungry."

Alex brought his chair up close to the bar for a refill, and found several bodies in front, unaware of him. Directly ahead was a red area and as he looked up to her blonde hair, she suddenly stepped back, laughing and bumped into his legs. As she started to fall, he leaned forward to put his arms around her waist and lifted her onto his lap.

Still laughing the blonde head half turned to say, "I'm so sorry. I had no idea anyone was in back. Are you all right? Spill your drink?"

"No, I'm fine. How about you?" He noticed the dark glasses, and got a whiff of fragrance as he loosened his grasp.

"I'm all right. Thanks for saving me."

"No trouble at all. I came for a drink, and see what I got instead! A blonde on my lap!"

Father Tom was closest and helped the young woman to her feet, and everyone present laughed at the episode.

Alex was the first to recover. "None of these clods will do the honors. I'm Alex Snyder, and I work with our hostess at the hospital."

"I'm Donna Edwards. My father works with the host at the institute."

"Now that we've been properly introduced, what are you drinking? Can I get a refill for you?"

"Yes. Thanks. A Tom Collins on the rocks. Straight. No gin or vodka. Just pure Collins."

Alex could tell immediately that Donna had a visual problem, so when he received the Collins glass, he placed it into her outstretched hand and noticed her face. He couldn't see her eyes, but her uncertainty in her movements confirmed his belief that she couldn't see very well at all.

When he had his drink, he said to her, "Here's how! Let's move out from here, it's too crowded. How about the porch where we can talk."

"Fine with me. Lead the way."

"Tell you what. I'll hold our drinks, and you get in back here and push me along. I'll guide and navigate. Help me over this little hump by the door. There. A few steps to the left over by the corner and we're all set. Give me your hand, come forward turn around and the chair is in back of you. OK. Here's your drink."

They were in the corner of a large jalousied room with comfortable chairs, lamps, and tables. Several other couples had come out to catch a breath of air.

"I could hear you across the room," Donna said opening up the conversation. "The survey sounds interesting."

"What makes it great is working with the students at the college. They are an inquisitive bunch, and Dr. Cohen is a peach, too."

They were into a good session when Donna's mother came to them. "Donna, I was in the other room when . . . are you all right?" She was anxious and had heard of the incident. Turning to Alex she said, "I don't believe we've met. Mabel Edwards. I'm pleased to meet you."

"Evening, Mrs. Edwards." Alex responded.

"Mother, everything is fine. I just stumbled and I'm not hurt at all. We're just chatting here out of the stream of things inside."

"If you need me, dear, just call." With that she departed to check on her husband. Alex thought her a bit of a worry wart.

Donna sighed. "Mother gets so concerned about me. I'm really capable of getting around fine. I suppose it's natural for her."

Alex agreed. "Mothers are the same the world over, and there's no way to change them. Mine just about drove me crazy when I came back from service all banged up. They wanted to do everything for me. I finally decided to get out while I could."

"What happened in the service, Alex?"

"It was over in 'Nam, the Army, and a hand grenade did the job on my legs, but I was lucky. It wiped out many of our guys. So now, I have wheels."

"When you left home, what then?"

"I bought a car and learned how to get in and out with the chair, then enrolled in graduate school and lived on campus. That just about blew their minds, but I became independent. Like us, parents have to live with the condition for a while, then get used to it."

"Yes, I know, but it's so hard to train them. My father can

handle mine, but mother hovers over me. I can almost feel her eyes on me now."

"Send her an ESP signal, and tell her I'm harmless."

"I don't know about that. The way you held me when I fell into your lap leads me to believe . . ."

"Yes?"

"You are nice, and I'm happy to have met you."

Alex smiled and quietly said, "Thanks. You know a corner of me that gives with you? What do you do for excitement?" He watched as her red lips formed the words, white teeth flashing amid smiles, and her dress pressed against strong arms and legs, swishing as she bounced a little on the chair.

"Mine is rather a simple life. I live with my parents a few miles down the road off Route 301, and I'm an only child. After I graduated from Trinity College in Washington a few years ago, I became a receptionist at a law firm near my father's office, and type briefs. We drive in together every day, I play the piano, read books in braille and enjoy good company."

Rita came over to announce, "The buffet is ready. Can I help you?"

"If it's OK with you, Donna, let's wait until the line thins out, then we'll eat. In the meantime, will you have that miserable bartender, your lovable Joe send out drinks for us? He knows mine, and a virgin Tom Collins for Donna. Also, save us a quiet nook for dinner?"

"Mrs. Evans, will you tell my mother to go ahead and eat?"

"Sure to both requests. I'll have Roger bring you drinks."

At the bar Rita said to Joe. "You should see Alex and Donna on the porch. They're getting acquainted fast."

"I know. I saw her when she fell into Alex's lap, and he brightened up all over. I'm happy for both those people."

Alex and Donna continued their chat over drinks and

talked about the current unrest on college campuses, music, books, and politics. She had dim light perception, and while he appeared in a blur, she could 'see' him through his deep voice, the texture of his tweed jacket, and the manly odor he gave off.

"Mr. Nixon won the recent election in a landslide over Senator McGovern, with his sixty percent of the popular vote," Donna offered.

"Yes, but I don't feel comfortable about him and the way he's running the country. He's sort of sleazy, there's something wrong there, and I can't put my finger on it." Alex shook his head.

"I understand, too, that when Judge Sirica opens hearings on the Watergate break-in next January, there will be a lot more than just the attempted robbery coming to light." Donna said. "My father told me that there is more than meets the eye, and a big scandal is brewing. In addition, Larry O'Brien has sued the Republican Party for millions."

"He's hurt programs I'm interested in," Alex said. "The social and behavioral sciences don't need another four years of cutbacks and retrenchment while the fat cats get fatter. I just hope we can survive. The trial will be interesting. The judge is a tough one, and I believe they call him 'Hanging John.' By the way, you mentioned the piano. What do you play?"

"Mostly classical, and I've done some concert work. Playing relaxes me. What about you? Anything musical?"

"Years ago, I took violin lessons, but now I wouldn't know an 'E' string' from a 'G' string, literally, that is." He laughed then looked around and said, "I think the line has thinned out. Want to go in?"

"Yes. Now I'm hungry, in fact starved. Let's go."

At the buffet line Alex said, "If you hold the plates, I'll serve and tell you what is on the menu. Oh, smell that food!"

When Donna heard the different selections available, she told Alex, who filled her plate and his own, then he balanced the plates in his lap while she pushed the chair out to the porch where they joined Al Burns and Rita at a table for four.

"Sit here, Donna on my right," pulling out a chair for her, then coming over so he was opposite Al, with Rita on his left.

Leaning over to her he spoke in a low voice. "The roast beef is in front of you, the corn directly north, the beets east and the spinach casserole on the west. Salad is northwest, water glass northeast. OK?

Al Burns watched with interest as Donna found and ate her food gracefully. He said to Alex, "Now that we're near the end of the project, what are you going to do with your spare time?"

"The fun part starts now as we analyze the data and write up the report. I'll have the students do most of it, but I'll supervise every aspect and make sure the content is correct."

Rita spoke up. "The data here will be important not only for the churches but for our hospital, the schools and other parts of the community. It has implications for all of us now, and for long range planning."

Alex glanced at Donna, who was doing all right except for the meat.

"Here, let me do a bit of carving for you," as he reached over to cut the beef.

Rita and Al exchanged glances, smiled and returned to their plates. "This is so good, Rita," Al said.

"It's delicious, Mrs. Evans," Donna piped in. "I'm so hungry, I'm making a pig of myself."

"No wonder, Alex has just about worn you out talking as he can do," she replied. "Can I get seconds for anyone?"

The talk at the table was lively, and they covered a range

of topics about La Plata and the state. When the election surfaced again, Rita said, "I just can't remember for whom I voted. I didn't want McGovern, and I dislike Nixon, but I went into the booth and pulled the lever. Where my vote went, I just don't know."

Alex laughed right out loud. "I've never known you to be confused before, Rita. You've spoiled my concept of you as 'perfect.' Welcome to the paisanos of the world."

All four got a kick out of this and laughed heartily.

Afterward, they joined the main body of the guests in the recreation room. Donna in back of Alex, pushing his chair.

Mabel Edwards came up to her daughter. "Did you watch your diet, dear?"

"Not tonight, Mother, I was too hungry. Tomorrow, I'll go back on it."

Joe Edwards inquired if Alex planned to write up the results of the survey for a publication.

"Oh yes, indeed. Dr. Cohen and I have already talked about this, but we haven't decided what journal to send it to. We both have ideas, but nothing firmed up yet."

"I'm interested in the whole project, and I know Dr. Whitlow would like to receive a copy of the results."

His wife stood alongside, looking first at Donna, then at Alex, who seemed to have captivated her daughter. During the evening, she managed to excuse herself several times to check on them, and found the two with their heads together.

Joe Evans joined the group, and putting his arm around Donna's waist said "We just happen to have a piano in the living room, and would you do the honors for us?"

"I'd be delighted, Mr. Evans. Alex, can you lead the way for me?"

When she was settled at the piano, Alex wheeled back to the bar to fix himself a Rusty Nail, and he could hear her fingers gliding over the keys on the "Minute Waltz." That was just to get her warmed up, for she played on request most of the popular tunes. Donna was a gifted player with a light touch, and knew the scores of most of the musicals.

By 11:30, the last of the guests were sallying forth into the cold night, and Alex asked if he could drive her home.

She leaned down to whisper, "Not tonight, I'd better leave with my parents. Mother's a bit upset with me, so I'll need to placate her. It's been such a great night. Thank you so much for being here."

"It's been swell. I'll give you a call, and we'll do the town."

"Yes. Make it on the weekend."

Alex stayed longer helping to clean up and had a final drink.

"Many thanks, folks, for inviting me. I sure enjoyed myself with the food, the drinks, and the company."

"Including Miss Donna?" Rita asked slyly.

"That's some dish, and no more will I say at this point, except good night."

It was past 1:00 a.m. before Alex arrived home, and long after that before he fell asleep.

Chapter IX

The December meeting of the ministerium was held at the Rectory of St. Dunstan's Church with Father Shane as host. All twelve members were present to review the results of the survey of the handicapped, since Alex had told Al Burns they could now begin to write the report.

They sat around a large table, with Al at one end and Alex at the other, to discuss the survey and to respond to questions. It was agreed beforehand that Al would give the highlights and implications for reaching out to provide religious services to those who desired them, while Alex would be more specific in his presentation regarding the demographics.

"First a moment of silent prayer for the success of our project, and for the welfare of our clergy who are called to serve the handicapped," Al said in calling the meeting to order. Then he continued, "Our committee thanks each of you for your cooperation and help on the project. Thanks also to Alex here, to Dr. Clare Cohen and the students at the college, and to the community leaders who gave of their time and efforts.

"Now to some highlights of the survey. We had over 7,500 responses to the survey, out of which we can identify over 6,500 persons with some type of mental disability and over 1,000 who have a physical or a sensory defect.

"We have given each of you a sheet containing a breakdown of the disabled persons by age range and type of condition which affects them. You will note the religious denomination and we hope to send these to you in the near future. You are aware that my Tommy is mentally retarded, so I was particularly interested in the number of persons so handicapped which we'll use not only for the churches, but will pass on to the parent groups and the school board for their planning. It goes without saying that we'll make the results of our survey available to every community resource, both private and public which makes a request."

Al continued on for another fifteen minutes, delving into the area of prevention for the conditions listed in the report, and in general made an interesting as well as informative presentation.

Alex lit a cigarette as he began his talk on specific aspects of the project. "Starting with the youngest in the population, that 500 children have mental problems, and almost 250 have a physical defect. While many are in programs, far too many are at home where mothers lack support and guidance in training them.

"We have so many teenagers with learning disorders, over 500 have a mental dysfunction, alcoholism affects 400 students and over 400 are hooked on drugs. The cause of much of this lies in the home where divorce or separation of the parents results in a one parent family unit.

"As we look at the population in their second decade of life, we see almost 3,000 cases of mental and physical disorders, involving emotional upsets, alcoholism and the use of drugs. A great many in this age range are using wheelchairs but they are not visible in the community. One wonders why they are not gainfully employed.

"We have discovered quite a few disabled people in their middle ages who are on waiting lists for the state hospitals, but what they need are group homes, so that they can receive treatment near their families and remain in the community.

"A definite lack among all levels of the handicapped was recreation facilities and social outlets. This is but one way in which the disabled feel left out of the mainstream of activity. They need to be accepted as persons in their own right, with integrity and responsibility and an opportunity to participate up to their physical and mental potentials."

Alex continued on for twenty minutes, going into great detail. He ended with the statement, "The family is the core of our culture, and indications in the survey are that many families are not living up to their responsibilities for the very young child and the youths."

In the general discussion that followed it was revealed that some churches had a surplus of teachers and rooms for Sunday School classes but few pupils. Others had more students but insufficient space and teachers. It was agreed that the wealth must be shared.

Rabbi Halpern, a recent addition to the ministerium, offered to help train the clergy in handling difficult pastoral problems in counseling and guidance. This was broadened into the need to explore a course at the college for pastoral counseling. Dr. Cohen was suggested as a good person to talk to at the college, and the rabbi agreed.

"Before we get away from the Sunday School classes," Alex said, "wherever possible absorb the handicapped into the regular groups, and not just assign them to special classes. It is good for the non-handicapped to see, hear, and talk with children who have a disability. Both benefit by this type of association, and they can be helpful to one another. Isn't this what churches are all about anyway?"

Alex had struck a chord in all present. Like so many, they were "segregationists," feeling that the disabled wanted to be with their own kind, and not mingle with the non-disabled.

"The mentally retarded can't keep up," someone said.

"I know," Al Burns replied. "They can in some classes, but with the lower grades, we'll make adjustments. Our Lutheran Church has done a great deal with the religious education of the mentally retarded, and has published many booklets for this group."

"I'm familiar with their work, and impressed with their activities," Father Tom said. "I'll browse around in our Catholic publications and see what I can bring forth. This goes for all of us here. Let's see what our respective churches have going in this area, and perhaps we can come up with a solid program of religious education for our slower parishioners."

Jake St. John stood up. "Earlier Alex mentioned the lack of recreation and social outlets for the disabled, and I feel that this is an important part of their activity which should not be neglected. Our church has a small gymnasium which we'll be happy to make available for physical education classes, recreational programs and social activities."

"That's a good offer, Jake. We'll be over to use it," Tom said.

Al noticed the two black ministers talking quietly, and when one looked up, Al said, "Yes Phil?"

Phillip Mason, pastor of the A.M.E. Church rose to say, "I want you to know how much this meeting means to Ted here and me. This is a very conservative community, and our black brethren have not had it easy, but a lot of progress has been made. Anyway, I shall be interested in getting the data on my congregation who are disabled, and pitching in to help them and the others, too. If we can help one another to look out for the disabled, we'll be showing real Christian love and concern. You can count on our A.M.E. Church to participate in every way."

As the older, portly, dark-skinned man sat down, his much

younger slim companion, Ted Queen rose to speak. "I agree with everything Reverend Mason has to say, and in addition, I'll make a specific proposal. For those churches which do not have ramps or railings to ease the entrance into the church, I have several carpenters among my members who I'm sure will be willing to give up a weekend or two to assist in building ramps where needed, and also install railings along the walls. Give me a call."

"That's what we need! Manpower to accomplish some of these structural changes. Thanks, Ted. We'll be in touch with you and the men," Al said.

During the course of the next hour, other areas of concern were mentioned, including the unmarried mother and the single parent. This opened up the question of sex information and education.

"At some point, gentlemen," Bob Steels said, "we're going to broach these areas for the adult person and youth who are disabled. These are topics we may shy away from, but sooner or later we'll have to face up to them. How do we respond?"

Dave Halpern replied, "If we get the course on pastoral counseling underway at the college, this will be an area which will be included."

As the meeting drew to a close, it was decided that Alex, Al, and Tom would meet with Rita at the hospital to review the data and pull together the community resources to share in the information uncovered by the survey.

Chapter X

Clare Cohen was hustling into her office just before the holiday vacation began and heard her secretary on the telephone.

"No, Jean, Clare hasn't come in yet. Wait, I hear her coming into her office now. I'll see if she can pick up at her desk."

Clare heard the last of the conversation and picked up the phone. "Hi Jean, all set for the holidays?"

A stifled voice returned her greeting. "Can I come see you now?"

"Sure, I'm free for a moment. Come ahead."

In three minutes Jean Matson was seated and with ambivalence written all over her face announced, "I don't know whether to be happy or just cry!"

"Take your time, Jean. What brings all this on?"

"My husband breezed in last night from work to tell me that he's being transferred to Oahu in the Hawaiian Islands late in January. He's been with the U.S. Coast and Geodetic Survey, and having been stationed in Washington for seven years, now it's time for him to move up to the next promotion, and that automatically means a transfer of duty station."

"So?"

"I'm sad because this means I'll be leaving the college.

I'm happy working with the students here, and the faculty has been so nice to me. The thoughts of moving give me the cold chills. With two children and a husband plus all the stuff we've accumulated, how am I ever going to do it. On the other hand, I'm happy for Hank and his promotion. Duty in Hawaii sounds wonderful."

"How marvelous that you're going all the way out to the Pacific! I'm happy for you, but sad that we'll be losing a competent instructor. We'll miss you greatly. Any target dates yet?"

"Hank says it will be late in January, so we do have time to pack, sell the house and get ready. I'm sure that I'll have no trouble marking the final exams and getting my records in before I leave."

After Jean left, Clare sat at her desk remembering when Jean appeared in her office five years ago, unannounced and just when she needed a sociology instructor. She developed the course on "The Sociology of Human Relations" and made it popular with the students in the Human Services Sequence. The only concern Clare had was that Jean relied too much on the text and there was a lack of projects in the community for real life experiences for the students. She was a good teacher and everyone enjoyed working with her. Now she'd have to find a replacement and organize a going-away party.

In the lunchroom, she joined Cynthia Heywood and they chatted about the holiday recess, shopping, and Jean's move to the Pacific.

"Clare, I want to bring you up to date on Tina and Andrea. Olivia Powers and I went to the house a few days ago, and you should see the progress that little girl has made. Her arms seem to be more flexible, and she can perform more self-help skills like eating, washing her face and hands, toiletting and bathing. Tina has done well in executing the exercises, and the two of them play on the mat and out in the yard, too."

"How about Rosa?" Clare asked. "As I recall, she was a real bottle neck and couldn't bring herself to let Andrea do anything for herself."

"Rosa gets uptight when Andrea makes a mess, but she's improved a great deal. She does a few of the exercises with Andrea, and next year we hope to have her do more.

"What has really helped her is being able to get out of the house. In addition to her regular shopping tours, she has been going into Washington frequently on Saturdays when I am working with Andrea, and has a new wardrobe from Garfinckles."

"How do you know all these things?"

"Tina keeps me posted. When Rosa is not at home, Tina has to sign for deliveries from the UPS man for packages from Garfinckles."

"She has done a complete about face in a short time."

"Definitely. Tina thinks she has drawn a bead on that professor she met at UVA when she went to see Tomas in the play last month. They have corresponded, and Rosa asked Tina if she would be able to spend a weekend at her house whenever she might take a trip to Charlottesville—to see Tomas of course."

"This is good news, Cynthia. Tina's presence is working out nicely for both daughter and mother. How is she reacting to all this?"

"I think we've lost a candidate for ballet. Tina has confided that she'd like to switch and become a physical therapy assistant. She likes this work with children, and hopes to make a career out of it."

"According to Alex's figures on the survey, there are plenty of patients who could use the service at home. Of course, eventually we'll want Andrea to improve to the point where she can be enrolled in a community based program and be among her peers."

"She is rapidly coming to that point, thanks to Tina. I must be off now, Clare. Have a nice holiday."

Back in her office, Clare called Dean Keyes. "Hello, Roger. Just wanted to call and wish you a very pleasant holiday."

"Same to you, Clare. Are you leaving town?"

"Yes. Tomorrow, I'm off to Florida, and will bring back a tan so you can admire it."

"Lucky girl. Have a swim for me."

"Another thing before I go. Jean Matson told me this morning that her husband Hank is being transferred to Hawaii in January. This leaves us with a big hole in Human Services."

"It sure does. Jean is a valuable member of the faculty. Any ideas about a replacement?"

"At the moment, no. You know how difficult it is to get faculty in the middle of the year. Most are on contract, and not available until the summer. I won't promise to look hard in Florida, but if I see any likely candidates, I'll give you a call. Happy holidays."

"Have a good time, Clare, See you next year. Wait! Have you seen Rita Evans lately?"

"Yes, last week. Why?"

"Would you give some thought to having Rita in your department?"

"You know she's full time at the hospital, and has been there just a few months. Yes, I'd love to have her, but that's an impossible dream. Nice try!"

Roger Keyes was a competent administrator, and he had the ability to recognize promising candidates for his faculty. The idea of going after Rita Evans was a challenge he would enjoy pursuing. Now there was a sharp woman.

The rest of the afternoon was spent on telephone calls

and paper work that had piled up. One good thing about the holidays was that he could wade through a mountain of white without too much distraction. Throughout, Rita Evans was on his mind and the mental wheels were spinning. As he drifted off to sleep that night an idea was born. He nurtured it the next day, and mid-afternoon he called Dr. Sargent at the hospital.

"Dave? Just want to send greetings of the season to you and the staff. It's been a good year for all of us."

"Hi, Roger. Good to hear from you. Yes, it's been a great year. We've had more 'ups' than 'downs.'"

"How about stopping by the house on your way home tonight for a short one. I believe you go right by the door, don't you?"

"Why yes. I'll be happy to pause, but briefly."

Roger arrived home that evening bristling with the damp cold and promptly laid a fire in the living room.

"Dave Sargent is coming by for a short Season's Greetings drink, Ruth. Shall I make one for you?"

"No thanks. I'm busy in the kitchen. Roger Jr. is due home any minute now from Princeton, and he'll come in starving. I need to be ready. Anything new on the campus today?"

"It was rather quiet, students finishing up and faculty getting ready for their recess. Oh yes, Clare Cohen told me that the Matsons are going to Hawaii in January. Hank is being transferred to Oahu, so we'll need to get a replacement for Jean. That might be tough, but I've got a plan."

The fire was roaring when Dr. Sargent lifted the knocker, and Roger welcomed him.

"Come in, Dave, and warm up. It's brutal out there. Here, let me take your coat and hat."

"Thanks, Roger. It sure is snappy. Your fire looks good and smells even better. I can stay just a wee bit, as we've got an engagement tonight. Our medical society is having its annual Christmas party and they throw a good one, plenty of everything."

"Can I offer you a drink?"

"Yes, a martini with Tangueray, my favorite gin," he said as they inched over to the bar. "Don't let the vermouth fumes contaminate the gin." He let out a laugh.

They relaxed in front of the fireplace, enjoying their drinks and discussing the mess in Washington following the recent election.

"Seems to me the White House is trying to bury a lot of skeletons," Dave observed. "That break-in trial in January will be something else."

"Yes," Roger agreed. "There will be some pretty red faces in the upper echelon before the trial is over. I enjoy the political cartoons by Herblock in the *Washington Post*. He sure gets to the essence with a few quick strokes of the pen. He's priceless."

After a slight pause, and before Dave rose to leave, Roger said, "After the holidays, I wonder if you and I can talk about an idea that may be beneficial to our agencies."

"Sure, Roger. Care to give me a quick fill-in so I can be thinking about it?"

"One of our faculty, Jean Matson, will be leaving late in January to accompany her husband on a new assignment to Hawaii and we've got to find a replacement. She teaches the Sociology of Human Relations course, and she'll be hard to replace."

"How do we fit into the plans?" a cautious Dave asked.

"That's what I'd like to talk to you about. Maybe something on a part time basis? A sharing of staff? I'm not sure yet."

"Good. It's worth thinking and talking about in January. Many thanks for the drink, Roger, I must be on my way now.

We'll get together soon. Merry Christmas."

❧ ❧ ❧

Late that same afternoon, Alex Snyder drove his car up the ramp to his house, paused, pressed the button and watched as the garage door opened, then drove inside. He opened his door, reached behind to haul out his chair and slid from the seat onto the chair. The garage door closed, he reached into the car to get a package, closed the car door, then wheeled himself up the ramp to the house. He was rather proud of his domain, and he was happy in it. Shortly after joining the staff, he purchased the house, chose the furniture, drapes, color schemes for the two bedrooms, living and dining rooms, and the kitchen. A carpenter made some adjustments in the kitchen so he could work at the stove, sink and closets. Everything was on one floor, with no steps to hinder his progress.

His bedroom was large with a walk-in closet, and the other bedroom was his study, with all his books and papers. Down the hall was a den with twin beds which would accommodate guests. A woman came in weekly to clean house, and in the fall and winter, he hired a boy in the neighborhood to keep his wood pile stacked in the garage and a supply near the fireplace in the living room. Alex was resourceful, had sufficient money to afford the luxuries, and he enjoyed the good life. He might be crippled, but that did not mean he had to live in a hole. He kept a well stocked larder, and his liquor closet contained the full range of liquors."

When he came home from work, he'd roll into the bedroom, get out of the suit, shirt and tie to don slacks and a sport shirt. Then he went out to the refrigerator for the ice cubes to float in Cutty Sark, his favorite scotch, while he pondered what he'd cook for dinner. Being sedentary, he was careful in his diet, for he knew he could easily grow a "pot," and he had no need for one of those. In all, Alex knew his dietary needs and was able to maintain his weight of just over 150 pounds for his five-feet, nine-inch height.

On this cold Friday evening, he took his drink into the living room, lit the fire, and turned on his stereo to listen to soft music. Time for relaxation and to enjoy his drink and cigarette. It had been a good day, in fact the week had gone rather well. As a social worker, he enjoyed helping others untangle their lives from a myriad of problems. There was the high school football player whose arm was shattered in an automobile accident, the five-year-old girl in pediatrics hobbling toward him on her crutches, and the man who had just been told that he could no longer play golf because of neurological damage.

Alex drank, smoked, and leaned back in his chair rethinking his own bouts with despair over his shattered life, and how he came to his present state where he could be of help to others in need.

After a while he wheeled over to put another log on the fire, then went out to the kitchen to place a small steak on a slow burner. Back in the living room, the fire was warm, the music soothing, and he thought of the recent party where he met the girl with the blonde hair and the red dress. Soon his mind wandered.

Donna was talking to him. "Nice place you have here, Alex, you should have invited me over sooner."

"Does your mother know you're out?"

"I really don't care. She's too protective of me."

"Now that you're here, how about a drink?"

"Sure. White wine?"

"OK."

With the drinks on a tray in his lap, Alex wheeled to the chair occupied by Donna, checked the fire and said,

"Cheers," raising his glass to clink hers.

"Thanks, Alex. This is great. Nice way to spend a Friday evening. Nice company, great music, warm fire and a good friend."

"Now that you're here, I hope you'll stay for dinner and enjoy my Delmonico steak, baked potatoes, tossed salad, ice cream, and coffee."

"Sounds great. I know I'll enjoy it. After talking about a range of topics, Donna stood up and said, "Alex where is the powder room?"

He led her to the first door on the left. "Fifteen feet straight ahead is the commode, and opposite is the wash basin. Towels to the right."

When she emerged, he said "Here is my study across from the bathroom, next is the den for guests, and my bedroom is further down here."

"Good. I was hoping you'd show me around."

When she entered his room, her hands on the handles of his chair, she said, "I can't make out too much, but I smell 'man' all over."

"Sure, I'm the only occupant."

"Alex, how do you get out of your chair, undress, and get into bed? Isn't it difficult?"

"Nothing to it. I slide onto the bed, take off my clothes, put them on the chair, and slip into my pajamas and, in no time, I'm in the sack."

Donna had come around from the back of his wheelchair to sit on the bed as he talked. She took his hand, placed it on her cheek, then found his face and kissed him.

When she leaned over to kiss him, Alex could see inside her dress to the firm breasts, and in a moment, he slid off his chair on to the bed. His movement caused them both to fall backward locked in an embrace.

Donna kissed him softly at first, and he responded

passionately. He could feel himself getting hard, and Donna was responding pressing her body close to his.

Suddenly a burning odor wafted into the bedroom.

"The steak! Damn! What a time for it to burn," he muttered as he came to, aroused by the crackling of the grease on the stove. Before he could move, he felt, then saw the damp spot on his trousers.

"Wow! What a dream! And a wet one at that! It sure was nice!"

As fast as he could, he made it to the kitchen to rescue what was left of the charred mess. "What the hell. I'll cook up another and have a drink while I savor that gal. Wonder what she'd really be like in bed. Not to worry, Alex, that'll never happen."

Back in his room, he changed his slacks and paused at the door of his study. We never got close to talking about my books here, but she almost got to see me in the flesh—the real flesh!" He laughed at himself.

It was almost nine o'clock when he finished his dinner, and went into the study to do some work. He found it hard to concentrate on anything, for the memory of his encounter with Donna came flashing back, and he had trouble putting it aside, not that he wanted to.

Finally, he tossed discretion to the winds and picked up the telephone. "Hello? Donna?"

"This is her mother. Whom shall I say is calling?"

"Hello, Mrs. Edwards. This is Alex Snyder. We met at the Evans' party recently."

"Oh, yes. Donna is in her room. I'll have her pick up there."

There was a brief pause, and he could hear Mrs. Edwards calling to her daughter. "Donna, a call for you."

"Hello. This is Donna Edwards." Not the low tempting voice he had heard before in his bedroom, but a reassuring quiet announcement.

"Hi. This is Alex Snyder, the guy you fell over at the party, remember?"

A full throated laugh came over the wires. That's more like it.

"Yes, I do remember and blush when I recall the incident. How are you Alex. It's good to hear your voice."

"Oh, I'm fine. Thought I'd give you a call, just on the spur of the moment to see how you're getting along."

"Very nice of you. I'm glad you called. That was a nice party, and I enjoyed meeting you, although the circumstances . . ."

"I couldn't think of a better way to meet a young woman than . . . well you know what I mean." He was thinking not so much of the encounter at the Evans, but what had occurred in his bedroom within the last few hours. He knew she couldn't see his crimson face over the telephone wires.

They talked idly for sometime, and when Alex asked if she was free the next night for a date, she readily accepted and put the telephone down all aglow as her mother knocked then pushed open her door.

"What did he want? Is everything all right, dear?"

"Yes. Alex and I had a nice chat, and he's invited me out tomorrow evening." She wanted to be alone to cherish the conversation, and her mother was an impediment to the reverie. It had been a long time since she had received a call from a gentleman friend.

"I hope you know what you're doing, Donna. He's crippled, and in that chair. How can he drive and . . ."

"Mother! Alex is a big boy now, and I'm a grown girl, rather a woman and I know exactly what I'm doing. You want to protect me too much, and I don't like it. Nothing can happen to either of us. We'll manage nicely, I'm sure."

Sniffing softly, Mabel Edwards retired to her own room

to get ready for bed and to worry alone. Donna was her sole concern, and if anything happened to her, she'd be lost.

Later, Joe Edwards came up in route to bed, knocked on his daughter's door, and opened it to her "Come in."

He came to the bed to kiss her good night. She put her arms around his neck and said excitedly, "Daddy, I've got a date tomorrow night. It's Alex Snyder, the man who works with Mrs. Evans at the hospital. He called and he's taking me to a pub."

"A pub? My daughter?"

"It's really a piano recital, in a beer joint, down the road."

"That's different. As long as it's respectful and the pianist knows some good beer drinking songs. Many an evening I spent in a joint singing along. Those were the good old days, and before I met your mother." His eyes twinkled, and he enjoyed joshing with his daughter.

Father and daughter got along famously. In their daily round trips to Washington for work, they joked, laughed, had serious conversations, and made a good team. Both knew that Mabel was upset over Donna's lack of vision, but the girl took it in stride.

She had her work, her music, good health, and a joy in living. She made more of her life than her mother with two good eyes. While Donna was an extrovert, always looking out, Mabel's world revolved around her daughter, and she was constantly worried that something might happen to her.

Her father was proud that she held down a good job in Washington and was an accomplished musician. He was concerned that there were no boy friends knocking on the door, and he knew that despite her good looks, her lack of vision precluded such relationships. She had a tiny bit of travel vision and could make out shapes and light, but everything was a blur. There was no clarity, and there were times, she told him confidentially she could see nothing. "Just darkness, and not a God damn thing."

"I'm happy you're going out, kitten. We're off, too. I'm taking your mother out, so if we should meet in some den of iniquity, let's pretend we don't know one another?"

"Daddy, I can't imagine mother in a den of iniquity. It would kill her."

"It might be the best thing in the world for her. She's too protected. Enough of this nonsense. Good night. Get a good sleep and be rested for tomorrow night. Never can tell what may happen."

"We'll be very proper, Daddy. 'Night."

Donna slept late that Saturday morning, had a leisurely breakfast with her parents, tidied up her room, and played the piano for a while. She knew every inch of the house, and though legally blind, she rarely made a false step.

Her mother announced that she and Joe were going out that evening and asked if they should wait until her young man arrived.

"No, Mother, I'll be ready, and when I hear his car, I'll go out to meet him."

"If there is anything I can do . . ."

"No. Nothing. I have everything under control. Please don't pester me, and don't worry. Alex isn't going to rape me the first night out!"

Mabel was shocked, but said nothing. Within she wondered what had got into my docile daughter?

As Alex's headlight swept the wide expanse of lawn and bounced off the living room windows, Donna heard the chimes of NBC on the radio announcing six o'clock and thought, "He's right on the nose. I like that."

Alex watched as his date closed the front door, walked assuredly on the side walk, turned left where she could dimly see the lights of the car, and made her way to the fender then opened the door of the automobile.

"Hi Alex! How goes it?" She settled into the seat.

"Great. You look pretty nice in that outfit, and I like your perfume."

"Chanel. It does have a fragrance. Well, now, where are we going for this recital?"

"A what?"

"That's what I told my parents. My mother didn't believe me, and my father knew I was joshing. Are we heading for the strip?"

"We'll drive by it, but we'll go to a favorite place I know. Besides, there are too many joints on the strip and none of them have ramps."

"Sounds OK to me. I smell wool, Alex. What are you wearing?"

"A tweed sport coat with a little green in it. Dark green woolen slacks, beige shirt and tie with green and grey stripes."

"Must look good. You don't mind if I ask these kinds of questions? My father always tells me what he's wearing, and then I can see him better."

Soon they came to Mike's Place, a white stucco building on Route 301 south of La Plata and about five miles from the Governor Nice bridge over the Potomac River.

"Donna, this is one of my close friends whom I met in 'Nam. After service he opened up Mike's Place and has done very well here. It's not a typical bar, for he serves meals and has a piano which he plays frequently."

As she pushed the chair up the ramp, she said "How did you know he was here?"

"I didn't. When I first saw the place, it was on a hot day, there was a ramp, so I came in for a cold beer. Both Mike and I couldn't believe it when we saw one another. He's great. You'll like him."

The interior was warm and pleasant. A fire place was glowing and about forty patrons huddled around tables or at the bar on padded seats. A waitress took their coats and led them to the bar where Mike held forth.

"Alex! Good to see you, and your charming companion."

"Mike, meet Donna Edwards. Donna, this is the guy I told you about."

"I'm delighted to meet you, Mr. Thomas."

"My pleasure, Miss Edwards. Pull up a bar seat, and I'll take your order. I know what this rogue usually has."

When the drinks arrived they toasted and snacked on peanuts and chips.

Mike was short, with black curly hair above bushy brows and a broad face opened to show off his gap-toothed mouth. Merriment was in his eyes when he sat at the piano to roll off a few tunes. Alex's eyes warned him to lay off Donna, no wise cracks or funny stuff.

Mike was curious about the blonde Alex had in tow. She was a beauty, had a great figure, was well dressed, but did she need those shades? He caught on as soon as he saw her fumbling with the glass and the peanut dish.

When the crowd thinned out after midnight, Mike prevailed on Donna to play the piano, and she willingly obliged. First a classical piece to warm up her fingers, then songs from musical scores.

"Interested in moonlighting, Donna?" Mike asked when she had finished Moon River.

Alex cut him off with a short "No way, man! She's got a job."

Donna's response was to dash off a few bars of "Good Night Ladies," then she excused herself to go to the powder room, with a waitress leading the way.

"Alex, you rascal. No offense. She's a great gal, and I'm all for you. Lucky man."

"Yeah, a wonderful person, warm and gracious."

The moon was dipping low at 1:30 a.m. when they arrived

back at the Edwards house.

"Thanks Alex for a wonderful evening. I don't know when I've had such a pleasant time."

Chapter XI

Beth was the snow watcher in the Evans family, and beginning in early December would come the repeated question, "Daddy are we going to have snow for Christmas? Do you think it will be a white Christmas?"

In 1973, the family's first December out from Washington, Beth got her wish.

Preparations for the holidays had been going on for days. Joe and the children had purchased the tree and green trimmings. Rita had all the presents wrapped and secreted throughout the house. Cookies, cakes, and pies were in the freezer, and the twelve pound turkey was in the refrigerator waiting to be transferred to the oven. A few last minute items remained to be purchased, but they were taken care of Christmas Eve morning when Joe and Rita drove up to Waldorf. Beth went along and when they came out from the store, the first flakes began to fall.

"I knew it! We'll have a white Christmas after all!" she exclaimed.

By the time they reached home, the steady fall had covered the ground making the roads slippery, and the driving dangerous. Roger and Joe Jr. were out in the yard having a snowball fight. The sky was a leaden gray, the wind whipping up the top of the snow, and it promised to be a good fall. Beth went into the yard to join the snow ballers, but when one hit her neck, and the cold water soaked her sweater and dripped down inside her clothing, she let out a yell and returned to the warm house to dry off and enjoy the snow from protective rooms.

The cocktail hour that evening was pleasant. The twinkling lights on the tree mingled with the glow from the fireplace, and the odor of burning wood danced with the smell of evergreen and a bayberry candle. The draperies in the living room were opened, inviting the snow covered trees outside to be a part of the household.

Joe had made a pitcher of martinis, gave one to Rita with a hug and a kiss. "Love you, dear. Thank you for everything." They sat by the fire, talked about previous Christmases, and were content.

One of the family traditions held that after the children had their baths, Joe would read to them from the battered red *Christmas Stories*, Dickens' *A Christmas Carol*, Moore's *'Twas The Night Before Christmas*, and other stories. When the children were in bed, Rita would bring out the wrapped boxes and place them under the tree.

It had snowed all day, a light powdery fall measured over fifteen inches out in the yard. The trees were heavy, limbs bent low, and shrubs were completely buried. The yard was a pretty sight.

"Joe, do you think we can make it out to St. Dunstan's for Midnight Mass?" Rita asked.

"Sure, no problem. The snow tires are new, and once we're out on the street, we'll be able to drive easily. I've heard the snow plows all evening, so the roads should be clear."

Bright stars twinkled above when they backed out of the driveway and drove into La Plata for church. The deep snow did not deter Father Tom's parishioners from Mass, and the church was filled to capacity. The priest gave a moving homily, and drew an interesting comparison between the present and the night the Savior was born, some nineteen hundred years ago. He always put a lot of thought into his sermons.

It was long after 1:30 a.m. by the time they returned home.

"I'll resurrect the fire, dear, if you'll arouse the children, then we can enjoy some eggnog, hot chocolate for the kids, and some of grandma's cookies and fruit cake," Joe said.

The gifts were many and varied. A wrist watch to Rita from a loving husband, who received books, shirts, and ties, while the children opened packages of games, books, and clothing. There was a mass of paper and ribbons on the floor, and Joe left it all to go to bed around three o'clock. He knew the family would be up until almost dawn, and he was tired.

It was 9:00 a.m. when he roused out of bed, and the house was quiet except for the boys in their room talking about their games. On the way to the kitchen, he saw two heads wrapped in a comforter under the tree, and when his coffee began to perk, Rita stirred. He brought a cup of black coffee to her, and she returned his "Good morning and Merry Christmas" greetings.

It was a beautiful, bright, clear day, shimmering in a white blanket. Mid-afternoon Al, Martha, and Tommy stopped by, then Alex and Donna for an exchange of greetings. Alex had no problems for Joe had made the house accessible with a ramp from the car port into the kitchen area.

The adults had eggnog and fruit cake, with Alex asking for the recipe for the cake. Beth offered, "Daddy thinks she puts brandy in it, but she won't give out the recipe."

Donna played a few Christmas carols, and led the singing of the entire group. Then running her fingers over her watch she said, "Alex, I think we'd better be moving along. The folks will be waiting for us."

"I'm ready. Thanks to everyone, and Merry Christmas. It's good to be with family at this season. Mine has gone to Florida, and Donna took pity on me. I'll be with her folks for dinner."

After they had left, Rita said to Joe "Did you see Alex when Donna was playing the piano?"

"Not particularly. Why?"

"He sat off to one side, sang a bit, but just ogled her. His eyes lit up, he watched every movement she made, and I think that the love bug has bitten him."

"What gives you that idea?"

"Why not? Alex has warmed up and those rough edges of his are smoothed over. Ever since they met here a few weeks ago he has been a different person. He told me they've gone out on dates to a lounge, shopped together, and now he's been invited to her house for dinner."

"Could be, love. Joe Edwards told me Donna has talked about Alex as they drive into the District. He thinks she likes the guy, but with her visual handicap, she's holding back."

"Her mother would not approve of this 'togetherness' I'm sure."

"No, Mabel is too protective, and won't let her be herself."

"Donna is such a pretty girl, and gifted, too. Maybe this is just a phase for both of them. At least they can have fun together, where alone they would be just that—alone."

"If they have part of the fun we had dating, they'll have a ball, and I'm all for them."

❧ ❧ ❧

Shortly after New Years, on one of the sleety, snowy days when one bent forward against the wind, Rita made her way to the office to be met by Billie Jean, who announced

"Dr. Sargent would like to see you sometime this afternoon."

"Call and tell them I'll be free about 3:30."

When she appeared at the appointed time, Dr. Sargent greeted her with "Come in, Rita. Have a seat. Coffee? Tea?"

"Thanks. Tea would be fine."

"First, I want to tell you how pleased we are with what you have accomplished in such a short time. You've made a nice impression on the staff and your ideas, such as the C.I.T., are excellent."

"I am happy here and enjoy the staff; they are all so cooperative."

"I called you in to talk about a plan which will involve you, and I need to get your reaction before any steps are taken.

"There is a vacancy on the faculty at the college, and in view of your education and experience, it has been suggested that you be considered for appointment there."

"I'm full-time here, the load is heavy, I supervise two workers, and I couldn't possibly see myself stuck in a classroom all day." Rita was slightly exasperated.

"Good thought. You're saying that there is more satisfaction in dealing with people's problems directly than through a textbook."

As she nodded in assent, he continued. "I've spoken with Dean Keyes at the college, and we'd like to pilot a program which would benefit all of us in the community.

"In brief, the college would invite you to join the faculty on a part-time basis to teach The Sociology of Human Relations in the Human Services Division. We can arrange your schedule here so that it can be done in the morning or late afternoon. You may want to do some lecturing here in the hospital.

"On our part, we'll arrange to send several staff to the college for courses to improve their proficiency or to help them begin work on the AA degree. We would be exchanging resources without any money passing between the two institutions."

"You've caught me off guard, Dr. Sargent. It does sound promising, and has potential. The opportunity to teach part time is inviting. Perhaps this would allow students to do a practicum here like Tina's work with Andrea."

"Yes. I've heard of that project, and I'm pleased with the results. The decision is up to you, and if you decide in the affirmative, I'll set up a meeting with Dean Keyes and Dr. Cohen."

"Thanks for sharing this with me. I'll need to think it over and discuss it with my husband. I'll let you know in a few days. Also, I should talk with Dr. Cohen to get an idea of what is expected in the classroom, the textbook, number of students, etc."

"Dean Keyes has mentioned this to Dr. Cohen, and she can give you the information you need."

On her way home, Rita drove by the campus, and wondered if she'd be able to handle both the hospital and college assignments. She'd need to talk this over with Joe.

Later that evening, Rita described the program Dr. Sargent outlined and what it would entail.

"If you are interested in teaching, along with your hospital work, that sounds like an ideal combination of theory and practice. You'll need to space your time, and not run yourself ragged. Students can be pretty demanding, and you'll need to do a lot of reading in preparation for class."

"I have a pretty good idea of the content, and it shouldn't take long to develop a syllabus. This would also be a great opportunity to develop practicum projects for the students, not only in the hospital but in many of the community's agencies."

"You sound as though you have already made a decision.

Go ahead and I'll support you, and help wherever I can."

As soon as Rita notified Dr. Sargent of her acceptance, he called Dean Keyes who passed the word on to Dr. Cohen. All were pleased with her willingness to join in on the program.

"I'm looking forward to this, Clare," Rita said a few days later. "I'll need some coaching as to the rules and policy of the college."

"Why don't you come over tomorrow and we'll give you all the information you'll need. Jean will be around for several more weeks, and she'll be able to tell you more about the students and what she has covered.

At the beginning of the second semester, Rita met her first class of eighteen students. Jean Matson had prepared them for a new instructor, and Tina had given them a rundown on the new "professor."

In her own quiet way, Rita introduced herself, her position at the hospital, and her background. She then established her expectations for the remainder of the term . By the end of class, the students knew they were in for a lot of work, but they would be learning a great deal from the assignments, the practicum, and from a competent instructor who would introduce them to new concepts and strategies in working with people.

Chapter XII

Joe Evans was up early to see the dawn wipe away the last vestiges of night and the beginnings of a spring day in early March. He roused Rita with a kiss and a greeting. "Wake up old girl. Here's the plasma and dried ink—your coffee and *Washington Post.*"

The newspapers, radio, and TV were full of the Watergate scandal. At this point, L. Patrick Gray was sitting on a time bomb, and the White House staff were pushing Executive Privilege as an excuse to refuse to testify before the Senate Committee. The debacle was horrifying and horrendous.

Rita was into the editorial page as Joe finished shaving, and as he emerged to dress she said, "Wait 'till you see the political cartoon. Herblock is priceless!"

"Tell me about it."

"There's R.M.N. sitting on top of a stinking garbage can overflowing with dirt, labeled 'Administrative Corruption' while a bulging lid has the caption 'Executive Privilege.' Everyone knows he's covering up something, yet he keeps quiet, indicating that he's protecting the office of the president."

At 7:30 the telephone rang, and Roger detached himself from the sports page to answer and call out, "Mom, it's for you."

"Hello. Oh, hi, Peg. What's up?"

"Sorry to call you at home, Rita, but we've got an emergency. Our C.I.T. will meet at 8:30. Come a runnin'."

As she parked her car, Father Tom Shane drew up alongside. "Morning rounds, Father?"

"Hello, Rita. No, I had planned to do them later, but Peg called for our C.I.T."

"Me too. Well, let's see what brings this on."

They met in Dr. Sargent's office Because this was a new program, he had volunteered to serve as chairman for the year. Rita, Peg, and Father Tom pulled up chairs while his secretary took orders for coffee.

"We admitted a white female, twenty-five-year-old patient at 4:00 a.m., five months pregnant and bleeding profusely as the result of a self-induced abortion. She found out that her investment broker husband has been running around with other women in D.C. and New York, where he frequently goes on business trips. They have no children and she wants a divorce and an abortion. When he refused, she tried to induce it herself so she'd be completely free of him. Now she's critical and may not survive.

"I've known her father-in-law for years. They're an old Catholic family, been into raising tobacco and horses for generations. I haven't been familiar with his son Ed, the patient's husband, but I hear he's gone wild over women and booze."

"How did she try to abort?" Rita asked.

"There's a powerful drug that just appeared on the market, and she got a vial from a physician in Washington. She was in tough shape when she was admitted, so I couldn't find out too much. She's sedated now, lost a lot of blood and tore up her pelvic cavity. The situation calls for a team approach, and I know how well each of you functions.

"Peg, the nurses will have to keep Mrs. Mitchell under very close supervision, for when she regains consciousness, she may try some other stunt to do away with herself. Rita, you'll need to track down her husband and talk with him, and when she recovers, talk with her about her family situation. Father Tom, I assume the woman is Catholic, and I sense you Romans disapprove of abortion, since it is murder. She'll need your comforting spiritual guidance.

"I'll take care of the medical aspects and keep you advised. She's still on the critical list, and it may be some hours before we'll know if she'll pull through. We'll meet again tomorrow morning, unless I call you in later today. Any question?"

❧ ❧ ❧

At the southern end of town in a housing development, Dr. Patrick Bolton was awakened by the chirping of birds, and opened one eye to see the clock, which told him it was 8:00 a.m. "Hell, what am I getting up for? It's my day off. Back to the sack"

When next he woke, it was noon, and he lolled in bed thinking of the buxom nurse he wrestled with the night before, making lots of love and having too much to drink. What a broad!

Pat was alone in the house. His wife Amy had gone to visit her parents in Texas and would be away for a week. This was great, for Pat now had the freedom to taste the night life in Georgetown, D.C.

Over a breakfast of juice, coffee and an English muffin, Pat thought about his agenda for the day: meet Dave Salter at three o'clock, then to the Saville Bookstore in Georgetown, and at five o'clock, meet Alice at the Three George's lounge for drinks, followed by lots of loving.

A navy blue blazer fitted well over his broad shoulders, covering a light blue shirt, red and white striped tie, while his long legs were encased in gray flannels just above cordovan weejuns.

He stacked the dishes in the sink, ran water over them quickly, walked through the comfortable living room and soon was out the door and in the seat of his "T" bird. The crocus and daffodils were in bloom, but he hardly noticed that spring was arriving.

He had made the trip to Washington so often that the car could almost make the proper turns and stops on its own. His mind wandered then paused as he thought of Ida, the girl he had last night. She was in her late twenties, unmarried light complexion, green eyes, luscious lips and big tits. She was a good nurse and had assisted him in the O.R. several times. When he had rubbed up against her, she had reciprocated, and he knew he could make it with her. They did, in a locked closet right afterward. She was all nurse, and in bed she was all woman.

Waiting for Dr. Salter in his reception room, Pat recalled when they had met a year ago at a medical society gathering. At the bar, one drink led to another, and soon they were sharing experiences, the older man giving tips to the novice. Once he attended a party at Dave's apartment, and spent the night sharing a bed with a luscious woman, but he was so drunk, he couldn't recall any of the details.

Dave Salter was in his mid-fifties, sporting 170 pounds on a medium frame, dark haired with a full mustache. The family were old Austrians who came to New York after World War I to raise the population by three sons. After Dave completed his medical studies and residency, he married the daughter of a prominent Washington businessman, but after a few years, it turned sour. They split, but with no divorce, since neither wanted one. They remained friends, even going out together occasionally.

The receptionist ushered Pat into Dave's office.

"Hello, Pat. Good to see you." Dave rose and came around the desk to greet and shake hands.

"Hi Dave. How goes it?"

"This is one helluva day. I'm up to my ears in fannies and butts, I don't know where all these women come from." Dave had a lucrative practice in OB-GYN, but had an unsavory reputation among his colleagues. He was out for a fast buck, and didn't care how he made it, or who he stepped on. In his work, he was precise and a competent specialist. In his off hours, he was a party man, which is one reason Pat was attracted to him.

"Anything I can do to help?" Pat inquired.

"Are you serious, or just being nice."

"Serious. I'm free for several hours, and happy to give you a hand."

"Good. We can knock this off quickly, then head for the apartment for drinks, dinner, and a couple of broads."

"Not tonight, Dave. I've got an appointment at five o'clock after I go to the bookstore."

A few hours later, at a nearby bar, Dave said, "My practice is growing, and I need help; could use an assistant. Interested?"

"I've got to stay at the hospital for the rest of the year, and when my residency is over, then . . ."

"You've got to finish the residency, but I mean on your days off like today, and in my other work, the abortions."

Pat thought hard and fast. This would mean a nice financial boost, and he could use the money.

Dave continued. "I've had several girls from down in your area coming in to get rid of 'IT.' If you're interested, I'll set you up in an office there. This will save them time coming up here."

"OK. Count me in. Sounds interesting. By the way, on that new drug you gave me last week. I administered it to

Mrs. Mitchell, and she's doing all right. I'll be seeing her tomorrow, and let you know how she is doing."

Later, Pat drove home congratulating himself on the arrangement with Dave. He could handle the assignments at the hospital and make moonlight arrangements for the abortion trade. No problem. The tricounty was conservative with staunch Episcopalians and devout Catholics all over the place. With the new drug Dave had given him for the private list of women in the area, his job would be so much easier.

He would need a nurse, for things did get messy now and then in these cases, and he'd need professional help. Perhaps Ida would be willing to join him in this activity. She'd be a valuable asset and her reputation as a nurse was good.

The next morning Pat was at the hospital bright and early. He was relaxed after his day off, and exhilarated over the prospects of the offer made the previous day. It would mean more money, the ethics and values be damned.

"Good morning, Peg," his voice cheerful as he passed nurse O'Bryan.

"Hi Pat. Enjoy your day off?"

Dr. Sargent came up the corridor. "Hello Pat."

"Good morning, Dr. Sargent. How goes everything?"

"We're in pretty good shape. We had a scare yesterday, but we're OK now."

The boss didn't scare easily. He'd been around a long time and had seen just about most everything.

"What happened?"

"We almost lost one of our prominent county citizens, when she was admitted hemorrhaging badly, but we stopped it. Our C.I.T. worked beautifully." He had been about to say a lot more, but he didn't want to reveal any pertinent information about the patient.

"Dr. Bolton, please call seventy-eight." The page interrupted his thoughts.

Over lunch at noon he was talking with two interns from Georgetown University Medical Center, and close by, several nurses were talking in hushed tones, and looking at the interns and hoping for some recognition.

As Pat got up to take his tray away, he heard one of the nurses say, ". . . Mrs. Mitchell almost . . ." He stopped but quickly kept going to the belt to deposit the tray. The interns would not be his concern this afternoon. Maybe it wasn't his Mrs. Mitchell, but he'd need to call her anyway.

"Hello. May I speak with Mrs. Mitchell? This is a friend calling."

The maid said simply, "She ain't here."

"Thank you." He hung up.

Pat was worried. Maybe it was his and Dave's patient to whom he gave that new drug. What if it IS her? Dr. Sargent had said the patient had severe bleeding. How was he to find out? AAAH, my friend Ida the nurse. She'll know and tell me.

As soon as Ida was paged she came to Pat's office.

"Hello, Ida. I'm glad you could get here. Close the door?"

"Hi Pat. I was finishing lunch when the page came." She looked beautiful today, red hair in sharp contrast to her white uniform stretched across those ample boobs and snug hips.

"Can you sit for a few minutes?"

"Sure, I've got the time."

"Who is the patient who was admitted yesterday with severe hemorrhaging?"

Ida was quiet, discreet, and professional. She got around and knew about everything going on. Despite the secrecy imposed by Dr. Sargent, she was able to check the admission records and the medical chart in the patient's room and learn her identity.

"No one is supposed to know about her and you are the only one who doesn't know, and that's because you were off yesterday. She is Mrs. Edward Mitchell, daughter-in-law of THE Sam Mitchell, prominent in local society. She almost died after taking a drug prescribed by some doctor. She aborted all right, but it tore her up, too strong a chemical reaction. I hear it's new and not fully tested."

"Wow! That's tough!" Pat was visibly shaken.

"Anything wrong?"

"No, Ida. I'm OK. Thanks for the info."

Later he went to a pay phone to call Dave and tell him what happened.

Chapter XIII

In his initial interview with Rita, Dr. Sargent had spotted her professional bearing in thought, speech, reaction, composure, and assessment. Once at the hospital, there was never any question about her judgement and integrity. Her basic concern was for the patient, the rights of the patient, and the best approach to solve the problem.

Rita knew her social work from the roots up. At one point in her life, she leaned toward the study of medicine, but the depression years precluded such a drain on the family finances. When a scholarship for graduate study in social work became available, she took it and became involved in this people-to-people field.

Her students at the community college soon became aware of her knowledge and sense of the practical. She used the text ordered by Jean Matson for the course, for it would crush her conservative heart not to utilize purchased and available texts. Next year she'd order a new book, one with a different approach. Aided by her husband, she had already begun to explore new texts.

At the outset, Rita and Clare had an understanding of the course. Clare Cohen had shown her the course outline, dealing with sociology as a base

Rita told her, "You know, my forte is social work, but I will not make this a course in social work per se."

"I know you well enough to recognize your professionalism and how you will handle the program. The students need not only the theory, but a sense of how it is carried out in every day life. We just don't have enough practitioners in the classrooms."

"I see no problem there."

"Let's see how the semester takes shape, and as problems arise, let me know. We can assist on any practicum assignments, and so far, you've done nicely."

"We could use a better title for this course. The present one does not sit right with me."

"I'm glad you mentioned it. It is a bit awkward."

The women had hit it off from the outset, and were at ease with one another.

The winds and rains of April had swept the sky clear of leaden clouds, spring flowers were already popping forth, and Rita had settled comfortably into her dual role. The students were a mixed group, mostly white girls, several blacks, an Asian girl, and five boys, two of whom were black.

"We've been discussing the role of medical services in our society. What are some of the impact points, the new emphases?" she asked.

Her students had done their homework—

"Care of the whole person, because the systems of the body are so interrelated, when you treat one, you affect the others."

"Prevention of illness. When you prevent something, then you don't have to get into a lot of expensive treatment."

"Using computers in medicine is taking advantage of the technology, and you can do a lot more things faster."

"The multi-discipline team approach uses many specialists to solve medical problems, and it is not just one person who does the job."

"No, I'd say that the interdisciplinary team approach is

much better for it means that these professionals have to work together, and blend their expertise in working out a patient's problems."

There were several other responses, ending up with neonatology.

Rita raised the question, "Sally, what does that term mean?"

"Well, it's when the baby is born, the doctor looks it over to see if it is all right, and if not, he puts it in the incubator."

Cindy added, "It's more than that, Sally. It's a new science just for babies. Like they've found the room should be darkened and not all those bright lights to frighten the baby, because inside the mother, it's been dark and comfortable and secure."

"And what else?" Rita was probing their minds.

Maybelle raised her hand. "They give the baby to a nurse to wash off, then give it to the mother so she can put it on her chest."

"On her breast, Maybelle. That's the correct term. Go on."

"On her breast, so the baby can feel the rhythm of her heart beat. The mother can examine the baby to see if it's all right."

"Supposing there is a defect?" Rita asked quietly.

"Well, that's where the neonatologist comes in." Cindy replied. "It's his job to know right off, so they can start treatment."

Rita looked at Zeke Campbell, the black football player, and asked, "What do they do with the father in all this? After all, he laid the keel."

Zeke was a tall, twenty-year-old, powerfully built young man, quiet and responsive. He burst out laughing, joining all the class in appreciating Rita's humor, done with a straight face and twinkling eyes.

"Oh, man!" He was convulsing, slapping his thigh, he got control and blurted out between laughs, "He's there at the launching!" At that, everyone cracked up.

Wiping a laughing tear from her eye, Rita said, "Well, we're in the groove today. Good to have a sense of humor. In this business, it's a prime requisite. Continue, Zeke."

"Well, now they're bringing in the father so he can be with his wife during labor and the birthing. Studies show that father has a big role to play, to be with his wife while she's in pain, and also to see the baby born, and to hold the new baby too. If anything goes wrong, or if the baby is malformed, the father is present to see it. If any treatment is needed, the father is there to give consent, along with the mother, if she hasn't gone back to sleep."

"Good work, Zeke. So, there is a place for the father in the birthing process. When an infant is born with a very large head, it is called?"

"Hydrocephalus," a voice rang out.

"Any other defects noticeable at birth?"

"Mongolism."

"Now it's called Down Syndrome." Rita was pleased with their rapid responses. They had paid attention and had done their homework. "What to do when this happens?"

The class was quiet for a few moments. One of the girls raised her hand. "This is where the interdisciplinary team comes forth and works with the parents. It means the neonatologist, a nurse, the neurologist, the social worker and maybe others work together to help the parents."

"Good work, Cindy. Much depends on the nature of the baby's defect, and the reaction of the parents."

"Can't the doctor make decisions alone?" Amy Dale asked. Her uncle was a physician in Baltimore, and she was aware of the authority of the doctor.

"Yes, Amy, in medical matters, the doctor alone does

make the decision. But in treating the whole person, sometimes these decisions affect the family. There are specialists on the interdisciplinary team who are knowledgeable about human dynamics and behavior and can provide information to the parents so they can make the proper decision."

"Sounds complicated to me," Sally said.

"It isn't," Rite countered. "Think about it. If you are the parent of a handicapped child, do you want just one person, a physician, to make a judgement which affects not only your baby but the family, or do you want the advice of several professionals who can provide information so you make the proper decision for your family?"

As the class became quiet, thinking of her last statement, Rita looked at her watch and said, "We're just about out of time. This has been an interesting session. For next week, I'd like to have you submit a brief paper on human sexuality. I want your own thoughts, no references from books or pamphlets, just you on paper."

After class, Mai Chon, an attractive eighteen-year-old girl of Chinese American parentage, asked her, "About that keel and the launching, that was funny."

"That's an old navy story. A young sailor married less than a year was attached to an airplane carrier which was getting ready to cast off, and he wanted to leave the ship. He asked the captain, 'Sir, my wife is going to have a baby, and I need to be with her.' The captain was a kindly man and replied, 'Son, I know the feeling. You were with her at the most important time, the laying of the keel. Fun, wasn't it? Now more experienced hands will be present at the launching to guide the little one on its way, and there's not a damn thing you could do even if you were there. Permission denied.'"

Both laughed again at the story.

It was late in the afternoon, so she drove straight home, and wondered what kind of papers the students would submit. There was Maybelle, a buxom lass who was "stacked," as the boys would say. Larry was known to be a "horney bastard." Zeke, the quiet one would turn in a good paper. Ellen was shy and bright, but "sexless," and Viki, a vivacious black girl whose pretty features and face attracted all the boys, especially Zeke. The papers would be interesting.

Over cocktails that evening they exchanged activities of the day. Rita told him about the class and the reactions of the students. Then she asked, "Joe, what does the term human sexuality mean to you?"

"I look upon it as the maleness or femaleness of the person. It connotes how he or she reacts in a physical, mental, emotional, and spiritual milieu. I shun the narrow 'sexual' interpretation, the procreative act as the common denominator. I look upon it as how a man conducts himself in relation to his manhood, a woman to her womanhood."

"That sounds a bit heavy, but I know what you're saying and I agree. Maybe such a view will eventually become accepted."

"I sure hope so. We still have traces of a puritan ethic which places our use of the word 'sex' in a derogatory mode. What we need is a new vocabulary to place it in a more positive vein."

"For starters, what would you call it?"

"Why not a simple 'human development'? That takes in the whole range of the person."

"How about 'humanality'?"

"Not bad. You're catching on."

They continued on with other matters, then assembled the children and sat down to dinner.

Out of curiosity, Rita explored the topic with her friends

at the hospital. Father Shane put it in a strict religious setting. Alex started out by putting it as an attraction to the opposite sex, said it's simply love for another person. Al and Martha Burns were closer to her concept.

"It's all those things concerned with a person and his or her spouse. The physical act of sex is a very small part of the term."

Peg O'Bryan had a narrow concept. "It's just plain unadulterated coupling—sex."

When her class met, she collected the papers and turned them face down on her desk. She'd read them later.

"Anyone care to give a thumbnail sketch in a word or two on the concept of human sexuality?"

The responses were as she expected and ranged from having sex, scoring, the macho male and sexy female, and what you do when you're married, to human development, from three students.

"This is a good start. The sex act is but one minor part of this term, and to me it means the total person and how he or she reacts, responds to love, sharing and loyalty to another.

"On the other hand, there are those whose totalness has been stunted and are unable to relate properly to persons of the opposite sex. Our Judeo-Christian culture asks that we have a genuine respect for one another. When this does not prevail and our human sexuality falls apart, there may be some unpleasant consequences. These include some of the following: families where the parents fight constantly, the sonless father who treats his daughter like a boy, arson as a form of revenge, muggers who prey on women, the girl who becomes pregnant to spite her parents, child abuse, battered wives, and the list goes on."

During the break in the period, Zeke Campbell talked with her. "That was a good session. You covered a lot of ground."

"Thank you, Zeke. It is a broad subject, and covers almost

every facet of our lives."

"Yeah, but it scares me."

"You? I'd think that nothing would frighten you."

"Not much physically. I can handle myself in any fight, but it is the segregation, it's tough to be black and in the minority. White kids have a better chance than we do, especially in this county."

"What does this have to do with your humanness—your role as a man?"

"A lot! I don't feel that I can make it like the others. There's too much going against me."

"Wrong! Look at all you have going for you. Good health, devoted parents, brain power which helps you in college, skill on the football team, respect among your friends, both black and white, people admire you. You have many assets."

"Oh, sure, I do have some things going for me, but I worry about the future. I don't plan on staying here all my life. There's no opportunity for blacks to get ahead."

"Isn't that why you're here, to improve yourself and move on? This college is but the beginning, to get your feet on the ladder, then move up. You might be able to win a scholarship, combining your academic and athletic capacities."

"Yeah, I'd thought of that, but it's such a long time and so much work."

"What isn't work? How do you suppose that people get where they are without work, sweat, and a lot of inspiration?"

"But, here in this place?"

"Who says you have to stay around here? There are forty-nine other states, as well as this one, where one can go to study, live, and work."

Zeke was silent for a moment then said, "I didn't mean to get into all this, Mrs. Evans. It just kinda popped out. Guess I need to do a lot more thinking about myself and where I'm going, but it sure is hard."

"Anything worth doing is hard, Zeke. Stick with it. If I can be of help, give me a call. I'll be happy to do all I can for you."

After dinner that night, Rita and Joe talked more about Zeke and his concerns.

"I have some books he could borrow," Joe said, "to give him some idea of the professions he might consider. Maybe some evening he could come for dinner and the three of us could talk about directions he might want to consider."

"I'm not in any hurry. Zeke has some work to do on his own first."

"Sounds as though this fits right into your current classroom discussion on human sexuality."

"Yes, and in its broadest scope. I thought about that driving home tonight, and I wonder if Zeke is aware of himself in this context."

Chapter XIV

June came quietly and dropped a carpet of soft late spring flowers on the southern Maryland countryside. Warm days, a cool breeze wafting off the river, stirring the oaks, maples, and elms, while fields of corn flapping their tendrils were characteristic of the month. But, it is also fickle. Hot sticky weather can suddenly envelope all living creatures, soaking them in their own juices, while the sun seems to glower, hanging in the sky for days, relentlessly beating all who venture out into its streaming rays.

School buildings are empty, classrooms silent, the occupants long gone on vacations to the beach or mountains; teachers to summer jobs or on a college campus for additional course work.

To celebrate the closing of another year, the faculty of the community college held their annual picnic on the Saturday previous to the final day of classes. Dean Keyes made his summer cottage available at the tip of the county where the Potomac River washes into the Chesapeake Bay. The cottage was a large, two story white frame structure, with a screened-in porch wrapped around three sides of the house, filled with brightly colored summer furniture. On the west side one could see the river rushing down to the bay; from the front, a clear view of the distant bay, while off to the right, trees formed a phalanx to ward off intruders.

Beyond this were the outer fringes of Cornfield, a small community of no more than 450 people.

A cove extending from the river for about a ten acre area served as home to a family of ducks, and protected the boats from the savagery of the Potomac when on a tirade, especially during the spring floods. Trees lined the perimeter, with bushes and willows sloping down to the water on all sides, except where an arch designated the paved road to the boat house.

It took the dean and his wife two years to put the property in order. The first year was spent on the house, and when it was liveable, he turned his attention to the dock area. He designed a large boat house to serve as an entrance to a new dock. On one side were lockers and shelves, and on the other an open space into which he could pull his cabin cruiser, and with pulleys, raise it up from the water and secure it from the elements of the winter. The dock extended about one hundred feet into the water with slips on each side and a loading ramp at the end to rise and fall with the flow of the water.

The land near the boat house was cleared and leveled so that a barbecue pit, picnic tables, and benches could be placed under an awning of pine trees. It was here that the faculty party was held on a glorious Saturday afternoon.

Clare Cohen invited Alex, since she considered him quasi-faculty, and told him he could bring a friend. He arrived with Donna in the front seat and a trunk full of cold beer.

Joe Evans came up to lift a case from the trunk. "I like your taste in beer, Alex. This is good stuff."

"I called in a debt from a pilot friend of mine. He was heading out to Denver, so I put the bite on him."

When Donna came around to the front of the car, Clare moved to her side. "How cool you look. I'm glad you could join these academic types. Away from the campus, they're even human. Alex, I'm going to introduce Donna around. OK?"

Alex rolled over to the bar and saw Rita sitting close by. He called to her, "Can I get you a drink? A beer?"

"No beer, it's too filling. Make it a cool Tom Collins."

When he joined her with the drinks, they talked while people milled around them.

"It's been quite a year, Alex, and I'm glad for summer and our vacation next month."

"It's been busy for both of us. Your arrangement with the hospital and college worked out well, and I certainly enjoyed working on the survey with the college kids. Now to enjoy the summer."

"Donna looks wonderful, I'm glad she came today."

"Quite a girl. Mabel tries to nix our friendship, but Donna has made up her own mind. Her father is a great guy, he wants her to get out and have fun. He's like your man."

"Mothers can be overly protective, but I agree, she is her own person. I take it that you like her?"

"You said it. She's number one in my book, and I'm going to keep it that way."

"How does she feel about this relationship?"

"I think she enjoys my company, but not much beyond that. She still has some of the dependency syndrome many handicapped get. I did at first, but that's all gone now."

As Clare guided Donna back to where Alex sat, she said, "Thanks for introducing me to the faculty and staff. They are all so nice."

Joe Evans came up with refills on their drinks and said, "How about strolling over to the boat house and the dock? I'm interested in the cruiser tied up there. Ever do any boating, Alex?"

"Years ago when I was a kid, we'd go sailing, but not lately."

As they entered the boat house, Donna said, "What a nice breeze here. I can see a dim light at the other end, and it smells painty and boaty in here."

As they walked into the boathouse, a young man came out of the cabin cruiser, saw the group on the dock and hailed them. "Hello. She's all ready. I've just finished cleaning her, and I'm to take guests out for a ride."

Joe introduced himself, Donna, and Alex, then said, "Thanks a bunch."

Broderick Keyes saw Alex eyes light up when he saw the boat and heard the invitation. Looking at the man in the wheelchair, he said, "We can get you on without any trouble."

In a few minutes, they had Alex aboard, then guided Donna down the ladder, and the two sat in the stern laughing at their efforts. He said, "Isn't this better than walking around up there? Let me describe this craft."

Joe went aft to release the lines, and Broderick ducked into the cabin to start the motor. Soon they cleared the dock, swung around and headed for the entrance to the cove, and out to the Potomac River.

As Broderick turned downstream and handled the wheel easily, Joe admired the fixtures and equipment inside the cabin, then engaged the helmsman in conversation. He learned that the young man was a student at Yale, and was waiting for his appointment as a government intern in Washington for the summer.

At one point they looked at the couple holding hands in the stern. Alex was pointing out something off the starboard beam and talking to her. In response to Broderick's question about Donna, he replied, "Yes she's legally blind, and you'd hardly know it. She's a college graduate, works every day in Washington and is an accomplished pianist. They're just very good friends, and we enjoy being with them."

When Broderick made a wide sweep to go back up the

river, Donna called out, "Where are we going?"

"Up the Potomac to Kitt's Point. It won't be long and you'll enjoy the breeze."

Joe took the wheel as they returned from the point, and soon they were entering the cove again. It took a little over an hour, and Broderick was ready to take another group out for a ride.

Alex said to Donna, "You've got a sunburn, and it makes you look even prettier. We'll have to do this again. You liked it?"

"Yes. Anytime on a weekend. Just give me time to get ready."

The next week, while reading an article on recreation for the handicapped, Alex noticed one on sailing, and how a double amputee trained himself to handle a twenty-five foot sail boat. He was intrigued. "Hell, if he can do it, so can I!"

The following day, he left work early to drive to a marina on the river to watch the boats getting under way, and to observe what is involved, and how to handle the operation. As a youth, he could take a sail boat out and race, and soon that knowledge came back to him. Still, he bought books and magazines on sailing, and returned to the marina to observe the boats. Nearby, he found a school that taught sailing, and approached the instructor for lessons.

The man took one look at Alex in the chair, and said, "No way."

Alex was determined to learn, and after several heated arguments, he convinced the man that he should be allowed to try.

After several lessons, the instructor was amazed at how rapidly Alex learned the "ropes." He could crawl up on the housing, bend on the sails, hoist them and secure the lines. Sitting in the stern, he handled the sheets, learned to tack, and soon the man was a believer in his student's determination to master the skill and art of sailing.

"I'd never believe it. The guy was clever and quick. He did it better and sooner than some of my regular students," he told friends later.

After a few weeks of practice, Alex was able to take the boat out alone and perform all the operations properly. There were a few problems, but he did not let them deter him from the goal.

Next he wanted to own a sail boat. Luck was with him.

Al Burns passed the open office door, looked in, and saw Alex bent over some papers on his desk. "It does my heart good to see a man hard at work."

"Hi Al, come in. I need a breather. What brings you up here?"

"One of my parishioners is here, and I stopped by to see him. How goes it with you?"

"Great, no problems. This visit fits in with some of your pastoral counseling?"

"Yes, and I'm pleased at the progress I'm making. Rabbi Halpern ran quite a nice course at the college. I'm going to continue it in the fall. He's fascinating."

"Many in the class?"

"Quite a few, about twenty, mostly men, but a few females snuck in. We have nine from our ministerium, including Tom Shane, Jim, and Bob. It's a good group, and some come up from St. Mary's county."

"How about the ramps Phil Mason and Ted Queen had put up at your church? Any takers for them?"

"You bet. Ten new parishioners come every Sunday with their families, and they are very happy to be regular churchgoers. That survey has really paid off."

"Glad to hear it."

"I've seen you tooling around with a blonde in your car. She seems like a real nice girl. Donna is her name?"

"Yeah, we've been out and around. We've been to a picnic, and even went boating on the bay. Joe Evans and Broderick Keyes helped us to go aboard, and it was fun."

"No problems getting into the boat?"

"Brod had a ladder, and I slid down it, and they helped Donna down, then we sat in the stern and enjoyed the ride and the scenery. This was my first time out on a boat since before the war, and it was great. It brought back a lot of wonderful sailing memories."

Al had never been sailing, and the nautical world was foreign to him, but he enjoyed talking with Alex, who confessed to a renewed interest in boating. "I've been to a sailing school, and passed all the requirements. Now I'll be able to rent a boat for my rides."

"You're serious about this stuff. I'm amazed." Al paused, pursed his lips, and was silent.

"Heavy thinking, Al? What's up?"

One of Al's parishioners was being transferred to Kansas, and among the items he was selling was a twenty-two foot sailboat. That evening, Alex called the man for more details on the boat, and a week later, Alex was the proud owner.

In the course of the negotiations, the owner, Will Berger, learned that Alex had been active in the survey of the handicapped. "I want to tell you how pleased we are that my mother can now attend services at the Lutheran Church. I understand that somehow you had a hand in that operation. My appreciation is reflected in a reduced price for the sail boat, and lowered monthly payments. Our whole family is indebted to you and all those who have made it possible for us to attend services together."

The boat was tied up at a marina further up the river, and Alex wanted it closer to La Plata. He remembered the dock area at Dean Keyes summer cottage, and knew that it would be ideal for him. Through his work with Clare Cohen, he had met the dean many times, and was on friendly terms with him.

The dean was cordial on the telephone. "Certainly, Alex. I'd be delighted to have you rent space at the dock, and feel free to use all the equipment and facilities we have there. I think it's wonderful that you have a sail boat and can enjoy the beauties of the Potomac and the Bay. Bring her in anytime and make yourself at home."

Alex could hardly wait to spring the news on Donna. In a short period of time, he had been able to take lessons, buy a boat and now he had a private dock with facilities. All this without Donna being aware of what he had been doing, despite their frequent meetings and dates.

During the last week of June, he had his boat tied up at the Keyes' dock and took it out alone to check it out and make sure that everything was "squared away." Then on Friday he called Donna. He could hardly restrain his enthusiasm. "Anything planned for tomorrow?"

"I was going shopping with mother in the morning, but after that, nothing special. What did you have in mind?"

"I'll pick you up around one o'clock, we'll take a ride, have dinner, and on the way back we can stop at Mike's Place."

"Sounds great. I'll be ready."

The next day he found Joe weeding the garden, as Donna emerged from the side door wearing a pink outfit, low cut shirt, slacks, and sneakers. Mabel seemed upset, petulant and tense, and barely returned his wave. Donna kissed her father on the neck, and came forward to the car.

Smiling and reaching in to shake Alex hand, he said, "I won't bother to ask what hell raising you two are up to."

"Nope, and would you ever be surprised!" Alex responded.

"Have a good time whatever it is. Take care of yourselves."

As they backed out of the driveway, Alex said, "What's your pleasure? Any particular place you'd like to go?"

"You're the driver, and I'll be the quiet passenger. Besides, you indicated to my father that you had some nefarious activity in mind. Sounds wicked. I'll just tag along."

"Good. Hold tight. Let's head on down to the point. It's a good day for a drive, not too hot, low humidity, a slight breeze and clear skies above."

It was a straight shot on Route 301 toward the Governor Nice Bridge, and in fifteen minutes they turned into Dean Keyes' property and drove on through to the boat house.

"Alex, where are we? My vision is nil, but I recognize some shapes. Is this the dean's place, and is that the boat house?"

"Yup. How would you like to go down to the dock and sit?"

"It's such a beautiful day for that. Yes, let's do it."

With Donna walking behind and pushing the chair they arrived at the door of the boat house, Alex unlocked the door, and they went through to the other end and came out on the dock. The cabin cruiser was tied up on the port side, the sail boat on the starboard. Alex's heart beat with joy as he saw it riding smoothly with the slow motion of the waves and as it stretched its mooring lines.

"Let's sit on this boat here on the right," smiling as he locked his chair.

"We can't. It belongs to someone, and if they come and see us . . ."

"Nothing will happen. It belongs to a friend of the Keyes."

"How do you know?"

"Because I am that friend. This sail is mine, bought and paid for!"

Donna was so happy she put her hand to her mouth, then

laughed and said, "You dog! When did all this happen? You didn't tell me a thing!" With that she leaned down, put her arms around his neck and planted a kiss on his cheek.

"It's for us, baby," and he held her so he could kiss her full on the lips. Donna responded with equal vigor.

"You're mean to keep this from me. I love it. Now, tell me about it."

"She's twenty-two feet long and seven in the beam. Light blue trim around the sides, a blue cover for the mainsail, teak housing for the cabin, and metal wheel for steering. The cabin is small but has a head, sink, small refrigerator, table and two bunks."

"Beautiful, beautiful," was all she could say as he talked. "I'm very happy for you. What prompted this nautical turn?"

"Remember that day when Brod took us out on the cruiser? You seemed to enjoy it so much, and as I used to sail when I was younger, I thought, what the hell, I'd like to sail again. So, I bought some books on sailing, went to school to learn the ropes once more, and had planned to rent a boat for us for weekend rides. When Al Burns had a parishioner whose boat couldn't sail to Kansas, I bought it. Here it is, just for us!"

"So you went ahead and hocked the family jewels! Great! I'd have done the same."

"I wanted to surprise you, Donna. I knew you'd like it. Now give me another kiss and get off my lap, we have work to do."

"Are you sure you can sail it?" She sounded a bit unsure.

"There is a certificate in the cabin that says I've passed the examination and I'm qualified to sail. The instructor was amazed to see me get around on the deck and in the cockpit. You just have to know what you're doing. Care to cast your lot with me and sail this tub?"

"I wish I knew how, Alex."

He leaned over, pulled her face to his and said, "Trust

me love, I can handle it," and kissed her full on the lips. She wrapped her arms around his neck again, returned his kiss and murmured, "I'm all yours, sailor, let's go."

He edged his chair close to the edge, locked the wheels, grabbed the top of the ladder, and in one swift movement was out of the chair and down the ladder to the deck. He called up to Donna just a few feet above him.

"Take hold of the ladder, turn around and I'll guide your feet on the steps. There," he said as she touched down. "Let's sit here in the stern for a bit."

She sat on a cushion, while a breeze ruffled through her hair. "How wonderful to be here. I never thought I'd be on a boat again, and to think that it's yours."

"Care for a drink to celebrate?"

"I'd love one, but where?"

"I was down here yesterday with a cooler and stashed some drinks in it, so they'd be cold today. Lemonade for you? And I'll pop a beer."

When he returned she said, "How did you ever manage to get a cooler and drinks down on the deck?"

"Dean Keyes and I rigged up a pulley on a yardarm that swings out over the dock. There is a basket in which I place various things, lower it to the deck and carefully tip it over, then bring back the basket for another load. It works well and fills the bill. Simple."

"I might have known you'd think up something like that."

As they sipped their drinks, Alex described in more detail the boat, its equipment, what makes it run, where are the sails, the boom, and responded to her questions.

"Ready to take her out, Donna? I'll show you what I want you to do."

He unlocked the motor, started it up to make sure it ran properly, then crawled forward on his hands and knees to the housing. He uncovered the mainsail, ran it up on the mast, and secured it on the cleat. The jib he took forward to the bow, hauled it out of the bag and bent on the sail, but did not raise it. While forward, he cast off the bow lines, and returned to the cockpit.

"Donna, hold this line and when I tell you to let go, throw it up toward the dock. Don't worry if you hear it splash in the water, I'll get it with a gaff when we come back."

He revved up the motor, then called to her, "Cast off!"

The boat slowly backed out of the dock area, then he steered it forward to the entrance of the cove. Soon they were on the river, where a westerly wind caught the sail and filled it. When Alex cut the motor, he told Donna, "Keep the wheel steady and we'll go straight ahead. There's no one else around. The wind is blowing off your starboard ear, and listen for any rustles in the sail. That's it! Stay there on course. I'm going forward to hoist the jib. Be right back."

After raising the jib, he laced the sheets outside the shrouds and through the pulleys, first on the port, then the starboard sides and sat in the cockpit as the boat leaped forward under the added sail power.

"See? It's easy. You can feel the wind coming off the starboard abaft the beam, and it's filling the sails. We're tight on course, because we don't have any ruffles in the mainsail."

"This is fun. Wait until I tell my father I was out sailing, and even steered the boat. He'll love it. Mother, of course will die of fright."

"Wait until you get comfortable with the boat, and get the 'feel' of it. I'll make a deck hand out of you yet."

Once out in the bay, Alex turned north around Point Lookout, at the very tip of Maryland, and hugged the shore keeping Deep Point on the port side. He didn't want to go up too far, as it was getting late in the afternoon.

"As soon as we get a good wind, we'll come about and

return to base."

When the boat rounded Point Lookout and headed upstream, a fast moving cabin cruiser sped by off the port side, sending waves to rock their boat.

"Bastards, they should slow down out here," he cursed at them, making a grab for the binoculars.

"I'll be damned! That's Dr. Bolton with a girl and another couple. He's much older, and the two girls look like teenagers. What are those old men doing out here with two kids?"

"Let's not worry about them. We're having a good time."

The sun was starting its descent when they reentered the cove, and Donna was at the wheel while Alex reached out with the gaff for the mooring lines and tied her up. Both worked together to clean up the boat and put away the sails in their coverings. Life jackets were stowed in the cabin, and everything put in its place.

"Donna, up the ladder with you, and I'll follow, to guide your legs."

Later in Mike's Place, Alex had a beer while they talked over the sailing activities of the afternoon. Donna wondered if her lack of vision would be an impediment, and make it harder for him to operate the boat.

"Nonsense, girl. What about my legs? So, we're even. Drink up."

"You are impossible, but lovable. Did you say we're having crabs and beer? I've never had either."

"This is a good time to start. Every good sailor finishes the day with crabs and beer. Not to worry, I'll help you."

There was a good crowd at Mike's that night, but they were able to get their favorite table. Later at the piano bar, Donna played both classical and popular numbers to rousing applause.

After midnight, Alex dropped her at home.

"I can't tell you how much I've enjoyed this day, Alex.

You're kind and considerate of me. Thanks." She kissed him warmly and opened the door.

Joe Edwards pulled his head from the refrigerator as his daughter entered through the kitchen door. "Well, you look pretty with your sunburned face and windblown hair."

"I've had such a wonderful day. I had three firsts today! I've been sailing, steered the boat, and had crabs and beer."

"I thought you smelled crabby when you kissed me. Wait a minute, you said sailing? With Alex? With his bashed legs?"

"Wait till I tell you. He's got the best little twenty-two foot sail, and you should see how he can handle it. We went out on the Potomac, then down to the bay and back to Dean Keyes' place where it is tied up. What a day!"

"I'm glad you had such a good time. We'll talk more about this next week as we drive into town. Your mother is fast asleep, and we'd better turn in and get some rest."

"Yes, I'm tired. Good night, Daddy."

Chapter XV

Donna was awake early on Sunday morning after a short night's sleep. The sun was up and she didn't feel sleepy, but she was sore. Muscles she didn't know she had ached for attention. "It was that crawling over the boat yesterday that did it! What fun being out on the river and the bay!" She rolled over, hoping for another snooze, but she was wide awake as she reviewed yesterday's events. Her thoughts centered on the skipper of the new boat. Alex was such a dear and considerate man. She never would have dreamed that she would go out on a boat, even taking the wheel, to say nothing of being with a man who had little use of his legs. But, he had eyes for her, and was willing to be her eyes, describing everything so that she might enjoy and see through his.

Men were a strange breed to her, and outside of her father and the lawyers in her office, she had little or no contact with them. Dates were nonexistent until she met Alex, and then her world changed. She was doing things she never dreamed of doing, like going to a tavern for crabs and beer, and sailing with a robust man.

In her shadowy vision he emerged faintly, dark around the face because of his beard, and low in stature since he always was in the wheelchair. Standing in back of him, resting her hands on the handles, she would occasionally measure the width of his shoulders—broad, strong and muscular—

and she knew his body was like an oak tree, powerful.

While she could barely make out the movements, Donna was amazed at Alex's agility, and his ability to get in and out of his car, collapse or open the chair, stash it in back of the seat, or haul it out, all in a matter of minutes. He was so quick!

His voice was low and clear, the words articulated precisely. Illness and confinement had opened up the world of literature and enlightenment. He was well read, and the authors ranged from Shakespeare, Chaucer, Hemingway, Manchester, and Michener to name but a few. He talked about these men and their works so readily with her.

Alex was an intellectual man, and gave evidence of this when talking about his graduate studies and his work at the hospital. Al Burns had once remarked to her, "Donna, you should see him (Oops, I didn't mean it that way!) on the survey. The guy's a whiz. He had those college kids eating out of his hand. I suspect they learned more from him than hours on end in the classroom. I like him, he's great."

"Yes, I know," she had responded, and to herself, "I do too."

She rolled over in the bed, still awake and sore.

As father and daughter drove into Washington the following week, they talked at some length about Alex and her sailing.

"Were you afraid to go out with him?"

"At first, yes. I was a bit terrified, for I had never done anything like this before. When he told me he had taken lessons, earned a certificate to sail, and said to me, 'Trust me, I can handle this boat.' I was willing to sign on. I could almost feel his competency. When he went forward to raise the jib, he told me how to steer the boat, and I did!"

"He sounds clever, and seems to know what he is all about. Anyway, it must have been a wonderful experience for you."

"Yes, it was. Mother doesn't feel the way we do. She was upset when I told her, and now she's going to worry every time I go out, even if we don't go sailing."

"Yes, dear, I know. She expressed her fears to me, and I've tried to allay them, but you have to be a mother to appreciate her feelings. She is concerned for you, and I guess she always will be. I'll try to keep her calmed down, and as long as you are comfortable with Alex in the boat, I'll not worry."

She was quiet as they drove along, seemed lost in thought, and knowing his daughter, Joe said, "Something on your mind? Care to share it?" They were close and had few secrets.

"Does liking someone mean that it could be love?"

"No, dear. We can be fond of a person, and like him a great deal, but that does not mean love. Love is reserved for a man and a woman who share a great deal, who are compatible, want to do something for one another, and in general want to be with the other person always."

"That's what I thought, but I wasn't sure. Thanks." She remained silent.

"Alex?"

"Yes, Daddy. He's such a good person, and has been wonderful to me. I have such good times with him. You know, he kind of acts as my eyes, and tells me about things I cannot see. He's perceptive and seems to know what I want before I say a thing. Since we met last year, I've gone out more and done more things with him than anyone else."

"He sure has been paying you a lot of attention."

"Look what he did for me last Saturday. Took me out on his boat, and I had a marvelous time. He didn't seem to mind about my blindness."

"True, love, but he also has a disability, and maybe it's hard for him to get dates with girls."

CHALLENGE 145

"I realize that, but he did take me out, and he's called me often for dates. I'm at the point now that I really like him, but I don't know if I'm in love."

"When the bug bites, you'll know it, loud and clear."

"What does mother think about me dating Alex?"

"She's afraid of this twosome. She knows you need some male companionship, but she shies away from you getting involved with him or any man."

"Is she afraid that I might get pregnant?"

"That plus the idea that you might get married to some guy, and with your lack of vision . . . well you know."

"Sure, Daddy, I know. I love her and respect her, but I need to live my own life and not always be under her shadow. I can get along OK. Guess I need more independence and to be on my own."

"Back to Alex. Ride along with it. See how far this thing goes. One or both of you might cool off and decide to go your separate ways. On the other hand . . ."

"Yes, then what?"

"Go with the tide and the winds. Life works in strange ways, and this might be just the thing for both of you. Why not? You complement one another and so far you seem to get along real well together. Enjoy!"

❧ ❧ ❧

In the privacy of the rectory, Father Shane was dressed in casual summer slacks and a blue shirt to match. The windows of his study were open, allowing a warm summer breeze to wash through the room, while he sat comfortably in an easy chair smoking a pipe and watching the Baltimore Orioles vs. Detroit baseball game. That Saturday morning he had spent bringing the sacraments to patients at the hospital, and now after lunch, he had a few hours of free time before he'd enter the confessional in the church. He smiled thinking of the children in the pediatrics ward who clambered over him, searching for the candy hidden in his pockets, then singing along with him as he left the room. He was a popular figure, loved and respected by patients and staff. It was a good life for Father Tom, and he was a happy man.

It was a slow game, and his head went back as he closed his eyes.

It was not for long as the ringing telephone jolted him upright.

"Father Shane?"

"Yes, speaking."

"Father, this is Sister Benedicta at the Carmelite Convent."

He could immediately picture the tall severe-looking nun with heavy Germanic features speaking from her office.

"This is a nice surprise, Sister. What can I do for you?"

"I wonder if you could spare a few minutes tomorrow after you conduct benediction services for us?"

"Sure, I'd be happy to, Sister. Any inkling of what I'm getting into?"

"It's about one of our novices, and I'm not sure how to proceed."

"I'll lend whatever assistance I can, Sister. Count on it."

The priest enjoyed his weekly visits to the Carmelites. Regularly on Sunday afternoons he conducted benediction, gave a short homily, and then had dinner with them. It was a refreshing interlude, uplifting.

The convent was located east of La Plata in a secluded area which led into an open field in the middle of which the nuns had a garden. The building was old, but had been recently renovated, repainted, and reinhabited by the nuns whose forebears had established it over three hundred years ago. Although vocations had decreased for the priesthood and sisterhood, there were many applicants for the Carmelite Order, and the Archbishop of Baltimore had assented to the reopening of the Cloister here. There were a few older nuns, but most were young, and he enjoyed listening to their voices as they chanted the office.

On Sunday after the service, Sister Benedicta led him to the parlor. She sat in one of the straight back chairs, and motioned Father Shane to a comfortable wing chair. Her hands were folded in her lap, although the nervous twitch of her fingers indicated that she was in a turmoil. The skin on he face was clear, the blue eyes bright, and an aquiline nose was perched just above compressed lips also indicate unease. Today, something was bothering her, but he waited for her to mention it.

"Father Shane, I hope you won't mind if I ask your advice about a matter that has just come up."

"Not a bit. You mentioned it had to do with one of the novices."

"Sister Margaret Mary is one of our younger women who asked for admission to the Order late last year. She has her degree in education and was a teacher in a high school, then a small college for a short period. She comes from a prominent family in Baltimore, where she has a younger sister in high school."

"She sounds like a welcome addition to the community, Sister."

"Yes, she is, and we have learned much from her in this short time. The problem is she wants us to reach out more into the community and do things we've never considered before."

"Such as?"

"Well, having some of the women come here for a series of spiritual talks like a retreat. She says she has gained so much from her stay here that she believes it would be beneficial for professional women to have an opportunity to spend a weekend here in meditation and prayer."

"What do you think about the proposal?"

"It is something we have never done before, and I'm not sure how it would be accepted by other members of the house, and by people out in the city. Do you have any thoughts on the idea?"

"As a priest, I can only say that any way we can get people to come together to pray, that is a good thing. Our fast-paced world doesn't allow much time to back off, sit down, and take a look at ourselves spiritually, to meditate on values and to ask ourselves: Where are we going? What meaning does this or that have in my life? We in the religious life have the opportunity to take these retreats, but lay people just don't have the time, nor the opportunity. I think Sister's idea is a good one. But what is the problem?"

"I guess I am the problem. In my thirty-seven years as a Carmelite, we've always remained a cloistered group, and shunned the outside world. With the recent Vatican Council and the openness of the church to new concepts, including the reaching out of the religious beyond their own parameters, well, I just don't know how to react."

"So this new young person comes along and in short order wants to accomplish something like this 'retreat' and it scares you?"

"Yes, Father. I don't know how to answer her."

"If you're not rigidly opposed to the idea, and would like some help, I'll be willing to give it some thought and suggest a few solutions."

"I would appreciate that, Father. It would help me and Sister Margaret I'm sure."

"All right. I'll give you a call in a few days."

On the following Tuesday, Father Tom cornered Rita and told her he'd like to talk with her about a proposal.

"Let's make it at lunch today in the cafeteria. Get a quiet spot and save me a place."

He was seated in a remote spot, a table for two, and had just placed his tray on the table when Rita came in with her tea and salad.

He began to talk. "I was at the Carmelite Convent last Sunday for benediction and ran into a minor hornet's nest. Seems as though a 'young upstart' nun is at cross purposes with the Abbess, and wants to have a retreat for the professional women in this area. She feels it would be good for them to come together for a weekend, but the Abbess isn't sure about it and tends to take a dim view of the whole idea. On the surface she appears ambivalent, but underneath, I suspect she'd rather have nothing to do with it."

"To me, it sounds wonderful! I can't conceive of her wanting to spike it."

"I agree, Rita, but while she might be dead set against it, she wants my suggestions."

"Since she is the boss, couldn't she just lay down the law to the young novice?"

"Sure, that'd be easy. But, she told Sister Margaret Mary that she'd take it up with me, since I am the spiritual director of the convent. The more I think about it, the more I like it. What about you?"

"Yes, definitely. Now that you have me cornered, what can I do to help?"

"I was hoping you would volunteer. First I'll call Sister Benedicta and suggest that unless she is definitely opposed, I feel a retreat for the ladies of the area would be a wonderful activity, and she should encourage Sister Margaret Mary. Then I'll invite us over to set it up with the four of us acting as a committee to plan the retreat."

"I accept. It's been too long since I've made one, and at this point, I need to back off before we get into the fall activities.

On Saturday afternoon, they assembled in the convent parlor, the Abbess a bit cool, the younger sister warm in her greetings to the priest and Rita. He opened with, "Sister Benedicta, I've asked Mrs. Evans to join us since she is in our parish, and holds an important job in the hospital. As I told you on the telephone, the idea of a retreat for the women is excellent and it's the kind of spiritual reawakening we need, and one which I'm sure the Archbishop will be pleased to hear is taking place at this convent."

At this, the coolness melted from Abbess, and she replied, "The Carmelites are happy to be of service to our sisters in this community and to the diocese." She had forgotten that Father Shane was close to the Chancellory, and she did not want to offend anyone there. She was aware of ecclesiastical politics.

Rita smiled at Sister Benedicta, and turned to Sister Margaret Mary, a woman a few years younger than herself, with bright blue eyes, an open face that shined, delicate hands and fingers extended in a warm handshake, and a lithe body buried in yards of black skirts. There was a white wimple around her face and a black veil over her head and down her back. She was charming, outgoing and had an engaging smile which exposed straight white teeth.

"You are in education? Where did you study?"

"Yes, and I loved it. Took my B.A. at Manhattanville, and the Master's at Columbia."

"I know the college well. I have a close friend who went there, and I visited her on one occasion. This idea of a retreat for the women around here is excellent, and I'm looking forward to it."

"Me, too! Now let's get down to the nuts and bolts." Father Shane smiled at Sister Benedicta who could only roll her eyes in disdain at the language of her young charge.

Rita opened it up with, "How about a Friday evening through Sunday afternoon and schedule it in about a month? The ladies could come from work and get right into it."

Father Tom said he had available devotions and spiritual talks ready for a retreat.

When Sister Margaret Mary said, "I think it would be good for Sister Benedicta to give a talk on our order, and on the role of women in carrying out the spiritual life of the family," the somewhat austere older nun softened visually. Maybe the retreat idea was not so bad after all.

The meals were planned to be light, and nonfattening, with coffee and tea breaks interspersed throughout. A light wine would be served before the evening meals.

"Whom shall we invite?" Sister Margaret Mary asked.

Rita answered. "I would like to see women of the area here who are professionals and some at home mothers, no discriminations, make it an ecumenical gathering."

"Amen!" Father Tom boomed.

"Of course, the sisters of the community will be present," Sister Benedicta stated.

"Why yes, and we could ask each one to serve as a guide or companion to our guests, especially to those who may not be of our faith," the young nun added.

In a rather short period, the planning was completed, and the foursome disbanded.

"The young nun is a smart one," Rita said to Father Tom as they drove away. "She'll put a lot of life into that convent."

"She'll still have to deal with the Abbess, and I noticed she warmed up considerably as the meeting progressed."

❧ ❧ ❧

There were more than several interesting family conversations which took place the following week in the town.

"Look, Bart, I'll be off next weekend after my tour, and you're in charge of the house and kids," Peg O'Bryan announced to the man in her life.

"What's the big deal? I'm here to help. What are you up to?"

"I'm going to the convent."

"The WHAT? CONVENT? God, woman, you're married to me. The kids?"

"Keep the shirt on. It's just for the weekend, and over to the Carmelites for a retreat."

"The Catholics? The Carmelites? You, an Episcopalian?"

"Why not? They're good people, and besides it's for the women of the area. An ecumenical gathering, and I'm all for it. And that hospital had better not call me for any emergency. Now, here's a list of things . . ."

Dave Cohen looked at his wife in disbelief. He had just come in from a brutal day in Washington, and he was tired. Clare had readily accepted the invitation and thought it a marvelous idea. She told Dave she was going.

"Clare, how can you? They take Jews? OK. I wish I could get away. Go, and God be with you. Say some prayers for me. I can use them."

The Rev Phillip Mason, pastor of the A.M.E. Church came home from the ministerium meeting to greet his wife with, "Father Shane told us today about a retreat for women at the Carmelite Convent. If you're interested call Mrs. Evans at the hospital."

" I met her once when I brought one of my students in to her office. She's such a lady. A retreat, huh? I've heard of them. Maybe that's what I need before school gets into full swing, and I go out of my mind. You don't mind if I go? You'll be without your high soprano at services on that Sunday."

Alyce was delighted to learn from Rita that she'd be

welcome to join in the retreat. She added, "I wonder if it would be proper for me to bring something?"

"What did you have in mind?"

"I make a creamed salmon, and if I do say so myself, it's good."

"That's a great idea. Some of the ladies may also want to bring their specialty. I'll pass the word."

Donna took Alex's call in her room. "I've just come in from work, and I'm pooped out. What's up?"

"Not too much. I'm here at home conjuring up nice things for us to do on the weekend."

"Sorry, sailor man. The weekend is taken. I've a date."

"A date?" Alex's voice registered his disbelief.

"Yes, a date to go on a retreat at the Carmelite Convent with women from this area."

"A retreat with the Carmelites? You, a nonbeliever?"

"It's as much a surprise to me as to you. When Mrs. Evans called, I was on the verge of declining, but then I thought it might do me some good. Y'know, a change of pace, a period of quietude, and a chance to sort things out."

"I know what you mean. Go ahead and make the most of it. Say a few prayers for me, I can use them."

Later she spoke with her father. "It would be wonderful if Mother could come with me to the retreat, but she gets so stubborn."

"You know your mother by now. She's shy, quiet, and doesn't venture beyond her own domain. Besides, she's not one for religion, especially the Roman Catholics."

"This is more than just a retreat for Catholics. It's ecumenical. Clare Cohen is a Jew, there's a Baptist, a Lutheran, one woman from the A.M.E. Church, all are going. It would do her good to be among the women of the area."

"I realize that. She's just afraid that one of the nuns will convert her, and we've never been much for religion in the house."

"She liked the nuns at Trinity College when I was a student there. I must say they were wonderful to me."

"I know you're disappointed, but go ahead on your own, and enjoy it."

Rita's message to those she called to invite to the retreat was simple, and included the chance to get away from the mundane. "You are not required to attend the religious services, but you'll miss the beautiful choir. Topics of interest to all include morality and values in our lives, behavior on the job, children and husbands in our lives, being a good neighbor, discrimination. If you have a specialty dish, bring it along for dinner Friday evening."

On Friday, the last weekend in August, Rita finished up early in the hospital, went home to get the salad she had prepared and rushed to the convent to help in the final preparations. She was at the door to greet the ladies as they arrived and to introduce each to Sister Benedicta and Sister Margaret Mary.

The chapel was small with pews to seat no more than one hundred people. An altar was made of dark mahogany, very plain with a crucifix in the middle, on a white lace cloth. In the center and above the altar was a stained glass window with Jesus Christ in the middle, flanked by St. Benedict on his right, and St. Scholastica on his left. Along the sides of the chapel were windows with images of women saints, and one of the Blessed Virgin Mary. The pews were comfortable with a curve to the back, and the kneelers were padded. In all, a peaceful place to pray and have solitude.

"As spiritual director to this convent, I am pleased to welcome you to this retreat," Father Shane began his introductory remarks. "You have come to find peace in prayer, to seek God each in her own fashion, and to renew oneself. I shall be saying more in the homilies, and conducting services for those who wish to attend."

The Abbess was brief in her remarks welcoming the ladies, and outlining the activities for the weekend. She thanked Sister Margaret Mary for proposing the retreat, and Rita Evans for her suggestions. "Wine and cheese will be served in the hall outside the dining room, and after dinner we shall reassemble here for the first period of meditation, while our sisters chant their Holy Office."

Dinner was served buffet style, with the specialty dishes interspersed with the food the nuns had prepared. When all were seated, the Abbess asked Alyce Mason to give the blessing. She had been asked earlier and was both pleased and ready with her prayer. She, from the A.M.E. Church, asked to pray over the food at the Catholic convent. The very idea warmed her for a long time.

A slight breeze crept up from the river to grasp at wisps of hair from the two women walking slowly along the path in back of the convent. Other women, either alone or in small groups, walked or talked quietly after the evening service to enjoy the soft air as dusk deepened.

Clare spoke to Rita. "What a wonderful idea, and even better was the service and the chanting of the nuns. Beautiful voices! This is an important piece of my life—to be with a fine group of women and retreat from the world briefly. This is just what I've needed."

"This will help all of us, and I find it refreshing," Rita replied. "I'm enchanted by this place. To think the nuns would serve wine, and that meal. I had to hold back on the food. Most of all it was the peace and quiet of the chapel. I did a lot of soul searching tonight."

"Sister Margaret was astute in her talk on the responsibilities of the professional woman toward her peers and subordinates. She has much to offer," Rita said.

"I like your Father Shane. I knew a rabbi like him years

ago, a great guy, both of them. Back to this world. All ready to come back to the campus and do us another great job? You sure made a nice impression on our students and faculty."

"All set and rarin' to go. My notes are ready and I have a couple of projects that I'll need to share with you. They'll fit in well with the subject I teach."

They passed Peg and Alyce sitting on a bench deep in conversation. Martha Burns walked by slowly, deep in thought, while Donna and her companion, a young nun, were singing a duet from one of the hymns. Was Rosa Donatti standing alone under a willow tree thinking of her daughter, her son Tomas, or the English professor at the University of Virginia?

Saturday was a "sleep-in" morning, with no rush to get going. Sister Margaret had suggested a juice and coffee bar at eight o'clock for the early risers, an 8:30 a.m. Mass for those interested, and the first session at 9:30, after breakfast. Peg knew how wonderful it was to loll in bed on a free Saturday, with no children around, no husband messing in the kitchen, and no TV to rouse them early. This was their weekend for peace and quiet.

There were several at the coffee bar, then out for a walk to witness the glory of a new day, the sun rising in a mist, as birds twittered in the trees. About eight of the ladies attended Father Shane's Mass, after which he disappeared until later in the day.

"If I had the guts," an unknown voice said, "I'd join this outfit. What a sea of peace and quiet. What I've needed for a long time. Do you suppose they'd take in an unregenerated bitch?"

"Hush your mouth!" from another unknown.

The schedule of activities followed without interruption, a light lunch, periods of meditation, talks by the nuns, and free time to sit in the chapel or walk the grounds.

During the afternoon break, Rita and Donna were sitting on a bench under the willow tree, and Donna was saying, "What do you think of Alex as a man?"

"He's one of my bright stars. I'd be lost without him on the staff."

"I'm sure he's a competent professional, and I know he's well liked by so many people. But as a person away from the work?"

"That would be hard to answer. I know him only in the office, and how he has taken on projects for the ministerium and with his college students. I can judge only that which I've seen and observed. On these counts, he's a great guy."

"Yes, I agree. I've found him to be wonderful."

"Something on your mind, Donna?"

"I think I'm falling in love with him, and I don't know quite how to handle it or my mother. Daddy's no problem."

"What do you mean?"

"Alex is the first person who has taken an interest in me and sought me out. We've done so many things since we met at your house. He has acted as my eyes, described things to me, brought me out on his boat—he's been so good to me. I think I could fall in love quickly, but I'm not sure how he feels. Between my lack of eyesight and his wheelchair, I'm not sure how we could ever make it."

"Have you discussed this at home?"

"With my father, yes, and he's all for it. My mother is something else. She's deathly afraid that I might go overboard, get pregnant and do something dreadful."

"How do you feel, down deep in your heart?"

"Other than my father, he is the nicest, most lovable person I've ever known, so gentle, kind, and considerate. I'm quite lost without him. I look forward to our dates and the weekends."

"It sounds as if he's very special to you."

"Yes, very special, but I don't know how he feels about me."

"I can't speak for Alex, but I suspect he's fond of you. Maybe you need to sound him out in a quiet womanly way. When he kisses you, return it warmly, with a dash of passion. He may need encouragement—give him an idea of your feelings toward him."

"You mean get him in a cove, throw over the anchor and . . ."

"Yes. You choose the time and place."

"If we get real serious and we marry, what about a family?"

"Do you want children? Can you care for them?"

"Not right away. I want to enjoy my husband and let him get accustomed to me first before we can think about children."

"Enjoy while you can."

"I have a question. Since Alex is in a wheelchair, does he have the capacity—is he impotent or not?"

"We're in deep water there, Donna. Frankly, I don't know and I don't dare ask him!" With that they both laughed uproariously.

"Seriously, you know what I mean. You're a married woman, and I haven't even seen him, it . . ."

"Yes, dear, you are at a disadvantage."

"Isn't this something awful to be talking about during a retreat, and in the garden of a Carmelite Convent?"

"Not at all. It seems to me that a retreat like this is for people to stop, take stock and sort out difficult areas in our lives, both spiritual and temporal. Talking about men, dating, love and sex are normal areas for discussion. Sex is not dirty, it's how we use the sexual function, and the connotations we place on the words and acts. Sex is fun, but only for marriage and it brings a lot of responsibility. If one partner cannot perform sexually, it may place a burden on the other, but this should not affect a sound, loving relationship."

"Thanks. I hope I wasn't desecrating this retreat by saying what I did." She paused, then continued.

"This helps me a lot. I'll have to proceed cautiously, and not scare the daylights out of the man."

"Not too cautiously, Donna. Live a bit dangerously. It won't hurt. Wear a loose fitting, "V" neck shirt or blouse, and if he gets you in a clinch and starts to explore your breasts, let him. Don't brush him off. It's just his way of showing that he likes and enjoys you. If you're sitting on his lap and you feel something hard coming up from his crotch, then you'll know he can 'get it up,' to use the vernacular. He is probably not impotent, but you can find that out."

"I think I can handle that. I've fought off just a few characters before, but with Alex, there would be no battle. I'd join him!"

After a pause, Donna continued. "If we should marry and have children, I wonder if we could manage them?"

"That will come in good time. If the good Lord blesses you with a little one, He will point the way for you to manage and cope. On the other hand, many couples who want them, never have them."

"Even if we didn't, I'd be blessed with having Alex to care for and live with and love."

"When you have a loving husband who shares with you, and you are compatible, you've got it made. I know."

"Thanks. You've been a big help. Now to get to work on an unsuspecting male who shall not be named!"

"Lucky man!"

It was time for devotions again and the two women retraced their steps to the chapel. Rita looked forward to the periods of prayer and solitude, so she could communicate with her God, and thank Him for a wonderful life. For Donna, it was a time for contemplation, thanksgiving and hope.

At the wine and cheese table before dinner a small group gathered. Peg O'Bryan looked at Rita to say, "It's so quiet here, I may lose my mind. I've never been so 'laid back' and peaceful. You know me, I'm always bouncing from one thing to another at home or at the hospital. Don't get me wrong, I love this place."

"I'll second that," Alyce Mason added. "It's such a relief to go for hours on end and not have someone tagging at my skirts wanting something. My, that Father Shane is a wonderful man, and me married to a minister of the gospel."

Martha Burns chimed in, "He was so good to my little Tommy when they first met. He's a dream, and these Carmelite nuns, just beautiful people."

One of the group said, "This is such a nice experience, perhaps we can do it again next year."

Sister Benedicta conducted the devotional service after dinner, and this was followed by a period of rest, prayer, and meditation while the nuns again chanted their office.

Before retiring, Rita and Alyce walked around the grounds, deep in conversation. "I sure have a different impression of Catholics, especially as I know and love these Carmelites. They have such a beautiful choir—we have one too in our church. Do you suppose we could join forces, and have a joint singsong?" She laughed quietly and then continued. "As you know, I teach at the high school, and I'm worried about our boys and girls. I hate to say this, but sex is a bit heavy among them."

Rita smiled, nodded, and knew what was coming.

"My girls, both black and white, are fully developed, and I draw no distinctions. Too many of them just flaunt themselves before the boys, and it's no wonder some of them get into trouble."

"I know. I see them in the hospital all the time."

"What can we do to prevent this, how do we help them stay out of a mess?"

"There's a simple answer, but it's terribly hard to implement."

"Such as?"

"Education. They all need to know more about their bodies, from top to bottom, and especially in between."

"Yeah, I agree, but where are they going to get it?"

"That's the problem, Alyce. This is a conservative community and any mention of sex, especially in the schools, is verboten."

"Conservative is hardly the word for it. We in the black community know this only too well. If the schools won't do it, where can it be done?"

"The logical choice is in the home, but parents are scared stiff of the subject, and don't know quite how to handle it. Their own sex lives may be a mess, they are embarrassed to talk, they know the four letter words, but not the more appropriate ones, and then they cop out. The result is the kids pick it up on their own, and most of their information is unreliable."

"I couldn't agree more, but where do we go from here?"

"Again the problem is how to face up to it. The schools won't, the parents can't, so that leaves . . ."

"The church? And me with a husband who is a loving one, but hates the word 'sex.' We need to pray long and hard on this one."

The next morning, Sunday, Mass was celebrated by Commander Edward Condon, a navy chaplain and uncle of one of the nuns, who was en route from Norfolk to a conference of chaplains at the Naval Academy in Annapolis. In his homily, Father Condon said, "God never 'promised us a rose garden.' As we find ourselves in confrontation with a number of problems, He gives us the grace and help to see through these difficulties, and we don't always come out on top. Life is not easy, but with faith in God, we can push on and survive."

Donna, sitting beside her guide and constant companion, murmured to herself, "It sure isn't easy, but this retreat has bolstered me."

The priest was in his mid-forties, dark hair graying at the temples, silver glasses on a bright, clear, blue-eyed face, with Boston-Irish characteristics. He had been doing parish work for ten years when, as a Navy Reserve chaplain, he was called to active duty.

"I find that many of the men I work with in the navy have a tremendous faith in God, and at times they face almost insurmountable difficulties. They always seem to come through, with a blend of faith, physical prowess, and good mental footwork, knowing they did as much as they possibly could. We should do the best we can and trust in God. That's all He asks."

As she left the chapel, Alyce tugged at Rita's arm. "I'm in a rush to get home and then sing in our church, but I think I have a solution to the matter we talked about yesterday. I'll give you a call tomorrow night. This has been wonderful, I'm a new person, and have been 'reborn' again."

After breakfast there was another meditation period, followed by a devotional talk. The final activity was benediction offered by Father Shane.

Sister Margaret Mary spoke with Rita as she left. "I want to thank you for your help in putting the retreat together. All the ladies have remarked how nice it was, and how much they gained from the experience."

"Sister, it was a pleasure, and I appreciate the opportunity to be here. Maybe we should think of making this an annual event?"

"Yes, that would be nice. However, I may not be here

next year."

"A transfer?"

"I'm not sure where I'll be, but I have my doubts about life in a convent. I'll need to talk with someone about it."

"How about Father Shane?"

"Yes, I know, but I think I need to talk with a woman."

"Sister Benedicta?"

"No, not her yet. I need help in sorting out some things before I go to her. She doesn't have patience, and is too ingrained in the order to listen to other voices. I want someone who is a Catholic, professional, and who is a good listener. Would you . . . ?"

"I'd be happy to be of service. Let's wait for a few days, then write to me."

Chapter XVI

Billie Jean rose from her chair, and crossed to the other end of the room to answer the telephone. "Hello. Yes, she's here, but we're in a staff meeting now. I'll give her the message, and she'll call later." As she returned, she aimed a meaningful glance at Rita who smiled and continued.

"We've finished our regular agenda on hospital related items, and now I'd like to have brief discussions on problems or concerns as you see them and as they relate to our community. Anita?"

"A couple of items come to mind. A great need is for sex education and information for our young people, especially the adolescents. Then there is racism, which still has a strong under current here. Minorities tend to get shoved around in a subtle fashion, but it's there nevertheless."

"Care to elaborate on these?"

"In the first one, it's no secret that we have our share of teenage girls coming to the OB-GYN clinic for prenatal care, and they have no shame at all. Rather, they seem proud of the fact that they are carrying a baby. A few, still unmarried, have come back for the second baby, and they haven't reached age twenty yet. This involves both white and black girls, although the number of blacks is greater than whites. This is a blot on our community, and I wish we could do something about it."

"You are not alone in your concern with this problem, Anita. At the retreat last month, one of the high school teachers brought up the same issue, and it is something that will be difficult to deal with."

"My second problem is racism, and it gets me down. I am an educated black woman working for this community, and I get pushed and shoved around in the stores. The clerks often will serve a white woman before me anytime, and it's a frequent occurrence. My money is just as green as hers. I get mad when I pick up the newspaper here and see so few pictures of black brides in contrast to the white ones. Little mention is made of black organizations, but there are pictures galore and big write-ups of the Masons, Eastern Star, Knights of Columbus, you name it.

"I'm human, and want to be recognized as such, not as a black, but as a person who contributes to this community and its people. That's my tale."

"Well spoken, Anita. We all share your concerns on this matter. Alex?"

"You're not the only member of a minority, I'm one too. A handicapped person goes through the same B.S. from the public, and I've heard similar remarks, only 'handicapped' is substituted for the word 'nigger.' When clerks give me a hard time, I leave my purchases on the counter and wheel out, never to return. I tell my friends and we just boycott the place. Hit them in the pocketbook, that's where it hurts."

As he talked, Anita and others nodded approval of his statements. He finished, flushed, pulled out a cigarette, his hand shaking a bit as he lit up.

"What I see happening all too often is insensitivity to others. As a handicapped person, I can see it, feel it, and it hurts. There is discrimination against people, minorities, senior citizens and the handicapped.

"This morning, I talked with an attractive fifty-eight-year-old patient who'll be leaving the hospital to return to an empty house. She'll drive her nice car, she has all the luxuries, but she is lonely and dreads going home. The one daughter who could help her is living with a man in Baltimore, and rarely comes to see her mother. She could easily offer companionship, but she is insensitive to her needs. This lady has made friends here among the patients, including a man about her own age, and I hope the friendship blossoms. I'm sure there are other older persons around who need companionship, and share their lives with others."

"You touch a chord in all of us, Alex. Thank you."

"Can I say something?" Billie Jean asked."

"Sure, you're one of us."

"I see a need for training mother's helpers to go into families to help out. I know of a little two-year-old-girl who is deformed and on crutches and cries a lot. There are two other small children in the house, and I suspect the mother is abusive to them. Maybe because she's worn out and could use some relief. Maybe we could prevent child abuse by training high school boys and girls to do this and give them an entre to the human services field."

"Thank you, Billie Jean, that's a good observation.

"To close our staff meeting, I'll add my pet problem. It is on the sanctity of human life, and how little value we place on it. Each of us has touched on this today, and I'll add my concerns about the unborn who will be aborted, sterilizing the mentally retarded, and denial of citizen rights to the disabled."

There were a number of calls to make, notes to review on cases, and folders for Billie Jean to file away. It did not take her long. Rita was a fast worker. All the while, she was thinking over the concerns expressed by the staff in their meeting, and as she finished up, closed the office and drove home, she mulled them over.

Anita was brief in her expression of sex problems among teenagers, but it was monumental, even in this small area. What are the parents doing about it? How do mothers talk with their daughters? Do fathers talk with their sons? Are any preventive measures taken? Who shoulders the responsibility for the baby?

At the other end of the age continuum, Alex's concern for the older widow with the rash, returning to her lonely house poses a problem. Companionship is what lonely people need, and to be wanted. Perhaps this woman could reach out and invite the man to her house for dinner, a movie, a talk—anything just to have companionship?

Alex should be aware of this. He is alone, but he is active in his work and community. How are he and Donna making out?

Billie Jean had a good point—how to provide respite for parents and give them a chance to go out for an evening? Could we develop a mother's helpers program? If not, why not?

As she arrived home it was 5:30 and Joe pulled up right behind her. While the children were involved with their activities—Roger on a scrub football team, Beth at a neighbors, and Joe Jr.—out in the yard, Rita and Joe relaxed as the dinner cooked.

"We're in review committee time now, and there are some interesting projects on the table. It's amazing what some communities develop to meet local needs and they're asking us for 'seed' money. A city in Texas wants their pregnant high school girls to complete the program and get the diploma. They have a home care curriculum that gives not only academic work, but care of babies and young children. The young mother learns how to care for her own, but could also get a job as a mother's aide."

"This is the kind of information I can use locally. We

have a mounting problem of teenage pregnancy, and we'll have to do something about it. What, I don't know, but maybe this Texas proposal and others may give us some clues as to directions to follow."

"I'll try to get a copy of the project, so you can examine it in detail. I think it has a lot of potential."

"Good, I'll appreciate that. By the way, do you know any studies about the marriage of blind people, either spouse blind or just one?"

"Not off the top of my head, but I can check our files in the office. What did you have in mind?"

"Donna thinks she may be falling in love with Alex, and raised a few questions to me during the retreat. Mainly they were about her ability to manage children if they should tie the knot."

"The idea of those two getting married would be wonderful, as they seem to be compatible, and if they are in love, why not? They appear to complement one another, and so far, their disabilities have not prevented them from doing things most people do. However, when it comes to raising a family, I'd have my doubts that Donna would be able to handle kids, especially during the day when Alex is at work, and she'd be alone in the house. There could be some terrible accidents everyone would regret."

"That has crossed my mind too, and I shudder at the prospects. However, the main thing is that if they are in love, there's nothing to prevent them from marriage."

"Except her mother. Mabel would fight that with all her strength. It's too bad that parents like her can't let go and allow the girl to enjoy the companionship of a man, and Alex is such a fine person."

"If it comes to that, Joe Edwards would step in and lay down the law. He's fond of his daughter, and realizes that she has to get out from her mother's influence. He is aware that Alex is a big influence on Donna now, and will continue to be, but Mabel is objecting fiercely to a secondary role."

"What you're saying is that if she really loved her daughter, she'd release her and let her fly on her own, now that the girl has found a stable male friend."

At the dinner table, Beth said the blessing and talked with her mother about dresses, while Joe and Roger discussed the upcoming Redskins game against the Dallas Cowboys. Joseph had a small toy truck with his glass of milk in it, guiding it around his plate and over the unused napkin. This was a quiet meal, with no outbursts or quarrels.

When the meal was over, the brothers helped to clear the table, while Beth rinsed the dishes and placed them in the dishwasher.

The father spoke to the boys. "When you're finished there, come out to the yard and we'll pass around the football." As often as possible, Joe tried to spend time with his sons, either playing ball, or outside, or in his workshop as he repaired a toy or piece of equipment.

"Thanks, Beth, you're a big help to me," Rita said as they cleaned up the room. "Did you have a good day in school?"

"We had a field day, and went down to the river with Mrs. Madden and saw the squirrels putting nuts away for the winter. Then we watched as the beavers built a dam on a little creek. Ruthie was with me, so we talked and sang on the bus going down and back."

"She is your age, isn't she?"

"Yes, and we get along fine."

"The family lives down at the end of the street, don't they?"

"Uh huh. Her sister is Alma and she goes to the high school, and her mother gives us treats when she's home."

"I'm happy you've found a playmate, little one. We're

all finished here."

The next morning, Rita slept in, for she had a 9:30 appointment at the County Health Department office, and would go directly there. As she drove down the street, she noticed two women standing by a car in front of Ruthie's house looking at a flat tire.

She pulled to the curb and called out, "Hi! Can I help? I'm Beth's mother."

"Hello. I'm Ruthie's. We've a flat tire and we're stranded."

"I'm headed uptown to the County Building, and I'll be happy to take you."

In the car, the woman introduced herself as July Rohm, and her daughter Alma. "This is kind of you, otherwise we'd both be late."

From the back seat, Alma said, "Do you know Mrs. Akers? She lives near us and works at the hospital."

"Yes, she's on the staff and is a good worker. At your school, do the students go out on any projects?"

"Not that I know of, but I'll find out. Here we are. Thanks for the ride."

"I hope you didn't mind that I raised the question to your daughter, Mrs. Rohm, but I need some information."

"Please call me Jule. Alma will be happy to get it for you. She's a conscientious girl."

As they parted at the County Building, Rita said, "Could we have lunch someday soon? I feel embarrassed about not welcoming you to the neighborhood. My husband and I get pretty busy with work and the children."

"Fine, you name the date and place."

"Howard Johnson's is just across the street, how about 12:30 tomorrow?"

Thursday was one of those crisp October days, a full sun riding in a cloudless sky, while the wind chased fallen leaves around the sidewalk. Rita walked down East Charles Street dressed in a brown tweed suit, with matching leather purse and shoes. She made an attractive figure, and her smile was all warmth for those she greeted.

Jule Rohm was already seated at a table in the far corner of the restaurant, and waved to signal her presence as Rita moved toward her.

"What a beautiful fall day," she said, extending her hand, "And what a pretty suit you have."

"Yes, it is a nice day. The suit? I picked it up in Garfinckles last spring, and it's just right for this weather."

Both women hit it off immediately. They found common interests in books, music, the theatre, Rita's knitting and Jule's crocheting.

"I'm happy we are neighbors," Jule said.

"Yes, and our daughters get along so well, too."

This opened the door for their backgrounds, and when Rita finished talking about the Evans family, Jule said that she came from Michigan.

"When my father died, my mother carried on the real estate business for a while, but then her arthritis forced her to sell it, and we moved to St. Petersburg, Florida. I met my husband-to-be there, and we had a good marriage until he took off with another woman. In the divorce, he left me the house, furnishings, the car, and a comfortable settlement."

"What attracted you to this area?"

"I came to Washington, went to law school, and got a job in the office of a congressman. When he was beaten, I lost that job and decided to come here to the peace of a small city, where I could bring up the girls in a better atmosphere than in a metropolitan area. We all love it here."

"We found the same when we relocated from Chevy Chase. It is a delightful area for all of us. Joe and I live a rather quiet life, and we enjoy the peace of our home, reading books which are all over the place."

"That sounds like our house. I brought most of ours from Florida, including my law texts, from the University of Michigan Law School. I've passed the Maryland bar, so I can set up shop here. For the time being, I'll get the house in order, enjoy the girls, travel a bit, and later decide what I'm going to do. It'll probably be in private practice."

When they finished, Rita said, "I must run now to keep an appointment. This has been nice. Let's do it again. Some evening we'll have you over for drinks and dinner. I'm sure Joe would like to meet his new neighbor."

In route back to her office, Rita thought how nice it was to have a woman her own age in the community, and as a lawyer, she might be willing to take on a civic assignment, as one way of getting to know the area and the people.

Later that afternoon, Rita had a conference with Anita King, who silently considered her supervisor a remarkable woman. She put order in a chaotic mess, and reached out to help the downtrodden and worked as hard as any on the staff. They huddled over Anita's problem cases for an hour, then turned to the concerns Anita had expressed the week before.

"As for discrimination, we all recognize that there is a great deal of bigotry in the county, but I see signs that it is diminishing."

"I know, Rita, but that doesn't help us now."

"Patience, my dear. Time works wonders, and we need both. How about the NAACP? Is it active here?"

"No. The chapter is located in Waldorf, but they don't do anything for us. It's dominated by a few old timers who don't want to rock the boat."

"I would suggest that you document every act of discrimination, and try to get witnesses for each incident. Keep a log of your activities, and don't frequent those stores where you have been humiliated."

"You're right, but it's so demeaning, and I feel so hurt."

"That's the only solution, Anita. In the long run it can be effective. About your second concern."

"The girls ask for trouble the way they flaunt themselves before the boys, and we see the results in our prenatal clinic. The boys are just as responsible for they invite the girls by their remarks."

"What suggestions do you have at this point?"

"Basically, information and education is but a starting point. That's going to be difficult to bring about, but somehow it needs to be accomplished."

"We may find a way around these obstacles. I have a meeting with Mrs. Mason, a teacher/counselor at the high school next week on this very subject. Care to join us?"

"Sure, count me in. She's the wife of the minister, and well liked. I've heard of her from some of my patients."

"In the interim, talk informally with your friends and get ideas as to how we can legitimately provide sex information to the kids and their parents. That might be a key to the success of our work."

As Anita left, Dr. Sargent appeared in the door, smiled at Rita and said, "I'd like to introduce the Reverend Donald Leyton, the Episcopal priest who replaces Father Jake St. John, who has been called to another parish. Mrs. Evans is our Director of Social Services."

Rita looked into the clear blue eyes set in a ruddy face, and took the strong hand he extended in greeting. "This is a pleasure, Mrs. Evans."

"We're delighted to have you with us, Father Leyton. I'm sure you'll enjoy our community."

"I've been showing Father Leyton around the hospital, and we've about completed the tour. May we come in for a chat and rest the feet?"

"Please. Can I order something to drink?"

"I'll have tea, with lemon," the priest said.

"Make mine coffee, black," replied Dr. Sargent.

Rita launched into a brief description of their work in the hospital and community, when the phone rang, and Rita answered it. "It's your office, Dr. Sargent."

"Tell her I'll be right there. I've been expecting this. Please stay, Father, and enjoy your chat with Mrs. Evans." He smiled at her. "You've done wonders for us here. Thanks."

When the door closed, Rita continued. "Among our community activities is the ministerium. Have you met any of the members?"

"No, for I've just arrived the day before yesterday. My predecessor said they are an active group and I am anxious to be with them."

"I happen to know most of them through the work of this office. Father Shane is pastor of my church, Reverend Albert Burns at the Lutheran Church, Reverend James Wilson at the Baptist Church, Reverend Steele, Rabbi Halpern, and Reverend Taylor are among the members."

"Excuse me, but did you say Father Tom Shane?"

"Yes, do you know him?"

"Do I know him! We were in Korea together."

"What a nice surprise for both of you. He's one of the best around here. Everyone loves him."

"The Bishop thought I needed a less active area, because of an illness, and that's why he assigned me here. What goes on here in the community aside from the hospital? Dr. Sargent thought you might be able to fill me in on general activities."

Rita thought for a moment, decided that she could trust this gentle soul and then said, "Let me give you a sample of some things we get involved with. The staff member who just left feels the need for sex information and education for young people, and the presence of racism in the community is a concern. Another staff member suggested that high schoolers be trained to become mother's helpers, to prevent child abuse. A third worries about the insensitivity to the needs of the handicapped and senior citizens. On the positive side we had an ecumenical retreat at the Carmelite Convent recently for eighteen women, and the local ministerium conducted a survey of the handicapped, to make their buildings accessible to those with ambulatory difficulties. It was successful."

"This is most interesting. I thought I was assigned to a sleepy town, but from what you indicate there is much activity going on."

"La Plata may look sleepy and a bit 'southern,' but the undercurrent is swift and we have plenty to do."

Father Leyton looked at his watch and said, "I must be going, and I do appreciate your 'insider's' look on the local scene. Do you have Father Shane's number? I must call him tonight."

Later as she drove out of the parking lot, she passed Father Shane as he entered to visit a parishioner.

"Hi, Rita, what's up?"

"Not much, just the usual stuff. By the way, give a call to the rector at St. Agnes Church."

Both cars were blocking traffic so they had to move on. Father Tom wondered what her parting shot was all about. He knew Jake St. John was about to leave, but why didn't she say his name?"

After dinner that evening, he called the Episcopal Church rectory.

"Hello. This is Father Shane, is Father Jake St. John in?"

"No, Tom, but I am. Don Leyton, just arrived here."

"Don Leyton? The guy I met in Korea? Now here in La Plata? I'll be damned!"

"Tom, you old son of a gun, it's good to hear your voice."

"I'm so surprised to know that you are here and at St.

Agnes. How did you know I was at St. Dunstan's?"

"Dr. Sargent gave me a tour of the hospital, and dropped me in the office of the Social Service Director, and I almost died when she mentioned your name. I was getting ready to call you, as she gave me your number."

"Ah, now I know why she told me to call your rectory as we passed in the parking lot this evening. This surely is a surprise. Say, how about coming over for dinner tomorrow night. Bring the wife. I'll have the cook throw more water in the soup."

"I'll come alone, Tom. My wife passed away several years ago, so I'm a bachelor."

"Sorry to hear of your loss, Don. I'll remember her in my Mass tomorrow. But, you are free? Good. See you about six o'clock. Great! I'm so glad you are here."

Father Tom was at the door when the bell rang, and he threw it open to greet his friend. "Don, my brother in Christ!" and both men embraced.

"Yes, we are brothers in Christ. It's so good to see you again. You look great, Tom."

"Here, let me take your hat. Come on in and relax."

They sat in Tom's study, both nursing scotch and water. Tom thought Don looked a bit haggard, with lines around his eyes, and not as bubbly as when they had last seen one another in Korea years ago.

"How long has it been, Don? I came out of service in '67 with this leg."

"Yes, I heard you were lounged up. That was about a year after we parted. I stayed in the Army until 1969, and right after that Elsie became quite ill, and it was all down hill from there on until she passed away. Boy, that really shook me up. I still miss her."

"I'm dreadfully sorry about her passing, and your loss. May she rest in peace. I prayed for her this morning."

"Thanks ol' friend. You were always so kind to me. She was a living saint, and I'm sure she'll keep an eye and a prayer for us here on earth."

Don's eyes misted as he talked about his wife, his hands shook a little as he reached for another sip of scotch. Tonight he was casual in dress, a plaid open neck shirt, slacks, and penny loafers. When he recovered he continued, "Dr. Sargent is in my parish and was kind to show me around the town and the hospital briefly. When he had to leave, Mrs. Evans gave me a run down on La Plata. She is a charming person."

"Bright, too, and one of the nicest people around here. We arrived here about the same time, and in her quiet efficient way, she has sparked things up in the hospital. You'll meet her husband, Joe, and their three fine kids."

"She was telling me about the kinds of problems breaking out here."

"Yes, I know all about them both from the parish and the hospital. You must have hit it off with her with a bang; she trusts you."

"It must be the honest mug I wear."

"On that one, I'll agree, and get us another scotch."

The two friends made short work of dinner—steak, mushrooms, baked potatoes, brussel sprouts, salad, and apple pie. A bordeau wine topped it off. Back in the study, they had coffee and continued catching up.

"Don, we've got a fine ministerium, and I hope you'll join us."

"By all means. When is the next meeting?"

"Next week. We laid off during the summer. We'll be at Al Burn's house, he's the Lutheran minister here, and a great guy. You'll like him and his wife, a wonderful cook."

"Sounds like my kind of guy. Who else attends?"

"The names won't mean much now, you'll meet them

next week. We have the Methodists, Presbyterians, a Rabbi, Baptists, and African Methodist Episcopal. They are a fine group of men."

"Tom, I was interested in some of the community concerns expressed by Mrs. Evans, notably the lack in sex education, the insensitivity to the needs of the handicapped and the elderly, and particularly the matter of letting the dying person die in peace and dignity."

"I'll say Amen to that, Don. These things worry me."

"Has the ministerium done anything about them?"

"So far, only in regards to the handicapped. As you've heard, we were responsible for a survey of the handicapped, and the results were good. For one thing, we got ramps built at the churches so people with mobility problems could get to services in their church. Community agencies now have data on the number and types of disabilities so they can now begin to meet the needs of those affected."

"What about sex education?"

"This is a terribly important problem for the community. We are aware of the great number of teenage girls who become pregnant, and we've got to do something to make them realize what they are doing to their bodies."

"You may not be aware of this, Tom, but I have a personal identification with two of these problems. My sister and I were children of devout and conservative parents who abhorred the idea of sex, and never mentioned the word in the house. Well, you know how kids are. This just presented a challenge to find out more about this word and what it meant. We lived in a small community and my sister was with a fast crowd. My parents found out about this and refused to let her out other than to school."

"This must have been a difficult time for your family."

"I felt close to my sister and she confided that she had missed several of her periods. Mother found out, somehow, and that really blew the place sky high. When my sister refused to have an abortion, they literally threw her out of the house. The young father came forward, and they were married. His parents were wonderful, and were concerned with saving three lives. As it turned out, my sister died giving birth, and my parents never went to the hospital nor to the funeral services.

"I cried bitterly when she was lowered into the ground, and it was a long time before I could speak civilly to my parents. Eventually I forgave them. But Tom, what ignorance, and what devastation to deprive young people of basic information about their bodies, and yet, how easily these tragedies can be prevented."

"That's a pretty sad story. Did the baby live?"

"Yes, and she's doing beautifully. She was baptized in the Catholic Church, and named Mary Cronin. Bill's mother adored Mary, and since she could have no other children, she had a ready made daughter. Bill's father was crazy over her, and she is a loved member of the family.

"Bill is now a successful lawyer, married a wonderful woman, and they have two fine kids. Mary is now in college, and the Cronins have loved and supported her every inch of the way. I visit both families every year, and am so proud of all of them. The whole family is just priceless!"

"That's a beautiful ending to what could have been disastrous. It only demonstrates how stupid we are when we don't provide sex education where and when it is needed," Tom said.

"Unfortunately, in the seminary, sex information is approached on a philosophical/moral basis, and what is needed is the realistic/practical."

"That reminds me of the experience I had once when asked to talk to a group of seminarians on sex information and education. Perhaps I was too forthright and picturesque in my presentation, for the rector scowled at me and 'harrumphed' loudly. Needless to say I was not invited back. After that I took courses in counseling, read a lot, and I think I'm competent to speak on the subject."

"Good! I may call upon you. Speaking of the Irish, how about a dab of Irish Mist, to go along with my coffee?"

"Sure, coming up."

Both men relaxed in easy chairs, Don pulling on a pipe, while Tom lit a cigar. They sipped on their Irish Mist and coffee and were quiet. Then Tom broke into the reverie, "Don, you mentioned two areas which had touched you. What was the other one?"

"That concerns Elsie and it tore me up all over."

"If the telling is too painful . . ."

"No, I want to share it with you, since it is a matter we ministers face frequently. It concerns the death of a loved one—the dying process.

"Elsie had been ill with cancer for some time but the doctors would not tell me how bad it was. Finally, it spread to her internal organs, and I was told that the condition was terminal but that medicine could prolong life, although it could not prevent the inevitable death.

"They kept her in the hospital for some time, and on every visit I made, she seemed to have an additional IV tube in her body. They tried all kinds of medication, and I suspect they were experimenting with new drugs or medicine. Still she did not improve.

"One day, she said to me plaintively, 'Don, I know I'm going to die, and I'm not afraid to meet my Maker. I want to go home and be with you to the end.'

"The medical men were furious with me when I told them I wanted no more heroic efforts with my wife, and that I would bring her home the next day. They tried to dissuade me and Elsie, but we were adamant on this."

Don leaned forward in his chair, his face brightened, and hands gestured as he continued, "Would you believe, Tom, that Elsie actually looked better and color came back to her cheeks in just a few days at home? Some days she came downstairs and we ate in the dining room. On one warm day, we had lunch on the patio, and we talked about our lives together, swapped stories about when we were kids and about people we had almost forgotten. Elsie loved flowers, and the ones she had asked me to plant were now coming up, and it gave her much pleasure to see them.

"The cancer was hard at work, and within two weeks she passed away, but it was such a peaceful departure. We said some prayers together, I kissed her, and we held hands until she lapsed into a coma, and I could feel her life slipping away. It was sad, but in a way, beautiful. We had our last moments together, in our house, holding hands and praying.

"This is 'death with dignity,' and I'm all for it. Someone once said, 'Let the dying die in peace.' There comes a time in life when death comes to everyone of us, yet we fear it, and try to hold it off. With Elsie, I'm just sorry I didn't take her home sooner and let her enjoy her home and flowers a bit longer."

"You've had a rough time of it , Don. I wish I had known and been able to be with you during that period. I always remember my friends and families in Mass daily, so in a way, I was praying for you, although neither of us were aware of the circumstances."

"Death is the most natural thing in the world, yet we all fear it. I guess it is the unknown we enter, and that can be scary."

Tom rose from his chair, stretched his arms and legs and went to the kitchen to heat the coffee. Returning with the pot, he noticed that Don was quietly sitting, and relaxing.

"What's up, ol' friend?"

"Nothing, I'm just content. Such a nice evening. You sure are a calming influence on me. I haven't had peace of mind like this in a long time."

"That's what friends are for. Remember, we've been through the trash of war together, and that makes believers of everyone, and close friends."

"Say, what about our former commander-in-chief, who got his hands in the cookie jar and made a stinking mess of things in Washington?"

"Trickey Dick and his mad machinations, stonewalling every move to make him confess? He's crazy as a loon to think that the American people didn't see what he was doing."

"Yeah, thought he was above the law, and accountable to no one."

"He wanted to go down in history, and he sure will—the first president to be forced out of office. What irony! He'll submerge, but you wait and see. He'll make a comeback, somehow and in some fashion."

"Sure, Gerry Ford pardoned him for all his transgressions, and he's a free man. Yet, he was the one who knew it all and had his finger in the pot all the time."

"Tom, you know for all his skulduggery, he was the former supreme anticommunist who made the breakthrough to establish friendly relations with Communist China."

"I often wonder how his Quaker brethren, those peaceful souls, looked upon him. Well, let's not spoil a nice evening thinking about the miserable wretch. We're not very Christian, are we?"

"It's been so good, Tom. I'm sure glad you are my neighbor."

At the door, they shook hands warmly.

Chapter XVII

Sunday mornings were a bit hectic in the Evans household, Joe was always the first one up and about. He made the coffee, showered, shaved, dressed, brought a cup of coffee and the front section of the *Post* to Rita in bed, then roused the children to get them going. He knew he'd have to make another trip to get the boys on their feet, while Beth would be in and out of the bathroom and dressing in her room. In the kitchen, he'd drink coffee and read the sports section.

When Father Shane emerged from the sacristy at St. Dunstan's Church for the nine o'clock Mass, the Evans family would be in their regular pew about ten rows up from the front. Joe would be on the aisle, then Joe Jr., Rita, Beth, and Roger. Joe and Beth were the singers in the family, Rita couldn't carry a tune in a basket, and she knew it, and Roger could but wouldn't. They were faithful in their obligations to the church, with regular visits to the confessional, and receiving Holy Communion on Sundays, except Joe Jr. who had yet to make his first Communion.

On this particular Sunday, Father Shane chose for his homily "Living and Dying with Dignity," using as his example the life of Christ.

"He was born in poverty, in a stable, was obedient to his parents, helped his father, a carpenter, and went around doing good for those in need. He cured the handicapped, fed the hungry and raised the dead, yet he could show anger, when he drove the money changers from the temple with a whip. He went to at least one party, a wedding, and saved the day by providing wine for the bridal party when they ran out. He was good, and lived a life of dignity.

"What about his death? This was ignominious, for in those days crucifixion was the epitomy of how not to die. Our Lord accepted the cross and didn't fight it. He embraced it and gave it meaning. The cross is now the centerpiece of the Christian religion, and many of our churches are laid out in the form of the cross. It is a symbol of love and dignity.

"Some people are granted the dignity of a peaceful death, while others die a slow demeaning death. Here, I refer to the terminally ill cancer patient, or one with an irreversible condition. Families are stricken with grief, for fear of losing a loved one. Professionals fight to save lives, sometimes at all costs, even when no hope for a cure is present.

"In any event, such prolongation of death in these terminal cases is undignified, unethical, and does nothing to insure peaceful living either for the patient or the loved ones. We need to examine our lives to insure that each day is lived in a dignified manner, and seek to insure that our passing from this earth to the next life will be done in a dignified way."

As they left the church after Mass, Father Shane was greeting his parishioners and motioned the Evans family to come over. He shook hands with the children and Joe, then said to Rita, "I'd like to talk with you this week."

"Sure, Father. I enjoyed your homily."

"I've been doing some thinking about this topic, and last week it was brought home vividly to me. I'll tell you about it later."

When the children dashed into Baldwin's Bakery for the usual Sunday treat for breakfast, Rita called out, "Surprise us and make it good!"

The Sunday breakfasts were more a brunch, and the family enjoyed sitting around the table afterward talking, except Joe Jr. who was off as soon as he could get away.

"Father Tom really laid it on today in his homily," Joe offered in the car while the children shopped for 'goodies.' "I wonder what prompted this type of sermon?"

"He'll tell me all about it this week at the hospital. He has a good point, though. I believe that some medical professionals are more interested in research than in the person under treatment."

"We need the researchers, pet; we'd be back in the dark ages without them. Look at the progress we've made because of research. I realize, too, that sometimes we open a Pandora's Box through research, when any one of us can 'pull the plug' so to speak, causing death."

"I don't think it is as blatant as that. He's saying that we should not go to heroic lengths to prolong life, and let the individual go forth in a dignified manner."

"Yeah, but who is to call the shots? There are ethical and legal questions involved."

"If the patient has command of his faculties, he can request it."

"Supposing the patient doesn't?"

"Then the next of kin, the spouse, a son, daughter, in concert with the best medical advice and legal counsel too, if that is indicated."

"The ideal way is for people to stipulate their wishes in a will or document while they are in good health."

At that point the children returned with a full bag. "We got some strawberry and lemon tarts, chocolate doughnuts and crullers," Beth said.

Rita's office was in the middle of the main corridor on the first floor, and was large enough to accommodate her desk and a large conference table with comfortable chairs, while the walls carried prints of historic Maryland and sailboats on the Chesapeake Bay. It was at the conference table that she waited for Alex to show on Monday afternoon, and when he arrived, late, he wheeled in taking a position opposite her.

"How goes it, Alex?"

"Fine, Rita. No serious problems in my patient load, but there are a few things we need to talk about."

With that, their heads went together, discussion flowed freely, and the give-and-take of professionals was evident.

She asked, "How about the college? Are you involved again?"

"Not yet, but I suspect there will be some project coming down the line and they'll be putting the bite on you for my invaluable services." He laughed a hearty belly full, and Rita joined him.

"I'm sure of it, and I'll be happy to keep you occupied and out of mischief."

"I'd like to continue what I had to say at the last staff meeting regarding what I see as the insensitivity to the needs of people, the plight of senior citizens and the functioning of the handicapped in society. In addition, what I see as the need for a gravely ill person who is going to die, to be able to go home and die there, if that is possible."

"That last topic is sure getting a workout. We got hit with it at Mass on Sunday. Father Tom and I talked about it over lunch today, and here you are bringing it up again."

"Is it a 'no-no' topic?"

"By no means, Alex. It is very appropriate, and something we should be aware of, especially in a hospital. We see so many ill patients, we may sometimes forget their humanness, and look upon them as statistics."

"Yes, and for professionals who have particular

interventions to ply, the patient reaction may be more important than the patient himself."

"You're saying that research comes first, then the person?"

"Absolutely."

"That's what Father Tom was saying. He told me about a friend whose wife was terminally ill, and they convinced the medical staff to let her go home to pass her last days with her husband in their home. I guess that got him going, although he said he'd been thinking about it for some time."

"We can't solve that one here, but you should bring it up in one of Dr. Sargent's cabinet meetings. Count me in if there is any way you think I might help."

"Good. About the insensitivity of people?"

"That's another broad scope problem that will need more than just a few of us to take on, but it burns the hell out of me when these instances take place. What Anita had to say is just the tip of the iceberg."

"Agreed, Alex, but it has to start somewhere, sometime. Someone has to assume leadership and get the ball rolling."

"But it's so huge, so overpowering."

"All the more reason to get a campaign started. Perhaps some people committing these acts are not aware of their insensitivity to their fellow humans.

"A campaign, here in this town?" Alex was incredulous.

"Why not? This is where these things take place."

"You have some ideas in mind?"

"You know I always have ideas. For starters, how about a guest column in the local newspaper, pointing out some of the ways people can be insensitive to others. Get yourself on the radio on a question and answer talk show. Stations are frequently looking for ways to involve their audiences. Another would be to get some bumper stickers . . ."

"Are you kidding? A bumper sticker for this?"

"Look at the crazy things they have on bumpers now.

Something like 'Be Nice to your Neighbor,' 'Have a Heart,' 'Be Sensitive,' etc. You'd be amazed at what might come out of something like this."

He looked at her and grinned. "You might just have the germ of an idea. I'll need to thrash this around some more."

"You might want to combine your concern for the senior citizens under the umbrella of insensitivity to others. This would knock off two birds with the one stone. It's worth exploring.

"You had another topic, the rights of the handicapped in striving to lead normal lives. Care to expand on that one?"

"The handicapped are frequently set aside as unusual, sometimes 'freaks' because they are not like others. They are not 'average,' they don't belong because they are different. The child with cerebral palsy who wears a headgear and is on crutches can't go to the regular school, so is put into the special education class. The person who has mental retardation stands a good chance of being railroaded into an institution, or if not that, he goes into a special education class. The idea of mainstreaming is unheard of in this section of the state.

"The adolescent who has a sensory deficiency is looked at askance, and is not allowed to participate in the usual sports or recreational and social activities of other young people. This puts them at a disadvantage and they suffer immensely unless they find kids their own age who are similarly handicapped.

"Older persons are at a disadvantage because of age, infirmity and a condition that prevents them from active participation.

"The parents of the disabled are often afraid to let their sons and daughters go out on dates, for fear that something dreadful might happen, like falling in love, getting pregnant, or wanting to get married.

"There is the question of sterilization of the mentally retarded by parents who are afraid that a daughter will get in trouble through a pregnancy, and worry about care for the baby. The list goes on and on."

"I share your concerns and feel for the parents of the handicapped. In spite of what you say, look how far we've come in our recognition of the needs of the handicapped. The programs begun by President Kennedy are bearing fruit, and both the mentally retarded and the mentally ill are much better off now than a decade ago. These things take time, and a change in the perception of the general public."

"Yes, I'm aware of all that, but I want more and the sooner the better."

He lapsed into silence for a few moments, and she was quiet, too.

He came back mentally to the room, fished out cigarettes, lit one and blew smoke rings.

"Any thoughts you want to share, I've a good listening ear."

"There aren't many people I feel free to talk to, but you are one, and my best 'ear' to confide in. It's about Donna. I'm falling in love, but fear to express it to her."

"She's a beautiful person and not alone because of her physical attractiveness."

"Since we met at your house, I've admired her, and on our many dates, I've come to know her much better. If I continue to see her, I'll be so deep in love, that I'll want to marry her."

"What's the problem?"

"I can't because of my legs and wheelchair. She's blind. What a combination. I couldn't do that to her."

"How does she respond to you?"

"I think she likes me, but doesn't want to push it. She might feel the same way I do, about our physical limitations."

"Think of the great times you've had during this period and what this relationship has meant to you both. You seem to complement one another, you are her eyes, and she is your legs."

"We have no problem with that. We've had loads of fun, and could continue doing just that. If we do, we might both fall deeply in love and then marriage would be the logical next step."

"There might be risks involved in such a relationship."

"Like what?"

"In view of your disability, suppose you couldn't fulfill her sexual needs? She is a woman with ample proportions, and I suspect could be passionate."

"Perish the thought. I know I'm not impotent and would enjoy the opportunity to make love to her. She has a great body, and I drool when she gets close to me. I know she can't see her body, but I suspect she knows she has ample proportions and carries her body well."

"Most women do, Alex. Some use it to flaunt, to seduce, and for others it is to be coy or graceful. I think Donna feels kindly toward you and is impressed by all you have accomplished."

"OK. If we were to get married and have a baby, I guess we could handle it, somehow. Donna needs to know where things are in a house, and she catches on quickly in her orientation to physical items. She can get down the ladder on the boat, and help me cast off, and work the sheets on the jib. She goes fore and aft without any trouble at all."

"Perhaps her mother would help out a little if a baby is born, that is assuming you two make it legal," Rita laughed to lessen the tension.

"Yes, maybe the ol' bitch will relent and bear a hand. Y'know, Donna has a tiny bit of vision, and can make out shapes, so between us we could manage. All that is in the future. I'll have to think that one over."

"Still have doubts?'

"Yes, quite a few."

Rita leaned back in her chair, closed her eyes and spoke. "I seem to remember a speech about rights of the handicapped and insensitivity to others. This is your life we're talking about, Alex. Are you afraid to fall in love? Are you to deny yourself the rights of a young man to consider marriage and a family? What about Donna's rights to fall in love and to make love with a man she admires. Who is being insensitive?"

"We're both handicapped! It would never work!"

"So far, it has worked for both of you. Nothing has prevented you from doing what you've wanted to do. Sure, you can't go dancing, but you enjoy music. She plays the piano and you sing. Neither of you play cards or chess, nor golf or tennis, but you can hear, see, and enjoy the competition. Joe and I aren't handicapped, but we do the same things you do. We're not athletic, but we enjoy the games, and we'd rather talk and read books than play cards or chess. It's a sharing of mutual interests, Alex, that makes love survive."

"Rita, if you weren't married, I'd take you on. You sure talk turkey to me, and that's what I need. This has been a good session, and you gave me the word. You've made me squirm, but I asked for it. I'm off to the pad and a couple of scotches to think over what we've talked about. Thanks a million."

"Anytime, Alex. I'm fond of you and Donna."

Rita fell asleep that night reviewing her conversation with Alex. On one hand he decries insensitivity to needs, yet he doesn't realize what he's doing to himself and a wonderful girl. If only he knew what Donna had confided to her during the retreat! He would blush. In the event he did become impotent, they could still make love and be fulfilled. They'd make a great couple, she's so pretty, and he's so masculine. Wonder what their kids would be like?

Chapter XVIII

Fire engines clanging and roaring down Route 301 roused Rita from her sleep at 2:00 a.m. The house was about five blocks off the main road, and she could hear more engines heading toward town. She rose, put on a robe and went into the living room to peer out the window. There was a red glow off to the right, and a pall of black smoke rose to partially obscure a half moon on the wane. As more fire equipment raced by, she went into the kitchen to call Andy Wright, the night operator at the hospital.

"Hello, Andy? This is Rita Evans. What's going on down there?"

"God, Rita, it's awful. Seems as though the whole town is going up in flames. We've got some injuries already."

"I'll be right down."

Rita hurried back to the bedroom to find Joe sitting up. "Am I dreaming or do I hear fire engines?"

"No dream, Joe, it's a fire in town. I just called the hospital, and Andy said there's a big fire downtown. The injured have been brought to the hospital and more are expected. I'm going in to help."

He leaped out of bed and pulled on some clothes quickly, as Rita was doing the same. "I'm coming along, and will drive you there."

Roger heard the commotion and came into their

bedroom. "What's the matter? I heard voices and then the fire engines."

Rita repeated what she had told her husband, then said, "Stay here and take care of the house. Don't arouse Beth and Joe Jr. We'll be back in the morning, if not before, to get you off to school. I'll tell you all about it when I get home."

As they approached the shopping area at the intersection of Route 301 and Charles Street, Joe said, "Look at those flames leaping up over there."

"Joe, we can't get down Charles Street. We'll have to find a way to get to the hospital."

"I know, dear, we can't cross hose lines, and there are fire trucks all over the place. What a fire! I haven't seen one like this in years!"

"Look over there on St. Mark's Street. The fire is raging out of control. Lord, I hope people in those apartments were able to get out before it's too late. Let's try the back road to the hospital. Hurry!"

Fire engines were thick on St. Mark's and Charles Streets. Hose lines were intertwined and zigzagged all over the roads, while flashing red lights on engines and police cars swirled in the night, causing grotesque figures to dance on stores and houses nearby.

Joe continued down Route 301 for about a half mile, and turned left on to a back road which led to the rear of the hospital.

In the lobby, Rita met Peg O'Bryan who said, "Quick. C'mon here and help me in Emergency. We've got our hands full."

"What happened, Peg? I couldn't see much from the car, and we couldn't get close out there to see what's going on. Joe parked in the lot, and went down to see the fire."

"An eighteen wheeler tanker was late getting to the corner to deliver a load and arrived about 12:30 a.m. He'd

been held up for hours on the Virginia side of the Governor
Nice bridge near Bowling Green. The station was locked
and when he went out back to take a leak, there was a roar,
then an explosion and fire."

"That's near St. Dunstan's, and an apartment . . ."

"Here, bandage this man's arm, while I do his leg. Yes, it
looks bad for the church, from what I hear. Stay here and get
into this white coat, and I'll tell you what I want you to do.
They'll be more patients coming in for us to care for. Stand
by."

At that moment another ambulance with siren screeching
roared up to the emergency entrance, doors swung open and
another victim was rushed in. Under a bandaged face she
recognized Father Shane, and heard Peg's voice, "Here, take
him in here. This bed is free."

The priest was unconscious. While Peg looked for vital
signs, Rita cut away some of the clothing from his body,
exposing raw flesh where he had been burned. A doctor came
in, shoved Rita aside and began his examination. "Severe
burns, Peg. Get the first aid kit, then we'll move him
upstairs."

Rita moved over to another patient to calm her down.
"Everything will be all right. We'll take good care of you."

Firemen overcome by smoke inhalation were brought in
to be resuscitated. The homeless crowded into the lobby
where Rita tried to make them comfortable. Coffee and
doughnuts appeared for the fifteen families with about 55
people, many of whom were children, all were white.

She was running ragged, going back and forth to a room
where the coffee and milk for the children were located,
and there was no one to help, for the medical and nursing
staff were busy with the injured. The families were huddled
close together, as if fearful of getting separated. As she
returned to the lobby with a tray full of milk, a voice halted

her.

"What can I do to help?"

Quickly she replied, "Take this milk and give it to the children," and went back to get another load.

After ten minutes of spilled milk, sloshing hot coffee, and sugared hands from the doughnuts, she stopped to catch her breath in the supply room, and her helper appeared in the door.

"You were most kind to come in and lend a hand to us, sir. I'm grateful. I'm Rita Evans on the staff of the hospital here."

The man's deep bronze face broke into a wide grin as he said, "So you're the Mrs. Evans my wife spoke about when she returned from the retreat. I am Phillip Mason from the A.M.E. Church across town."

"How nice to meet you, Reverend Mason. Your wife and I had several chats while we were on the retreat. How good of you to come here and help during this disaster. I wish we met under better circumstances."

"Helping one's fellow man is the best of circumstances, and I enjoy doing it."

The interlude was broken by calls for refills and other activities.

The fire continued to gain momentum down the street, fanned by the wind. Additional fire companies arrived and they were dispatched to set up a wall of water beyond the church to stem the flames.

It was 3:30 when Rita saw Dr. Sargent talking to Peg O'Bryan in the corridor, and he beckoned to her. "Rita, David Morrison, manager of the Howard Johnson Motel just called to say he had plenty of rooms and he'd be happy to make them available to those who have been burned out and have no place to go. Can you handle this? Peg and I have many patients to attend to here with burns, fractures, smoke inhalation, and God knows what else."

She crossed the lobby to where Reverend Mason was talking to a family and asked, "Are you available when you finish?"

"I'm ready now for anything you have in mind for me."

"We need to get these homeless families over to the Howard Johnson Motel where the manager has offered rooms for the rest of the night. I'll need your help in getting them organized."

"Good, let's get on it."

They looked first for the families with babies, and very young children, then those with other children, and with Reverend Mason leading the way, carrying a little girl sound asleep, the procession wound down the street, stepping over hose lines and in between fire engines. Rita brought up the rear with the senior citizens. At the main intersection, a policeman stopped traffic to let the group pass over to the motel.

"Mr. Morrison? I'm Rita Evans from the hospital and Dr. Sargent told me about your kind offer."

"Yes, and we're happy to help. There's a wing of empty rooms on the second floor, and we can put up the larger families together."

An hour later, Rita walked back to the hospital through the smoke and stench of burning rubber and wood. The engines were still pumping water, but the fire was pretty much out. She had left Reverend Mason to attend to any details, and he was to call her if any problems arose. He had been a tremendous help to her, the families were pleased with his comforting words, and his efficiency in getting things accomplished was appreciated by all.

It was 4:30 when she reentered the hospital; the lobby was strangely quiet, but there was still much activity in the emergency room. Peg had that place under control, and Rita was able to assist her in a few details.

"Peg, how is Father Tom?"

"You know the Irish. You can't kill them, and he's one of the tough ones. He has several bad burns on his face and left arm, some contusions but nothing too serious. He was unconscious when the firemen found him in the church trying to save sacred vessels and vestments, but the smoke got to him, and he dropped. He'll be OK in a few days."

Joe found his wife in her office about five o'clock doing paper work in preparation for the telephone calls she'd have to make to relatives of the injured and burned out families. He came around her desk, leaned over to kiss her smudged cheek and tired face. "You look all tuckered out, dear. Come home and get a rest."

"I can't, Joe. There's too much to be done. I'll be all right here. You go and get the children ready for school, tell them what happened, then you get to D.C. for your work."

"No way I'm going to the office today. I'll call in and tell them about the fire, and my need to be around to help out. I'll return here about 9:30. Can I bring you anything?"

It was mid afternoon before she could get away from her desk to see Father Tom, whose face was covered with bandages, and his left arm draped in a white cloth above seared flesh. He tried to smile in greeting.

"You people sure know how to keep a guy in the sack. Peg was about ready to handcuff me to the bed when I wanted to get out. How're you doing, Rita?"

"Hi Father. I feel like you look, almost dead on my feet. I'll survive. You had quite a night of it."

"That's the understatement of the year. I got knocked for a loop, and it's a good thing some fireman dragged me out of there. I hear there's nothing left of the church and the rectory, just the walls."

"Yes, I heard it is a total loss."

"The Archbishop called and will send down an auxiliary bishop to find out what we do next. 'Not to worry,' the boss said. 'I'll assign a young priest to help until you get on your feet.' I hope to be up and around before he arrives."

"Any other visitors?"

"My old friend Don Leyton came in late this morning, and offered to help in any way. Good man, Don. Guess I'll have to find a hall to say Mass in for a while. The good Lord gave us a fire, and I'm sure He'll help with the resurrection. Could be a blessing in disguise. Who knows?"

In a few days, city officials had things sorted out. It was as Peg had told Rita. The gas truck blew up at the station, probably caused by a spark from the motor near the fumes of the hose. When the truck blew, the station followed, and that started flames, which caught the apartment and houses, then the church. The driver was lucky to have escaped with his life.

The police cordoned off the entire area. There was nothing left for the occupants of the apartment building or houses to retrieve, and they had only the clothes on their backs. Fortunately, there were no deaths, for the people were evacuated quickly. Father Tom lost all his possessions in the rectory, plus the entire contents of the church.

The public and private agencies turned to and helped the victims by offering clothing, furniture, and equipment, while social services assisted in locating living arrangements for the homeless. Some went to live with relatives, others with friends, and a few had to stay at the Howard Johnson Motel for a longer period.

Several days before his release from the hospital, Rita went to his room and found him sitting up in bed. "Hello, Father Tom. How goes it today? I hear you'll be released soon."

"Hi, Rita. Yes, so I hear." He seemed a little down. "I'm

a bit worried about all that has to be done, and I'm not sure just where to begin. I've lost everything in the fire."

"It was devastating to everyone concerned, but the community will do all that it can to put things back together again."

"Yes. We have wonderful people here, and this makes us realize that we are our brothers' keepers."

"I'm amazed at the outpouring of help from so many groups offering to help the homeless people."

"I've heard of that. Yesterday, our ministerium held an informal meeting at this bed and offered help to me and our parish. I've had offers to say Mass in their churches and halls. I'll be eternally grateful to them for their generosity."

"Joe asked me to give you a message."

"OK. Let's have it."

"The day you are released, we'll pick you up to have you come to the house for dinner, and bring your toothbrush."

❦ ❦ ❦

"Now, I know how the apostles must have felt when Jesus gave them their marching orders, 'Take neither purse nor script . . .' and here I am with not much more. Rita, that was some meal. Perfect all around."

Bandages and all, Rita picked him up on the day of his release, to bring him home and feed him. The family had gathered around the table to welcome their guest and enjoy his companionship. As the children helped to clear the table, Joe asked, "What now, Padre?"

"I'm starting to get a handle on things, and sorting out the priorities for the church, rectory and my personal life."

"Your car was destroyed . . ."

"Beyond all recognition. The junk man took pity on me and hauled it away for free. Then out of the blue, nice things happened. A parishioner visited and stated that her husband had a protracted business trip to the Orient and she would accompany him. Would I consider 'house-sitting' and using their car so both would not deteriorate? Their generosity nearly floored me, and of course, I accepted. The house is modest and roomy, and the car a year old Pontiac Grand Prix. The Lord sure looks out for His servants."

"Until you move into their house, we'd like you to occupy our guest quarters here. Between our two cars, we can offer you transportation."

"This is most generous, and I appreciate all that you've done for me. I accept with the provision that you'll allow me to participate in some way."

"We'll handle that later. How about saying Mass and getting vestments?"

"We'll have Mass at the National Guard Armory, and between the Archbishop, who is sending vestments to me, and the Carmelite nuns, who are making a new set, I'll be covered. The local ministers have offered me space for classes and meetings. They've been just wonderful."

Rita dropped in to say, "Your clothes and books?"

"I'll have to order from the skin on out. My insurance covers most of that outlay, but my books are another thing. Some I'll never be able to replace."

"We have a modest library here, and I want you to feel free to use and borrow to your heart's content. No deep philosophical tomes, but interesting literature."

"Thanks, Joe, I'll take you up on that. The major activity now is to start on a new church. I've some ideas I want to pursue, and I'll have to discuss them with the Archbishop, and he's a progressive man. Also, I'll call upon the parish membership, for this is their church and they'll be using it long after I'm gone."

"Good thinking, Father. I'll be happy to suggest some

names along with those you already know, for we have some
bright lights in this parish."

"I also plan to nudge the ministerium for ideas for our
new church. Those men are great and I have respect for my
co-workers in Christ."

"That's a surprise. I suspect many of them would want
to change their churches if given the chance, but not to
reconstruct a burned edifice. Would you face any criticism
from our parishioners?"

"I doubt it. Not many people are aware of the constant
dialogue and interaction we clergy have. I'd like to get away
from the standard Gothic architecture we have in many of
our churches. It's nice, but quite expensive. We need a solid,
but modest building, and not too elaborate."

"What about the interior design?"

"The Vatican Council suggests the alter be close to the
congregation, and I like that. It brings the celebrant and
people together. I've seen some of the newer churches, and
I'm impressed with their simplicity, few statues, no candles,
no alter rail, a pitched floor, etc."

"I suppose it's too early to ask if you've got a tentative
cost figure?"

"Lord, yes. I don't even dare to think about that. Much
will depend on the size of the building, kinds of materials
and labor."

"Will the Archdiocese help out financially?"

"I'll have to sound out the boss on that one. Maybe he
can get some low cost financing for us."

"I have a suggestion for ideas. In addition to the men,
sound out the women and young people of the parish. Many
will be parishioners for a long time, and this will give them a
feeling of belonging, and a sense of partnership. Too often
we ask the men, and forget other important people."

"That's a real good idea, Joe. I'll remember it."

"In this house, we have some good candidates in Rita, Roger, and Beth. They're still young, but one never knows what gems they can come up with."

Later over coffee in the living room, the men and Rita continued their conversation about the new church and Father Tom's rehabilitation activities, while he remained as a guest. The Evans family was delighted that the priest would stay with them, and the children especially enjoyed having him around.

Chapter XIX

It was late on Friday afternoon, Billie Jean straightened up her desk before leaving and put a note on her door for Rita, advising her of an early Monday appointment which would delay her arrival in the office. She did not want to interrupt Rita in her conference with Alex.

"I'm happy to see Father Tom back on his feet and making rounds of his patients, Rita was saying.

"Yes, we all missed his cheery self bouncing in and out of rooms, leaving a trail of happiness. It must come from being Irish," Alex said.

"He has a positive outlook, and neither the burning of his church nor the rectory has him down. Add to those are the facial burns and other lacerations from the fire. I know I couldn't handle these as easily as he has."

"The community is all behind him, and I know he's already planning a modest replacement for the church."

"Yes, he's shared some ideas with us at home."

"It must be nice to have a star boarder. That is generous of you and Joe."

"It's nothing, Alex. We have the room, he's burned out, and he's just a wonderful person. Enough of that. What's with you and the lady friend?"

"Tonight, I dine with her family."

"Checking you out?"

"I'm checking them in, Donna and her father. Nice people. The mother?

She's a drag. What a dame!"

When Alex pulled up in the driveway at the Edwards' house, Donna was near the carport, and came over to him.

"My, you smell nice," and she leaned in to get a closer whiff and kissed him. "It's so nice out, we're eating on the patio out back."

Joe Edwards came up to the car as Alex got out and settled himself in his chair, as Donna started to push him along.

"Hello, Alex, welcome to the pad. We're all set for a nice evening on the patio."

"So Donna told me. Sounds great."

Once settled out back, Joe asked Alex, "How about a thirst quencher?"

"I 'll take a scotch and water on the rocks."

Sitting next to him under the umbrella table, Donna said, "You're pretty snappy tonight."

"How can you tell?"

"By the tone of your voice, the feel of your coat, and your general bearing. I may not see, but I have good senses and perceptions."

As they talked, Alex noticed how nice the patio was laid out with flowers neatly tended, the comfortable lawn furniture, and the trees in the background. Joe did all of the gardening and maintenenace himself. "I need to get out in the dirt and make something grow. It's a nice change from the office."

When Joe came to the table with the drinks, he sat down to join the conversation. He had heard of Father Tom's return to work, and his plans for a new church, plus the efforts of the community to help him in numerous ways. Both Joe and Alex were Baltimore Colts football fans, and they gave Donna a hard time, as she was loyal to the Washington Redskins.

"Daddy, you know I've always rooted for the 'Skins. Sonny

Jurgensen has it all over Johnny Unitas."

Before they could continue, Mabel Edwards came out the door, bearing a tray of cheese and crackers. She greeted Alex cordially, passed the dish around and sat with them. She told Alex that the dinner entree was one of Donna's specialties, and hoped that he was hungry. She was a gracious hostess and turned to talk to Alex about his boat.

"I hear you have a boat. Have you named it yet?"

"No, but I'm working on it. You haven't seen it yet, Mrs. Edwards. How about coming out for a ride? The weather is still good."

"Not me, young man. I like boats, but only from dry land. Thanks just the same." Mabel was not rude, but she was not about to accept any favors from this young man. She knew what was on his mind, and his intentions toward her daughter. She would fight in her own way to keep them apart.

Joe was in Donna's camp. He approved of the relationship with Alex, for he recognized her need for male companionship, and to get out from under her mother's domination. Their daily rides gave both father and daughter time to exchange thoughts about her dates and both considered Alex a fine person.

When the conversation turned to financial matters, Mabel's ears perked up. It soon came out that Alex had a comfortable portfolio in stocks and bonds, and kept a close eye on the stock market. He bought shares regularly and reinvested the dividends. This gave Mabel insight into his financial status, and she thought that with his disability pension, regular salary and investments, he was doing all right, and would be able to support a wife — but not her daughter as the wife.

After another round of drinks, dinner was served.

"This is delicious! Wonderful! You made this Donna?" Alex asked.

"Simple," she replied. It's called crab Kodiak, and the

hardest part is picking the cartilage from the crabmeat."

"Maybe you'll help me make it sometime over at the house," he said.

"Sure, anytime."

Mabel excused herself to enter the house to plug in the coffee. As she left, Joe noticed that her face was a crimson red. He knew what she was thinking.

Alex learned that Donna had made the salad and set the table with its nice china, cut glasses for the white wine, and prepared the vegetables. After dinner, the group sat talking, while Mabel cleaned up inside. "Busy tomorrow, Donna?" Alex asked.

"No, I'm free. What do you have in mind?"

"Care to sign on as a deck hand, and we'll take the boat out?"

"Sure, what can I bring?"

"Nothing. I've got all the fixings. Pick you up about 10:00?"

Saturday morning was beautiful It was a warm southern Maryland Indian summer day, giving a lingering look at what had been glorious for months and before the winds of autumn shake loose the leaves as a harbinger of winter.

Donna had emerged in a white skirt and pale green loose fitting shirt, and white sneakers. Alex had on a red striped shirt, white slacks and top-siders. Joe Edwards waved to them, "Have a good time" as they backed out of the driveway.

As they drove south along Route 301 they chatted, noting the crowds going into the shopping center clothed lightly, taking advantage of the warm day. "What a glorious day to be alive and to be able to go sailing," Donna remarked.

"It couldn't happen to finer people," Alex replied as he caressed the car along the open roadway.

At the dock Alex parked his chair, locked it and soon was swinging over the side to let himself down onto the boat.

"Wait a moment, Donna until I get settled, then come down. I'll guide your feet on the rungs."

He was at the bottom of the ladder, and as she descended, a gust of wind lifted her skirt, and he had a glimpse of pink panties and strong well molded legs. Inaudibly he gasped, said nothing, but admired.

"Oops! Did I show?"

"Not to worry, just a puff of wind. Everything's under control."

In short order, they were under sail. Donna now knew the boat and her assignments. Alex had set the sails, revved the motor, Donna cast off the lines, and they were in the cove, then out to the river.

"We'll head north today, go under the bridge and head over to the Virginia shore. We haven't done this before, and it's rather pretty there."

"We have plenty of supplies?"

"I came down early this morning to fill the gas tank, put the beer and ginger ale in the cooler, and the sandwiches and fruit in the fridge. We have no worries for the day."

They had a fair breeze as they sailed up the Potomac, under the Governor Nice Memorial bridge, and edged over towards Dahlgren, the site of the navy's weapon station, and from there down toward Potomac and Colonial Beaches. Over a beer and a ginger, they talked about their work and books. Alex told Donna how much he enjoyed her father, and their mutual fondness for football.

No mention was made of Mabel for a few moments until Donna spoke up."

"I try to understand her, but it's so difficult now. Formerly, it didn't mean so much, but since you and I have been going out so much, I know she doesn't see it as I do."

"How do you mean it?"

"I think she fears that I'll leave her and she doesn't want

our relationship to end."

"Have you been that close to la mere?"

"No, but she sees me as her one goal in life, to care for me."

"You're doing all right, what with your job and music."

"Alex, don't you see what I'm saying?"

"Tell me, I'm a male, not very perceptive."

"She's afraid that we'll fall in love and get married! I'll be leaving the nest, and then she'll lose me to you."

Turning in his seat to look at her he said, "What's so bad about that? Do you think you could love this ol' sad sack, crippled and all?"

"Come over here you silly man." With that she nudged close to him, put her arms around his neck and drew his face to hers.

They kissed softly at first, then with passion. He couldn't get enough of her soft lips, and she his lips among the beard. They had kissed before in the car, but never like this. Donna had whipped off her glasses, and beads of perspiration lined her brow. Alex's heart was beating rapidly, and he placed one hand under her right breast to cup it, and feel its softness. There was no question but they were hungry for one another, tongues meeting at the lips, then poking inside to explore. Alex's hand reached inside her loose fitting shirt, found the bra and slipped his fingers in to caress her breast. Donna kept her head on his neck, and joyful tears slipped out of her eyes.

Suddenly, Alex, said, "Let's head into this deserted cove and have a drink to cool off and relax. I'm all steamed up!"

While Alex fished the anchor out of the locker and heaved it overboard, Donna went forward and dropped the mainsail, and began to secure it.

"Now let's have a frostie and settle down."

"This is so wonderful, Alex. I feel so free and easy with

you."

"I must confess that I never anticipated anything like this, being with a person I could respect, admire and love."

"Because of our particular situation, my eyes and your legs?"

"And your mother who looks daggers at me."

"She is not involved. It's me. This is between you and me."

As Donna leaned forward, her shirt fell out and he could see the bra holding her full breasts. He reached in to hold them.

"That's all right, Alex, go ahead, feel me. This is a part of love. She leaned down to kiss him again and held his lips together.

After a few minutes, Alex raised up and said, "Let's get comfortable." He scrambled forward to the cabin and emerged with a blanket and a pillow, which he spread on the floor of the cockpit. As he was doing this, Donna had removed her clothing, and helped him to smooth out the blanket. He couldn't help but admire her firm body, as he took his slacks, shirt, and clothing off. She could dimly make out his body, and moved closer to him, and met his embrace. Once again they kissed passionately, and soon under the warm rays of the sun, their bodies glistening with perspiration, they made their mutual commitment to love. They had hungered for one another so long, and now to have surrendered so completely, they could wish for no greater accomplishment. It was pure ecstasy!

After a while, they separated, lying quietly side by side each with their own thoughts, the boat rocking listlessly, while the sun gazed on down, the only witness to their peace and happiness. Alex broke the silence.

"Donna, let's go overboard for a swim and cool off."

"Like this, in the buff?"

"Why not? No one is around to see us. There is a small platform off the stern, and I've used it several times. Here I'll help you. There, feel the platform? Sit there and then let yourself into the drink."

He rolled off the platform and swam around enjoying the cool water, and watching her. When she eased herself into the water, he swam with her, came up behind, put his arms around her cupping her breasts once more.

Soon it was over, and they were back on the deck. Alex brought towels and dried her off first, then she did the same for him. "I can feel a lot of hair, Alex. I wish I could see all of you."

"The best part is the body and shoulders and head. The legs are shrivelled and not much to see."

"I have a confession to make, Alex."

"What's that?"

"I wondered if your Army accident had left you impotent."

"You wondered if I could perform? And now?"

"I'm too modest to say, but a quiet 'WOW' will suffice. Let's eat!"

They munched on the sandwiches, and drank their liquids. As crumbs would fall on Donna's bare breasts, Alex would reach over to brush them off, and watch as the nipples would rise.

"You like that, don't you?"

"I'm just an admirer of good scenery."

They took a nap after lunch, and then made love again. "I could do this forever, Alex. It's so good to be here with you."

"This is a wonderful life, a great life, and you're the nicest thing in it."

As they sailed back to the cove, they were silent each nursing their individual thoughts. "What do you make of all this, Donna?"

"I don't want this day to end. It's been precious."

"Yes, fabulous. We'll have others, but fall is on us, and our sailing days are nearing an end for this year."

"Alex? I think I think I'm falling in love with you."

"I've already fallen, and I'm very happy. Today was everything I always wanted— to make love to you."

"It was for me, too."

Chapter XX

Amy Bolton awakened early this morning, but did not open her eyes, nor did she stir as Pat dressed quietly and left the room. She heard him in the kitchen opening the refrigerator for the orange juice, then the faucet gorging water into the kettle for coffee, followed by opening the front door for the *Washington Post*. Soon he'd be gone for the day, leaving her alone.

She was a pert little woman, two years younger than Pat, who had swept her off her feet in Birmingham and married her right after finishing medical school. Dark brown hair crowned her small stature, and she carried her 105 pounds gracefully, small breasts fronting a short waist, with nice legs always encased in smart hose and soft shoes.

Soon after the marriage, she knew she had made a big mistake, for Pat became absorbed in his medical work, and he had no thoughts of a family. He told her in no uncertain words, "Amy, children are a drag. I'm too involved with my work to want them around. They take up too much time. We'll just forget that for a long time." He was brusque.

She could not remain idle, she was too vibrant for that. From her savings, she took a real estate course, passed the license test, and became an agent in a local office. As the area expanded, she soon was starting to make money for herself, which she put into her private account.

Amy's concern this morning was her husband. Pat was finishing up his residency, and planning to set up his practice in La Plata, with the help of Dr. Salter of Washington. This was a man she had disliked the first time she met him. It was at a matinee at the National Theater in Washington, followed by dinner at Hogates on Maine Avenue, on the waterfront. David had a 'wandering eye' for any female he saw, preferably young girls and young women.

In the powder room of Hogates, Mrs. Salter said to her, "You know, of course that Dave and I are separated, have been for years. No divorce, we're good friends, and he takes me out for dinner occasionally. We seem to enjoy each other's company, but that's as far as our relationship goes. He lives his life, and I have my own."

As far as the Salters were concerned, that did it for Amy. No more would she be in their company. She had her doubts about Dr. Salter, who was being helpful to Pat, but she had more misgivings when she'd overhear their telephone conversations and the word 'abortion' kept cropping up.

"Amy, someone has to do these operations, and it is a lucrative business," Pat had told her when she questioned his work.

She had other worries, too. Frequently when Pat went to Washington to help Dr. Salter, he'd stay overnight and sleep in Dave's apartment with some woman, or hole up in a hotel sharing a bed with a female. Traces of lipstick and perfume on his clothing were mute evidence of his philandering.

During the first year of their marriage, their sex life was good and fulfilling to her. Then it became joyless, when Pat began to plead tiredness and their sex tapered off. She felt that they really had no marriage left, and theirs was a union of convenience.

When Pat left the house, she arose, showered, dressed and went to the kitchen for coffee. She told herself, "I'm too young to put up with this nonsense. I'm making money in real estate, and this is not the happiness I dreamed of when I married. This life now is a drudge!"

As he finished up his residency, Pat visited his patients at Powell, the nurses, Ida and Peg, spoke briefly with Dr. Sargent and left, muttering, "Get me out of this place soon!"

He drove north on Route 301 toward Washington to keep an appointment with Dr. Salter, and he looked forward to working with this older man.

"Come in, Pat. Just the man I want to see," Dave Salter greeted him.

"I'm ready for anything. My tour at Powell is just about over, my patients there are in good shape, but I'll have to look in on them a few more times."

"Don't burn the bridges, Pat. You'll need to keep on good terms with that outfit and staff, just in case of emergencies."

"What do you have in mind?"

"Let's talk over lunch."

When the martinis came, Dave said, "I think we have a couple of nice deals coming up in your neck of the woods."

"You had indicated that you'd help me set up an office there, but the other deal?"

"First, let's settle the office thing. Your wife is in real estate. Could she find a nice place setting close to the hub of activity with plenty of parking space?"

"That should pose no problem. Should we be in the center of things? What with the kind of work we'll be doing?"

"Hell no, man, but reasonably close to activity. We can't be stuck out in the east end of nowhere. We can check out possible sites Amy locates."

"How about the other deal?"

"I can't go into much detail now, Pat, but I can assure you that when it comes off we'll get rich, very rich. The activity requires a place on the river, down in your general area. Perhaps we can drive down there soon and look it over."

"Sounds mysterious to me, but I can wait. You haven't disappointed me yet."

"Good. Are you free this afternoon? How about giving me a hand with the patients. I don't anticipate any emergencies. Afterward we can have drinks and dinner at the apartment, and invite some nice friends over."

Pat was agreeable. This was a good relationship with Dave who paid well, and would be a help to him in his practice. Pat knew he'd have the best of liquor, and a delicious meal, followed by cute young girls, all ready for a "tumble in the hay."

Chapter XXI

Rita had finished the lecture for the day, and with a few minutes left raised the question, "Any areas for discussion? Problems?"

The class was silent on this mid-November afternoon.

"Let me share a few thoughts on a topic which came to our attention at the hospital the other day. It is abuse, and a problem which occurs over and over, and on all levels of society.

"The metropolitan papers in Washington and Baltimore carry many of the lurid details, and you've probably read some of them. The most revolting are stories where children are the victims.

"For your assignment, I'd like a paper from each student describing how you were involved in an abuse activity. This might be something you observed, a friend was a victim, or a circumstance where you have knowledge of what went on."

In the parking lot at the Safeway store, Rita met Jule Rohm unexpectedly and they greeted one another warmly.

"I've just had a wonderful offer, Rita. A job opened up in the office of the State's Attorney, and I've decided to hang my hat there until I get on my feet. It's too good to pass up, and it'll be good experience for me."

"I'm happy for you, Jule. Shall we have lunch again soon?"

"Yes, I'll give you a call."

At home, she put away the groceries, talked with Beth, and gave Joe Jr. some milk and cookies. Joe Sr. came in with a rush, kissed her quickly went to the bathroom, then returned much relieved. "Had to go bad."

"Joe, does your office have any information on abuse? Any studies been done on this? We started to talk about it as a form of the deprivation of the rights of the individual, and I've asked the class to submit their personal involvement in one situation, through observation or participation."

"We have some reports on rejection of children by parents, desertion of the family by a father, and a few cases of abuse as noted by hospital staff when a child is admitted. Let me ask our librarian to haul out what she has on the topic."

At dinner, Roger said to his father, "I heard you and Mom talking about abuse, and I think our soccer coach abuses us kids."

Joe's eyes bulged at the very thought, but he smothered it and asked, "In what way?"

"Well, he's wearing us out in practice. He has us doing the same things over and over. We get all tired out, and he's still on our tails."

A relieved father replied, "Son, the coach is stretching you, and challenging you to do better. He's getting you ready for another match so you'll be ready to go against perhaps a better team."

"I agree, Roger," his mother said. "There are many forms of abuse, but what the coach is doing is not abuse as we know it."

"Well, maybe, but he sure gives us kids a hard time."

"Hang in there, Roger, do as he says, and you'll be a better player."

❧ ❧ ❧

One Friday evening after work, Rita called her neighbor. "Jule? I was wondering, in lieu of a luncheon, are you free to come to our house tomorrow evening for dinner? I'd like you to meet the other members of the Evans family."

"Yes, that would be fine. We are all so busy with our work, we don't have much chance to relax and get to know one another. I'll be there at 6:00. Thanks."

Joe met Jule at the door when she arrived. "Hello, Mrs. Rohm. Do come in. Rita is in the kitchen, busy as usual, and will join us shortly."

"Thank you. Please call me Jule."

"I'm Joe. Let's go into the den and relax. May I offer you a drink?"

"That would be fine. A Manhattan on the rocks."

This gave the neighbors an opportunity to know one another, and they talked about their children, doings in Washington, the recent antics of Congress, and their work. Rita came to join them, "I see you two are getting acquainted, and I hope have solved all the problems of La Plata, the state and possibly the country."

"If we did that, we'd have no work to do!" Joe responded.

"I'd hate to put myself out of a job I just started," Jule said.

"How do you like the new job?" Rita asked.

"It poses a real challenge. Even in this short time, I'm getting busy with juvenile and family cases. I believe that this is the area I'll be handling, as more of them come to the court, and I'm enjoying the work."

"We seem to be on a parallel at the hospital, for we are seeing more family situations, particularly with young high school girls coming to the OB-GYN clinic for care," Rita said.

Jule added, "Then they come to our attention filing a

paternity case against the father, and the families get into the act."

"At the college, we've started to talk about abuse of children, and I think we'll expand that to include all kinds of abuse, including battered spouses. Have you had any of these types of cases?"

"A few have started to trickle in, and they're the forerunner of more to come," Jule added.

"It seems to me that these problems indicate a breakdown in the family as a unit. When there is abuse of children and spouses, and teenage girls become pregnant, and delinquent youths run wild, the family has lost its role as a stabilizing force for the children," Joe said.

"Part of the problem is that these are one-parent families, and there is no father, or male figure present to provide authority," Rita said.

"Another facet is that dependency breeds dependency. Illegitimate children grow up to have illegitimate children, and these, in turn, have more." Jule said. "I found that out when I was working in Washington."

"What steps should we take to solve these problems?"

Joe replied, "We've got to look at the whole problem, not just the pregnancy, delinquency, or abuse. People, starting with the young in junior and senior high schools need to recognize and shoulder their responsibilities to society."

"Prevention then is an answer," Jule said.

"First we need to provide information, and education to use that information, so that people know and understand what they are doing."

Joe responded. "Then prevention can take place. The big problem is how to get the information to them, and educate them."

Rita spoke up. "Jule, sometime soon, would it be possible for you to join me and another member of the hospital staff in a discussion of abuse at the college? I feel it is important for the students to learn what is taking place in the community to prevent or treat some of the social ills that trouble us."

"I'd be happy to. Let me know when."

"When you mention social ills, keep in mind that the use of drugs in our society is fast becoming a major problem," Joe said. "We are beginning to see the effects of drugs on the behaviors of young people in our studies."

"I know it's prevalent in Washington, but do we have it here in this city?"

Jule answered. "Not yet, but a few of the lawyers tell me that there are users and pushers around, but they haven't been caught and brought to court up to this point."

❧ ❧ ❧

When the class assembled the following week, Rita opened with this statement. "I'll collect your assignment papers at the end of class, and in the meantime, I'll ask for volunteers to give a brief oral report on an instance of personal observation of an abuse. Yes, Dorothy?"

Dorothy Redmond, a shy, short girl of nineteen, with ebony eyes and skin, rose and in a low rapid voice said, "I know of a girl who baby sits for several families, and when the parents are not at home, she threatens the kids with a strap. She's mean and beats them if they cry. I pity those children, and I'll bet she will be a mean mother when she grows up and gets married."

"What does this do to you? Have you reported her?"

"It makes me sad. No, I wouldn't know how to report her."

"Thank you, Dorothy. Yes, Sam."

From his height of six feet, Sam Cochran looked down on his classmates, and in a deep voice related how he likes to visit his cousin in New York where they play basketball. "My uncle, Ben's father, married a woman with a daughter, and both of them hate his guts. Ben has a terrible time, and gets the short end of the stick for everything. His stepmother gives her daughter all the 'goodies' and Ben ends up with nothing. It's a case of pure rejection, and I think that's a form of abuse."

Gloria Bricker had to struggle to inch her very large, black body out of the chair to stand, and in a halting, emotional voice claim, "We blacks get taunted by whites all the time. I mean, it's kind of subtle, but it goes on all the time. We don't get those nice cushy jobs the white folks get. I went for a job as a clerk, and I knew I was qualified, but the manager gave it to a white girl, and I was there before she was. That's the pits. This is class abuse, and I resent it."

"We all resent this kind of treatment, Gloria. Yes, Tony?"

"That's the same kind of treatment many minorities get," Anthony Alvarez said. "My parents came from Puerto Rico five years ago, and my father has a very strong accent. I work with him in the summer on a construction job, and the guys give him a bad time because he doesn't understand English too well, and people have trouble understanding him. He's a good worker, but he gets discouraged when anything like this happens. I think this is a cruel form of abuse."

Holding a clipping from the *Baltimore Sun*, Patty Donaldson rose, shook out her flaming red hair over her small shoulders and said, "I don't have a personal experience, but I found this piece in the paper. It's about a woman who turned her house over to her son and his wife, in return for them paying the bills, etc. Well, they locked the woman in her room and practically starved her. They were terrible to her. A younger daughter heard about it and took her mother out of the house, then had her brother and his wife arrested and brought to court. The judge threw the book at them, and sent them to jail. I think that's a case of terrible cruelty and awful abuse to your own mother."

There were other personal observations of abuse. A Viet Nam veteran told them how some of his buddies while in 'Nam took a young girl out and gang raped her. Another stated that the speeders on Route 301 were abusive toward others when they endangered the lives of pedestrians and motorists when they raced down the road. Natalie Shaw, a buxom blonde of twenty years, told of several characters hanging around the campus trying to sell marijuana and drugs, which is an insidious way to abuse young people.

Emily Shaw was almost in tears as she related how her close friend got in a family way. The boy denied it and, before he could be accused in court, disappeared. Troy Holland rose to say he was ashamed to say how his father beat his mother and him, until one day his mother let him have a two-by-four in the head, and while he was unconscious, she called the police.

"This has been an interesting session, and I want to thank you for your comments. Some of you had to bear your souls over these incidents of abuse, but they only bring out how painful it is to the victims.

"We have been able to bring these things out into the open, and look at them. The next step is to think of prevention, and how can society avoid some of these atrocities. Perhaps we can never eradicate abuse, but we may be able to take steps to diminish the impact.

"In the next few weeks, I hope to invite some friends to our class to share ways of preventing abuse, and some methods of treatment. Class dismissed."

Chapter XXII

"May Almighty God bless you, in the name of the Father, the Son and the Holy Spirit. The Mass is ended, go in peace to love and serve the Lord."

With that, Father Tom finished the second of his two Masses in the Armory, and preceded by his alter boy, Roger Evans, left the alter to remove the vestments. Joe, Rita, and several parishioners helped to dismantle the alter, folding up the chairs, moving the table to one side, and restoring the open space to its original state for the next drill by the reservists.

When he had everything in his bag, Father Tom came to the family and friends to say, "Lord, you people are wonderful! I don't know what I'd do if you weren't around. The whole community has rallied, and it's not only my parishioners, but those from the other churches, too. It's a great feeling, and I'm most grateful for all you've done these last few months."

"You're part of the family, Father," Rita said, "and we enjoy helping out."

Joe reached out to shake hands and said, "Good homily today, Padre. Speaking of family, how about joining the Evans at the ranch for brunch?"

He was about to decline when Beth looked up at him, stuck out her little hand to grasp his, and said, "Please, pretty please? We'd like you to come with us."

"All right, I can't refuse that request. I'll be there in an hour."

Beth met him at the door when he arrived. "I'll take your hat and coat and put them in my room. They'll be safe there, Father."

"Thank you, little one. I'll say an extra special prayer for you."

"Sit right down, Father," Rita said. "You know the routine. The coffee is on the table and help yourself. Sit in your usual place."

The Evans family made the priest right at home during the period he spent prior to living in the Rollins' house. He had long chats with Joe, and thoroughly enjoyed the children, all of whom respected his need for privacy.

After breakfast, Joe said a conflict in their schedules prevented them from attending a recent meeting of the parish council. Father Tom replied, "We've talked enough here that I think you know my feelings regarding the new church, and at the council, I shared with them the things I want to see in the building. It should be modest, not a long time expense for the people, and yet, I want a nice house of prayer for the Lord."

"I like the plan for a southern orientation, so we get the warmth of the sun in the winter time," Joe said.

"Having the alter in the middle as the focal point is what I like," Rita added.

"One added feature that all will enjoy is the air conditioning unit which uses the ducts for the heating plant. The men in the ministerium told me, 'even if it costs a few more bucks, do it now, while you can.' We'll worry over the costs later." Father Tom was pleased with this addition.

"Alex tells me that you are planning ramps and rails all around for people in wheelchairs and those with mobility problems," Rita said.

"He'd murder me if I didn't do all that and more for the disabled."

"Are you working on plans for the new rectory?" Joe inquired. "No doubt you'll want to finish the church first, and then do the house. Right now, you've got a pretty decent pad to live in."

"The rectory is a long way off. For the present, the Rollins house suits me. It has plenty of room, all very comfortable, and the lady of the house left a full larder. I'm doing just fine."

Rita said, "If I was to be away from this domain for over nine months, I'd sure want a reliable person to 'house-sit' for me; I suspect they feel you are reliable."

"I manage to carry an honest face, and that helps."

They talked until three o'clock when Father Tom looked at his watch then announced, "I have a baptism at four o'clock, and later I'm off to see Don Leyton. He has invited me to join in a discussion with a men's group at his church. He's such a great guy and I admire him."

Joe and Rita walked with him to the Pontiac, and bid him adieu as he drove out of the yard.

"He sure has recovered from the wounds of the fire," Joe said.

"Even more so from the loss of the church and house," Rita added.

"Turkey Day is coming up soon, gal. Any plans for inviting guests for Thanksgiving dinner? If Father Tom is alone, let's ask him."

"By all means. He's popular around town, so we might have to stand in line. Anyone else you'd like to invite?"

"Not at present, but give me time."

🍏 🍏 🍏

Ivy covered the stone walls of St. Agnes Episcopal Church, one of the oldest buildings in town. It was organized during the colonial period, and its male parishioners fought in the Revolutionary War, the War of 1812, the Civil War, and the recent struggles around the world. It was a beautiful Gothic structure, with stained glass facing the main street. The parish house was in the rear, and it was here that Father Don led Father Tom to the room where the men were gathered.

Edmond Flint, a prominent attorney, came forward as the clergymen entered the room. "Evening, Don, we are all just about assembled. There'll be about twenty-five in attendance."

"Hi, Ed. That sounds like a good number. Let me introduce Father Tom Shane, Pastor of St. Dunstan's Church. He's my guest tonight."

"Hello, Father Shane. Glad to have you with us. You'll find this an interesting group."

The rector spoke up, "Father Tom and I were G.I.s in the Army in Korea for over a year, then we went to different assignments. Despite the horrors of war, we had a great time there."

Several men drifted to the group, and one man, Vernon Deming, held out his hand and said, "I'm a veteran of that mess, too."

Father Tom responded with, "Glad to shake hands with a buddy."

Dave Morrison came up from behind and clapped him on the shoulder.

"Hello, Father, decide to join the Episcopalians?"

"Hi Dave. Good to see you. No, I'm not joining, just being available in case you need to brush up on your Latin. I want to thank you again for being so helpful to the people who were burned out in the fire. It was mighty generous of you and the staff."

The president of the group brought forward a man to introduce him. "Father, this is Martin Garrison, who has just moved here from Laurel. He's a good church worker."

"I'm pleased to meet you, Mr. Garrison. Don't you live down the street from me? I'm at the Rollins house, temporarily. You look familiar."

"That's me all right. I've seen you around, and I'm happy to greet a new neighbor."

After the meeting was opened with a prayer by Don Leyton, the president asked for reports from committee chairmen. One of these was the plans for feeding the poor of the parish at Thanksgiving, and for both food and gifts at Christmas. Dave Morrison and Andy Heller reported that their committees had made a good start on their assignments, and stated that no one would go hungry on either festive day.

After an hour of reports and discussion, Don Leyton rose to speak. "We are all reeling from the recent fire and I know that some of our parishioners are victims. We'll continue to help them out. But what has happened to the folks at St. Dunstan's and to you, Father Shane? Can you fill us in?"

"Thanks, Don, for giving me this opportunity to come to St. Agnes and personally thank you for being so generous to the victims of the fire, including those of my parish who were burned out. I thought Dave Morrison's gift of housing and food the night of the fire was most generous. Others here were equally kind. I appreciate and thank you for all that you have done for us. As to Thanksgiving, our members have been caught up in the effort to clear the church and get ready for the rebuilding program, so we've not given it much thought."

The president responded. "St. Agnes parish will be very happy to assist your parishioners in providing food for the needy at Thanksgiving."

"Let me share this with our parish council, and I'll get back to you or to Don Leyton. Thanks again for your offer."

As the group filed out of the room at the end, a man held open the door for Father Shane and said, "Can I speak with you for a moment? I am Ralph Stone."

"Certainly, Mr. Stone. Let's walk over to my car."

"To begin with, I was brought up a Catholic, but haven't been practicing it for a long time. My wife is an Episcopalian, and when the children came along, I joined her church, so that as a family, we are all of the same faith. Growing up in a parochial school, the nuns pounded us with the notion that we'd be 'lost' if we didn't remain Catholic."

"The recent Vatican Council changed a lot of those old ideas, Mr. Stone, so have no fear. The important thing is that you and the family are spiritually close to God, and living in accordance with your beliefs."

"We are a happy and contented family, Father. My wife is a volunteer at the hospital and tells me often how much she respects you and what you do to help the patients, and the cheer you bring to them."

"Thanks for the compliment. I'm only doing the job as I see it."

"I know you are building a new church, and since I represent several building and supply firms, I can expedite the sale and flow of materials once you are ready. Here is my card in this envelope. Call me anytime."

"Thank you, Mr. Stone. I'll be in touch." At home, the priest tossed the envelope on his desk and retired. The next morning, he opened it to file the card, and found a generous donation in the amount of $500.00 for his building fund.

"What a surprise this is! May the Lord be generous in His blessings to the Stone family."

❧ ❧ ❧

The snow began rather quietly on Thursday morning, and what had been forecast as a light layer, changed in mid-morning to a full blown storm. At noon, the radio reports warned that the area could be covered by as little as fifteen inches or up to two feet by the end of the storm. That might be on Friday, or later. The schools let out early, and the road crews were already out with the plows trying to stay ahead of the drifts.

Rita, Father Tom, and Alex were in the cafeteria enjoying lunch when Billie Jean came to the table to talk briefly with Rita. Father Tom had told them how much he enjoyed the discussion group at St. Agnes. "They are a fine group of men, and I wonder if at some point our parish men might hold a joint meeting."

"Rita," Billie Jean broke in, "we just received a call from Emergency that Mrs. Edwards was admitted."

All three looked startled, and Alex was first to say, "What happened?"

"The resident was still examining her, no diagnosis yet."

"What about the family? Joe? Donna?" Alex asked.

"I'll call Joe right away," Rita said. "He'll tell Donna."

As she left, Father Tom said to Alex, "Let's finish lunch. This might be a long day."

And it was a very long day.

It was almost 4:30 p.m., when a haggard Joe, followed by a flushed and tired Donna, reached the hospital to be met by Rita and Alex .

His hat and shoulders covered with snow, Joe asked, "How is she? What happened?"

Alex took Donna's hand, and when she bent down he kissed her and said, "She's doing all right now. Rita will explain."

"Joe, Mabel had a stroke at home late this morning. A neighbor stopped by to return some books, and peering in the window she saw Mabel lying on the floor. She pushed the door in, took her pulse, and called the ambulance immediately. Dr. Jenkins has been with her, in a semiprivate room on the second floor. Leave your things here in my office, and we'll go up to see her."

"We had a terrible time getting here. This blizzard is a rough one. First of all, your message was garbled, and then when I found out what it was all about, I had to battle the roads and crazy drivers to pick up Donna at her office. There was an accident just over the line in Prince George's County, and that held us up. We're lucky to be here now!"

At Mabel's room, Dr. Jenkins talked with husband and daughter. "Come in here. Mrs. Edwards is resting comfortably, but she is sedated. She has suffered a stroke, but we won't know the full effects until I can complete a series of tests and examinations. I do know that her left side is affected and she was unable to speak, but that may be only temporary. We'll know more in the next few days."

Joe sat by his wife's bed, and held her hand. Alex met Donna as she emerged from the room, sat on a chair and cried softly.

Rita went over to Alex, sitting next to Donna and said, "I'll have to leave now before this storm gets any worse, and it's bad enough now. Let me know if you need me tonight. See you tomorrow."

Father Tom came to the waiting room to sit with Donna and Alex. He held her hand, and comforted her with soothing words. There was a TV in the waiting room, and all three watched as the weather reports warned of the continued storm, and advised motorists of road conditions.

Finally, Alex said, "Let's get something to eat. I'm hungry." Donna agreed and went in to see if her father would join them. He said he wasn't hungry, but went out to see Father Tom, who said he had to return to the house. Joe thanked the priest for his comforting words and returned to the bedside.

As Donna and Alex finished their snack, Father Shane came into the cafeteria, covered with snow. "It's a lousy night out there, and I can't get the car started. That blizzard seems worse. Can I bum a ride?"

"Sure thing, Father. Sit and drink some coffee, to warm up. We'll get you home."

When the trio returned to the waiting room, a nurse was coming out of Mabel's room and talking to Joe. "Dr. Jenkins called and said that your wife would remain in the coma, and for you all to go home and get some rest. There is nothing anyone can do for her at the moment."

Alex took charge. "Let's get out and see what the storm is all about. Father, here are my keys. Will you bring my car around to the covered Emergency Room entrance? I don't have runners on these wheels, then I'll give you a lift home. Joe, can you make it all right?"

"Sure, Alex, no problem. Many thanks for your help."

"Alex, you're a dear," Donna said, leaning down to kiss him. "I'll see you tomorrow. Good night."

Ten minutes later, as Alex was getting into his car, Joe came out to say, "The nurse told us that she heard on the police CB band that an eighteen wheeler is jackknifed on Route 301 about two miles from here. No one is hurt, but traffic is all tied up, and the road will be closed for hours."

"Know what you're going to do?" Alex asked.

"We'll walk down to Howard Johnson's and get a room."

"In this blinding storm? No way. I have a better plan. Squeeze in."

He let Father Tom out at his house. "I'll pick you up in the morning and get you to the hospital. We'll worry about the car later. Night."

"I'm sorry to put you out like this, Alex. I believe the truck overturned a few miles from where we live. Now what?"

"I'll tell you in a few minutes."

Donna spoke up, "I'll bet I know," and then was quiet.

It seemed as though the snow fell faster, as the wind swirled it all over the place. Alex knew his car and how to drive in snow despite the drifts on his street. Soon they were at his house, and as he came up the driveway, he hit the button and the garage door opened. As the door closed on the storm, he remarked, "Am I ever glad to get in safe and sound."

Within minutes, they were inside, turned on the lights, and removed wet coats and hats. Alex gave the order. "We need the fireplace going. There's wood by the side there. Donna, put on the kettle for coffee, while I break out the ice cubes for drinks.

Around the blazing fire, Alex announced, "We bunk here tonight. There are twin beds in the guest room. I have tooth brushes, towels and plenty of food and drink. Let's enjoy the storm inside."

"I capitulate!" Joe said. "I'm just too tired and worried to offer resistance. I can only say I appreciate this. Donna can speak for herself."

When the eleven o'clock news came on, it showed the havoc the storm was wreaking all along the eastern seaboard, as it moved up from the south. In the Washington and the south county area, the snow measured fourteen inches and was still falling fast. The storm would continue all night and into Friday.

When Joe went into the kitchen to call the hospital, Alex said to Donna, "I have extra pajamas, robes, and slippers for you and your father. I've put them in the guest room. Be comfortable and relax. You'll rest easily there."

She whispered in his ear, "I'd rather share your bed tonight, but under the circumstances . . ."

"Be gone, woman, before I accept and your father comes back to hear this!"

Joe came in from the kitchen. "The nurse says Mabel is still in a coma, and apparently resting comfortably. Alex, I think I'll have a night cap, and then turn in. I'm tired. Where's Donna?"

"She's in the powder room. I've laid out pajamas, robes, and slippers for the both of you. She'll get comfortable and join us."

"You sure are prepared for emergencies. What with the food, drinks, clothing, toilet articles, you're set for a siege."

"In the morning, use my electric shaver. You'll find towels in the bathroom. Help yourself to whatever you need."

Later, when Joe had turned in, Alex shut off the TV and turned the stereo down low. He sat on the sofa, with Donna curled up, her head on his chest, content just to lie there quietly.

"What are you thinking, dear?" he asked.

"Mother's stroke will bring some changes in our lives, and I don't know how it will affect us."

"It's bound to change things, but we'll work it out. Think positive."

"She's so active around the house, I'm afraid of what this will do to her. I've known of people who have had strokes, and some are completely devastated, their personalities change, and not for the better."

"The big thing is to have faith that it will not be as bad as you think. We'll see what the doctors say before jumping to any conclusions. One never knows what's in store."

"You're such a rock, Alex. I don't know how you keep on the cheerful side despite all that you've gone through. I'm happy to know and to love you."

"Hey, look at what you've accomplished with your life. You work every day, play the piano, help sail a boat, and enjoy seeing life through others' eyes. You're a remarkable person. Not many people can say the same about their activities."

"Right now, I'd love to see me in your new pajamas. Where did you get all these things?"

"My mom always sends me loads of stuff at Christmas and my birthday. It's light blue, with dark blue ribbing, and the robe is a dark navy blue"

"I know it's dark because it doesn't shed any light, but both are so warm. Thanks for sharing them."

They sat for a bit longer, then he said, "We'd better turn in. We've had a long day, and we need a good night's sleep. We'll need to be ready for the morrow. It's Friday already. Good night, dear."

"Good night, Alex. You're a wonderful person."

Joe's senses were struggling even as he tried to regain consciousness. His right eye opened to see a strange digital clock on an unfamiliar night table reading 7:15 a.m., then it slid over to a window splashed with snow, and a wall with frames and pictures, one a toreador dodging an enraged bull. His body was warm under the down comforter, but that was the only right thing about this setup.

Then, all at once he sat bolt upright. Mabel's stroke, the blizzard, Alex and the jackknifed truck all came back in a rush. Now he knew, and the senses were in tune. His nose caught the familiar coffee aroma, so he rose, pulled on the robe and slippers, and shuffled to the kitchen.

"Good morning, Alex," he said from the doorway.

"Hi Joe. Good morning. Have a 'cuppa,' as they say down under."

"Thanks. I had a wonderful sleep, the bed was so comfortable. I see and hear our blizzard still howling around."

"I called the hospital ten minutes ago, Joe. The nurse said your wife is still in a coma and stabilized. Nothing unusual happened during the night."

"That's a relief. Maybe we can get over there later this morning."

"This storm will have to let up a bit. The radio indicates we're in for another day of it. But, one can't believe all the weathermen say."

When Joe finished his coffee, he returned to the bathroom to shower, shave, and put on his robe again. "I'll wait until Donna is up, then I'll dress. How's the coffee holding out?"

"There's plenty. Care for breakfast now?"

"No thanks, just the coffee. I'll have something when she gets up. I like the layout of your house, Alex. It is ideal for you."

"I had to make some adjustments for the chair, but I can get around pretty well. A woman comes in to clean up once a week, and a boy to stack my wood. I like it."

Joe remarked, "I wonder how the padre is doing this morning? He sure is one fine person, and I admire him greatly. He was most comforting to us last night, and seemed to take things in stride even with this terrible weather."

"He's a prince, and the more I see of him daily at the hospital, the more I like him. We have frequent talks over coffee, and he comes out with some plain common sense, bordering on sound moral values. He lives a truly Christian life. He's not just words, but a man of action."

"Yes, Alex, I know the type. When I was an enlisted man in the navy, we had a guy like him. He was a chaplain from Boston, Father John Flynn, and he was a corker! A real man's man, tough when he had to be, but gentle as a kitten when working with the wounded."

"Pretty heavy stuff going on here," a small voice piped up from the doorway. "Good morning, guys!"

"Well, sleepy head, glad you came to at this hour of the day. Alex wanted to feed me earlier, but I held off until you could join us."

"Any word about Mother?"

Alex replied. "I called the hospital earlier, and there's been no change. All's well, so far. We'll call later after the doctor sees her."

"Thanks, Alex, you are a gracious host. I near died when I went to bed. That was a great sleep. OK, how about food? I'm starved."

When Joe left to change into his clothes, Donna came to Alex, put her arms around his neck and gave him a kiss. "What would we do without you? Such a warm reception, big heart, wonderful host, and my dear friend."

"You'll swell my head and spoil me, girl. Let's get some food ready for us. Will you do the eggs? We're on the third pot of coffee, but there's water in the kettle for your tea. You know where the wheat bread is for toast., and the bacon is where it should be. I'll give you a hand there on the stove."

When they were seated at the table, Donna said, "I'll change after we eat and clean up. What's on for the day? We're going to the hospital?"

"That depends on the weather," Alex replied. "It's still snowing, and no let up in sight. Let's see how the morning goes. You can call the hospital soon, and get the latest word on your mother."

Joe polished his plate with a sigh, drained the last cup of coffee, and said to Alex, "I'd like some exercise. If you have boots, a heavy cap, and jacket, I'll clear off your driveway, so when we do go out, it will be easier walking and driving."

"I've got all the makings, but you don't have to do this. Some kid will be around soon to clear me off."

"Let him save his strength for some one else. I need to get out and do something. The shoveling will do me good."

"Don't argue with him, Alex. He's a big boy, and will enjoy playing in the snow."

Alex called the hospital again, and let him talk with Dr. Jenkins, who somehow made it in to care for his patients. "There is no substantial change, Mr. Edwards. She is comfortable, and we'll know better after we complete the neurological and cardiovascular tests to determine the damage to her systems. It's still pretty bad out there, and if there is any change, we'll call you at Alex's house."

Knowing that Mabel was in good hands, Joe bundled up and took it easy shoveling the front walk and the driveway. As he did so, he thought of Mabel and her stroke, the relationship of Donna with Alex and how it might eventuate, his work, and what changes might be in the wings with a wife who might be crippled.

After two hours of solid exercise fighting the snow, Joe announced, "Well, I'm done," as he reentered the kitchen, red faced and puffing.

"You're on the payroll whenever we have a snowstorm," Alex said. "Just come over and shovel me out. You've been volunteered."

"Daddy, are you all right? I hope you didn't tire yourself out."

"I'm fine. Best thing I've done in a long time. This puts me in shape to do our place when we get home."

After he had a hot drink, Joe said, "Alex, do you suppose it would be too much trouble for us to get to the hospital? I'd like to see Mabel and sit by her bed."

"Sure thing, Joe. It's still snowing, but it has abated. The streets are clogged, but my heavy car has no problem getting through."

While Joe parked the car, Donna wheeled Alex up the ramp, entered the emergency area and went down the corridor to the elevator. As they passed Peg O'Bryan's door, a white coated Father Tom emerged.

Alex broke out in a laugh. "We're sure hard up for help when we have to drape the clergy in a white coat and put him to work."

The priest roared with him, and replied, "I'd make a good saw-bones. The kids up in pediatrics thought I was good with them. I cured a dozen cases of tears and sniffles."

"You look good, Father, I think," Donna added.

"Donna, your father is coming?" Peg said from her door. "Good. Dr. Jenkins is still here and has completed some of the tests. I'm sure he will want to discuss the results with your father."

"I'll bring you up to your mother's room, Donna, then I'll be in the office for a while. Later, I'll meet you in the waiting room."

Chapter XXIII

When Rita told Clare Cohen that she was having guest panelists in for a discussion of abuse, Clare asked if she could bring in some of her students to join the group. " I'll get us a larger room and a table."

"First, let me introduce our panel who have agreed to respond to questions on child abuse. Mrs. Jule Rohm is a lawyer, Mrs. Margaret O'Bryan is the Chief Nurse at Powell Hospital, and Reverend Albert Burns is pastor of the Lutheran Church.

"Several weeks ago, we opened up the area of abuse, relating incidents we had observed. Today, our focus is on prevention, and our guests will respond to your questions."

With her brunette hair in a long ponytail reaching down her back, Pamela Durkin shot up her hand, then rose to ask, "What can we do about a man who beats his wife and children? I know, because my father does it in our house. Not to me anymore, because I'm big, and I fight back at him. I'm worried for my mother and younger sisters."

"Has anyone tried to counsel him?" Dr. Cohen asked.

"No, because he wouldn't go. I tried to talk to him, but he is too stubborn."

Jule Rohm said, "This sounds like he should be arrested and brought to court. What he is doing is against human rights, and he could be prosecuted for physical harm as well as mental abuse to others. Is his employer aware of his actions to the family?"

"No, I don't think so. How do we get him to court?"

"It seems to me," Peg O'Bryan said, "if he injures a member of the family, and we see that person in the hospital emergency room, we could then ask the mother to file charges, and have the police pick up the man."

The minister wanted to know if he had financial problems, and if this was causing him to be upset and he took it out on the family. Pamela replied that she thought money was part of the problem. "I don't know about his job, but when he comes in with liquor on his breath, I know we're going to have trouble."

When Peg O' Bryan asked if her mother had gone to their pastor for counseling, Pam said, "Yes. Only once. He was no help at all. Now she won't return to that church ever again."

"If you like, Pamela," Reverend Burns said, "I'll be happy to suggest a minister who is also a pastoral counselor. He may be of help to your mother and the family."

"Thank you, sir. I'll tell my mother."

"I'd like to hear the panel talk about social abuse," Sam Cockran, the lanky basketball player said.

"What did you have in mind?" Dr. Cohen asked.

"It's like when black people are taunted by whites and down graded along with other minorities. There is an arrogance toward those who don't hold the same views as we do. When a majority group does not give the minority group a chance to express its views, and proceeds to steamroller right over them. Some politicians waste public funds on their own projects, and this is an abuse. This, in turn, deprives children, the handicapped, and the elderly of needed services."

Jule Rohm replied, "The best way to get rid of those politicians is not to reelect them to office. If their actions are flagrant, petition for a recall. Yank the rug out from under them. Another method of preventing these social abuses is to expose them in the media, where all can see what is taking place."

Al Burns added, "We clergymen can alert people to wrongdoing by speaking out from the pulpit. Of course, the very people who should hear the words of warning, may not be present in the congregation."

Patty Donaldson's hand shot up like a beacon over her red hair. "What can be done about the sexual abuse of young children, especially if the abuser is the father or a relative?"

"That is a very hot potato," Peg O'Bryan replied. "We are starting to see a few of these cases in the hospital and it is tragic."

"This is most dangerous, for one must have positive proof before such a charge can be made," Jule Rohm said. "Mothers must be very sensitive to what is going on in the house. They must talk clearly and forcefully with their daughters about their bodies."

Dr. Cohen added, "Children are never too young to know about their bodily functions. They should be warned never to let anyone feel or touch their private parts. If that should happen, the child should be trained to talk freely about the incident. When parents are open about sex and tell children what might happen, this can serve as a preventative."

"These adults are pretty sick people," Al Burns observed. I'm also aware that abuse occurs when a woman seduces a young boy or a youth. This has happened."

Beverly Olson, a striking blonde, asked timidly, "What about rape, and how does one prevent it?"

Jule responded, "Simply know who are your friends and their reactions to talk of sex, those who are willing to 'put out' and the ability to ignore peer pressure when someone says, 'everyone does it.'"

"Be in off the streets at night, and beware of places which might be dangerous," Al Burns warned. "When we know that someone has loose morals, that should be a signal to stay away from that person. Those who choose to play with fire sometimes get badly burned."

"One way to prevent rape, Beverly, is not to bum rides with strangers. When I see girls on Route 301 with their thumbs up, I wonder if I'll see them again in the hospital, victims of a rape attack. It happened too often," Peg O'Bryan said.

Dr. Cohen added, "Girls who dress suggestively in brief shorts and go braless are sending out signals to males who are just waiting for another conquest. Girls need not be saints, but they shouldn't swagger and flaunt their bodies unless they are looking for some action."

"There is an increasing number of rapes committed by relatives and friends of the girl," Rita said, quoting from studies she'd read about. "One must be extremely careful and trust only the most reliable persons."

"Listening to all this," Al Burns said, "I realize what a miserable job we do in educating our children and ourselves in the facts of life. We have an explosion of information in all spheres, wonderful channels of communication, yet we fail to prevent these atrocities on our children and adults. What a shame!"

"We all agree with what you say," Jule stated, "and somehow we must take the bull by the horns and begin to educate and train if we are ever to do a decent job of prevention."

"Who will do the educating?" Peg asked.

Rita answered. "It should start in the home, where the parents are comfortable with their own sexuality, and can feel free to talk about sex with their children from an early age on. Then the school has a responsibility to conduct courses in human development and family life, beginning in the junior high. The children then will begin to know their own bodies and the functions of their sex organs."

Gloria Bricker stood and said, "That could never happen in my house. My father deserted us, and my mother would be scared to death to talk to us about sex and all that." Several students nodded their heads in agreement.

"Somehow, we've got to get the message out to parents about their responsibility, and to youths to be aware of what they are doing to themselves," Al Burns remarked.

"A serious form of abuse occurs when a girl aborts her fetus. I feel this is an abuse of the girl's body, and an abuse of the rights of the unborn to live. Murder is the ultimate form of abuse," Peg O'Bryan stated.

Rita rose to say, "Our time is running out, but before we close, I'd like to mention another form of human abuse, and that is the use of drugs and chemical substances. This is a self-inflicted abuse which can be most damaging and injurious to the body. I am beginning to read more about the victims in the *Washington Post* and the *Baltimore Sun*, and the stories are not good at all."

Peg added, "We see a bit of that in the hospital, with patients spaced out, the victims of killings or gunshot wounds."

"Our juvenile court now has a few cases on the docket, and I know the police are aware of these substances, but they haven't been able to track down the pushers," Jule said.

"It must be easy to get," Ruth Miller said. "I told Mrs. Evans I was approached by a character who wanted to sell me some stuff, and I told him what he could do with it."

"I heard about that man, Ruth, and I passed the word to the dean. It is bad enough for adults, but to entice young people into trying it is simply awful!" Dr. Cohen was visibly upset with what had been attempted.

As the meeting ended, Rita was pleased to see her students crowding around the panelists asking questions and receiving personal answers.

Later at home, sitting by the fireplace, Rita said to Joe, "Somehow, I feel something was lacking in our session today. We just did not come to grips with the hard realities of child abuse."

"Were they beating around the bush?"

"The closest we got was when Al Burns remarked disgustedly that we'd done a lousy job in the education of our kids as to their sexuality. I kept hoping he'd lay the whole mess open and decry the fact that children are bearing children and they don't have the slightest notion of what it's all about."

"How long was the session?"

"About an hour and a half. Why?"

"Perhaps the panel needed a longer period to warm up and tear into the meaty things."

"I don't buy that. They're all professionals, and can articulate their positions quite readily. I am disappointed that it didn't turn out as I had hoped."

"Better luck next time."

"If there is a next time, I'll have Mrs. Mason, wife of the minister and a counselor at the high school. She'd blast the system of welfare dependency, and the sexual delinquency of the teenagers. I'd have on the panel persons who advocate sex education classes, and lay the whole thing out on the line. We know that parents are scared to talk about sex to their children. I'd invite the police to come and tell about their efforts to locate the drugs that are coming into the county."

"You'd need a long night and a large auditorium to pull that off. What you're thinking of sounds great."

"Too bad that Rabbi Halpern could not make it. He

would've been a nice addition to the panel. I'll have him next time, if and when."

"Rita, any news on Mabel Edwards? How is she doing?"

"The final evaluation is that the stroke has left her with little use of her left side, and no speech at present. She has started therapy to regain the use of her limbs, and the speech therapist starts her treatment next week. It will be a long haul for that lady."

Chapter XXIV

The holiday season was ushered in by another blizzard starting on the Sunday before Christmas, and ending on December 24. It left a carpet of soft white to cover the remains of the preceding fall. People took it all good-naturedly, did the shopping, cleared the walks and carried on. The snow hardly hampered the round of parties, and the Evans held their usual bash on the Sunday before Christmas, hosting their many friends from the hospital, college, and community.

The Edwards family was represented first by Joe and later by Donna, escorted by Alex.

"You go, Donna, and I'll be here to take care of your mother."

"Daddy, you need to get out and see your friends. It'll be good for you. Alex is coming and we can help her as needed."

Joe recognized his daughter's stubbornness and knew he couldn't get far unless he compromised. "All right. I'll go first, have a drink and a snack, and I'll be back in an hour. Then you and Alex can shove off." And that's where it stood.

Mabel was a sorry sight. She had to be waited on hand and foot. She had never had a good personality, and the stroke made her outlook worse. She was petulant, and made her wants known by pointing or ringing the bell by her bed or wheelchair. Even the bell had a sharpness to it.

The new year came quietly to the house. Alex came to

keep Joe company as they watched the various football games, and Donna kept busy in the kitchen preparing dinner. Mabel alternated between the bedroom, the living room, and the family room where she managed to interrupt Joe's concentration. She'd nod to Alex as he sipped on a beer.

Mabel's stroke had changed their lives considerably. Donna resigned from her job in Washington to stay home and care for her mother. She missed greatly her talks with her father as they drove back and forth, her companions at the office, and her paycheck. To compensate for her loss of income, Joe gave her a stipend and said he'd let her use his charge plates for her clothing.

Alex was her staunch ally, and was always available. "Alex, dear man, I don't know what I'd do without you. It's such a help to have you around."

"Well, girl, I do have a strong back . . ."

"I mean your moral support. Mother can be so demanding, and real mean at times. I don't know how Daddy stands her. He's a walking saint to put up with all this nonsense."

"I think you're the saint. Here you are all day in this house doing nothing but looking after your mother. I know how difficult that can be. I remember what a rough time I gave my therapist and my mother when I first came out of the service. It takes time to get acclimated and oriented to a different life style. Fortunately, this is a rambler, so you are not up and down stairs."

"There are some bright spots."

"Tell me."

"You. Your daily telephone calls and your visits here. You're like a rock, and I've come to love you more each day. Your patience spreads over to me, and I gain by it. The weekends are better, for then Daddy is home, and we can get out together."

"Yes, love, but only when we're not knee deep in snow."

Joe had rearranged the carport so Alex could drive in without getting wet from the rain or snow, and he had easy access to the kitchen. It helped Alex, and Donna, for he realized how much she relied on his companionship. Also, he enjoyed talking about sports, politics, and literature with the young man.

Frequently when they went out, they'd go to Mike's Place or to Alex's house where they'd sit by the fire and talk.

"Though I can't see, I can tell when she is bitchy, then I stay out of her way, until I hear her bell. It's a help to me, Alex, to be able to talk over these things with you. It's not as bad now as when I first started to care for her."

"We need to give her time. Remember, this is a whole new way of living for her, and she's not accustomed to being an invalid, nor is she able to comprehend why she can't walk and talk as she used to be able to do. If she can regain her speech, that will make her feel better."

During the first three months of the year, she made marginal improvement through the weekly trips to the therapist. She could do some things with help—wash her face and hands, brush her hair and go to the toilet. With the onset of April, Mabel could see the spring bulbs popping out of the ground, and she yearned to get out there and dig in the dirt. Alex and Donna were no good at this, so Joe added gardening to his other household activities. In a way, this was good for him, as he needed the change and the exercise.

Late in the month, Alex called Donna with a request. "I've written a paper for one of the journals and it needs to be typed. I can't ask the girls in the office, and I wondered if you'd be interested in doing it."

"Yes, Alex. I'd be happy to do it for you. Can you bring it over on Saturday?"

When she finished typing and Alex proofread it, he sealed

it, ready for mailing. With Joe at home, they went to the dock to see the boat, and insure it had weathered the winter storms. Alex confessed he had been down several times and could hardly wait for warm weather to take her out.

He asked, "Are you going stir-crazy at home without any challenge?"

"Yes, and I can hardly wait for the time when we can go out to relax here. Why?"

"How about setting yourself up as a piano teacher and take on some typing at home. You could pick up some quick change, and this would relieve the strain of what you're doing."

"I do have a challenge, and that's keeping up with my mother. I need to anticipate her requests, and I can feel the progress she is making. I know what you are saying, and appreciate what you want me to do."

"As your mother progresses, you need to back off a bit and not do for her the things she is capable of doing for herself."

"I know. There is one problem and I doubt she'll let go of that."

"Yes, and it's me. She'll hold on to you as long as she can. I thought that since both of us are in wheelchairs, she might go a little easier on me, but I still see fire in her eyes. She hates the thought of losing you to anyone, and she sees her role as being available to protect you. If the truth be known, she is an insecure person, and relies on you for support."

"Back to your suggestions for my work, as piano teacher? And typist?"

"You have great musical talent, and only you can decide if you'd be able to teach it. The typing, you already can do that."

When Donna didn't reject the idea of teaching piano

completely, Alex knew he had her thinking, and they continued to talk about initially, he had an idea. "How about your playing at a dinner club, like Mike's Place?"

Donna howled at that. "What a crazy idea! It would be fun, though."

"OK. We'll table that. About your typing, when you were in Washington, D.C. you used a recorder to transcribe letters, memoranda, etc. Why not set yourself up at home as a professional typist for the business men around town?"

"La Plata and the area is growing rapidly and I feel there is a need for this type of business."

"Keep talking, you get more interesting with every word."

"I'm just throwing out ideas for you to think about. Talk it over with your father, and see what he has to say about this or any other idea for you. You might want to establish an answering service, and there's a need for that here."

"This is all so sudden, but you are correct. I need to do something with my time, and if I can do it at home, and still care for Mother, that would work out fine. I'll need to talk it over with my father. If I do go ahead on a project, you'll have to give me a hand, and serve as manager until it gets underway."

"You can count on it."

❧ ❧ ❧

As chairman and host for the April meeting of the ministerium, Bill Taylor, pastor of the Methodist church opened the session with a short prayer. "Heavenly Father, look down upon your appointed ministers gathered here, bless our efforts as we talk about activities affecting our lives and those we serve. We thank you for bringing us safely through a rugged winter to enjoy the burgeoning spring. Amen."

The men sat in his large oak-panelled study, filled with

books on theology, psychology, and literature, as a bright late morning sun filtered through the tall windows of the Victorian house. It was a comfortable setting, the eight men scattered around the room, each nursing a coffee cup served by Grace Taylor, wife of the host. She was a charming lady, as tall as Bill, filling out a grey tweed suit, tapered fingers well manicured, and short hair graying at the temples.

"I know we all welcome back Phil Mason after his lengthy illness. We have a few items left from our last meeting at Ted Queen's house."

When they had completed the old business, Tom Shane rose to speak. "I'm happy to report, gentlemen, that the plans for the new St. Dunstan's Church have been approved, we've been able to secure a loan at a reasonable rate, and our council is deep into plans for the ground-breaking ceremony. You and your families and parishioners will be extended invitations for a Saturday ceremony.

"I need to express once again to each of you how much I appreciate your help to us following the disastrous fire which wiped us out of house and home. You all have been magnificent, and I know I speak for my parishioners in extending heartfelt thanks to you and yours."

Phil Mason heaved his bulk from a chair, and looking at Tom said, "You have done so much for this community, you rate all the help we've provided. We'll do more. You have been a source of enlightenment to all of us, and I know for sure the joy and peace you've brought to so many of the patients in the hospital, irrespective of their religious persuasion."

All the men clapped in approval of the statement, and Tom murmured his "Thank you, thank you."

Al Burns was recognized for a comment.

"Gentlemen, I believe we have a problem in our midst, and it relates to the sexual behavior of our young people. I'm sure we've all had parents come to us quite upset over the sudden news that they are about to become the grandparents of an illegitimate baby. The tragedy of the news is the mother is still in high school, and even worse if she is a junior high school student. While we decry such behavior on the part of the girl, not too much attention or fault is laid at the door of the boy responsible for this fatherhood. What it comes down to is children bearing children."

There were murmurs of agreement in the room.

"I heartily agree with Al's portrayal of the problem," Jim Wilson said. "This touches the whole community, and as leaders, we have a stake in it."

Ted Queen offered, "We have a large share of our black teenagers coming up pregnant, they drop out of school and wait at home for the welfare check to bail them out."

There were similar tales from others, and Bill Taylor said, "We know the problem. What do we do about it?"

Don Leyton raised his hand. "This is a conservative community, and in the short time I've been here, I've noticed a less than liberal outlook on a number of matters. The people tend to keep things like this to themselves, hide them, make the best of the situation, and hope it doesn't happen again."

"But, they do, Don," Phil Mason replied. "My wife is a teacher and counselor in the high school, and what she tells me about the behavior of the students would make you blush."

"I consider myself a liberal in many things," Tom Shane said, "but a conservative in the basics of life. What we need is a program of prevention to ward off these tragedies to young lives."

"What do you have in mind, Tom?"

"For starters, a sex education program in the schools."

"Wow! Wait 'till the school board hears that," Jim Wilson said.

Bill Taylor joined in with, "That's a bombshell! It's

needed, I grant, but will it fly?"

"If it doesn't, then something has got to be initiated to stop this delinquent behavior," Ted Queen said.

"This is a topic which has to be approached carefully. We might just have to sneak up on the school board," Don Leyton proposed.

There was silence, during which lips were pursed, heads scratched, solemn faces looked out the window, and realization dawned on them that they would have to come up with an action program.

Tom Shane asked, "How would it be if we devote a single Sunday soon to talk about the sanctity of the family, the values of a happy married life, and the need for a healthy outlook on sexual activities?"

Al Burns responded, "That's a good beginning, Tom. I'd go a step further and ask if any of the school board members are parishioners of our churches. If so, could not we, as pastors, sound them out regarding their opinions about sex education classes in the schools?"

Others wondered about board members who were not churchgoers, and those who believe that these matters belong in the home. Phil Mason asked who would teach these classes in the schools, provided they were approved. Few counselors or teachers were equipped to talk about human reproduction.

"I'll approve the proposal that we devote a sermon on this subject," Bill Taylor said. "I wish Rabbi Halpern was here today. I'm sure he has some good ideas to share with us. I'll call him tomorrow when he returns from his trip."

Don Leyton got the floor. "We are embarking on a monumental undertaking, and it appears to me that we need more hands on this wheel, persons outside our religious profession. This calls for more than a clergyman exhorting the faithful from the pulpit, for it affects everyone in the community."

"Who do you suggest?" Jim asked.

"A social worker, teacher, physician, lawyer, parent, editor, to name just a few."

"We know enough people in our congregations to tap them as needed," Bill replied.

"At the hospital, we have Rita Evans and Dr. Sargent as potential members," Tom added.

Jim Wilson spoke. "I'm a friend of the editor of the paper, and I think we should use the radio also to get our message across."

Don cleared his throat, and with a furrow on his brow rose to say, "Whether by design or not, we've been skirting around several topics which impinge on the subject of sex, and these are sterilization as a permanent prevention for birth, the use of birth control devices, and abortion, the killing of the fetus. In our pluralistic society, we have seen these terms come into common use, and whether we agree or not, they are facts of life."

"What are you getting at, Don?" Bill asked.

"Simply that we need to address these terms in any educational program which is undertaken. Personally, I abhor sterilization, especially for the handicapped, birth control is necessary for some parents, and as for abortion, I consider it murder. We can't expect everyone to agree, for we all have our own values, and we need to respect the other person's belief."

"I have complete agreement with Don on two of these—sterilization and abortion," Tom said. On birth control, the Catholic Church takes a different stand and believes that self-control in matters of sex . . ."

"That is difficult, Tom," Jim Wilson interposed. "We have many unwanted babies now, whether by married couples, or by sexually active young people."

"I realize that, Jim, and I can understand your position.

This still doesn't make it right. As Don just said, we each have our own values and moral standards, based on our religious persuasion, and we can't force these beliefs on others. If you and I were to appear on a program discussing these topics, we'd be forced to present our individual viewpoints, even though they clash."

Al Burns spoke up, "I know of several childless couples in my congregation who would be happy to have one of these unwanted babies. Trouble is, the adoption agencies are so tied up in bureaucratic regulations and policies, it takes years to get a child."

The chairman looked at his watch and announced, "Gentlemen, it is getting late, and Grace has notified me that lunch is ready. We've had a good discussion on a long overdue topic, and while we've not solved the unsolvable, we've made some dents in the approach to prevention."

"May I suggest the following. I will ask Rabbi Halpern to make available to each member a few ideas on sex education and human development which we may want to incorporate in our sermons on the family.

"Next I'll ask Al Burns to serve as chairman of a group to include Tom Shane and Ted Queen to seek persons in the community willing to form a larger committee to inform, educate, and train our young people in matters pertaining to human life, reproduction, and the responsibilities inherent in bringing a child into this world. All of us should make available to Al and his group the names of people we feel are responsible leaders, with an impact in the community. We should get some of the school board members on board, if you'll pardon the pun.

"Any questions? Do we have agreement?"

There was no dissent.

"Thank you. We go forth in unison. Phil, will you give us the benediction, and include the blessing for our luncheon?"

Chapter XXV

"Pat, I've been thinking about our marriage, and it just isn't working out. You are involved in your practice—late hours and overnights in Washington. We don't see one another enough to maintain a decent relationship."

"Do you want a divorce?"

"No, at least not now. I need to get away for a while, and try to sort out some things, especially my life, and what I want to do."

The Boltons were at home having a late Sunday brunch, sitting in the dining room. Outside, a warm wind caressed tender blades of grass, tulips waved their red and gold bulbs on tall slender green shafts, while buds on the dogwood trees were ready to burst forth.

Amy was busy in her real estate work, and was doing quite well. She had found an office for Pat's OB-GYN practice, and some waterfront property on the Eastern Shore which he was interested in buying for investment purposes. A steady growth in the population meant housing for new residents, plus stores and offices to support them. Her commissions were increasing to the point where she knew she didn't have to depend on her husband's income for her livelihood. She had saved enough money to defray her own travel expenses.

"I'm taking off this week to attend a reunion of my college sorority, then I plan to go home to see my father. After that

I'll be on vacation for two weeks. I'm caught up in the office."

" All right. Shove off and have a good time. The change will do you good. Wish I could get away, but the practice is increasing, and I'm doing more work for Dave. I'll hold the fort. Any decision you make about us will be fine with me."

Outwardly, he was being nice to her, but inside, he was thinking, what a break! Maybe she'll decide to split, and I'll be in clover!

Wednesday evening was quiet in the Bolton house. Amy had packed and left by late morning, and when Pat came home, the silence was eerie.

Earlier he had called Washington. "Dave, I'm alone in the house. Amy has taken off on a trip, and will be gone for about three weeks. How about spending the weekend here?"

"What kind of bait are you offering?"

"There is peace and quiet. We can discuss our medical concerns, there is the waterfront activity and all that it implies."

"Mundane stuff! Any interesting action?"

"I was leading up to evening activities. There are a couple of beauties around, new comers to town. Both are good looking and stacked in all the right places. You take it from there."

"Now you're talking. I'll be there Friday evening."

Although he specialized in OB-GYN, Pat took on a few family practice patients just to get going, and here he came into contact with a few children, the young marrieds, and some middle aged women. He recognized that some of the latter had no serious problems, but needed attention once they were on the examining table with feet in the stirrups and spread wide open for stimulation. Pat was a willing operator, and made these patients happy.

He lured away from the hospital Dixie Baxter, a woman in her late twenties whose husband was on the road a great deal driving an eighteen wheel rig. She knew Pat was horny, and enjoyed playing with her buxom fullness, legs and thighs. They had fun together frequently.

When teenage girls came for examinations, Dixie was in attendance to assist, but never demurred when Pat took his time to admire the budding youths and their bodies. She had a good job, and knew that later she'd have Dr. Pat all to herself. His marriage to Amy was in name only, and she knew it.

The waterfront property seemed to be ideal. Dave had come down to see it when Pat told him of the location on the telephone. "Dave, I've found the perfect spot. It's on a cove south of the Governor Nice bridge, and owned by an old lady whose husband died a year ago. She came to the office, and when we got to talking, she said she wants to sell the property and move to Connecticut with her sister."

When Dave visited, he found the property was a deal, but the house and barns were about to fall down. Built in 1910, the two story house had seen better days, and a strong wind could knock it flat.

The first floor contained a small living room, dining room, and ancient kitchen. On the second floor the bathroom had a rusty tub, two bedrooms, and a den, and all ceilings had water spots. Outside, there was a small garden patch and a tool shed leaning against a tottering barn which contained a ten- year-old Buick. The property contained just under four acres, most of it in trees and shrubs, right on the river, where a solid dock was the most recent addition.

Mrs. Fielding, the owner, told the doctors that her husband wanted to do nothing but fish. "He bought a boat, and one day the damn thing blew up and him with it. He died the next day from burns. That was over a year ago. Now, I want out."

She was asking ninety-five thousand dollars for the property, buildings, and Buick, all in one deal, but for cash, she'd come down a bit. Dave talked with her lawyer, brought the price down, and within a few weeks became the owner with Pat having a minor interest.

"First thing, Pat, we'll bulldoze the house, barn and shed. Then we draw up plans for a ranch-style house with a southern exposure facing the river. That'll make a great view, and we can see the river traffic as it goes by en route to the bay."

Recently, Dave had revealed his activity in the drug scene, and this was why he wanted river property. "As we build the house, we'll need a secret place to stash the drugs as they come in off the river. This will also be great for our clinic practice, away from the center of things in La Plata."

Pat's thoughts brought him through his encounters with those "bitches" at the hospital, the tirades with that bastard Sargent, and the arguments with Amy. He felt sure that soon he'd be free from her and live his own life.

He could work well with Dave in medicine, the drug trade which would make him rich, and the girls, especially the young ones. I must be oversexed, he thought, but it sure is good any way you can get it. Too bad Amy never got the same kick out of sex that I do.

On Friday afternoon, Pat told Dixie, "Let's clean up and get out as soon as the last patient leaves. Any plans for tonight?"

"Yup. My ol' man's due in about eight tonight. Sorry."

After he closed the office, Pat shopped at the food store, the bakery, and the liquor store for supplies for the weekend. At home, he put away the groceries, poured himself a stiff scotch, picked up the paper and turned on the TV for the evening news. Five minutes later, his mouth was open, the eyes closed, the newspaper on the floor, and the ice slowly melting in the glass. A soft snore was no competition for the blaring news on the tube.

Dave pulled his Fleetwood Cadillac up in the driveway in back of Pat's car. It was just after eight o'clock and as he rang the bell, he could see his host sprawled out in the easy chair. Pat sprang up as the bell shattered his dream, and he came to the door.

"Hi Dave! I don't know what happened to me. I started to read the paper, and the next thing I know you're ringing the bell."

"Some guys are lucky. You young ones get all the breaks. Where do I stash my bag?"

An hour later, both were sitting in the kitchen refreshed. Dave had changed into slacks and a sweater, while Pat had on shorts and a sport shirt. Dave made his own martini— vodka on the rocks with a splash of lemon, and Pat was nursing a scotch, while keeping an eye on the dinner.

It was a comfortable kitchen, well stocked and equipped, and big enough for a large table and four chairs near the side entrance.

"What's new in D.C., Dave? I haven't seen you in over a week."

"As usual I'm busy day and night. I seem to be getting a full share of the abortion business, and I want to transfer much of that down here as soon as we get set up. The regular practice is on a normal basis. Between the White House and Capitol Hill, the squabble rages daily. We've got a lot of 'crazies' running loose there, at both ends of Pennsylvania Avenue. How are we doing here on the property?"

"The other evening I drove down to walk all over the place. Rather than bulldoze the house and shed, I'd suggest that we leave them and temporarily use the house for storage of the drugs. Also, if crews had to stay overnight, they could use the old house. Let them be for a bit."

"Near the path leading to the dock is an open space. With some clearing of the trees and shrubs, we could place the house there and it would give us a great view of the river."

"I see. You've got a point in your planning. Smart thinking. The house and shed could serve many purposes."

"I've got some ideas for the house, too," Pat continued.

"You've been a busy bee with plans. Shoot."

"A long low rambler will serve as a summer house, or I may take up residence there as a live-in caretaker. We'll need four bedrooms, large living room, dining area adjacent to the kitchen, clinic space and a garage large enough for three or four cars."

"I agree with the idea of you living there for safety and security. A long open deck out front with a view of the river is a must, for parties add sun bathing."

"Tomorrow we'll look over the scene and mark off how we'd like the house to sit with the proper orientation."

As they ate dinner, Dave told about his connections for the drug trade. "We'll need to get the timing down on the deliveries. A ship coming up the Chesapeake Bay could be met by a Boston Whaler, which could off load the drugs and make a run for the dock. We'd probably do it mostly at night or at dawn. We can start soon, and use the old house as a base.

"We'll need to be careful, for the Coast Guard patrols the bay and the Potomac regularly, and we don't need to run the risk of getting caught."

"Do you have plans to sell the old Buick?"

"No. That old buggy has a lot of life left, and it also has plenty of trunk space, which we'll use. Once we get it revved up, we'll need some one to deliver the stuff to my office in D.C."

"I know a guy in town who'll be glad to make a buck. We'll disguise the packages like medical supplies, so the driver won't know what he is hauling," Pat said.

After dinner, they continued their planning over coffee

and liqueurs. Dave made several calls to Washington concerning his patients, then announced, "Pat, it's been a long day for me. It's almost midnight, and I need my beauty sleep. See you in the morning."

Chapter XXVI

A brilliant sun bounced off his vestments, giving a dazzling effect on this Easter morning, and the congregation crowded around as he stood away from the entrance to St. Agnes Episcopal church on Charles Street. Don Leyton had a good feeling about the service, and his homily on the risen Christ who had died and then risen for the sins of mankind.

"A wonderful service, Rector" was spoken frequently as beautifully dressed women, spring-suited men, and children reached out to shake his hand in greeting.

"Thank you, thank you," he responded, reflecting his pleasure with a smile, and hoping to see many of his flock again soon. Too many came occasionally, some only at Christmas and Easter.

One of the last to emerge from this historic edifice was Jule Rohm and her daughter. After the recessional hymn, Jule sat in the pew near to the rear to explain the church and alter to her daughter, then walked down the aisle pointing out various memorabilia.

"See, these marble tablets were erected to the memory of people who were living here during colonial times, and who were staunch supporters of the church. Over there are memorials to fathers and sons who died in the Revolutionary War, and further on are the names of men who were in the War of 1812, The Spanish-American War, then World Wars I and II. On the other wall we see the names of the men who fought on opposing sides of the War Between the States. This is one way we commemorate the sacrifice our people made so that our democracy might live on. It is a beautiful tribute."

As they left the church, she saw the rector bidding the last of his congregation adieu. They walked over to greet him. "That was a moving service, Reverend Leyton."

"Thank you. I'm happy to see you, and your daughter."

"I'm Jule Rohm, and this is Ruth, my daughter."

"How do you do?" he said, extending his hand to Jule, looking straight into her eyes, and then to Ruth who smiled at him. I hope we'll see you again."

"Well, Reverend Leyton, I'm new to the area, and I thought it time I renewed my ties to the church. I was brought up in the faith, but somehow let it slide. Now I want to get back and let my daughters enjoy the richness and peace that comes through a devout life."

"We welcome you and your family, Mrs. Rohm."

"The older one is Alma, a student in high school, and she's spending the weekend with a friend."

"I know how important it is for young people to have friends they can stay with on weekends. I'll be happy to welcome her here. If there is anything I can do to assist, please let me know."

Ruth addressed him. "You have a beautiful church, and mother just showed me around inside. All those names and the history of them . . ."

"I'm happy you saw them. In another part of the church, we have a museum of history, the part St. Agnes Church played in the history of southern Maryland, and in the formation of this country."

Peering through his glasses at Jule, he inquired, "Do you have the time? Are you alone, free?"

She sensed the intent of the question and replied, "Ruth's

father left us some time ago in Michigan. Yes, we are free, but we don't want to impose on you."

"Not at all. I am delighted that Ruth is interested in history. We have some unusual artifacts, newspaper clippings, flags, etc., which I'm sure you'll find interesting as a newcomer to this area. Come along."

Don removed his vestments and spent over an hour with them in the museum room, pointing out to Jule and Ruth the array of items, from flints to old pistols, flags, parts of uniforms, newspaper clippings, and old pictures. While doing this he kept admiring Jule, whom he thought to be a striking woman. Her height, weight, and firm figure, so nicely dressed in a tailored suit, gave her the appearance of a devoted mother and her child, who was well mannered and nicely dressed. He was impressed with them.

As they finished in the room, Jule spoke. "You are so generous to give us this time, and I do appreciate your thoughtfulness in providing Ruth this historical background to her new state."

"My pleasure, I assure you. I believe the rectory has a cold Coke for a thirsty little girl, and a cup of coffee for her mother?"

The protestations were mild, so he led them into the house, where they sat in the small dining room.

"I'm a bachelor, also the cook and bottle washer. The Coke is on the way, and the coffee will be ready in a moment. Care for a Danish? I'll just put them on the table."

It was close to mid-afternoon when Don escorted them to the door. "This has been delightful, Mrs. Rohm. I want to thank you and Ruth for such a nice visit, and making this Easter a happy occasion."

"You have been most kind, Reverend Leyton. We appreciate your generosity in showing us around St. Agnes, and also your culinary abilities," Jule laughed quietly.

"The Danish was fresh out of the bakery, and I should know how to brew a cup of coffee, I've been doing it for so long."

"Well, good-bye and God bless."

"Bless you, too. Good-bye."

Don took his forty-four-year-old body into the study, shed his jacket, collar and vest, picked up the newspaper, skimmed the headlines, then put his head back to close his eyes in thought.

As Jule drove along Route 301 toward the river to see the sailboats, she thought, "What a beautiful Easter this has been." I have more joy and hope than I thought possible. Was it the service, the minister, or both?"

✷ ✷ ✷

On Holy Saturday afternoon, Father Tom heard confessions at the Carmelite Convent. The youngest novice, Sister Margaret Mary was the last to enter the confessional, and when she was absolved, she identified herself and said, "Father, I need to make a decision now."

"About what, Sister?"

"Whether I should remain as religious or not. I'm confused as to what course I should take."

"Do you feel that the life of a nun is not for you? Is the Carmelite Rite too severe? If the latter, there are other less restrictive orders."

"I feel content spiritually, Father, and if I were to leave, I'd not join another order. I know I can maintain my relationship with Christ wherever I am. Here, it is the subservience of the mind and body that seems to strangle me. There are books I want to read, journals I'd like to receive to stretch my mind, but I can't. Occasionally, I'd like to sleep in to indulge my lazy body."

"I had the same feeling in the seminary, at least regarding 'sack time.' We all need to break out of the mold every now and then, but when we are in a restrictive society like the Carmelite, we have to go by the rules. Have you given it enough time here to recognize that this is not the way you want to spend your life?"

"I know, but, it's so hard to conform, and I've tried."

"Are there ways I can help your spiritual life, any prayers or devotions you think I can suggest?"

"No, Father. I would like to talk with someone who is in the world and can give me some guidance. Do you think that Mrs. Evans would be able to talk with me?"

"I'd be happy to inquire of her. First, it seems that you have made up your mind to leave the convent, and in that event, you should discuss this with the Abbess."

"I've had a talk with the Abbess, and she was kind and understanding. She suggested that I talk with you."

Father Shane was invited to remain for dinner, during which he noticed Sister Margaret Mary with head lowered over her meal. The nuns showed the priest the new vestments they were making to replace those lost in the fire. He was pleased and expressed his appreciation to these devoted women.

Before he left, he talked with the Abbess, who said, "Sister Margaret Mary is a very bright young woman, full of zeal and integrity. I would truly hate to lose her, for we have much need for her kind to replace us older ones, but I recognize she can do more good out in society than in here. Yes, by all means ask Mrs. Evans to come see her. Sister needs information as a bridge to the outside."

A few days later, Rita was finishing a conference with Alex when Billie Jean stuck her head in the door to announce Mrs. Rohm.

"Good! I'll see her right away. So long, Alex."

"Come right in, Jule."

"Thanks for seeing me right away, and on short notice, but I think this case deserves our cooperation."

For over an hour their heads were locked in on a rather messy case in which the courts and the hospital had responsibility. There were some arguments, a great deal of discussion, and finally a solution.

"We're now into lunch time, Jule, care to join me in a salad and tea in the cafeteria?"

"Yes, I am a bit hungry, but I must watch the waistline."

There was one clean table left, and as they sat down, Father Tom showed up with his coffee and a sandwich. Rita welcomed him to join them.

"This is a pleasure, ladies."

"Father Tom, may I introduce Mrs. Rohm, an attorney on the staff at the court."

"How do you do? Glad to know you."

"I'm happy to meet you, Father Shane."

There was a bit of idle chatter, and talk about work when Father Tom paid Rita a compliment. "Mrs. Rohm, when you work with this lady, you have a winner. In my book, she's tops!"

Rita came right back with, "Jule, don't believe this Irish rogue. He's the one to work with, despite his blarney. He gets thing done, and if I wasn't married to a gem, I'd take on this . . ."

"I've heard glowing reports about Father Shane. Last Sunday, Reverend Don Leyton sang his praises loud and clear."

The priest blushed and hid his face in the sandwich. Then after a few moments he said, "You know the rector at St. Agnes? He is one fine person. We served together in the Army in Korea, and it pleases me that he is now in the area."

"I am, too. He was so nice to us when I took Ruth to the Easter service. Later he showed us around, and gave us coffee and a Danish plus a coke for Ruth."

"That's like Don, a gracious guy. Well, ladies, I must be off. Rita, will you be in the office later today? Good. I'll call Billie Jean for an open time."

Rita had looked at Jule as she talked about her visit with Don Leyton, and felt that something special had taken place in her friend.

Late in the afternoon, Father Tom knocked on the door.

"Come in, Father, I've been expecting you. What's up?" Rita was cool, efficient, and as she spoke, her hands were busy with papers on her desk. But she looked right at the priest, and gave him her attention.

Father Tom was relaxed as he sat in the chair in front of her desk. He reached into his pocket to pull out a pipe, then the tobacco and matches and lit up, while talking. "Recently, I had a talk with Sister Margaret Mary, a novice at the Carmelite Convent, the one we met last year. She needs help to make a decision about her future. That's it in a nutshell."

"That doesn't surprise me. Last August I had a chat with her, and she didn't seem happy. I wasn't sure if she was so new to the convent that she had difficulty coping with a strict regimen or what."

"I believe that she has a deeper problem. She tells me that her spiritual life is secure, and physically she appears robust. It is her emotional life that appears to be blocked, or it could be her mental state."

"In what way."

"She claims she has no challenges, can't read the books and professional journals she would like."

"Is she at odds with the Abbess? The other nuns?"

"Not that I am aware of. Of course, the Abbess holds her and the nuns close to the rule. She is no exception."

"How do I fit into this picture, if indeed I do?"

"Sister Margaret Mary feels that as a woman of the world, you would understand her needs. She admires you greatly, ever since the retreat, and would appreciate very much if you could talk with her."

"I'd need to get permission from the Abbess."

"The Abbess told me she'd welcome any assistance you could provide. Just call and make the appointment."

"Fine, that's easy. I like both nuns. Any clues to a deeper problem you suspect she's beset with?"

"Not a one. Say, I like your friend Mrs. Rohm. Nice person."

"She's a colleague and a neighbor. When she moved in, I had wondered if she'd be one of your parishioners, but she tells me she'd like to rejoin the Episcopal Church."

"She can't go wrong with Don, he's such a super guy. Life dealt him a severe blow when his wife passed away. They had no children, but he's fairly young yet."

Rita remarked, "I think I know what you're thinking, Padre. Jule had lights in her eyes when she told how gracious Don was to them on Easter, and what a nice way he had with Ruth."

He paused, relit his pipe, then said, "I must say they'd make a good match. She is a stunning woman, and if I wasn't in the cloth, I think I could go for her myself. Too bad Rome takes a dim view of its clergy in the marriage state—maybe it's just as well."

"Oh, I don't know. I think you'd make a wonderful husband and a devoted father to children. As you said, it's just as well. We don't have to share you with some female. We've got you all to ourselves."

"You talk about me with blarney? Belay the compliments!"

That evening, Rita greeted Joe as he came in, coat slung

over his shoulder, and looking mighty warm.

"You look beat. Freshen up and I'll get the drinks ready. The kids are around somewhere, and dinner is a half hour away. They'll show up when they smell the food."

"Have a good day, dear?" he asked moments later.

"Pretty good. Had a session with Jule Rohm, and later the padre joined us at lunch."

"What's Jule up to these days? We haven't seen much of her lately."

"When she went to the Easter service at St. Agnes, Don Leyton gave them a tour and a drink. She's impressed with the rector."

"And . . . ?"

"The padre feels kindly toward his colleague, Don, but if he wasn't a Roman, he might consider making a play for her himself."

"Wow! Woman, what are you saying? Father Tom has an eye for the gals?"

"Any man worth his salt would look at Jule. She's stunning, professional, competent, carries herself nicely— why she'd do any man proud! You can look and admire, but that's all. You're already spoken for and hog-tied!"

"I must agree, she is a fine specimen. Sounds like cupid wings are fluttering, and you'll be on the sidelines to make sure they don't falter."

"They just met a week ago, don't rush things. By the way, I have an invitation to go to the Carmelite Convent soon. I'll be talking to one of the novices about a decision she has to make on her future."

"From what I see and hear, the church is losing more religious than they're bringing in. There is a lowered enrollment in the seminaries and convents, priests shedding their collars for wedding rings, and nuns on the picket lines as social activists. What are we coming to?"

"When Pope John opened that window, and the Vatican Council concurred, many flew out, but I'm sure we have a stronger church now. With so many changes taking place, it's a whole new ball game."

"Who said a ball game?" Roger dashed in at the end of the conversation. "Dad, are we going to the opening of the Orioles next week?"

"Sorry, son, no dice. I'm off on a trip Monday. Maybe we can make a game on the weekend."

Beth and Joe Jr. trooped in, sweaty, dirty and hungry.

"By the time you get cleaned up, dinner will be ready. Now git!" Rita stood up and clapped her hands in command.

As they undressed for bed, Joe took note of his wife's fine figure, glowing with health, a firm waist, full breasts, solid hips and good looking legs. She easily slipped out of her clothes and into a nighty.

"What's with the Edwards family these days? See much of Joe?"

"Occasionally in staff meetings. Now that Donna is home caring for her mother, Joe goes in early and comes home early."

"I see Mabel briefly when she comes in for her physical therapy. I hear her attitude is pretty poor, and she is not making the progress the therapists think she should be making."

"She's not a happy woman, sort of dour. All she can see is her daughter, and I'd say Donna is quite capable of taking care of herself. That woman will get a big dose of her own selfishness one of these days."

"Alex indicated to me that he has just about convinced Donna to open up a message service in her house. She can do that and still look out for her mother."

"That's a great idea. She needs an outlet, and Alex is good for her. He'll make her happy and guide her along. They are a good combination, each complimentary to the other. I feel sorry for Joe. Bet he hasn't come close to Mabel in ages. He needs help."

"Joe Evans, are you hinting at something? I caught you looking at me a short time ago when I was getting into my nighty. Does this mean . . . ?"

"What? A romp in the hay? It's spring, y'know."

"Yes, I know, the sap flows. Now be quiet, put out the lights and get in here. Don't keep me waiting!"

Chapter XXVII

"Daddy, Alex will pick me up after dinner, and we're going out to shop. That will save you the trip. He needs some things for his house, and if you'll give me our list, we can take care of it. You add on the items to those I already have."

"Are you sure? I don't mind doing the shopping."

"Yes, we enjoy it, and I've done it several times with him. It's easy. He guides me pushing the chair, and tells me the location of the items high or low on the shelves where he can't reach them. It's fun shopping."

"All right. I'll have the list and the money when he comes. You are quite a twosome, and seem to get along easily."

"It's more than that, Daddy. I love the guy. He makes me feel so important and wanted. At this point, I know his house as well as ours, and I am tremendously happy. This is a special relationship."

For a moment Joe said nothing, then, "How goes the business? Any luck today?"

Joe had transformed a corner of the family room adjacent to the kitchen into an office for Donna. A telephone jack was installed near the desk where her typewriter and braille machine sat on top. She could get from her desk through the kitchen to her mother's room easily when she heard the bell, so she could still work and care for her mother.

"Yes, several new customers are lined up and I am

encouraged. We should keep the advertisement in the paper for some time yet. I love to hear our ad on the radio. Alex has other ideas to get the word out. So, it looks pretty good."

"I'm happy for you. I must say, however, I do miss you traveling with me to and from D.C., and our chats."

"Me, too, but now we have our talks at home."

"With you at home, I don't worry about your mother. You're doing a good job, but I don't think she is responding as rapidly as I had hoped."

"Give her time. Tomorrow, Alex and I are going sailing all day, and we'll have dinner at his place. In the evening, we'll go to Mike's Place, and I'll tickle the ivories for a few hours."

"I must go down some evening and see this joint, and catch your act."

"You'd love it. Everybody joins in to sing along. We have a great time. Mike tells me his business is picking up."

The waves lapped quietly against the hull as Alex and Donna came along the dock. Donna went down the ladder first to unload the baskets when he lowered them. It was an ingenious method and expedited loading supplies.

Once on board, the supplies in their proper place, Donna took her place near the forward lines, and when Alex gave the command, she cast off.

As the boat moved backward, then forward out of the cove into the river, she scrambled aft, holding onto the lines. She settled into her seat on the stern next to the captain, and gave him a smooch. "That's for being a good boy, so far, and there's more to come."

"I can hardly wait, baby. Don't get too comfortable, for I'll need you to help. Take the wheel and keep it steady on course, while I raise the topsail and the jib."

"How about me raising the topsail. You can tell me if I'm not doing it correctly. I've raised and lowered it at the dock several times."

"OK. You've earned the chance."

Donna moved forward, found and unleased the lines, pulled with all her strength to raise the sail to the top.

"Good girl. That's great. She's snug, too. Come back here and take the wheel while I raise the jib."

Under a partly cloudy sky and a warm sun, they made headway down the river and out into open water.

"What a glorious day," Donna said, her arm resting on Alex's shoulder. "It couldn't be better, and you've made it possible."

Alex started to respond, but she stopped him with, "No, dear man, you're the one who has opened my eyes and brought me out of the dark, so I can appreciate all this wonderment—the air, sun, flapping of the sails, the wind in my hair and the warmth of the sun on my body. But, most of all, the love you give me and the companionship."

"It's a great life, and you're still responsible for much of this. We've got work to do. Hustle your butt forward and get us a couple of frosties. I'm thirsty."

The westerly breeze brought them out to the bay, where they turned south and hugged the Virginia coast. About one o'clock they dropped the jib to laze in the water for lunch. Alex popped a beer and had a smoke while Donna prepared the lunch of crab meat, ham and cheese, salad with brei, and croissants. For dessert, it was fruit, grapes, berries, and pears.

The captain spoke. "You do well in the galley, slave. I'll keep you."

"Ah, my master, I bow, and seek only to serve you—with cooling water." And with that she leaned over the side, and flipped a handful of water in his direction, hitting him in the face. Alex roared with laughter.

Donna cleaned up after lunch and put everything away. She sat next to Alex, who was working on his second brew.

"It's so lovely here—peaceful and quiet, the sun bathing my body."

"There's nothing to prevent you from getting 'sunned' all over. Here, let me help."

Donna stood to remove her shorts, shirt and bra, then off came the panties. Alex looked at her body, the long tanned legs, firm buttocks, flat tummy, raised breasts with nipples standing straight out, glowing face and short blonde hair.

"Hey, gal, you look great—my tan goddess. Now relax."

"What's good for me is just as good for you. Now strip."

She helped Alex remove his shirt, and he shrugged out of his shorts, to reveal his thin legs and large torso. They sat in the sun, listening to music from a radio station.

"Donna, move forward and get the blanket and pillows so we can stretch out."

In a few minutes they were enjoying the full effects of the sun on their entire bodies. Donna ran her hands over his torso and legs as she poured lanolin on his body, "So you won't get too burned."

When she finished, he took the bottle from her. "My turn now, to give you the oil treatment." Carefully, he poured the lanolin over her body, rubbing it in, and as he did so, he admired every inch of her being.

Alex leaned down to plant a kiss on her brow as he finished. She looked up at him, raised her lips to his and folded her arms around his neck. Both were aroused, and in a few moments, they were locked in a passionate embrace.

"I'm going to roll over, Donna, so you'll be on top."

Later she said quietly, "Oh, Alex, what joy! What made you think of that position?"

"It's more comfortable for me. People who are handicapped need to find the best way to perform. Does this offend you? Were you hurt?"

"No, it was fun, and I came sooner than I expected. Any

way we can make love and enjoy, that's what we should do." She kissed him again, and they repeated their love making.

The sun was starting its westward decline when they hauled anchor and began the return voyage.

"Alex, what a wonderful day. Everything was just perfect."

"Ah, yes. Our love making? You like?"

"That's one of the parts of our relationship, and I feel so good about it, not degrading or awful. Guess I'm in love with you and everything we do is so wonderful."

"You know I love you, Donna, and wouldn't do anything to demean or hurt you. One of these days, though, we'll have to get serious about marriage and some wedding plans."

"If it wasn't for Mother, we'd be married quickly, like yesterday!"

"As soon as she recovers sufficiently to become more independent, we'll make definite plans."

Inwardly Alex knew that Mabel would hold off her recovery as long as possible in the effort to keep Donna to herself. Somehow he'd have to circumvent that eventuality.

As the boat came up the river, and about four miles before they reached the Governor Nice bridge, he noticed activity on the Maryland shore.

"Over there, off to the right, near the old Fielding place."

"Yes, I can hear voices. What's going on?"

"Can't tell yet. Maybe we can get in close. No, we'll drop the sails and motor in that cove there. Go forward and drop the mainsail. I'll cut the radio."

As the boat entered the cove, Alex could see a large sailboat tied up to the pier. Beyond that, through the trees and shrubs, he could make out some construction going on with two men hammering on studs.

"It looks like a long place, but I can't figure out what they're building. Wish I could get closer, but that's out of the question."

"Too bad, Alex. Let's head for the ranch."

"I heard that Mrs. Fielding had sold the property, and had I known it was available, I'd have put in a bid for it. The house is a shambles, but the property is valuable."

"How did you know about this place?"

"When I first came to this area, I met up with Mr. Fielding, and we had some common interests. He was quite a guy, and we got along real well. We came down here often, and that's how I came to know the place."

After dinner at Alex's house, they drove to Mike's Place, where Donna played to an enthusiastic audience. Alex sat nearby, looking at her face and fingers as they rippled over the ivories. He loved and admired her so much.

Damn that mother of hers for throwing obstacles in our path, he thought. Donna is all mine, if only that bitch would let her go. I'll bet she's staving off recovery because she knows I want her daughter. Selfish! Mean!

🍎 🍎 🍎

On the answering service, Pat heard Dave's voice. "Pat, it's 2:00 p.m. June 8. I'm sailing down, leaving Washington at eight o'clock Saturday morning. Should arrive in mid-afternoon. Meet me at the dock with the food stuffs. Lay in enough booze and food for four. Got us a couple of beauties. Ciao!"

It promised to be a great weekend, and Pat would have to do a lot of shopping. Since Dave would leave his boat tied up at the pier, he'd need to drive them all back to D.C. on Sunday evening, and return on Monday morning.

Saturday was perfect for sailing, clear blue sky, warm sun,

and a good wind. Pat loaded his car at noon and headed south on Route 301 to the property. He wanted to have plenty of time to look over the construction of the house and to check out the old Buick. He put the perishables in the refrigerator of the old house, and gave it a quick cleanup.

The shack was liveable, but lacking in the amenities. Mrs. Fielding had just walked out, taking only her clothes and a few personal possessions.

Pat blew the dust off the seat of the old Buick, inserted the keys and there was no response. He lifted the hood, checked the oil, water and gas, and made a few adjustments in the carburetor. He tried it again, and after a few coughs, the motor growled and turned over. A tune-up and a paint job would make it feasible as a transport vehicle, and the locals would not recognize it.

The contractor was proceeding rapidly on the house. He was from Baltimore and even had his trucks pick up all the materials there, as precaution for security and the prying eyes of people in La Plata. The house was roofed over so work could continue in inclement weather. All the wiring and plumbing was intact, and so far nothing had been ripped off, a sign that the area was isolated and the building unknown to thieves. The exterior needed grading and seeding, some trees and shrubs removed and the driveway cleared and paved. He stood outside the living room, facing the river, and knew that the deck covering the entire front of the house was just what he and Dave wanted.

Pat was about to leave when he saw the tops of the sails on Dave's boat with their numerals showing just outside the cove on the river. He estimated that it would dock in less than an hour. Right on time, 3:30 p.m.

It had been a busy week in the office. His patient load was increasing, and Dave had referred his patients from the Waldorf area to Pat, saying, "Dr. Bolton is my associate and has an office in La Plata. This will save you time and headaches in parking."

Amy had returned from her vacation refreshed and looking wonderful. Two days later, her mother called to say that her father was in critical condition, from an injury suffered in an automobile accident. "Pat, I've got to go home to see him. I'll keep in touch," she said and left without kissing him good-bye.

There was no doubt about Dave's seamanship. He nestled the thirty-four foot boat right up to the dock as slick as could be. One of the deck hands cast a line to him, and as she did, her bikini bra broke, and a large boob fell out of its sling. It surprised and amazed Pat, so that he almost dropped the line, but recovered to run it forward and secure it to a piling. The other girl jumped to the dock carrying the stern line. Dave busied himself killing the motor and beginning to secure everything.

"Welcome, Pat. We had a glorious trip down, and our estimated time was right on the nose. Tessie and Bessie are my crew, picked up in Georgetown. Tessie is a summer student at American U., and Bessie goes to the University of Maryland. They needed a job, so I hired them for the weekend."

"Good to have you with us," Pat said, wondering who would be his "deck hand."

This was solved when Tessie, she of the broken bra, came to him and said, "I'm sorry about the almost missed line, but I'll throw you another."

With that, everyone roared.

By the time they had secured the boat, it was five o'clock and time for the cocktail hour. After the second round, Dave couldn't wait to see the progress on the house.

"Get yourselves freshened up girls. Pat and I will be right back. I want to see what's been going on here."

Dave and Pat toured the new house, and comments raged back and forth. In all, Dave was pleased with what had been done, then they headed back. As they came up the lane, a dark cloud loomed over the western horizon, blocking out the sun, and a sharp breeze rustled the air.

"Damn! I thought we'd have dinner on board, but we'd better check the radio and get reports on this storm. What the hell! Maybe it'll blow over soon."

The weather news on the radio confirmed Dave's fears, so both men returned to the boat to retrieve some items of food and clothing.

Bessie was the cook, Tessie the salad maker, Dave the bartender, and Pat was in charge of ice cubes.

The girls were sexy from the first. Bess was short, had thick brown hair, fine features, and two breasts that sloshed around in a loose fitting shirt. Tess, the younger, had black hair, a small friendly face, straight waist, and the broken bra had been replaced with a shirt Dave had given her, which hid nothing. Her frontal equipment bounced up and down as she moved around the small kitchen. Pat had rampant thoughts looking at her and them.

The rain began as they started to eat dinner, and it came in torrents. All four were feeling no pain, and didn't care if it rained all night. Occasionally slashes of lightning followed by the boom of thunder echoed around the dining room, but none of the four seemed to mind. Dave had his hand under the table between Bessie's legs, while Pat reached inside Tessie's shirt to cup one of her breasts. At one point, she opened the shirt, so he could see and get a better grasp of her "equipment."

The rain continued to pour down, and the radio kept warning people of the serious thunderstorm, and the dangers of washouts.

Dave stood up and asked, "Pat, are those oilskins still

around here? I'm going down to the boat and make sure it's secure in this storm. Stay here and help the girls clean up, and make sure the ice cubes are plentiful. This will be a long night."

When they finished, Bessie went upstairs to take a bath. Pat and Tessie sat on the sofa in the living room.

"So what are you studying at Maryland this summer?"

"Two courses, one in math, the other is computers. I'm a sophomore at Vassar, and after graduation, I want to work in a computer company."

"Oh, one of those brainy girls. Aren't computers complex?"

"Hell, no. It's fun. The way of the future."

"I guess it's fine for some activities, but medicine, law and a few other professions will be safe from it."

"That's what you think. I'll bet you haven't the slightest inkling of what computers are all about, and they can and will affect our lives."

"You're right, and I don't want to know all about them."

Dave came in the back door, stomping his feet and dripping water all over the kitchen floor. The boat's all secure. It's a good thing I went down, two of the three lines were loose, so I tightened them and placed additional bumpers over the side near the pilings. Whew! It's a lousy night, and I'm soggy from head to foot."

Tessie helped him out of the oilskins saying, "Bess is taking a bath. Go up and join her, and soak in the tub. You'll feel better."

Pat made a drink for him, "Here, Dave, take this along."

When he had left, Pat embraced Tessie, reaching inside her shirt to cup her breasts. "God, you're built like the proverbial shit house."

"And with every brick in place," she finished for him.

"I've got more, too.

"You amaze me. A good looking girl with brains, and a great body."

In a little while, after Dave and Bess had finished in the bathroom, and retired to a bedroom, Pat and his girl ascended to the second room. They undressed one another and fell on the bed, where the rusty springs gave evidence of heavy movement.

It was a bright clear and cloudless sky on Sunday morning when the two couples awoke and, after breakfast, sailed down the river and had lunch aboard the boat. In a quiet cove, they cut the motor and anchored. Between making love and swimming in the nude, they had a fun afternoon. Pat was absorbed with the size of Tessie's big knockers and couldn't keep his hands off them.

They returned to the dock at 8:00 p.m., secured the boat, and made ready to return to Washington. Pat stopped by his house to get a change of clothing, for he'd spend the night with Dave, and return by the afternoon for his appointments.

Dave told him privately, "I expect a big shipment in a couple of weeks and it'll be a whopper. I'll clue you in on the details as soon as I have them."

"I approve your choice of deck hands. That Tessie has quite a repertoire, with all the equipment that goes with it. She has me dazzled. Are they for hire again?"

"For a couple of college kids, they are swell. Next time, I'll get other recruits. I don't want anyone getting too close to this operation. Once is enough. We keep this thing under our hats. Don't go after Tess. There'll be others as good, if not better."

🐾 🐾 🐾

She shifted from one foot to the other, then altered her stance, thinking all the while, I should have brought one of our aluminum chairs to sit on, but maybe I need this discomfort as an act of self-denial. Offer it up for the suffering souls in purgatory, as my dear mother used to say. Oh, well, it's just for an hour or less. Perhaps he'll give us a fast job today.

Rita's attention was diverted to the front of the congregation. Father Shane, preceded by the cross bearer, her eleven-year-old son, and two acolytes, came over to the altar, a table covered with a linen cloth, he bent down to kiss the altar, then moved to the front to say, "In the name of the Father, the Son, and the Holy Spirit. May the peace of Christ, and the blessings of our Heavenly Father be with all of you."

He welcomed the parishioners to "this annex to the new St. Dunstan's Church," the parking lot where Mass would be celebrated in good weather.

When it rained, they'd go back to the armory. The parish council had approved the idea of holding Mass outdoors, and suggested people bring their own folding chairs. As protection from the searing sun, umbrellas and hats should be worn. When he had mentioned what he planned to do, at a ministerium meeting, one man said, "I'm afraid my congregation would give me the air if I proposed such a thing. Go for it, Tom!"

While Rita followed along with the prayers and the readings, during the homily, she let her mind stray to the talk she had with Sister Margaret Mary in the garden at the Carmelite Convent.

"I'm so glad you could come, Mrs. Evans. I've been upset for some time, and felt I needed to talk with a mature woman."

"If I can help, I'm willing to listen and assist, but not for your spiritual needs. The Abbess and Father Shane are better qualified in that department than I am."

"Yes, I am aware of that. Let me tell you what this is all about. My father runs a lucrative contracting business near

Baltimore. It is small, but he is known for the quality of his work, and his crew are skilled, fast workers. He has given my mother, sister, and me a good living—we want for nothing in a big house, plenty of food and clothing, and every financial need is met. The major problem is that he's a beast in his physical and mental behavior toward us. For days, he'll not speak to us, and we never know what to expect. He's a big man and uses his strength to abuse each of us. He started to abuse me sexually when I was ten, but as I grew, I fought him off, and wouldn't let him near me.

"How horrible for a little child."

"I didn't want to tell my mother for fear she'd go to pieces. He continued to beat her so badly, that she was beginning to lose her mind. I had wanted to go away to college, but I couldn't because of him, and what he'd do to my younger sister and my mother. I was a 'day drag' at Notre Dame, but I did leave for my master's at Columbia in New York.

"I took courses in psychology so I had some inkling of human behavior, and knew how close my mother was to the brink of insanity."

"Could you not have taken legal action against him? Was there not a reliable person you could have gone to for a discussion of steps to prevent a continuation of his depredations?"

"I tried, but no one would believe me. The pastor of our church told me I was lying. A police inspector said I was out of my mind, and others gave me no help. You see, Father is a respected man in our area and above suspicion. I was at the point of believing I was the one to blame, that I was making up these weird stories. It was all so hopeless.

"Finally, I decided to join the convent, sort of as a deal with God to expiate for the sins of my family, principally my father. I felt that if I made this sacrifice of my life, the Lord would somehow get through to my father and change him around. I thought that going into a restrictive order, that it would be a greater sacrifice and move things along quickly."

"And it didn't?"

"No. Now I know better."

"Did you confide any of this to the Abbess when you came to the Carmelites?"

"Oh no, I couldn't. I didn't want anyone to know anything about my father. I made excuses for him when he did not appear at any of the ceremonies here. So, it passed over. My mother and sister did come to see me on occasion."

"Sister, you've carried a terrible burden. No wonder you've been so upset and distraught."

"Recently, I learned that mother has been admitted to Sheppard Pratt for treatment, and I doubt that she'll ever be normal and regain her sanity."

"Have you seen your mother?"

The nun replied that she had received permission to visit her mother again this weekend. She was also concerned for her sister who graduates from high school in June, and seems withdrawn, perhaps from the trauma she has endured.

"When I saw my father at the hospital, he was apparently a changed man—but I'll never trust him again."

"I assume that you've made the decision to leave the convent, and prepare yourself for a new life."

"Yes. I want to start over, and take care of Clara, who is eighteen years old. I can't bear to think of her alone in the house with him. I'm sure he has abused her, and she's not able to defend herself. I need to get her out of the house as soon as possible."

She confided that she liked what little she had seen of La Plata, and had some money left from her grandmother's estate. She could work as a typist and receptionist until she could find a job in education. As for Clara, "Father has money and must support his minor daughter. If he refuses, I'll threaten him with a law suit, and bring him up on charges. He'll pay or risk public censure, and he couldn't stand that."

"That's settled then. Let's plan a course of action so you and Clara can get your respective lives in order."

Father Shane finished his homily, and as the congregation stood to recite the Apostle's Creed, Rita came back to the open air Mass, and smiled to herself as Joe walked down the macadam aisle, one of four ushers to pass the collection plate.

When the service was over, the Evans family walked toward their car. Rita felt a tug on her sleeve, and a low voice said, "We saw you and wanted to say hello."

Rita turned to greet the Misses Pucci, Marion and Clara, arrayed in bright dresses. "Why good morning, Marion. I just caught myself, before 'Sister' could pop out. You look great, and you too, Clara."

Joe shook hands with the young ladies. "Good to see you both, looking so pretty. You're a sight for sore eyes."

"We miss you both," Beth said looking with adoration at Clara.

"I miss you, too, she replied searching for Roger and Joe Jr. who were in the car already.

"Why don't you follow us home, and we'll have a typical Sunday brunch at Rancho Evans?" she said, acknowledging Joe's nod of approval.

"You've been so kind to us already," Marion replied. "I don't know how we can ever thank you for taking us into your house for that week after we returned from Baltimore. Also helping us to get settled into the apartment. We'll be in your debt forever."

Beth piped up, "Tell us all about the new apartment, and yourselves over brunch."

"Don't be so curious, Beth. Please do come. We have loads of room and food for all. You can help clean up, and we'll talk then."

Joe added, "Sure, come along. When you finish in the kitchen, I'll put you out in the garden to help me. It's a corporal work of mercy."

The two sisters reflected their American-Italian parentage, with dark complexions, black hair and dark eyes. Clara was the shorter, thin and quiet. For one emerging from the cloister, Marion seemed to throw aside all caution in her dress and demeanor. She was bubbly with excitement, her dark hair swinging with the motions of her head. When she laughed, pearly teeth were exposed, and her face shone with merriment, dark eyes sparkling.

"I feel as though I've been reborn, the world is brighter, I have my sister safely with me, and my mother is totally unaware of what is going on. I'm at peace," she had told Rita a few days after leaving the Carmelite Convent with the blessing of the Abbess.

Chapter XXVIII

The Reverend Albert Burns, ruddy of complexion and looking dapper in his brown seersucker suit, tan shirt, brown and yellow striped tie, and penny loafers, stood in the conference room of his church to open the meeting.

"I am happy to welcome the eight members of our community to this meeting to explore ways we can help one another to work with our adolescents as they confront their sexual behavior. Our concerned ministerium has had several meetings on this problem, and we recognized that the subject goes far beyond the purview of religious leaders, and involves everyone in the community.

"Reverend Taylor asked me to serve as temporary chairman in seeking you as persons willing to be members of a community project. Since we are all leaders, anyone present could serve as chairman of this group. I am asking each of you to take a slip of paper from this basket, and the one who has the slip with the words 'Lead us' will be designated as chair of this committee. The other slips are all blank. Comment? Discussion? No, we'll proceed."

Rita Evans raised her hand. "Dr. Sargent is honored but could not be with us today. He asked that I represent him. I'll take two slips, and if he wins, I know he'll be happy to serve."

Jule Rohm picked the leadership role, and Al Burns

congratulated her. "I'm sure you can count on our individual and collective support."

"I am surprised but ready and willing to do the best I can. Let the record show that we begin our discussions at 10:00 a.m. on Thursday June 15, 1974 in the conference room of the La Plata Lutheran Church. We owe a great debt to the ministerium for initiating action on the topic, and I ask that you convey our appreciation to your members.

"As professionals, we have a stake in what happens to our young people. Sex need not be a dirty word, but it is a fact of life, and is but one part of human existence. We impact differently on the community as lawyers, social workers, ministers, teachers, etc., and we come with a store of knowledge gained by education and experience. Let me ask, then, that we identify ourselves, and state briefly how we approach prevention and treatment as twin goals of the program.

" To begin, I am Jule Rohm now on the staff of the Family and Juvenile Court, the mother of two daughters, deserted by their father. In my legal work, I can attest to the damage wrought to young people by an abysmal lack of information on bodily functions, sexual misbehavior and irresponsibility for their actions."

"All of you know me as Rita Evans, on the staff of Powell Hospital, as Chief of Social Services. My concern is similar to Jule's, but it goes beyond the young people. This starts with the family, its values, mores, understanding and perceptions of human life. Dr. Sargent asked me to pass along his concern over the lack of information about proper hygiene, illegal abortions, and preventive procedures. We both see the great need for information as a prime preventive mechanism."

"I am Reverend Al Burns, pastor of this church, married with one son who happens to have Down Syndrome. We know that Tommy will face serious problems as he matures into young manhood with its normal developmental needs including sexual thoughts, desires, and actions."

"As a teacher and counselor at the high school, I have long wanted to see a committee like this organized in this area. I am Alyce Mason, married to the Reverend Phillip Mason, pastor of the A.M.E. Church. Our two children are grown and married. We need all the information we can get, all the education, training, and sex education possible. Many of our girls flaunt their bodies, with low cut dresses, high skirts, and 'come hither eyes.' The boys are just as bad, patting the girls on their fannies, peeking inside their blouses, or making passes at them. We've got to have prevention and more treatment procedures."

"There is not much that happens in a community which escapes the eyes of the editor of the local paper, and I am that man, Ken Patrick, single with no children. If we were to prevent these activities, the parents will have to be part of the effort. Our paper will be happy to participate by providing space for informational articles."

"I serve a black Parish, the Baptist church on Leland Street, and I am the Reverend Theodore Queen, Ted for short. My wife Sharon and I came here nine years ago, and we've seen everything described this morning. I agree with every approach and what has been said. I know many households where the single parent struggles to raise her children alone, because there is no husband either because he is dead, in prison, or has deserted. One has to understand the culture of many of these youths who have no male role models and develop their own to show off their manhood and womanhood. Many are handicapped in the classroom, when white teachers cannot understand their 'street' language and their poor educational backgrounds. When these kids drop out of high school, without a diploma, this means failure in the market place, leading to frustration. I've said enough for now."

"I am David Halpern, rabbi at the synagogue, married, and the father of three children. As a psychologist also, I'm interested in the behavior of people, and seek to know what motivates humans to do what they do. We've mentioned prevention and treatment, both laudable targets. Prevention in the home? Sex information by parents takes place only when parents are comfortable with their own sex lives, and few talk about sex to their kids. Sex education classes in the schools? Great, but that will come when school boards stop haggling over 'to be or not to be.' This leaves the church or synagogue to do the job. I'm glad our ministerium has taken the bull by the horns and has gotten this show on the road. It's long overdue."

"Thank you for your comments and suggestions as to how we may get going on preventive and treatment activities. We need to be more specific in each of these domains. Can we have your suggestions?" Jule asked.

"We should start out," Rita said, "by helping the family to identify its perception of human life, values, functions and interrelationships between men, women, adolescents, and children."

Ken Patrick said that they should make the community aware of its responsibility to inform, educate, and train young people about proper sexual behavior by articles in the media.

Mrs. Mason suggested the library as one source in the community to help avert unwanted pregnancies, making available literature on contraceptive devices.

The other members rose to add to what they had already said.

Jule summarized by saying, "Our purposes relate to the role of the family, the need for the community to be aware of its responsibility, and to marshal all our resources to prevent, then begin to treat the problem."

At the coffee break, Rita found herself next to Dave Halpern and Alyce Mason at the tea urn. "The ministerium has pulled off quite a coup in getting this group together and talking as we have done so far," she said.

"Yes, I'm pleased with the progress to date," the rabbi responded. "The fireworks will explode when we get into some personal and touchy subjects where there is a wide divergence of thought."

Alyce broke in, "If the whites go messing around with the black families and they try that sterilization stuff, there'll be loads of trouble."

"Wonder what our next steps will be?" Rita asked.

David Halpern sipped his tea and replied, "We need more influential people on this committee, and I'm going to suggest it."

"If I had my way," Alyce said, "I'd get some kids in here to tell it like it is. They'd give us a touch of what it's like out there on the streets, especially for the black kids. We need more input from the consumers."

When the group reconvened, Jule opened with, "In talking with several members over coffee, it appears we are thinking about three major areas of concern, and our purposes fall into these categories: the family, the school, and the religious life, embodying the church or synagogue. Since we have so much to cover, I suggest that we split up into three groups so we can narrow our concentration into these areas. In addition, may I ask that we dispense with the formalities and go on a first name basis. Yes, Dave?"

"Jule, I'm in agreement with your statements. But, we've made a serious error in not having representation from the school system. I would like to see a member of the school board and a principal present."

There was general agreement to this suggestion.

Rita spoke up. "I'll be willing to lead the group on the

family, and I can speak for Dr. Sargent who gave me his proxy to speak for him. He'll also serve on this section."

"Count me in on the family group also," Dave said.

"Ken, are you willing to head up the school group, and Al, will you do the honors for the religious side? Yes? Thanks."

"I want in on the school group," Alyce said. "I'd like to suggest that we get some students in here. After all, they are one of the targets, and they need to have some input. Maybe they can tell us a thing or two!"

"That sounds reasonable, Alyce. Ted will you join me on Al's group? And we'll find out what happens when a lawyer tangles with two clergymen."

Jule then reviewed the subcommittee chairmen, and those who would serve on each section, including the representation of the school system and students. "I'm also telling the chairmen to add other prominent persons to their committees who can make a contribution to our deliberations. Our task is too great to limit us to a few members. I say the more participation we can garner, the better off we'll be."

Dave raised his hand. "In addition to its particular domain, I think each group should have certain generic areas for discussion. I'd suggest that we each ask what other community resources should be represented on the overall committee."

All agreed this was a good idea, and such topics rolled out as: What specific role does each of the three groups play in alerting their constituencies regarding sexual behavior? Could we develop a lexicon of proper terminology to replace the 'four letter' words used in street language for sexual activity and body parts? What are the ways each area can help to prevent aberrant sexual behavior for adolescents and adults? What literature is available which may be shared so that parents, schools, and the clergy may use them and hand out to those seeking information?

Jule looked at her watch and announced, "A little voice inside me is indicating that . . ."

"Lord, you're not 'P.G.' already?" Alyce said laughing, at which everyone joined her.

"No, I'm not, " Jule continued blushing, "but I am hungry. We are well into the lunch hour, and we've accomplished a great deal. Let's call it quits for the day and meet again in three weeks. In the meantime, group leaders should confer with their members, and add new members where you think it's appropriate. Many thanks for your cooperation."

Chapter XXIX

Although she had slight light discrimination, Donna said that her eyes hurt when she was out on the boat, so she always donned dark glasses. The summer months were glorious and made for sailing. At least two or three evenings a week and on pleasant Saturdays they were out on the river, lunching, swimming, and relaxing. It was the same on Sundays.

"I am amazed at how the message center has grown, my typing work too. I am out of the red, and starting to bank money."

"It was time for a new business in the area, and you hit it correctly. This place is growing so fast. I'm happy for you."

"Everything is real good, except Mother's attitude. She is so stubborn, and Daddy is just the opposite. Even when he gets home at night, he's there to help her, and he wants to lend a hand to me, but I've got it well under control."

"Yeah, I'm aware of her antipathy. She looks at me with a mean eye, and I know exactly what she's thinking, 'Butt Out!' It's entirely different with Joe, just one swell guy. Be a good girl and hustle into the cabin and fetch us a couple of drinks so we can enjoy this breeze and sail down the river."

Donna knew the boat so well that she could get to the cooler and return without stumbling. She had a good sense of direction and could pace off distances; rarely did she bump into anything in her own house, Alex's house, or on the boat.

The relationship with Alex was one of the best things that had ever happened to her. There was only one man in her life growing up, and that person was her father. She practically adored him, and the feeling of this father for his daughter knew no bounds. Mabel was a possessive mother, and having few friends, focussed her attention on Donna, who needed to be let out of the cage her mother insisted on putting her.

When Donna met Alex, she faced a dilemma. I am attracted to this fine person, but how can I break away from Mother, who needs me psychologically and who depends on me. Can I share this man with my father, whom I admire and love so much? The answer was not long in coming.

As the two young people dated and the relationship grew into love, the adults began to see their daughter drifting away from the nest, a happy young woman whose face beamed with freshness, and whose body took on a lithesome bearing. She found true happiness and was not about to give it up.

Mabel was the first to recognize what was happening, and in many ways tried to drop obstacles in their path, unsuccessfully, as it turned out. Joe took the opposite and more positive course. He saw that Alex was making his daughter happy, and that was enough for him.

Selfishness ruled the mother, while the father was the soul of generosity, and this was not lost on Alex, a keen judge of human behavior. He knew that he had Donna, and nothing could stand in the way of their happiness.

In contrast to the adults, there was a symmetry in the interaction between Alex and Donna. At first, both sought companionship without regard to their handicaps. They were two young people who enjoyed each other's company. As the relationship deepened, each gave more to the other. Alex brought her out of an inner self and exposed her to a world she had never experienced with a man—sailing, talking, allowing her to know his house, convincing her to open a message center, and giving her a dignity she could call her own. On her part, Donna lifted Alex out of his one-man world into caring for a single human being. His were professional relationships with a single person or with groups. There had not been the one person he could dote on or even love. There was still a part of him which decried the fact that he was disabled, a cripple in a wheelchair. Donna was more perceptive and saw the man in all his goodness as he cared for and shared with her. The externals were extraneous, and soon Alex began to forget those psychological negatives and responded to this fresh young woman who gave so much of herself.

What started out as friendship slowly grew into a deeper relationship, then into fervent love out of which emerged a team, each caring, each complementing the other.

"Alex we've talked about my family, but I really don't know too much about yours. You've mentioned them in passing, but I'd like to know more about them."

"My father is a lawyer, and they tell me I look very much like him. He's about 170 pounds, on a five-foot nine-inch frame, dresses well, and a humorous but bright guy. Mother is a tiny woman, smiles a lot and enjoys taking care of Dad. She used to be a teacher in high school, but gave that up when we children came along. I have an older brother in the navy, who flies planes off a carrier, he's married and has one child. They live in San Diego. My sister Grace is married to a wonderful guy who teaches in a community college in New Jersey. There. That's the lot."

"You've told me all that in short pieces, but what I'd really like is to see them. They must be wonderful people to have produced a man like you. I'd like to know as much about your family tree as you know about mine."

"You have a point. I guess it's about time we took a trip and made the introductions."

"Could we make it on a Sunday?"

"Sure. That will be good all around, especially if we can get Dad off the golf course for a day. I'll call and set up a time for us to go visiting. Maybe Grace and her husband could come and join us. Let me work on it."

❧ ❧ ❧

It was on a stifling hot day in mid August when Billie Jean asked Rita, "It's about the retreat you had last year. I've heard such good things about it. I'd like to go if you are having it again this year."

"Yes, we'll have the retreat, and you need to go. I've been doing a number on you, and your behavior suggests you should take off and repent all your transgressions."

Her secretary was about to retort, when Rita smiled then laughed. The girl sighed, "Lord, I thought you had caught up with me!"

Peg O' Bryan cornered her late that same day. "What's the dope on the retreat for this year? It's about that time, isn't it? I can't wait to get back to the peace and quiet there— no phones, no kids, and no husband."

"I've told Billie Jean the retreat will be on the second weekend before Labor Day, starting Friday afternoon and ending on Sunday. We have other staff ready to sign up, too. Our success last year has spread to many more people."

She was delighted when Jule Rohm inquired about it. "Yes, you'll be welcome. Let me know if you can arrange your schedule. There aren't many vacancies left."

One morning Alex joined her for coffee. "Donna wants to know if she is invited to the retreat. She has raved over the success of the one last year and told me how much good she had from it. Give me the details, and I'll pass them on to her."

"I need to call her about some other things, and I'll fill her in on the details for this one. This is all girl talk. No offense? How are you making out with Donna?"

"She's one great gal. She means a great deal to me, and as soon as I can, I'll marry her off, assuming I can kidnap her away from her mother. I'm sure she'll give me the ladder to get her out of the house. A super person."

In the Safeway store, Rita bumped into Marion Pucci, "Hi! How is the world treating you and Clara?"

"Hello, Rita. We're doing just fine. Clara has been accepted at the college, and is looking forward to classes there, beginning in September. Who knows, she might be one of your students."

"She's bright and needs the companionship of her peers. I think college will do her worlds of good. Yes, I'd enjoy having her in class."

"Do you plan to have the women's retreat this year at the convent? It was such a success last year. It should be an annual affair."

"Yes. I talked with Mother Benedicta the other day, and she welcomes the idea of having the ladies of the community return."

"It was exciting last year for me, but now? I don't know if I should go back even for the weekend. Do you think I should?"

"This is something only you can determine. You'll need to think about it, and then ask Mother Benedicta if she would have any objections."

"You're right. If I go, I'll try to bring Clara along with me. It will do the both of us a lot of good."

Two days later when Clare Cohen called about the retreat, Rita gave her the dates and told her that she would need to have the names of the faculty members who wanted to attend soon, in order to let the convent know the number who would be present.

When they met at the elevator, Rita greeted Father Tom warmly. "Hi! How goes the battle?"

"Hello, Rita. All's well here. The Archbishop is pleased with the progress of the construction and said he'd be available for the consecration of St. Dunstan's in December. Parish contributions for the church are coming in at a good rate, and the Rollins family is due back just about the time the rectory will be finished."

"That's wonderful, I hear you'll be with us during the second annual retreat for women at the convent."

"Yes, and that reminds me to brush up on my war stories for the ladies. That was a nice group last year."

"We'll have a few new faces this time. Marion Pucci decided to hold off this year. She told me that Clara will be attending the college in September, and that will be good for her. That will help to bring her out of her shell."

"Yes. Once she gets into her studies and the social activities, she should blossom forth. Speaking of the college, are you teaching there again this year?"

"Sure thing. I like the combination of practical work here, and the theoretical at the college. I'm happy that this has worked out so well, and the hospital and college are pleased. Everyone gains."

"You bring a lot of vim to your work, and I'll bet the students like your approach. Well, I'm off."

When Joe came home that evening, he laid a bulging brief case on the table and said, "Hi, love. Have a good day?"

"Very productive. And you?"

"So so. I've brought you the material you asked about for the sex committee. Interesting stuff. You might want to use some of it for the ladies retreat. The sample is small, but it has some good ideas for discussion."

Rita handled her many responsibilities well. Foremost of these was her role as wife and mother. She kept an eye on Joe's waistline, and prepared the proper low-fat items he should have. She loved and admired her children and with pride watched as they grew. Roger would soon be twelve and starting junior high, Beth's dark blonde hair was getting lighter and she'd be bleaching it out. Joe Jr. would start the third grade next month. My family is shooting up before my eyes, she thought.

Across town, Marion and Clara busied themselves getting dinner ready. They were compatible, friendly, and concerned with one another. Marion did not take on the role of mother, but treated Clara as an equal, sharing in the household duties, shopping, and cooking.

When Marion left the convent, Rita brought her to a group of new townhouses under construction. With money from her grandmother's estate she made a down payment to hold one of the houses, and in the meantime took a small apartment.

When Clara graduated from high school, Marion immediately brought her to La Plata. At the commencement exercises, she sat next to her father and told him of her plans for herself and Clara. He was not to interfere in any way with their life, except that he was to defray Clara's college expenses. He agreed, adding, "Once you get back there, I'll treat you both to a vacation at Ocean City. It'll be a good change for you. You should think of getting a house instead of renting an apartment. Real estate values always appreciate and you'll have more privacy in your own house. If you decide to go that route, I'll give you a big down payment."

Marion shuddered to take anything from him, but he was her father, he was wealthy and could afford any amount. She would accept his offer, but nothing else from him. As far as she was concerned, he was out of her life and Clara's.

For a month they lived at the Carousel Hotel on the beach at Ocean City, lolled on the sand, got sunburned, strolled the boardwalk, and sent the entire bill to Mr. Pucci. When they returned, Marion took a temporary job as receptionist in a new hotel in Waldorf, while Clara took care of the apartment. It was a quiet period for both. They had fun looking at materials and ordering furniture for the new house, which was ready for settlement and occupancy late in August. Marion had no financial worries, and she could meet all current expenses from the estate money, her investments, and her job.

Mother Benedicta met her at the door, a smile on her broad face and a warm greeting. "It's so good to see you again, Mrs. Evans. We have been waiting all day for the ladies to come, and everything is in order."

"I came a bit early to see if there was anything I could do." Rita responded. "Here's a cake for the table."

"Why, thank you. I'll have to pass it up, for I don't need any more pounds. I should go on a strict diet."

"This year we have eighteen retreatants, and more wanted to come. I'm happy to say that this retreat for women is becoming very popular."

"It's good for all of us, and I'm sorry we can't accommodate more, but space is at a premium. Maybe we should have another retreat in late winter or during Lent. We'll talk about that later."

By 5:30 p.m. all the ladies had settled into their rooms and were ready for the introductory service, conducted by the Abbess and Rita.

"After a few short prayers here, ladies," the Abbess said, "we'll adjourn for wine and cheese. Dinner will be served at 6:30, and the first service will be conducted by Father Shane at 8 o'clock."

Clare Cohen joined her with a wine glass. "At least eight

other faculty members wanted in on this, but only four made it. No room at the inn. Be warned that next year they'll be breaking down your door as soon as the word is out and the time for the retreat is announced."

"I'm sorry for them, but the Carmelites can put up just so many. I've talked with Mother Benedicta, and we may schedule another retreat possibly in the spring. This is getting so popular."

"On another subject, did you hear about Mrs. Bowie and the terrible accident she had last week?"

"Yes, and I feel so badly for her. I talked with her husband after she was admitted to the hospital. She's in bad shape, a lot of internal injuries besides a concussion and a broken leg. She comes from an old line family here, and they are such a nice couple."

"I hear that she'll be laid up for months, and will probably miss the entire year. The dean has asked me to help find a replacement for her. I've called several people, but they've all declined. If you happen to know anyone who is qualified and is able to come in on short notice to teach a basic English composition course at the instructor level, will you let me know?"

Father Shane was at his best that evening. He started by telling a few humorous stories to set his audience at ease, then was serious as to the purpose of the retreat. "This is a time for meditation, reflection, and for self-examination. As we pray, we cement our relationship with God. I will be here for most of the time, and will be happy to talk individually, as the need arises. There will be confessions for the Catholic women, and all are welcome to participate in the services. I know all the nuns will see to your every comfort. A warning! The food is fabulous and it will not be a sin if you overstep your diets."

Rita paid attention for while, then she drifted and she

thought of her family, the college, her students, then she paused when she came to Mrs. Bowie. "Who do I know to take over for her?"

It was after 9:30 p.m. when she called Marion. "I've just learned of a vacancy in the English Department at the college. Are you interested?"

"Tell me more. What is the area?"

"English composition and some literature."

"I'm working at a leisurely pace, and enjoy it, but if there's an opportunity at the college, I might consider it."

"Sleep on it, and let me know Sunday evening when I get home."

At breakfast the next morning, Rita told Clare of her conversation with Marion.

"I remember her from last year, when she was Sister Margaret Mary. She was such a pleasant person. I do hope she has the qualifications and can join the faculty."

"She has a master's degree in English, and I think she taught for a brief period at a small college. It would be great if she accepts."

The retreat was again successful, and the ladies commented on how much the experience meant to them. "I'm signing up now for next year," was one comment.

When Marion called Rita on Sunday evening to tell her she was interested in the vacancy, she said, "See Dean Keyes first thing tomorrow morning. He'll have all the details. Bring a resume of your academic background and your teaching experience. Good luck. Let me know how you make out."

Chapter XXX

"Our committee is happy to welcome the new members," Jule said, "and I'm sure we shall all benefit from your suggestions. We begin then on this windy, rainy day, the eighteenth of July at 10:00 a.m. in the board room of the Episcopal church, by introducing our new members. Rita, will you tell us about the people who have joined your subcommittee on the home?"

"First is Dr. Sargent who needs no introduction, as he is well known as the Chief of Staff at Powell Hospital, and is keenly interested in the activities of our city.

"Mr. Ben Adams has just completed his first term as a member of the General Assembly. He is married with two children and has lived in Waldorf for fifteen years, the last ten of which he has been a partner in the oldest law firm there.

"Miss Lettie Rogers is vice president of her sophomore class at the high school. She is also a candy striper at the hospital and a delight to our patients."

Ken Patrick stood up. "I'll introduce the lady I talked into joining this committee, but Mrs. Mason deserves the honor of bringing to you the two people she suggested.

"Mrs. Cameron Price is a member of our school board on which she has served for three terms. The Price family has been involved in community affairs for many years, and many of you know her husband, the owner of our largest hardware store. Mrs. Price is a member of many civic organizations."

Alyce rose to introduce her two new members. "Mr. Timothy Borden is the principal at the high school and is a wise counselor, a disciplinarian, avid sports fan, and one who loves the field of education. He is married and raised two children in the same house they bought when they came here fourteen years ago.

"The other is Sydney Cook, one of my former students who is now at the college in his sophomore year. He works at the public library year round, and is an asset to the community."

Al Burns took his cue and rose to say, "To balance Mrs. Mason's male members, let me present two females. The first is Mrs. Beatrice Jackson who manages her home and takes care of a good husband and a ten-year-old son. She shops not only for her family, but for others who are unable to get out.

"The other is Miss Meredith March, whom I met when she came to our house to help our Tommy with his school work. She is a junior at the high school, does well in her studies, and is on the track and swimming teams. Meredith has a slight handicap but you'd never know it. We are proud of her."

"Thank you Rita, Ken, and Al for making available such excellent representatives of the community to add to our discussions. I'm sure the subcommittee chairmen have told our new members how this group has evolved from discussions by the ministerium, and what has gone on in our previous meetings. In brief, we are focusing on three major areas which impinge on the subject of human sexuality: the home, the school, and the church. We also identified areas generic to the overall group, but which would serve as a starting base for each of the sub groups. These include the use of community resources, appropriate language, the range of sexual behaviors, prevention and literature for parents and adolescents. It is time now for reports from the three sub groups."

Dr. Sargent rose, removed glasses from his tanned face, swept back a wisp of grey hair from his brow and began. "I've been the designated speaker for our group on the home. To begin with, those of us who work at the hospital see all the negative things that go wrong in the home, for we're the ones who have to patch them up. A partial list includes the battered wives, the alcoholic husband or wife, the physically abused children, malnutrition, the teenage pregnancies, the unmarried mothers, etc. I can assure you there is a steady increase in our work with these cases. Our group talked about the need for a positive climate in the home as a basis for a good relationship between parents and children. This allows parents to speak freely about changes taking place in the young bodies of their children, especially around puberty. Do they know the proper terms for the private parts of their body? Are they comfortable with their own sexuality? Their own sexual behavior? If there is embarrassment to talk, lack of discipline, and no cooperation, there are bound to be repercussions when sexual misbehavior results. This is where prevention begins, and where parents must assume responsibility. Correct information and communication between parents and children at an early age will allay the fears of later years."

"Well done, Dr. Sargent," Jule said. "I hope your busy schedule will allow you to attend all our meetings. Ken, your school group?"

"I am surrounded by educators," the editor of the paper said, as he rose with a smile on his young face, and holding a sheaf of papers in his outstretched hand. "They are wonderful, and range from the policy making Mrs. Price, the overworked principal Tim Borden, the teacher-counselor Alyce Mason, and the student Sydney Cook. Each one gave me quite an education in the multiple activities which go on in the training of our young people.

"Well, what happened? Smoking, alcohol, and sex were our topics in descending order of frequency. Of course the school board had outlawed them, but it was up to the principal and teacher to police the students who were the violators. We talked a lot about prevention, but it's hard to keep kids from smoking in the toilet areas, when they smoke all the time outside, and what to do when kids show up in class with beer on their breath

or 'half lit' from a night of drinking. Most of the students dress properly, but a few are walking sex objects with their short skirts, braless bodies, and the boys with tight fitting jeans accentuating their crotch equipment. Small wonder we have teenage pregnancies, and the fathers go blameless.

"Marijuana and drugs were discussed briefly, and I am aware that harder drugs are coming into our area. That's all for now."

Al Burns gave his report, which centered around moral principles, ethical standards, and personal values for the young. The parent representative was appalled to see so many children out on the streets late at night and wondered if their parents knew where they were. She was concerned that the churches were apparently doing so little for them and the delinquents who roamed the streets at will. The student said that she didn't watch the violence on TV, as it gives kids bad ideas. He noted the positive influences in the community for young people, but said that what was needed were more adults willing to volunteer their time to help these programs.

"There is a mix of the positive and negative here in our town. While we focus on the sexual misbehavior of young people, we feel there are many forces which can be brought to bear on the overall project. There needs to be a coordinating force and its purposes should be announced far and wide to the entire community."

Jule resumed her role as chair person when Al finished. "Our groups have done their work well, and we are grateful for the information provided. We have much work ahead, and it will be no easy task. Any comments to open our discussion? Yes, Mrs. Price."

Seated plump in her chair, glasses riding a big nose on a broad face with hair neatly tucked in place, the school board member was in command. "I'm impressed with what I've heard so far about sex education in the home. If it is your hope that the board will sanction sex education classes in the school, provide birth control pills and condoms to our youth, I for one will raise a loud and vociferous 'no' vote. Schools are meant for academic training, the three Rs, and not how to prevent making babies.

"My husband and I raised four children, all are now grown, and when it was time, we read books, learned the proper language and it was easy to discuss sexual matters."

Sydney Cook, a short stocky lad with tousled hair asked, "When did you start to speak to them about sex?"

"Whenever they asked a question. We began when they were about age twelve or so."

"Does that include your daughters? What about the beginnings of their menstrual periods?" Mrs. Jackson asked.

"When Ellie, my oldest, had her first cramps, I talked with a nurse friend, got all the information then explained things to her."

"I think that was too late," Meredith said. I bet she was pretty scared when she first noticed the cramps. My mother told me all about this when I was eight or nine. She prepared me for it, so I was ready."

Rita stood to add, "Meredith has an excellent point. Parents should anticipate these functions of the body, and alert the child beforehand. The trouble comes when there is not a responsible adult to guide them, and answer their questions. Too often children get their sex education on the street, from peers or from trashy publications that deal in nude photographs."

"How do we deal with parents who are not articulate in these matters?" Ted Queen asked. "My parish contains many mothers who are hard working good people but don't know how to go about doing these things, what these mothers have done for their daughters."

Lettie Rogers, the cute strong voiced sophomore turned to him. "Do you have a mother's club in your church? If so couldn't these ladies talk to the women who have teenage daughters and give them the facts of what's going on? Or is there a doctor or a nurse who can help these women? Girls I know in school who have babies soon get over the pleasures of birthing, and are sorry they have to miss the fun of school."

Ben Adams, dressed in summer slacks, sport shirt, and white shoes, was impressive in his demeanor as he spoke. "In the General Assembly we are worried over the increasing teenage pregnancies which the taxpayer has to support and the sooner we take preventive measures the better off we'll be. These pregnancies are but one of the social ills we can't afford."

The principal sat wearily in his chair, glasses on and off his tanned face, and looking as though he wished to be far away from this chatter, out enjoying his fishing boat. He rose to say quietly, "I've noticed a gradual deterioration in the moral fiber of our young. Many sass the teacher, reject the discipline imposed, have poor attitudes, and we've already noted the drinking and now the drugs. If I had the answer to the prevention of these activities, I wouldn't be here, nor would any of us. As to the sexual behavior of our girls and boys, I would strongly advise sex education classes, provide birth control information and devices for those who are sexually active, establish classes on the physiology of the body, name the parts, etc. Kids think this is 'fun and games,' but when the financial and social responsibility hits home, it's a different story.

"Perhaps we should be more stringent with financial aid after the first pregnancy, hold the grandparents responsible for maintenance. Such preventive measures are caustic and tough, but who says this is an easy world? We must teach our children the dangers of playing with fire."

With flashing eyes and a slow red creeping up her neck, Mrs. Cameron Price looked at Mr. Borden as he sat down. She said not a word, but a look conveyed the message, "You're skating on thin ice, Timmy!"

She had an ally in Alyce Mason who had great respect for her principal, but could not agree with his approach. "This is too radical, the school board would never go along with it. How would we implement such a program? School counselors are overburdened as it is. Oh no, never!"

As a stillness settled over the room, Jule scanned the faces to see who else would respond. It came from Sydney, the black student at the college, with a large round face, nice demeanor, broad shoulders encased in a faded shirt and dungarees.

"I think Mr. Borden has a point. When I was there in high school some of this stuff was going on, but not as flagrantly as now. It's easy for students to apply peer pressure on a girl or boy and say, 'Go on, man, she's an easy touch,' or for the girls to say, 'It's fun! Wait till you try it. Wow! Then you show off the baby!' Of course, the boy goes free unless she nails him, or her parents raise hell with his parents. Kids need factual information and warnings of what happens when they go too far. Parents and the schools don't do enough talking about these things with kids."

"Sydney is right in what he says," Lettie spoke up. "Not all the kids act that way. There is a fast crowd hanging together and they're the ones who do all this stuff. Most of us are too busy with our classes and sports to mess around. We have goals to work for. I know if I did anything like that, my parents would . . . I don't know what, but it would be awful. They've trained me to be good, and I want to stay that way."

In her slow, halting voice, which was the only outward manifestation of her mild retardation, Meredith rose and bashfully said, "If we want to get some answers, why don't we ask some of these kids who do wrong to come here and tell us how we can help them not to do those things? It wouldn't hurt for us to try." She paused as though to collect her thoughts then went on. "Maybe we could talk to their parents and find out how they feel about it, and how we could help them prevent this stuff. Maybe they don't know how to tell their kids what to do."

Al Burns nodded in agreement and said, "Our students here are taking the ball right away from us, and it's great to see them tackle this problem. We've been looking at it from our perspective, but they are in on the ground floor, and can say it like it is from the kid's standpoint. More power to them."

Dave Halpern had been pensive throughout, and Jule noticed that he had been making notes on a legal pad. Finally she recognized his hand and he stood, tall, dark haired, and looked around the room. There was a professional air about him as he spoke. "It seems to me we are talking about a panorama of behaviors which are influenced by a triangle of forces in the home, school, and church. In each, the adults affect the children in a positive or negative vein. Where students have not had parental guidance they have gone astray in their sexual behavior. We are reluctant to initiate sex education classes to prevent more unwanted illegitimacies, and we must commend our students for telling us 'like it is.' While we did hear of some moral convictions, in the final analysis, how do we reach the ears of those kids who are most concerned? And their parents?"

Ken Patrick immediately stood up, aroused to action. "As a representative of the media, it is time we went public, and let this city know what is going on in our midst. Rabbi Halpern says we need to reach the ears of those most concerned, and I'm suggesting a series of articles in our newspaper on the topics we have been discussing."

"Who would write them, Ken?"

"Why anyone here," he replied. "I think you should call for volunteers, and between us we could carve out a series which would be readable and informative."

"I feel strongly about what we've been doing here," Dr. Sargent said, "and I'll volunteer to do an article on the medical aspects and give the harmful effects on the body of sexual aberrations."

He was soon joined by other volunteers, including Dave Halpern, Rita Evans, and Ben Adams.

The seventeen-year-old Meredith March, not so hesitant now, and heartened by her earlier statement, rose to inquire, "Could we three students here write something for the newspaper directed at students? They might read it better if it came from us rather than from adults. Maybe we could write an article for the student paper, too."

"Yes, let's do it," Lettie said happily, looking at Sydney. "Are you game?"

"Sure," he replied. "It might not do any good, but it's worth a shot. We can write it and let Mr. Patrick edit it, and make suggestions."

"I'll help with anything you put together," the editor said.

"Thank you all for your presentations, suggestions, and discussions," Jule said in closing the meeting. "I'll notify you of the next meeting. Don't forget to invite other people in the community you think would like to participate."

Chapter XXXI

Marion parked her two-year-old Pontiac in front of the house, and in back of a somewhat battered 1970 Ford convertible. It had never been there before, and she wondered briefly about it. She sloshed her way up the front walk carrying a briefcase bursting with papers and books. It had been a good day, but she was glad to be home and out of the freezing December weather.

She had been fortunate in getting the house, and with the money from her grandmother's estate and what her father had given her, she had a comfortable mortgage and a low interest rate. A renter took her apartment as soon as she vacated it, so she lost no money on the quick move.

A short mile from the campus, the town house was on the end of a row, containing two floors and a ground level family room. It was an all electric house, with minimum maintenance, and standard equipment. Bedrooms on the second floor, living and dining rooms on the first with closets, while the family room and utilities were on the ground level.

As she entered the front door, she heard voices in the family room and called down, "Hello, I'm home. Be down in a minute."

When she descended, she found Clara upset, red-eyed and sniffling. "What happened, Clara?" she asked.

"I was mugged and robbed, minding my own business,

when it happened."

The young man sitting next to Clara spoke, "I'm Kyle Richards, and I saw it all. I was about three hundred yards behind her, when I saw an old jalopy with three guys in it. They stopped, mugged her and took her pocketbook, and scattered her books. By the time I reached her they were driving away, but I'd know that car again. I took Clara home, and stayed so she'd have company and not be afraid. We just got in a few minutes before you."

Marion took Clara into the powder room to examine her for bruises, and freshen her up. "Do you have any internal injuries? Any soreness on your body?" she asked.

"Just a few bruises. I guess it was the shock of the attack and how sudden it occurred. I think I'm all right."

As they returned to the room, Marion said, "You'll make it. The bruise is not too bad, but it'll be splotchy for a few days, then get black. How about some wine to lift your spirits? Kyle?"

"No thanks, but I'll have a beer if you have one."

"Sure enough. I'll be right back with both."

Over their drinks, Marion and Kyle eyed one another. He could see she was pretty, wore her clothes well in a smart manner, had nice legs and a generally good appearance.

Marion saw a typical college kid, a nice clean cut looking youth.

"Tell me about yourself, Kyle."

"I live in Waldorf with my parents, this is my first year at the college and I'm nineteen. I was on the football team, and now I'm out for basketball. That's all."

"You have the dark complexion and looks of an Italian-American. I'd have taken you for a compatriot."

"You'd be right. We are of Italian heritage. My father wanted to be known as an American, so he changed our name to Richards. When I came along, my mother named me after one of her favorite brothers who was killed in World War II. She's of English stock."

"Do you like college?"

"Yeah. It's a challenge, but I like the sports best."

When it was time for him to leave, Marion and Clara thanked him for his kindness, and invited him to come for an old fashion Italian meal soon.

"I was born hungry, just let me know."

As he drove home, Kyle thought how fortunate it was that he happened along to rescue Clara. She was a quiet girl, rather bashful, pretty in a way, and not throwing herself around as he saw others girls doing. He had no steady girlfriend, although with his good looks he could have many. Kyle was too busy with his books, sports, and an occasional job running medical supplies into Washington for a Dr. Bolton. Trouble was, he never knew what night he'd have to make a run, but the doctor paid good money.

As they prepared dinner, Marion and Clara talked about classes and activities at the college. Clara told her sister that Mrs. Evans had asked her about taking on a project with a woman who has a visual handicap, and runs a business from her house.

Two days later, Kyle was waiting for her at the entrance to their history class, and greeted her with, "What a gorgeous shiner! A beaut! You should have it photographed."

Clara smiled then laughed, " Yeah. It's great. I've had all kinds of compliments on it."

"We lucked out, gal. Here is your purse or what's left of it." He held out a brown paper bag.

"How wonderful! Thank you so much. I don't suppose there's anything left . . ." She pulled out a small damp purse to examine its contents.

"I had to go back several times and just when I was about to give up, I saw it quite a way in from the road."

"They took my bills and the change, but left the other things intact. Thanks again, Kyle."

"You broke? Need some cash?"

"That's sweet, and I appreciate your offer, but I'm OK. My sister gave me some to hold me over. I wish I could do something for you."

"Sure. Come out Saturday and cheer us on when we play Anne Arundel College. If we win, you can buy me a drink afterward."

"Count on it. Win or lose, I'll do the honors."

In class, she thought of Kyle, and how good he'd been to her. He was so nice, but some girl already has her hooks in him. I'll play it by ear and see what happens, she thought.

Later that afternoon, Donna welcomed Clara to the house and introduced her to her mother. "This is Clara Pucci, sent here by Mrs. Evans as part of her outreach program, and she'll be learning how the visually handicapped function. I think we'll get along great."

Clara was impressed and, within a short time, the two formed a close bond. They talked freely, as Donna showed her the office and her braille machine. "I'll show you how it works, and what a help it is to me."

That evening, she talked a blue streak to Marion, telling her all about Donna and her message center and typing service. "She transcribes cassettes and the next day the business people pick them up." Then she explained how the message center works.

"I remember her. We met at the retreat over a year ago, but I was not aware that she had her own business. She must be quite smart."

"She is, and wait until I tell you this. She has a beau who is in a wheelchair, and he drives his own car. He's a social worker at the hospital and the two of them go out a lot. That's a neat combination, the way they can help each

other. Donna near floored me when she said that Alex has a
sailboat, and they go out on the bay. I'm going to like her and
this assignment. It'll be fun."

❧ ❧ ❧

Dr. Bolton was busy, very busy in his La Plata office every
day. The increased population meant that more people
needed medical attention and he had a full waiting room
daily. Friday evenings, Saturdays and Sundays he reserved
for patients needing an abortion, and this trade too, was on
the increase. Dave Slater had referred many patients to him,
and some weekends he came out to relax and work. No names
were given, no questions asked, and things were wrapped
up quickly and quietly.

A new Porsche in the garage, custom made suits and
shirts, ties and shoes were indications that Pat Bolton was
getting rich. His star was on the rise, and he was a happy
man.

❧ ❧ ❧

In midtown, Father Tom Shane was in the throes of
"birthing" his new St. Dunstan's church. At least twice, and
sometimes three times a day he was inside the structure
talking to the contractor, or watching a carpenter or other
workman as they put the final touches on his "baby." He
referred to it many times in his Sunday sermons in the armory,
for when the cold weather arrived Mass was moved indoors.
Most of the parish agreed that the parking lot Mass was quite
an innovation, and they enjoyed it.

The new church was modest in design and decor.
Outside, the walls were frame, a flat roof, and foundation
planting made it an attractive building. The focal point of

the interior was the altar, a marble slab, with a large crucifix suspended over it. There were no statues or vigil lights. Modern stained glass windows admitted some light, while a deep red carpet flowed down the middle and side aisles. The pews would be wide enough for comfort and the kneelers padded.

Early in the month he called the chancellor's office in Baltimore.

"Jerry, this is Tom Shane in La Plata. How goes it?"

The chancellor was an old friend who welcomed Tom. "Good to hear from you."

"I want to let you know that we're on schedule and the contractor will turn over the church to us on Thursday the eighteenth of December. I want to be sure the boss knows he's due here on Sunday the twenty-first, so he can consecrate the place."

"Don't worry, I'll put it on the calendar. He already told you he'd be down, so this confirms the date and place."

"You show up in your best monsignorial robes, to add dignity and all that stuff. I need to show off my high ranking ecclesiastic superiors."

"I'll be there in my finest. Wouldn't miss it for the world. I'm glad you're near completion, and the hard part is now over."

"Almost. The crunch comes in meeting the bills, but I have a great parish here. We'll make it. Thanks. So long."

His next worry was that a storm might foul up the ceremony, and he knew the aging Archbishop didn't like to travel in the snow. Well, he'd pour on the Hail Marys as a preventative.

In their meetings, the members of the ministerium were united in lending a helping hand to their popular priest. "Tom, we have room at our house if you want to put up any of your old buddies when they come for the affair," and "Our ladies do a fine job in cooking, and we'd be happy to have them help out your food committee." The offers were generous and they pleased the good father.

* * *

It had been a long hard day and Rita was tired. There had been an emergency C.I.T. meeting early in the morning, followed by conferences with the medical staff. Dictation to Billie Jean had consumed an hour, there were numerous telephone calls, and a quick visit to the college for a luncheon meeting with Dean Keyes and a host of other activities. Her desk was a mess, and the conference table was piled with case records. When Alex wheeled in late in the afternoon, she welcomed him. "I hope you'll be nice to me today, nothing heavy, for I'm about worn out. It's been one of those days."

"I've nothing too urgent or bothersome. How about I send down to the cafeteria for some tea? One of the candy stripers can do it."

He talked casually as they sipped tea, and he watched as the tension left her face, and she was relaxing.

He asked, "Are you and Joe booked up for Saturday night?"

"Not that I know of at this point. Why?"

"Donna and I would like to invite you and your beloved to Mike's Place for dinner on Saturday night. My treat."

"Sounds great, and I'll talk to Joe about it tonight. I enjoy hearing Donna play, and we had a nice time on our last visit there."

"Donna is also inviting Clara, the student you assigned to her."

"She is such a sweet girl. I thought it would be good for

her to know Donna and work out with her. Yes, that would be fine."

"Clara's friend Kyle Richards will be along too, and that'll make a party of six. We should have fun. I do have one business matter. Anything we can do about the increasing number of wives who are being abused by their husbands? It wouldn't surprise me if these guys are beating and sexually abusing their kids. I'd like to blow these characters apart."

"That's a police matter, and we can't interfere. We can help these women to bring charges in court, but the evidence has to be patently clear."

"Anything the Health Office can do? Any regulations for the care of children who are so injured?"

"That place! It makes me sick! The head man there is an old political hack who doesn't do a darn thing, but sit on his butt. He's got good staff, but they can't move. He makes all decisions himself, and rules with an iron hand."

"So I've heard."

"I'll be having lunch with Jule tomorrow and I'll ask her what might be done, if any laws can be invoked."

"OK. If I can help, let me know. What's with Dr. Bolton these days?"

"All I know is he has a busy practice on Route 301, and he's separated from Amy. She's in Waldorf and he's living in a new house down by the river."

"Yeah, I heard that, and he's making a bundle of money. There's a rumor around that he and a doctor from Washington are doing abortions at the house. The girls come in on Friday evenings, get the job done, and by Monday they are back at work or whatever, safe and sound again. That's illegal, and if true, I wouldn't put it past that S.O.B. He's a greedy one, and I'm glad he's gone from here."

"Right on all counts. He'll shoot himself in the foot one of these days. I wouldn't trust him with anything. Amy must have had a living hell with him. She's better off alone. Keep you ears open, and I'll do the same. If he's doing abortions and gets caught, that'll be the end of him."

At lunch the next day, Rita asked Jule about the protection of wives and children against abusive husbands and fathers.

"I'll have to research the law. I'm not aware of any particulars statute on the Maryland books, but it's worth a look-see. I'm all for prosecuting any male who is abusive to his family."

"The corollary, of course, is that some women might be accused of beating up on their husbands."

"Of course. The law usually applies to both sexes where there is a violation. Perhaps the Bill of Rights of the U.S. Constitution provides an answer to this. I'll check it out and get back to you."

Chapter XXXII

The procession moved slowly down the aisle, and as Father Shane passed, he dropped a quiet wink of recognition at Alex sitting in his wheelchair near the altar. Alex returned the wink, then squeezed Donna's hand. She was sitting in the pew next to him. As head usher, Joe had told him, "This gets underway at 12:30, so you'll need to arrive early, and I'll find a good place for you and a pew for Donna close by. We're planning a large turnout, and seats will be at a premium."

Archbishop Edward Sheehy had arrived about 10:00 a.m. in his Cadillac, accompanied by the chancellor, Monsignor Jerome Scanlon, and two of Father Tom's classmates in the seminary. They had a hearty breakfast in the new rectory, which gave them a chance to see the pastor's quarters.

Some of the local priests were present to talk briefly with the Archbishop and to participate in the ceremonies. The noon time start also allowed members of the ministerium to finish their services so they could join in the festivities. After all, Father Tom was one of their own, and this was a big day for him.

It was a bright sunny day, with a gentle but cold wind blowing robes and vestments. The precession formed outside the church, with the cross bearer flanked by acolytes holding two large candles in brass holders. As they entered the church, the choir of some fifteen voices on the right side of the altar burst forth with the hymn "Come Holy Ghost."

It was a beautiful sight, as two by two the men proceeded to the altar. Phil Mason in red robes with Jim Wilson, Al Burns and Don Leyton in white surplices, Ted Queen and Rabbi Halpern and the other members of the ministerium. They were followed by two military chaplains, priests from the surrounding counties, two assistant priests to assist the Archbishop, then Monsignor Jerry Scanlon side by side with Father Shane, and last of all the Archbishop walking slowly with his mitre as a cane.

While the choir sang and the procession came up the aisle, Alex had a tumble of thoughts which had brought him to this place in the church. At first he admired the new chaplain, then was impressed with the man's humility and work among the patients. When Father Tom revealed himself as a veteran of Korea, and wounded in action too, that did it. Here was a war time buddy.

While he was not religious, Alex frequently felt there was something missing in his life, and he asked himself many unanswered questions, How did I escape fatal wounds in the war? What got me into a work through which I could help others? When I became complaisant, how did this wonderful girl happen into my life, and she has a disability, and we draw close to one another? How does all this happen to me? Who or what is doing the manipulating?

One evening in November, Father Tom came for dinner and a few hands of poker. Alex had everything in order—drinks, steak dinner, salad, a fire going—when the priest arrived. They had a round of scotch then sat for the meal. Afterward, it was to the fireplace in the living room for coffee and liqueurs. They talked about local and national politics, sports, the Army-Navy football game coming up, basketball and hockey.

At one point, there was a long pause, broken by Father

Tom who said, "Alex, is there something wrong? You're not your usual self tonight. You seem to be out there somewhere."

"I can't put my finger on anything definite, but I feel as though there is something missing in my life."

"Seems to me you've got everything going for you—health, car, job, money, and a nice lady friend."

"Yes, all those and more, but they are the externals. There's more to it than that. Physically I'm in top shape, considering these."

"Mentally, you're no slouch. I've seen you in action."

"Yeah, realistically, I know what I can do professionally and I've ruled out any physical obstacles, so that leaves the one remaining facet—the spiritual."

He sat quietly while Father Tom went to the kitchen to refill their coffee cups. Then he continued, "I've been asking myself a lot of questions and I don't seem to be getting any answers. I've taken to reading the *Bible* lately, but while that helps, it isn't enough. I'm still searching."

"You're not alone on this. I've been a priest for many years and I still have questions and need answers. It happens to all of us, even clergymen."

"That's reassuring."

There was another pause as they drank and smoked—a pipe and a cigarette.

Father Tom raised the question, "What about religion? Have you sought counseling from any of our clergy?"

"No, I haven't. You are the closest clergyman I've been to. Early on, some of them gave me a rough time." He showed discomfort by inhaling great drafts of the cigarette, blowing out smoke rings at the fire, and taking out a handkerchief to wipe his brow.

"You see, I was raised a Catholic, but haven't been near a church for many years. I fell away, and like a lot of young people in the sixties, felt that I didn't need that stuff. When

I was injured so badly in the war, I thought God was punishing me for my lapses and disregard of Him. So, I fell further away from religion."

More silence, more coffee, and more smoking.

He told the priest that after the war, he felt defeated and hated everything related to religion and the clergy. He knew he had broken his devoted mother's heart, and then left home to attend graduate school, where he softened up a bit. Here, he found he could help people in trouble through these human services programs. At Powell, he lost the hard edge, and became a softy.

Having Donna in his life has been the best thing that happened to him. He said he envied her experience at the retreats, for she radiated goodness when they were over.

The rustle of the congregation sitting down brought him back to the present. Reverend Mason ascended the pulpit and in his deep voice, with arms stretched out from his red robe, said, "We of the ministerium welcome this opportunity to salute our brother in Christ, as he presents the new St. Dunstan's Church to his superior, the Archbishop of Baltimore for consecration. On behalf of all the clergy of our city, we beg God's blessing on this pastor, Reverend Father Thomas Shane, on his parishioners, who are our neighbors and on this edifice."

A few minutes later, Don Leyton approached the altar, bowed to the crucifix then to the Archbishop, and ascended the pulpit. "I am the newest of the pastors in La Plata, and one of the first to greet and hold me in a brotherly hug is one of the finest men I've known. We have been close friends going back to our days in the Army, and I am happy to be his neighbor now, and close associate in religion. May I compliment you, Archbishop Sheehy on your appointment of Father Shane as pastor of this flock. He is a shining example of the Good Shepherd, for he cares not only for his own parishioners, but as chaplain at the hospital, he cares lovingly for all who come under his spell. As to this church, I marvel at its beauty, for in its simplicity and warmth it reflects the character of its shepherd. He is truly a great person."

Alex glanced at his friend in the sanctuary and didn't fail to see a red glow on his face. "I'll bet he's saying, 'Let's cut out this stuff and get on with it.'"

He reverted back to his session with Father Shane at the house, while the chancellor, then the Archbishop stood to make their comments.

In the reverie, the priest was saying, ". . . and you think a retreat would be helpful to you?"

"I'd like the experience, and if a retreat would do for me what it has done for Donna, that would be fine. However, with this wheelchair, I don't think any of those places are accessible."

"I know the superior of the Manresa Retreat House in Annapolis, and I could call him for you. Lacking that, I'd be willing to provide routines of prayers and devotions over a few days for you."

"Sounds good, Father Tom." At this, the priest recognized that Alex was in spiritual pain, because he always addressed him informally.

When the bells signalled the consecration, this brought him back to the church, and he followed the prayers in the booklet. When the Host was raised, he lowered his eyes and prayed quietly, "Lord, have mercy on me a sinner."

After a pause in their dialogue at the house, Father Tom said lowly, "Alex, I feel for you and I'm trying to empathize with what you're going through. I'm about to make a suggestion which might help, but you may reject if you desire."

There was silence for a few moments.

"Would it help if you went to confession? I know what

comfort and peace of mind the confessional brings to those who have been away for some time."

Silence again.

"Yes, it would, Father. It's been so long since I've gone and I've done such a load of things, I'd take a whole week to count them up. Now? Here? And no confessional?"

"You'd be surprised to know how much we've changed. Sure, it'll be an eyeball-to-eyeball thing. Leave it to me, and I'll guide you along, and we'll do it together. Ready?"

"Lord, what have I got myself into? Let's get at it."

When he opened his eyes, it was to see Father Tom standing in front of him, chalice in hand, and the Host raised above it, saying, "Alex, receive the body of Christ." He responded, "Amen," and opened his mouth to receive his Saviour.

He held Donna's hand during the service, and at the Kiss of Peace, he gave her a warm loving kiss, saying, "The Peace of Christ be with you and me."

The evening of his confession found him sleeping more peacefully than he had in years. Father Tom left the house rejoicing, "I've found a lost sheep!"

After the Mass, the Archbishop with his attendants took almost an hour to consecrate the church, intoning numerous prayers and a long litany of the saints. Afterward, Donna wheeled Alex to the armory where a luncheon for the entire congregation was held.

"Donna, what did you think of it?" Alex asked once inside the large drill hall.

"Other than being long, I thought it was a beautiful and moving ceremony, very meaningful. His friends sure poured it on poor Father Shane. He must have been embarrassed."

"I'm sure of that, but he's a big boy and can handle it. Speaking of the devil, here he comes now. Hello, Padre."

"Hi, Alex, Donna," he said reaching for her hand to shake

it, then Alex's. "Quite an affair! Here, let me introduce friends of mine, Monsignor Scanlon, and Fathers McGlinchey and Burke."

They crowded around the wheelchair shaking hands and talking. The monsignor and Father McGlinchey told him they were veterans of Korea, and kidded Father Burke. "He was too young, just a kid then, but we bolster his spirits with our war stories."

"I must compliment you on your devotion to this young man," the monsignor said to Donna. "Father Shane has told me about you two."

"That must be some of his blarney he tosses around. Seriously, Alex is a wonderful person, and I'm not letting him out of my sight." At that, they all had a good laugh.

Father Shane left to visit with another group, and the monsignor said to Alex, "The Archbishop asked if you would come to his table."

"Be delighted, Monsignor."

As the group approached the boss's table, Alex could see Joe and Rita smiling and laughing as they talked.

The Archbishop was a chubby, short man with a kindly face, like a Santa Claus without the beard. He reached out to greet warmly both Donna and Alex, and talked at some length with them. He said he had heard of the survey of the handicapped and Alex's role in it. He told them that he too was a veteran, a chaplain in the navy during World War II, the Pacific Theater.

Alex said, "There are enough of you chaplains around to organize a Maryland chapter of veterans!"

After they laughed, the Archbishop said, "We can't be veterans, for we're still at war. Now we're fighting pornography, abortion, sexual behaviors, etc."

"We're part of the war too, against disease, infections, ignorance, and mental aberrations," Alex replied.

"I'm pleased you think so much of Father Shane. He came off today with a truck load of accolades. I envy him."

"You do?" Alex was amazed at himself carrying on with the man.

"Yes. He's out working with people. I'm inside shuffling papers and mediating squabbles. I'd rather be a parish priest with my flock administering the sacraments, watching the children grow up, marrying them and burying the dead."

He paused, smiled, took their hands in his and said gently, "Take care of one another. God bless you both."

As they left, the Reverend Phillip Mason was leading the members of the ministerium over to chat with the Archbishop, and soon there were peals of laughter coming from that corner of the room.

Alex and Donna joined Rita and Joe at a table for the lunch, and Joe told them how pleased the Archbishop is with Father Tom. He said, "If he does too good a job, I'll make him a monsignor and place him in a bigger parish with more responsibility."

Alex retorted, "We'll just have to cut him down in size. We can't afford to get rid of him. We'd just have to break in a new one!"

"I'm sure Father Tom is a happy man, and glad everything went off so well. It seems as though most of La Plata had a hand in getting the new St. Dunstan's Church off to a great start." Rita said.

On the way home later, Donna said, "Now that you're a 'born again' Catholic, does that change us?"

"Not in any way, girl. I still love you even more so."

"Could I go to Mass with you on Sundays?"

"I'd love the company. Anytime you say, we'll go to the nine o'clock Mass then take off and grab brunch somewhere, or get it at my house."

"As you know, we're not religious people, but I'd like to

tag along, and see what happens."

"Your parents won't object?"

"Mother will, but Daddy will encourage it. Besides, I'm old enough to make up my own mind, and do what I want. I have no problems on that score."

Chapter XXXIII

Rita opened one eye, a sleepy clock registered 8:20 a.m. and her snoring husband turned over to face the wall. After five hours of sleep, she was still tired, but she had lots to do, so she bounced out of bed to shower and get ready for the day. Joe would sleep for another hour and the children were already out in the family room playing with their gifts.

I can hardly believe this is our third Christmas in La Plata. Where has the time gone, and what have we to show for it? Plenty! she thought, asking and answering her own questions.

Midnight Mass at St. Dunstan's had been beautiful. Father Shane was in his glory, and gave an excellent homily on the birth of Christ, and how this event must relate to our own lives. The Evans family had greeted Alex and Donna and other friends, including a few non-Catholics who always went to midnight Mass. At home, she and Joe had eggnog, while the children had hot chocolate and fruitcake, followed by the opening of their gifts.

Joe retired first, then Rita, leaving the children to stay up as long as they wished.

She was nursing a cup of coffee when Roger came to the kitchen asking for milk and a pastry. "The other two aren't hungry. They've been munching on candy and nuts."

"I'll need your help today, big boy. We've got company

coming later."

"OK, Mom. Let me know."

"For starters, as soon as your father is stirring, come here and I'll give you some coffee and the paper to take to him. Let's pamper the ol' boy today. He rates it."

It had been a busy week for her, beginning with the dedication of the church, then cocktails for the staff, and preparations for Christmas. When Dr. Sargent complimented her on all she was doing, she replied that she had a helpful husband, cooperating kids, and a willing staff. "I enjoy keeping busy."

Today there would be the casual drop-ins, and later dinner for Father Tom, Jule, her children, Don Leyton, and the Pucci girls.

In mid-afternoon, when Joe Jr. heard a car in the driveway, he dashed out followed by Beth. "It's Alex and Donna!" she yelled.

Joe Jr. helped Donna wheel the chair in, while Beth took Donna's free hand.

"I knew you'd be around, Alex, so I have the ice cubes ready to plop into whatever spirits you want," Joe said in greeting.

"Merry Christmas, Joe, and you, Rita," Donna said as she emerged from the kitchen.

Rita gave Donna a big hug, and said, "My you look pretty in that red outfit."

While the women chatted, Joe led Alex into the family room. "Did the ol' boy fill your sock with coal, or was it miniatures?"

"He was kind to me, left a big snow shovel and an axe."

In the kitchen, Donna sat while Rita worked, and she said, "It's happened, I'm ringed! Look at my left hand."

"It's a beautiful ring, Donna. I'm so happy for you," and threw her arms around the girl. "Alex is such a fine person, and I know you'll both be happy."

"He surprised me, and he was so cute about the ring. He buried it in a box which he made me open after midnight Mass, and when I found it, I cried."

"Do your parents know?"

"Daddy was happy, but mother hardly looked at it, then went into one of her deep freeze silences. I could have brained her."

"Any plans for the big event?"

"Nothing definite, yet, maybe in late spring."

As Donna and Alex left, Father Shane met them in the driveway. "How are the love birds this fine Christmas day?"

"Merry Christmas, Father," they said in unison.

"Beautiful Mass last night, and great sermon," Donna finished.

"We're always trying. Have a blessed day."

Marion and Clara Pucci arrived next, and after warming themselves by the fire, they enjoyed talking with the children and Father Shane. The last to arrive were Jule, her daughters Ruth and Alma, and Don Leyton, who had picked them up in his car. On Christmas Eve, Don held a candlelight service at St. Agnes Church, which the three Rohms attended.

It was a lively group, and between drinks and a huge dinner of a standing roast beef, Yorkshire pudding, and endless vegetables, they all left the table "full, fat, and fancy" as Joe said. With two clergy on board, Joe had Don say the benediction, since Father Tom had said the grace before the meal.

"What do you make of Don and Jule?" Joe asked Rita later.

"They make a nice couple, both are alone, decent people and professionals. Don is alone, and Jule needs companionship and a male model for her daughters. It all adds up."

"Hon, Jule is divorced, and I don't think the Episcopalians are in favor of a divorced person marrying, and Don is a priest."

"Trouble. I hadn't thought of that."

"If they are in love, maybe they'll find a way. More power to them."

❧ ❧ ❧

Early on Christmas morning, Marion and her sister drove to the hospital in Baltimore to visit their mother, bringing her a nightgown, slippers, a robe, perfumes, and soaps. Mrs. Pucci hardly recognized her daughters.

"It's just as well," Marion said to Clara. "Mother's in a world all her own, and has no more fears. She had enough of them, living with him."

"Do you suppose he'll visit her later today?" Clara asked.

"You never can tell what he'll do, and I don't care. If he does come, she won't know it."

For the two girls, this was a far better Christmas than previous years.

❧ ❧ ❧

Joe Edwards was waiting for Donna when Alex brought her home after the midnight Mass. Mabel had gone to bed earlier, tired out. He had read, watched TV, had a scotch, and remembered the many happy holidays in the past, especially when Donna was a little girl.

"Merry Christmas, Daddy," she called as she came in the door.

"Merry Christmas, Joe," Alex called out.

"And a merry merry to you both. Now how about a drink to take the chill off the night air?"

As they raised their glasses, Donna said, "Wait, we'll drink to this. Daddy, Alex has asked me to marry him, gave me this ring, and I've accepted him." He gave her a warm hug, a kiss, and shook Alex's hand.

"I'm happy for you, little one, and you too, Alex."

They bantered one another about, Alex saying that she'd been on the streets long enough and he wanted to make an honest woman out of her. Donna countered with a comment about women he'd been chasing, who would hate it when he was out of circulation.

Joe asked, "Any date set for the wedding?"

"No, Daddy, we need to talk about it, figure out vacation times. We'll let you know."

At breakfast in the morning, Donna said to her mother, "After the Mass last night, Alex asked me to marry him, and I accepted. See the ring he gave me?" she said as she extended her left hand.

Mabel looked at it briefly then said haltingly, "Pretty. Rushing it?"

"Two years is a long time, and we're both in love. I know how you feel, but I'm the one who will marry him. Please be kinder to Alex, for he will be part of this family. He's a good, decent man, and while you don't care for his religion, that's his concern not yours."

Mabel ignored her daughter, and said to her husband, "Going to room."

Donna burst into tears. Her father took her in his arms, "Don't cry. Your mother is upset, but she'll get over it. Don't let this ruin your day. Maybe she'll calm down by dinner time."

"She can be so mean, and especially on a day like this when I'm so happy. Alex will be over later to take me to the Evans' for cocktails, then we'll be home for dinner. At least she can be cordial to her future son-in-law."

Christmas dinner at the Edwards house was a subdued

affair.

❧ ❧ ❧

Dr. Bolton treated Christmas like it was any other day of the week. His radio played all the usual songs and hymns, and the TV had many references to the holiday season, but the occasion had no real meaning. Dave had flown to Miami, and Amy had gone to Texas to be with her family. He had learned this when she called him earlier to wish him a Merry Christmas. She was not bitter about their separation.

On Christmas Eve Pat had two customers for abortions. Both were not married, from out of state, and had told their families they were taking a trip for the holidays and would not be home. Both families were conservative, Sybil from a strict Baptist household, and Eileen of Irish Catholic heritage.

The two girls were willing patients, in their early twenties, and Pat availed himself of the opportunity to "tumble in the hay" with each before the operation.

Pat was alone, and was able to perform the operations without any assistance. Afterwards, the girls slept, and left the house on the morning of the twenty-sixth of December, free of any embarrassing encumbrances.

Two days later, a large shipment of drugs arrived, and Pat was able to store it until he could repackage some of it as medical supplies and have the driver take them into Washington when Dave arrived back from his holiday.

Chapter XXXIV

The New Year is usually depicted as a naked baby with a streamer around its body with the year printed on it. 1975 was no different. But the babe could use a stocking cap, ear muffs, a fur coat and boots, for the temperature hovered around ten degrees, and a raging wind swept clouds of snow before its path.

In February, the temperature rose into the twenties, and for a few days it hit thirty, but as usual, the month dealt out some of the worst weather of the year—cold, raw, wet, and nasty. Even though there was a carry over into March, once this spring month began, people sensed an upsurge, a reawakening of the spirit. Winter would soon be over, and as soon as the bulbs popped up out of the ground, they could live once more.

Another sign of spring was the beginning of Lent, and from Ash Wednesday on, Alex could be found attending the seven o'clock Mass at St. Dunstan's church, with Father Shane celebrant. Frequently Rita could go, but her time was limited, for she had to get her children ready and off to school.

Rita called Clare Cohen. "Pass the word to the ladies on the faculty that Mother Benedicta has decided to have a retreat during Lent for those who could not be admitted last fall."

"That's wonderful. I know we have many who will be

pleased. Are you going to make it? I can't, there's a schedule conflict."

"I'm booked up too."

The nuns had a full house, and the sequence of events followed the prescribed routine. Marion and Clara attended, along with other college faculty, and staff from the hospital. Everyone found it an enlightening experience, particularly the non-Catholic women, some of whom were leery about what to expect from being with the nuns for a weekend. Mother Benedicta allayed all fears, her nuns served wonderful nonfattening meals and provided a peaceful atmosphere. Since it was Lent, they stressed the penitential aspects of fasting, prayer, and good works.

Late in March, Jule Rohm called a meeting of her committee.

"I'm happy to call to order this fifth monthly meeting of the committee on March 23, 1975 at 10:30 a.m. in the board room of the County Office Building. We have as honored guest, the mayor, Mr. Mark Long, who will talk with us later. Also we have a new member, Detective Sergeant Michael Garrity of the Maryland State Police, assigned to the Waldorf Barracks."

Jule then commented on the impact of the committee in La Plata and the surrounding areas. She asked Ken Patrick to tell the group what he had been involved in with the media and inquired as to Ben Adams' activities.

"Several months ago, we talked about 'going public' with some of our discussions here, and we had volunteers in Dr. Sargent, Rita Evans, and Ben Adams to write columns. Our series has been a success, and we judge that by the number of telephone calls and letters from our readers who are in support, and a few who disagree. But, that's what our democracy is all about."

He summarized briefly Dr. Sargent's portrayal of sexual

misbehavior by saying that a girl in her early teens is not ready to bear a fetus, since she's still growing and needs all systems to function to prepare herself for maturity. Smoking, he said, impedes muscular and respiratory functioning, and delays growth of the body. Drugs and other chemical substances were devastating to both the body and the mind.

"Rita's pen," he said, "was deft, descriptive, and decisive as she wrote about the social aspects and what it does to a family when a young member is caught between parents and peers."

He quoted her as saying that when the young girl becomes pregnant, she is the one who bears the social scars, while the young father too often goes free. In the long run, it is the community that suffers and pays and pays for years to come.

"Our legislator, Ben Adams, brought our statistics and reports to the General Assembly, and our work has been recognized and is appreciated. He brought back to our group corroborating figures and studies to show that we are not alone in facing the dangers of the areas we are working on." He stated that prevention at the source is what is needed, and the family is at the center of that preventive activity.

Ken's final review was on Dave Halpern's articles on the behavioral aspects, citing facts to show that the adolescent is not yet prepared physically, mentally, or emotionally to understand the nature of his or her sexuality. "The kids just don't know and understand what this is all about. These are children who do not know how to handle their fears or cope with peer pressure. Some individuals, even in adulthood, don't know how to handle their passions, and then we as community members must pick up the pieces from the ravages of the sex maniacs, the child abusers, the wife beaters and the sex murders."

Ken concluded, "We plan to continue these articles in

the *Star*, in the hopes that this community wakes up to the dangers presented by our children when they take matters in their own hands by unabated sexual activity, drinking to excess, and ingesting drugs and chemical substances which abuse their minds and bodies."

"Thank you, Ken, for the report and review of our columnists' articles. Our student members have a report to give. Lettie?"

"First off, the three of us will give the report, each taking a portion. We decided early on that since this is neither an elected nor appointed body, we don't make policy, but as volunteers we'll make suggestions. We went to the student leaders in our schools and told them what our committee has been discussing, and how important it is that students protect themselves from disaster through sex, drinking, drugs, and smoking."

Lettie told how well she and Meredith were received by the school counselor, faculty adviser, and the student council. Sydney rose to say that he followed the same course at the college, and it was favorably received.

All three students stood, as first one, then the other would talk.

Lettie continued, "What we wanted to do in both the high school and college was to write articles for the school newspapers about the dangers of sex activity, pregnancy among the girls, drinking alcohol, and the use of drugs. Since I work in the library, I can get a lot of information about handouts, books to read, pamphlets from pharmaceutical companies on sex things, and pass out this stuff to the students."

Meredith picked up on this and said, "Sydney couldn't say it, 'cause he's a boy, but it's the kind of booklet companies put out for girls when they begin to have their periods and their bodies change. My mother told me all about it, so I was ready. I guess boys need this kind of information around puberty and they need to know what's happening inside them." She concluded by saying that she worked in the recreation department, and she could put a lot of these freebies on the information table for the kids to take.

The three students were serious as they made their presentation, without notes or papers. They were together, and when one finished, another would carry on, as they made particular points. Lettie told about trying to get the kids in school to develope a 'Code of Behavior' so all could live up to it, and "If students in high school and college would sign off on it, then maybe we wouldn't have the problems this group has been called together to discuss."

Sydney told of efforts to have Dave Halpern help them in wording behavior activities such as discipline in controlling passions, obedience to parents, and teachers. This would call forth a respect for self and others, not a pressure from peers to do what is harmful, like "going all the way with a guy or a girl."

Meredith said they wanted something in the code of behavior about having pride in themselves, and to set goals for their school and social activities. "Of course, it means that the kid wouldn't go out drinking and come to school drunk, and to stay away from the 'creeps' who sell drugs and get them in trouble."

As they finished and were about to sit down, Lettie said, "I almost forgot. We hope to get rid of the dirty 'four letter words' and replace them with the proper terminology. We need to clean up the language in this sex business." Then all three sat.

The committee was silent for a few moments.

Jule broke the hush. "That presentation was absolutely wonderful. We owe you three members a standing vote of thanks and appreciation. Everyone stood and clapped, those nearest the students moved over to pat them on the shoulders.

When the hubbub ceased, Jule said, "I believe the mayor wants to have the floor."

"Ladies and gentlemen, I had planned to make a token appearance, but the reports have been so interesting that I stayed longer than I planned. You've brought the essence of your endeavors right down to rock bottom and laid it out for the students to take a look at themselves. I commend your efforts, and I'll do everything I can to support your activities.

"I see Mrs. Price taking notes, and I'm sure the school board will get a full report of what these young people here are trying to effect. I've read the articles in the *Star*, and trust that you'll continue them.

"Madame chairman, I thank you for inviting me, and I hope that I'll be able to come here once more. Keep up the good work."

After a coffee break during which the members stretched their legs and surrounded the students, Jule called the committee back to order.

"May I introduce our newest member, Detective Sargent Michael Garrity who lives in Waldorf with his wife and three children."

He filled out every inch of his brown uniform, all two hundred pounds on a six foot body, clean cut, short hair, and every inch a figure of authority. He was a native of the Free State, played sports in his high school, and made All American tackle at Notre Dame. Mike was a no-nonsense policeman, feared no one, and dared to haul drunken legislators out of their cars and into court. He applied himself to the job, studied hard, and was on the way up in the hierarchy of the State Police Force.

"First of all," he started out in a surprisingly gentle voice, "I am pleased to be here as a member, and I hope duty will allow me to attend all the meetings. The first speakers were quite impressive, but I must confess that the students here have done a remarkable job in their presentations, and what they hope to accomplish. We are all in this fight together.

"As a police officer, I get to see the seamy side of life, and it is no different here than in other parts of the state. Here, you are starting to do something about the thugs who try to ruin our young people. Believe me when I say that I'm out to get the 'pushers' of drugs and alcohol."

He went on to recount some lurid details of cases where young people were involved in accidents which were related to drugs and alcohol, and their parents had no idea what they were up to.

"There is an increase in the arrests for drug use, and we know drugs are coming into this area from Washington and Baltimore Harbor. We're on the watch for every possible source, and maybe we can catch some of these pushers 'red-handed' and track down the distribution source.

"I'm happy to see a group like this in action. Good luck, Thank you."

"We appreciate your coming, Sergeant Garrity, and hope you can join us frequently. If we get any leads, we'll let you know," the chairperson said.

When Rita's hand was recognized, she said, "I've heard a rumor at the hospital that this committee was going to recommend that a health service be established at the high school as a preventive measure for the unwanted teenage pregnancies. We need to nip this in the bud.

"From the knowledge I have, these 'health services' are no more than birth control clinics for the students, and I believe they tend to legitimize sexual activity by providing birth control pills and condoms. Some will say that if these kids are sexually active, they must be given information and aids to prevent a pregnancy. In other words, 'if it is going to happen, let us guide them.'"

She went on to state that we should approve programs that teach adolescents the facts of life, and that sex activity is for the mature body and mind. Parents need to teach and train children about what is and what is not acceptable behavior. "Health services and birth control clinics teach the wrong lesson—that it is OK to have sex," she concluded.

"For the most part, I agree with Mrs. Evans," Mrs. Price said. I am against the clinics. However, I would like to see the curriculum of any sex education program and know who is going to teach it before I'd give it my approval."

"I must agree with the ladies," Don Leyton said. "There is a moral issue here. Such services as Rita mentioned can dispel ignorance, but of greater importance is a careful, sensitive program that fosters proper behaviors. It should encourage positive attitudes and prepare our youngsters for adulthood, and the responsibilities when they too become parents. As I see it, these services and clinics condone behaviors for the young who are not ready for them. Our three students are on the right track. Let's give them every possible support. The kids might be more successful than the whole bunch of us put together."

"On that note, we stand adjourned," the chairman announced.

Chapter XXXV

April in New York City is one of the nicest seasons of the year. Signs of spring abound everywhere, tulips bring forth their finery, daffodils wave in the soft wind, men shed heavy topcoats and women array themselves in bright clothing.

It was lunch time in Sal's apartment, and the houseboy had just served broiled fish and a salad for the two men.

Gi spoke. "We've had the La Plata operation covered during the last few months, and it looks as though our friend Angelo has been siphoning off a little here, a little there. I figure it's enough to amount to about 900,000 dollars in street value. Now, that's a lot of dough!"

"You know what we're supposed to receive and what we actually get?"

"For every shipment, I have the figures, and that's what I come up with. Angelo's screwing us!"

"Sure sounds that way. What else?"

"The two docs are doing OK. They don't bother us and Angelo pays them off for the use of the dock and storage in the house. Within a day or so after they get a shipment, they have a college kid who runs their stuff into the older doctor's D.C. office, all wrapped up in medical packages so he doesn't know what he's delivering. He's the son of the man in Waldorf, brother-in-law to our Baltimore contact, who's keepin' tabs on Angelo.

"When our stuff comes in, Angelo hides it in the house for a day, then drives into Baltimore to deliver it to our distributor. But, he slices off a hunk for himself. The kid's father is pretty smart, because Angelo doesn't know he's being watched, yet he's got the place well under control."

"We better be sure that it's Angelo's hand in the cookie jar, and not the kid's father before we move in."

"Not to worry, boss, I'll be sure as hell before I make a move."

"As soon as you're positive, take care of it. Let me know."

"OK. I'll check it out personally. If it's true . . ."

"Gi, it's your baby. We can't have thieves stealing from us."

❦ ❦ ❦

It didn't take long for Angelo to know something was amiss at the house he was building for the two doctors. He'd been around, built many a house, and got to know people and their foibles. He wondered about a house with four bedrooms, a four car garage, a medical clinic, and other things, like a secret room off the utility room near the garage. Keeping his ears and eyes open, he learned many things, and the words abortion, girls, operations, and drugs came to his attention several times. He made no mention, but kept quiet. "I'll be a dumb Italiano and make like I don't know from nothing," he told himself.

One Saturday when no one was around, or expected, he bulldozed out of the ground a large deep hole, west of the old house. By nightfall, he had made an underground cache, waterproofed and fitted with a lock, and covered over with the same earth he had shaved away. It was difficult to know just where he had disturbed the earth—Angelo was a master craftsman. He knew and he'd keep the secret from everyone.

It might come in handy someday. If not, so there was an empty storage shed area.

Blanton Richards, owner of a gasoline station in Waldorf was a family man who could always use a few more bucks, so when his brother-in-law in Baltimore called and asked him to do a light surveillance job south of La Plata, and the money was sound, he accepted. "We want to know all about this guy, Angelo, his movements and what's with the house. We pay well."

Blanton's son Kyle was already running errands for the doctors who owned the property, and driving to Washington occasionally for them, so between them, the place was under good surveillance.

Kyle, unaware of his role and what was taking place, could describe his activities in the house and how he picked up medical supplies from Dr. Bolton, and drove the Buick into Dr. Salter's office in Washington on request, but not during his college class time. He told his father that Dr. Bolton always went to Washington every Wednesday afternoon, and usually stayed there over night. This tidbit and other gems were fed by Blanton to Gi's ears in New York.

When it became apparent that Angelo's fingers were very sticky, Gi decided that he had to take a look and action, if it was indicated. Through his contacts in Baltimore, Gi made sure that Angelo would be engaged in a meeting in Baltimore on the Wednesday he'd come to La Plata. That was also a day on which Dr. Bolton would be in Washington, and he'd have the property to himself to prowl.

The second Wednesday in May was warm, clear, and a typical spring day when Gi arrived at the Baltimore-Washington International Airport to pick up his rental car and drive south to Waldorf. It was just after noon, when he checked into the Howard Johnson Motel, registered, and went to his room to rest and read the local papers.

Mike Garrity was leaving the dining room after lunching with a fellow detective when he saw Gi enter the lobby and step to the registration desk. He noticed the tall fair-haired man, and the face bothered him; he couldn't fathom it, but he felt unsettled. He was sitting in his unmarked car in the parking lot, making notes of his conversation over lunch, when bells rang loud and clear in his head. The unknown stranger in the lobby was a New York mobster. Mike remembered being with a college classmate, an FBI agent in New York, watching a Giants-Colts football game two years ago. "See those guys over there," Bruce had said, "wrapped in blankets drinking beers? Gangsters, Sal Bocelli and Luigi Falk, both are tough nuts." The face of Gi reappeared in the motel, and it was the same person. Mike thought, "What's he doing in my territory?" He called the station and told the chief that he was on a lookout, and he'd report in later.

Mike returned to the motel, found a friend on the registration desk and said, "Veronica, can you give me a look at the form of the gentleman who just registered?"

He took the name, tag number of the rental car, and ran it through headquarters. It revealed only a "John Doe" from New York. This was a handful of nothing, but he knew that gangsters from New York did not visit La Plata idly. He called the chief. "An interesting man is visiting our fair city today, and I think he bears watching. I'll call in later and let you know what this is all about."

When Gi left the motel later that afternoon, Mike was discreetly on his tail, and followed him directly to the old Fielding property. From a safe and secluded place, he watched Gi easily enter the new house, and remain there for half an hour. Then he walked over to the old house, admitted himself, and when he emerged, he followed a path to a secluded section of the woods and suddenly disappeared. Five minutes later he came up again out of nowhere. Mike scratched his head in disbelief. When the rental car left, Mike followed him back to the hotel.

Gi had no trouble at all in picking the lock on the side door of the doctor's house. He admired the equipment in the kitchen, and the furnishings in the living, dining, and bedrooms. In the clinic, he looked at the pad on the desk with notations for patients and the word "ship" for a week hence. He was aware that this was the date for a large shipment to be off-loaded from a European vessel making its way up the bay to Baltimore.

When he went down the steps into the basement, he found the utility room in back of the area set aside for four autos. It was not long before he found what he was looking for—a small room used to store drugs. Although empty, he could detect a lingering odor, and knew then that he was on the right track.

After he finished examining the new house, he closed and locked the kitchen door and walked the several hundred yards to the old grey house.

"Might as well not have a lock on this place," he said as he pushed open the door, walked around on both floors, and sniffed but found nothing of value there. When he emerged, he noticed a pathway leading to a small open area to the west of the house, and followed it. There was a dog walking around, and being a lover of animals, he bent to pet it. The collie had his nose on the ground, and began sniffing and pawing. Gi noticed a plank underneath, and with his foot brushed the leaves and sticks away to reveal what looked like a trap door. He picked the lock, raised the door and pointed his flashlight into the darkness. It was large enough for him to enter, and when he did, there was his evidence of where his missing shipments had disappeared. "Doggy, I should get you a fat T-bone for this."

Gi disturbed nothing, left everything as he had found it,

and returned to the motel.

In the previous fall, Mike had gone to the college to watch the football team practice, and when possible, he attended their home games. He knew the coach, and several of the players, including Kyle Richards.

Kyle admired the policeman, especially when he knew that Mike had gone to Notre Dame, and made All American.

As Mike got to know Kyle, he asked him to keep him posted on any news of drug pushers near the campus. Kyle had signed the college students' Code of Behavior, and abhorred the drug scene, Mike was aware of his feelings, and knew he could trust the young man.

On the Saturday after he tailed Gi, Mike drew up to the Gulf station to fill his tank, and saw Kyle at the adjacent pump. After they had exchanged greetings, Mike said, "You still hauling supplies for the doctors to Washington?"

"Yeah. Whenever Dr. Bolton calls. He's got that old Buick he wants me to drive, and it's a beauty—powerful, great motor."

"Do you know a guy named Angelo at the house?"

"Sure, he's the contractor, and he comes by occasionally to do some touch-up work for the doctors. Why?"

"Oh, nothing, I guess. I'm suspicious of the place."

On Monday night, Kyle called Mike at home to tell him that he overheard Dr. Bolton say that a big operation was coming up on Wednesday night. Kyle had been around enough, and knew the doctors and the house to have his own suspicions aroused, so he called his friend.

"OK. Thanks, Kyle. I appreciate this. It may be nothing at all."

The day Kyle had indicated was the same date Gi had noted on Pat's desk calendar—Wednesday April 28.

In her own quiet way, Clara had become interested in Kyle. He was not like the other college boys. He was smart, a good athlete, always smiling, well dressed and he enjoyed talking with her. Kyle was attracted to this dark haired girl who was always well prepared in class, and unlike some of the sassy girls who practically threw themselves at him. He'd have none of them.

They found themselves increasingly in one another's company, and they found it a compatible relationship.

"I have tickets to the concert Wednesday night in D.C., Clara," he said to her over the telephone. "Can you make it with me?"

"Yes, I'd love to go."

When they drove down to the doctor's house, Kyle parked his Ford near the barn. "We have to take the Buick there in the barn, and when it's revved up, it's smooth. I like it. I'll leave mine here and pick it up tomorrow."

When Kyle went into the house, Clara walked into the barn and looked around out of curiosity. She heard a car coming along the road, and a few hundred yards away, saw it enter the driveway and disappear down into the garage. It was driven by a fifteen-year-old girl she knew through mutual friends, and she thought the girl was brash. I wonder what she's doing way out here? Clara thought.

In the house, Kyle met Dr. Bolton in the kitchen. "Hello, I'm ready to take off for Washington. The packages all set?"

"Hi Kyle. Good to see you. Yes, we've put them in the trunk. When you get to the office, give them to the secretary. She'll know which ones to put in the refrigerator. The packages are all marked. Dr. Salter is with me here tonight. Have a good trip."

Kyle went back to the barn, opened the door for Clara, and they backed out, then headed for the driveway. Just before they turned left, a car drove in. Clara was crunched down in the front seat, but froze when she saw the driver, and lowered herself so she wouldn't be seen.

The driver of the car was her father, Angelo Pucci. What's he doing here? she thought. Kyle was talking and she answered perfunctorily, but inwardly she shivered. She had never wanted to see her father again.

🖤 🖤 🖤

Early that Wednesday, Mike had asked the station to detail a man at the Baltimore-Washington Airport to check the flights from New York, and specified what he was looking for. Early in the afternoon, he received a call in his office. "Mike, this is Allen Hicks, your ol' side kick. A man answering to the description you gave came in on an Eastern flight thirty minutes ago, picked up a Chevy rental from Avis, and when I last saw him, he was heading south. Hope he's your man. Good luck."

Mike put down the telephone, and sat deep in thought for several minutes. Then he went to the chief's office, closed the door and laid out his plan. The chief agreed with him.

Back in his office, he called home. "Hi, dear. Don't hold dinner for me. I need to follow up a lead, and it may be a long night. Don't worry. Kiss the kids for me."

Mr. Michael Garrity was an idle pedestrian looking at a newspaper on the corner of Route 301 and Charles Street when the Avis rental pulled up for the stop light in late afternoon. Mike recognized the car and driver, Gi, as he crossed the intersection and parked the Chevy in the Howard Johnson parking lot and went inside to register. Casually, Mike followed, and entered the coffee shop, where he could see Gi as he signed in. Veronica was on the desk, and provided the information he requested, as he left to go to his unmarked car, parked where he had a good view of the entrance and the parking lot.

❧ ❧ ❧

"We've got a hot number tonight," Pat said to Dave as he saw Judy drive into the garage. Dave had come in earlier in the afternoon, had a nap while he waited for Pat to return from his office and enjoyed roaming through the house, admiring the entire layout. After they had drinks on the deck, Pat served a delicious broiled fish, green vegetables, a salad, ice cream, and coffee for dinner.

She parked the car, and ran up the stairs to the kitchen, where the two doctors were cleaning up. Judy Ashton was fifteen years old, but had the body of a much older woman. Blonde hair cascaded over her shoulders, make-up obscured her fine features, and a tight sweater accentuated her full breasts. Light blue slacks hid her slim legs and stockingless feet were tucked into soft tan shoes.

"Hi, everybody! What's up? "She was cheerful and bouncy, as she dropped her purse, sat down, then fished in it for a cigarette and blew a cloud of smoke around her face.

"I'm glad to see you so pert, Judy," Pat said. "This is an old friend of mine who'll be with us tonight."

The older man and the young girl exchanged pleasantries, cautiously, each eyeing the other.

"Tell me about yourself, Judy," Dave said to make conversation.

"There's nothing much to tell, really. I'm fifteen and go to the junior high school, and live at home with my parents. Father is a lawyer in Waldorf, and my mother keeps busy playing bridge all the time. I have an older brother in college, at William and Mary in Virginia, and a younger sister about ten years old. That's it."

"Tell me what happened to get you in this situation?"

" Well, I guess I'm pretty active. I've been going with a

guy five years older, and I really like him. We got to messing around one day out in the woods, and I was pretty hot for him. We got to wrestling, and I wriggled out of my bra, and he saw my big boobs. The next thing was he showed me his, and I showed him mine, and we wrestled some more with him inside me. It was some afternoon, let me tell you!"

She continued on to relate that a few days later, while the family was out shopping, her uncle came to visit. Judy took him to her bedroom to show him something, and the next thing she knew they were both under the sheets. She was fond of this uncle and they had a good time.

"Well, I missed my periods and having read some books, I checked with Dr. Bolton here, and he said I was pregnant. So, here I am to get rid of the little beastie!"

"Do you have the money to pay for this operation?"

"Sure, right in my purse. I scared the shit out of my uncle when I told him, and he gave me the money in cash so I could get this done as soon as possible."

"Did you use any protection—the pill or a shield?"

"No, too much trouble. I thought I was too young to have a baby. Wow! Was I ever wrong!"

"How do you know it was your uncle who did you in?"

"I don't. It could have been the guy I wrestled with, or it could be another guy who laid me a while ago."

"But, what . . ?"

"I just knew that I was pregnant, and the guys I've been with have no money, and couldn't pay for the abortion, so I laid it on my uncle."

As Judy reeled off this tale it was without a shred of embarrassment and she laughed, smiled, and lit cigarettes one after another. She sort of took delight in her sexiness and said that she had the "hots" for boys ever since she was ten years old. She found a slick pornographic magazine and was so excited by the pictures that she seduced a neighbor boy her own age. Judy also overheard her parents talk about her favorite uncle as being "oversexed," and since then she had caught him looking at her several times. When he came to visit, that's when she decided to try him out.

Dave said, "Didn't the uncle object when you told him?"

"He swore up and down he wasn't the one. I just told him I'd have to tell my father about us in my bedroom, and that did it. He's rich and has plenty of moola. He paid me in cash, all of it."

Pat came back into the kitchen and told her, "Why don't you go into the last bedroom on the right, disrobe and put on a gown that's on the bed. I'll be in soon to get you ready for the operation."

When she left, Dave shook his head. "That girl is a wily schemer, smart and way beyond her years. Even at my age, I'd hate to tangle with her physically."

"She's a knockout, buxom as all hell, and I'll bet she gives a guy a real workout."

"Take it easy, Pat. Relax. She's a kid. There's a penalty for using minors."

By nine o'clock, Judy was back in her bedroom, the operation was complete, and the anesthesia would keep her unconscious for many hours, until the following morning.

§ § §

Veronica was on duty at the registration desk when Mike called her at 8:00 p.m. Any information on our friend in room 145?"

"None. He left a wake-up call for 9:45 p.m., so he has some more time to snooze."

"Good. Thanks for the info." He had spotted the Chevy still parked in the lot when he drove in, but he wanted to be sure the quarry was still in the motel.

Mike knew he had plenty of time, so he returned to the barracks to talk with the chief, and to check out his plan. He also talked with another trooper and told him what he wanted to accomplish. They poured over a map of the area, and traced the back roads around the property.

It was pitch black when he returned to the property, using a little road unknown to most people. He parked in a secluded place, well off the beaten path, and walked through the woods, looking for a place where he could hunker down and not be seen. Yet, he wanted a place where he could view the new house and the old house. He selected a spot about one hundred yards away, which gave him a perfect position to see everything he hoped would be happening. Mike settled in for a long wait.

He had a hunch that the drugs would come in off the river and be lugged up to the house. With the New York mobster in town, it was a safe bet that he was in on the smuggling. So, he waited, hoping to see the Chevy come to the driveway and join whoever was in the house. He wondered what led people into the drug scene. Power? Prestige? No, it had to be money, and there was plenty to be made in the racket.

The thought struck him that perhaps his quarry would not come to the house, but stay at the motel and meet Angelo there. No, not plausible.

Since he had made the trip from New York, he'd want to be in on the action. These and a myriad of possibilities fled in and out of his mind. Down deep, he had a gut feeling that his man would show up around eleven o'clock and he wanted to be ready for him.

On the other hand, if this caper turned out to be a false alarm, he'd be a very embarrassed trooper with a red face. It was a chance he had to take, and he had felt so positive, that he requested backup from the barracks if he should call them on his radio. He had also asked the U.S. Coast Guard to keep a watch on any small craft entering the river and this cove that evening. They were not to intercept, but let it come in. If such a boat were to be halted and boarded, he'd notify them by the barrack's short wave radio.

The waiting was boring, and he was cramped. He looked at his watch—10:45, and a little later it was eleven. What went wrong? It was close to 11:30 when, way off to the left, he thought he saw a movement among the trees. His eyes had become accustomed to the dark, and his night vision was fairly good.

He kept looking, and sure enough could make out the figure of a tall man in a dark suit. It was too dark, and he was too far away to determine anything else. The figure approached the woods near the house, then stopped and squatted down on his knees. He's doing the same thing I am, Mike thought. What's this all about?

He was diverted by a low whistle and a flash of light coming up from the dock area. Lights came on from the house, and three men emerged to walk down the path leading to the dock. "This must be it!" he said to no one.

Mike looked to his left to see what effect this movement had on the mysterious intruder. He was surprised at how fast this man moved. As soon as the three men were out of sight, he stood up and ran from his hiding place carrying a bag. He ran down the sloping driveway and disappeared inside the garage.

Mike was tempted to run after him and find out what he was up to, but something told him to stay put. If this was Gi, why didn't he go directly and openly to the house when he first arrived? Why did he wait until the men left the house before he entered? If he's part of the mob, he should be down on the dock helping to carry the stuff up to the house.

While these thoughts rattled through Mike's head, Gi

was a busy man. He knew he had to act quickly and get out before they returned. He had three small powerful time bombs in the bag, and running up the stairs to the clinic, he placed one in a drawer of a medicine cabinet. Back down in the utility room, he opened the door to the storage area and placed the second bomb behind a stud near the ceiling. In the recreation room the third bomb was dropped in back of some books on the shelf. He left as quietly and swiftly as he had entered. He was out of the house in five minutes flat.

Mike watched as the intruder returned to his hiding place, still carrying the bag, although it appeared empty, unlike the fullness it had when he carried it to the house.

"Now, what in the hell is that all about?" Mike was perplexed.

Soon the flashlight's beams indicated that the men were coming up from the dock, carrying large sacks which they took into the garage.

When they emerged again after five minutes, Mike heard one man call out, "Dave you can stay here. Pat and I can get the other sacks, then the boat can shove off."

This was enough information for Mike to bury his head inside his coat and call to the barracks. "Chief, it looks as though a big deal is coming off down here at the Fielding place. Alert the Coast Guard to intercept and hold the boat that's just leaving the dock. Also have the squad cars be on the alert for a 1974 Blue Chevrolet, an Avis rental. You have the number. There's an intruder to the left of me, and he may be involved. If I don't get him, he might come out on one of the back roads I indicated to you on the map. This whole thing is weird."

When the two men came back up from the dock, one carried his sack into the garage. The other man came over to the old house, then beyond it and tossed his sack on the ground. He leaned down. Mike could hear a click, a door

was opened, and the sack dropped inside. He then closed the
door, clicked the padlock, returned to the driveway, and
disappeared inside the garage.

Mike checked his watch which indicated 12:13 a.m., and
in the distance he could hear the TV playing and laughter
coming from the house."

"Well, lads, this has been a good night's work," Angelo
said. "It's one of the biggest loads we've taken in, and I want
to thank you both for helping to get it up here. The boss will
be mighty happy when I tell him how neatly it came off!"

"Will you tell him also about your secret stash, or does
he know about it?" Pat asked with a straight face.

Angelo glared at him, but before he could answer, Dave
forestalled it when he said to Pat, "You'd better check on
our patient, and make sure she's all right."

Pat knew what Dave was doing, and he was glad to see
the little girl. He hated Angelo's guts, and the sooner they
were done with him, the better for both doctors. Would that
time ever come?

After they were alone, Angelo gave Dave an envelope
filled with cash. "Here, Dave, this is your part of the deal.
Split it with that snotty-nosed friend of yours. He's got to
mind his own business, like I don't mess with what you two
are doing. You handle your own business, and I'll handle this.
All we need and want is the use of the dock and temporary
storage for our stuff. OK?"

"Sure, Angelo. Don't mind Pat. He gets upset
occasionally. He's all right. We can do our stuff and you do
yours. No problems."

When Pat returned to the room, his nod to Dave indicated
that Judy was still asleep. He said cheerfully, "Hey, now that
we've finished, let's have a drink to celebrate, and enjoy
ourselves."

Johnny Carson was loud and colorful as they mixed the

drinks and sat back in easy chairs to have a few peaceful moments.

Outside, Mike looked at his watch, 12:29, and scratched his head, saying, "I don't get this. What's going on?" He turned to swing his head in an arc to look to the left to see if the mystery man was still in his place, but he never completed the arc.

A thunderous roar, followed by a blast of air and a blinding flash lit up the night air as though it was high noon. Mike was knocked flat on his back as the blast took the air out of his lungs, and he was out cold for about two minutes. When he came to, it was to gasp and choke for air to clear his chest, and he found himself wiping smoke from his eyes.

As his eyes cleared, he could see the raging inferno in the house, then he looked for the mystery man, but no one was there. He stood up, regained his balance, and called in to the barracks. "Chief? All Hell's breaking loose down here. My man has gone, must have just left, so have the squad cars pick him up. Call the fire department and get equipment here on the double. We've had an explosion, and the new house is in flames. I'm going to see if I can get inside and find anyone alive, but I doubt it. This place is a flaming torch."

Since he was down wind, and still choking on the smoke, he placed a handkerchief over his nose and made a wide detour around so he could get as close to the house as possible. The garage and kitchen belched flames and smoke, so he circled around to the front, broke a window to allow smoke to escape, but found that the fire was creeping into the living room. With his flashlight, he could see the smoke filled room, and the hallway. "I'd better get the hell out of here before the place falls in and buries me," he muttered.

It took the local fire department fifteen minutes to arrive, drop a hose into the cove and start to pump water on the blaze. In the end, there were three different fire companies on the scene.

The chief of the State Police came tearing down the road before the second fire engine arrived. "Mike, are you all right? What happened? God, look at that mess! Come over to the car and fill me in."

"First, did the boys find the Avis rental?"

"Yes. King and Halliday called to say they picked up your man on a back road, and he's now at the barracks."

"Good. I was afraid that we'd miss him, and he'd get away. To make a long story short, I played my hunches and they were right. When I spotted this guy in town, I figured he was up to no good, and somehow he was involved in smuggling drugs. Anyway, when I followed him, he was just casing the joint and planning his strategy. Then this evening, I was surprised when he didn't go down to the dock and help to bring up the sacks. Instead he hid in the woods, and planted bombs in the house when they all went down to the dock. I was still wondering about his role in this whole affair, and everything was so quiet, I couldn't figure it out. That's when the place blew sky high, and I lost the mystery man.

"He sure knew what he was about, and had this place well targeted. Why he bombed the place and the three men I still don't know. Maybe we'll never know. Now that I remember it, one of the men carried a sack up from the dock, and instead of bringing it into the garage, he brought it over into the woods. We should check that out soon."

Chief Duckworth and Mike continued to talk and put together some rationale for the acts. They decided that the doctors were a front for the mob, using their house and dock. One of the men was taking his private slice of the pie, and Gi came to La Plata to check it out. When he found stealing going on, he decided to kill the whole scene, house, occupants and all. If he could make a safe getaway, no one would know anything about drug smuggling on this quiet patch of Maryland.

"Well done, Mike. You sure pulled it off. Feel better?"

"Yeah. Let's see what the fire boys have come up with. There won't be anything left there but charcoal."

They walked over to where the fire chief, Sam Goodwin was standing,

"Good to see you, Clyde. How come you troopers are out at this hour? Come to warm yourselves by the fire?"

"Sam we wanted to be close by to help in case you need us."

"Whoever pulled this off sure knew his business. It'll take us another hour or so to bring it under control. As far as we can tell, the entire ground floor and the rooms over it— kitchen, dining, living rooms, and clinic are gone. Over on the far wing, the bedrooms have suffered water and smoke damage."

A fireman came to his chief. "We found a girl unconscious in the far bedroom. We're bringing her out now."

"Smoke inhalation? Burns? Get a paramedic here to look at her. Call the ambulance anyway and prepare to take her to the hospital."

Mike asked, "What about the men who were in there. I know there were three of them in the house."

Sam replied, "It's too hot to get inside, but if there was anyone near that ground floor level, then it's bye-bye. Not a chance of anyone surviving that place, the blast and fire were so fierce. As soon as possible, we'll look and let you know."

Mike led Clyde away and said, "Let's check out that disappearing act I saw earlier. It's over here beyond the house."

Their flashlights pierced the darkness as Mike led the way. "It should be just about here." It took them another five minutes before they stumbled on the hidden storage area.

Mike shot off the padlock with his gun, and they opened the trap door to look down inside. Mike lowered himself and with the flashlight poked around the bundles. Clyde followed and inside some of the ten sacks of marijuana they found packages of heroin, cocaine, and hashish. The chief said, "There's enough here with a street value of over a million bucks. A guy could retire nicely and not have another worry."

"Whoever had that in mind, if he was one of the occupants, is retired all right, but not as he had planned," Mike responded. "Maybe I was right, someone had his own pile to sell. I'll hold off judgement until we see what is left inside the house, for I saw them carry sacks into the garage."

Clyde said, "I'll shove off now and get back to the barracks. I'll want to talk to the man we have in custody there. You stay here and see what develops, then go home and rest. I'll see you sometime tomorrow, and you can tell me what else turned up. Thanks for all you've done. Good night."

"Night, Clyde."

Chapter XXXVI

Households in La Plata heard the morning radio news in amazement.

Rita was in bed drinking her morning coffee when she heard the news about the fire and devastation. Joe was coming out of the shower, when she called to him, "Listen to this tragedy."

Peg O'Bryan was parking her car in the hospital lot when she heard it, and then hurried inside where she met Dr. Sargent as he came off the elevator. "The forensic guys are in the morgue. Meet me there in ten minutes," he said brusquely, as he dashed off.

Alex, rolling out of bed, could only say, "I'll be damned!" Father Shane's reaction: " Lord, mementoes for the dead at Mass today." Donna was too busy getting her day in order to turn on the radio. Marion and Clara slept in and missed it.

Kyle, who was speeding toward an early morning class and thinking of the concert the previous evening with Clara, did not turn on his radio."

Janet Garrity hushed her children. "Be quiet. Daddy's still asleep. He had a long night."

At the State Police Barracks the chief was working on some loose ends of his draft report.

Ken Patrick and a reporter were hard at work on copy for the paper. When the *La Plata Star* hit the streets, the headlines

blared forth: BOMBS BLAST HOUSE, THREE MEN
DEAD

The opening paragraphs gave the substance. "Three men
suspected of smuggling drugs died in a fiery bombing which
destroyed the new house on the old Fielding property. A
fifteen-year-old girl was carried unconscious from the raging
inferno."

Pictures of the garage entrance, and the gaping holes in
the roof showed what had been the interior. Smoke was still
rising slowly from the charred remains as the photographer
took snaps of the four bedroom house on the river.

By the following Monday, the medical examiner, the fire
department, the state troopers, Powell Hospital staff, and the
drug enforcement police had concluded their separate
investigations. The suspect in the case, one Luigi Falk, was
turned over to the States Attorney for possible prosecution
for the murders of the men in the house he allegedly bombed.

The post mortem by the medical examiner revealed that
the three men had suffered severe concussions to the body,
decompression of air in the lungs, major burns on the face,
arms and bodies, lacerations from objects hurled into space,
and internal injuries. The force of the explosion was severe
and caused death rapidly.

There was no opportunity for any of the men to escape.
The bombs were placed so that the men sitting in the
recreation room received the full effects of the blast. From
bits and pieces of personal effects, he identified the deceased:
Patrick Bolton, M.D., co-owner of the house, white male,
33 years old, wife Amy, living in Waldorf; David Salter, M.D.,
co-owner, white male, about fifty years old, married; Angelo
Pucci, white male, about fifty-five years old, married, two
daughters living in La Plata, wife a patient in a Baltimore
hospital. Mr. Pucci had completed building the house late in
September.

Chief Sam Goodwin's report noted that there was extensive damage to the house when three bombs were placed strategically in the basement area, and on the first floor. When they exploded, they tore out the inside, and heaved upward causing fire to the entire area. The fire raged out of control for three hours, and the heat was so intense, that firemen could not get close to the building. Damage is estimated to be in the neighborhood of 100,000 dollars.

Dr. David Sargent, Chief of Staff at Powell Hospital, stated that Dr. Bolton had been on the staff at Powell, and he was able to pass on some information to the medical examiner on him. "Miss Judy Ashton was carried unconscious from the building, and brought to the hospital. An examination showed that she suffered no ill effects from smoke or the blast, but she was sedated following an abortion that night, probably performed by the doctors Salter and Bolton. We've had rumors that illegal abortions have been performed, and now they will cease."

The terse statement by Clyde Duckworth at the state police barracks merely indicated that when a gangster from New York was identified as a drug figure, a detective trailed him to the house, saw him run into the building and come out. "Shortly after that, an explosion, then flames engulfed the house, causing the death of three men and doing great damage to the building. The man causing the fire has been caught, and the Coast Guard intercepted the boat which had brought drugs to the dock on the property."

The Drug Enforcement Agency identified the New York man as Luigi Falk, known to them as an assistant to Sal Bocelli, a well known dealer in drugs along the east coast. The report spelled out that when the New York mob learned that Angelo Pucci had been siphoning off some of the drugs for his own purposes, Luigi Falk came to La Plata to wipe him out, and in the process he murdered two other men, who were guilty of running their own drug smuggling net.

✄ ✄ ✄

Marion and Clara were stunned when a state trooper called on them at their house to inform them that their father was one of the victims of the fire at the Fielding property.

"How did you know where to locate us?" Marion asked.

"Papers on his body gave us your address and telephone number."

Later at the morgue, they identified their father and made arrangements for the funeral and burial in Baltimore. Father Shane assisted at the Mass to lend comfort to the daughters. Angelo's two brothers and a sister, plus a few business associates, were present at the private internment. Afterward, Father Shane accompanied the Pucci daughters to the hospital, where their mother gave no indication that she knew or understood that she was now a widow.

Marion realized that she was the only person who could settle her father's estate, and turned to an old friend she had known in school.

"Edward, I'm so happy you could see me on such short notice."

Ed Manson was gracious, "Please accept my condolences."

"No doubt you've read the accounts in the papers. I'm sure his death was instantaneous, but nevertheless horrible. I need some legal help. Are you available?"

"Let's chat a bit first, and see what's involved."

"First, I assume he had a lawyer, but I'd prefer to have my own, one I can trust. I've seen some of his papers and the will, under which he leaves everything to my mother, and provisions for Clara and me. As you may know, Mother is a patient at Shepherd Pratt, has no concept of what has taken place, and is incompetent to act. Since I am the oldest daughter,

I must accept responsibility for the estate, his business to conduct, bank accounts to be settled, pay the bills and examine the portfolio of stocks and bonds. I'll need to spend time here to do all this, but I'll need legal guidance."

"On the basis of what you say, I'll be willing to assist in every way. I'd suggest a day or so each week to make a dent in it, and prepare documentation for the court. I'll talk with your father's lawyer, and then give you a call to set up our first appointment. I'll also talk with the manager of his office regarding current activities, and outstanding bills.

Lawyer Manson had his work cut out for him.

❧ ❧ ❧

It was late morning when Amy received the telephone call, "This is Mrs. Bolton. How may I help you?"

"This is the state police barracks, Trooper Ryan calling. You are the wife of Dr. Patrick Bolton?"

"Yes, but we have separated and now are preparing for a divorce."

"I'm sorry to be the bearer of sad news, Mrs. Bolton, but your husband was one of three victims who perished in an early morning fire. I would appreciate your cooperation in coming to the coroner's office at Powell Hospital to identify the deceased as your late husband."

In less than an hour, Amy was in the office of the coroner, and when the examiner lifted the sheet, she glanced at the burned tissue and scars and said, "Yes, that is Dr. Bolton," and to herself, "Have mercy on him."

There were no close relatives. His parents had died years ago, and a sister had married, left Ohio and had not been heard from. Amy went to Pat's office, and told the nurse they'd have to close up and refer his patients to another physician. She took his valuable papers home to examine them, and asked a lawyer friend to assist in these activities.

Although they were separated, and she had lost feeling for Pat, she could not be callous, and accompanied the body to Ohio for a brief service and internment.

Pat had made no will, and there were few if any resources to bequeath to anyone. There was a paper showing co-ownership in the house with Dr. Salter, on which he had put up ten percent of the cost, and he was making his regular monthly payments. There was a healthy bank account, but when she paid the many bills for clothing, sports equipment, and the car, the account was nearly wiped out. The burned car in the garage was a total loss, just a shell of its former beauty. She had to make up the difference for the costs of the trip to Ohio and the funeral. In the end, Pat Bolton died penniless.

When she returned from Ohio, her first call was to Dave's wife. "Mrs. Slater? This is Amy Bolton."

"Yes, Amy. As soon as I heard about David, I had to make arrangements for services, and then when I called your office, I was told you had gone to Ohio to bury your husband. I'm so sorry at how this whole thing came about."

"Since our husbands were partners, there are a few things we should discuss. I wonder about lunch soon. I have to go into Washington . . ."

"Yes, by all means. How about the day after tomorrow, at O'Donnell's on upper Connecticut Avenue at one o'clock?"

They embraced, wept, commiserated and talked, and agreed their husbands met untimely and terrible deaths. Nonetheless, both women never would have condoned the drug smuggling and abortion business of their husbands.

"About the house, Amy. David had told me a little about it, and he was trying to help Pat get on his feet, by allowing him to be co-owner. It's all paid for, you know, and Pat was making his regular monthly payments. Now, however, the house is a total loss."

"As far as I am concerned, I don't want any part of what would be Pat's share of the house. He had some assets, and I think we can pay off his bills. I'll let the lawyer handle that, and I'll ask him about Pat's share. As far I'm concerned, count me out."

"I feel the same way, and my lawyer will have to advise me on it. This will be part of David's estate, and that will probably take some time in the probate court. When it's all over, I plan to sell the place. Like you, I want no part of it."

It was late when Kyle brought Clara home from the rock band concert that night. They kissed briefly, then he left, for they both had classes in the morning. Sometime after midnight, he thought he heard fire sirens, but he turned over and went to sleep. In the morning, his mother fed him breakfast and said his father had already gone to work. He was thinking of a presentation he had to make in class and did not turn on the radio.

In the afternoon, he returned the Buick to the Fielding property so he could pick up his own car. As he pulled off the dirt road on to the driveway, he saw all the cars and TV equipment trucks. Then he noticed the ravaged house, and smouldering wisps circling upward. It was incredible! He parked the Buick in its usual place, and walked back to get a closer look at the damage. He asked one of the firemen close by, "Do you know if Dr. Bolton is around?"

"Nope, not here. He's dead, in the morgue at Powell Hospital."

"What? I can't believe it! I saw him last night, and did an errand for him."

"He was here until about midnight, then his world fell apart. This place was bombed, blasted and torched. He was one of three who didn't make it out of the house alive."

Kyle was speechless. He couldn't believe what the man said. He stayed for a little while looking at the ruins, then went to his Ford, dropped the top and drove to Donna Edward's house, where he knew he'd find Clara working out on her practicum for the blind.

"Clara, have you heard the news about the fire?"

"Sure, but the details are still sketchy. I heard that the place is in ruins, a total loss."

"I was just down there to return the Buick and pick up my car. I stayed for a bit, then I wanted to get out of there. The police are still conducting their investigation, and we'll get the sordid details later. Are you ready to leave here? I'll give you a lift home."

A sorrowful Marion met them at the door. They embraced and cried.

"What's wrong?" Kyle asked.

"Come in. We've had sad news," Marion said. "Our father was killed in the fire last night."

"I was just down there, and learned that Dr. Bolton was a victim, too. I'm sorry for your loss. Let me know if there's anything I can do."

"Nothing right now, Kyle. Thanks. If we need you, we'll call."

❧ ❧ ❧

Mike Garrity was at his desk when Kyle was ushered in.

"C'mon in. I was thinking of you today. Thanks for the tip."

"Hi. I've just come back from the house, and it's a royal mess. Clue me in on what happened."

The detective gave him a complete review of what happened the previous evening at the house, the bombing and the fire. The man responsible was in the brig at the barracks.

"Mike, am I involved in this?"

"Sure, up to your neck! You were the paid messenger, weren't you?"

"Like hell! I only delivered medical packages for Dr. Bolton to D.C."

"Cool down, Kyle. You were just the innocent one. Some of the packages were medical, for sure, but some were drugs, illegal stuff, and you were kept in the dark."

"How?"

"We've had Dr. Salter under observation for several months, and we were tipped off that you were the messenger bringing in the drugs from here to his office. When you'd drive the Buick into the garage under the office building, and take the packages up to his office, there was another man in the garage who would remove more packages from the secret compartments of the Buick while you were gone. You never knew what you were carrying."

"Now I know why Dr. Bolton wanted me to use the Buick instead of my Ford. Pretty clever! What would have happened to me if I was ever caught by drug enforcement agents?"

With a straight face, Mike replied, "Court, jail, and up the river."

Kyle looked at him in disbelief.

"No, Kyle, we'd have protected you. You will have to be a witness for us when we bring Mr. Luigi Falk up for trial."

"Anyone else implicated?"

"Yes, his boss in New York, and we know who he is. I hope we nail him good. For the present, the drug scene in southern Maryland is kaput! Over! No more!"

❧ ❧ ❧

A sleepy Lawrence Ashton picked up the telephone by his bed to answer the jingling bell. "Yes?"

"This is the state police barracks calling about your daughter."

"What about my daughter? She's here in bed."

"Mr. Ashton, I'm sorry to disturb you at this hour, with the news that your daughter, Judith, is a patient at Powell Hospital in La Plata. We brought her out of a burning house about 1:30 a.m., and she is under the care of staff at the hospital."

Wide awake now, he sat up in bed and shook his wife Mae. "What's going on? Is it Judy? Is she hurt?"

Quickly they dressed and drove to the hospital. A nurse led them to the bed of their daughter who was coming out of her sedated state.

"Mother, Daddy, am I ever glad to see you!"

"Can you tell us what happened, Judy?"

"I went to see this doctor, and he put me under so he could operate, and the next thing I knew, I was being carried out of a burning building."

Mr. Ashton motioned to the nurse and both went out to the hall.

"Nurse, what's this about an operation? For what condition?"

"The resident on duty did a complete examination as soon as she was admitted, and his finding is that your daughter had an abortion last evening."

"An abortion? Last night? And we knew nothing about it? What doctor performed it and where? This is a fifteen-year-old child!"

"I'm afraid, sir, that I can give only the medical information. Perhaps Dr. Small can provide further medical data as you require."

"Was it done here at the hospital?"

"No. We think it was performed in the house that burned down late last night. The state police have all the details on the fire."

"Thank you, nurse. I'm sorry to be so rough on you. I'll get the information I need later."

When he returned to the room, Judy had lapsed into slumber, so the parents drove home arguing all the way.

Lawrence Ashton was fiery mad. He gripped the wheel of the Lincoln Town Car so hard his knuckles were white, and there was sweat breaking on his brow. He could hardly speak, but he choked out at Mae, sitting as far away from him as she could up against the door. "Damn it all, woman, how could you ever let this happen to our daughter? She's but a child, and to think this took place right under our eyes!"

Mae had a handkerchief out and was crying into it, and between sobs, she said, "Don't you put all the blame on me! Remember, she's your daughter, and you had her for twelve years before I came along. You and your first wife brought her up like this."

"That makes no difference, you are her stepmother, and have a responsibility for her welfare. I can't believe this! How could it have happened?"

"I wish I knew. I can tell you this, Judy's never liked me."

"Have you ever encouraged her to like and respect you?"

"I did try, but with no luck. Ever since you divorced your first wife, Judy has hated me. She thinks I was responsible for the divorce, and has held that against me ever since."

"Damn it, that still doesn't mean we can't control her actions. If I ever get my hands on the man who impregnated her, I'll kill him! What a thing to do to a child! Jesus!" and he gripped the wheel harder.

Sweat was oozing from his armpits, as they drove another two miles. He blurted out again, "So you've never been close. But have you ever talked to her about her body, her menstrual periods and about sex?"

"I did try, but I got nowhere. Judy knew all the answers."

"That's no damn excuse at all, Mae. Girls her age need to have a mother to tell them the facts of life. Mostly they get it from the streets and that's wrong. As result of your negligence, now we have a child, our child, who's gone through an illegal abortion! Doesn't that make you mad? Wouldn't you like to throttle the doctor who did that to your Judy? Every time I think of it, I boil up all over again."

"You're just as responsible as I am, more so."

"What me? Talk to her about sex? You're crazy, woman."

"No, I'm not. You could have told her about boys who want to sow their wild oats, and about grown men who prey on unsuspecting women. There's a lot you could have told her about sex. Judy also needs a strong father, one who is close to her. But, no, you're always out at some meeting in town or away on a trip to a convention or off playing golf."

"Mae, I'm a professional person. There are things I must do to maintain my position and put bread on the table."

"There are more important things in life, like caring and loving one's children. As for the table, how often have YOU missed dinner because of a meeting. When you're home, you put your nose in the paper or a journal instead of talking with your daughter. That's what I mean."

"I don't see you staying around the hearth to be available when she comes home from school. It's out with the 'girls' playing bridge, attending luncheons and drinking martinis most of the afternoons."

He was still hopping mad as they neared their big house on the outskirts of Waldorf. He said in a somewhat calmer voice, "I wish this town had a sex education program for kids.

We sure need it, when parents like us won't or cannot explain the facts of life to them. One of my friends tells me that in La Plata there's a group talking it up for the school. It sounds interesting. Have you heard anything about that program?"

"No, Lawrence. It's too late to continue this. I'm tired. I will tell you this, you need to discipline her. She has too much liberty to roam around unfettered and don't ask me to take over your fatherly responsibilities."

"There you go again, preaching . . ."

Chapter XXXVII

"Aren't you glad you're not stationed at the Vatican, in Rome, Padre?" Alex asked jokingly.

"I'm happy to be right were I am, and couldn't think of a better spot. Why do you ask?"

"You'd have to push your 190 pounds into a tight cassock, and wear a biretta. In this humid weather, you'd melt off some of that flab . . ."

"Now wait a minute, Alex," Rita said over her iced tea, "Father Shane is well proportioned, and if he had to wear a skirt, he'd do it up proud."

"May I come to the rescue, Father Tom?" Peg asked. "As a nonvoting member of the Romans, let this Episcopalian say that I approve of the decision by the Pope, the Vatican Council, or the bishop to let you guys wear regular black suits short sleeve shirts, et al."

"Saved at last, Peg. Thanks!" Turning to Alex he asked, "What brought all this on?"

"Last night, I was reading where a priest on vacation in Rome was in 'civvies' when the Pope came by, and he recognized the priest. He chewed him out in a nice manner, of course, and after that, he had to get back into his cassock and biretta."

The four were enjoying lunch at the hospital on a Friday, getting ready to wrap up for the weekend. They all got along quite well, but never lost their professional touch when it was needed. Three of them were members of the C.I.T. and when the team was in action, voices were raised, and the "fur would fly," but these instances were rare.

Father Tom was excited about his new church, and found the rectory a comfortable place. During one of the Parish Council's meetings, the question about a housekeeper for him was raised.

"As you know, my last housekeeper left before the fire to care for her ill sister in Texas, and now . . ."

Joe Evans spoke up, "Father, would you consider having a group come in to provide maintenance for you and the church?"

Curious glances from the members prompted Joe to continue. "Studies in our office indicate that the mentally retarded living in group homes in the community are gaining success in providing indoor housekeeping and outdoor maintenance for banks, offices, corporations, etc. How would this council feel about exploring such an arrangement for St. Dunstan's?"

Father Shane was the first to speak. "I'd love it."

The Parish Council approved, and Rita was delegated to explore the possibilities. She found that the St. Mary's County Association for Retarded Children had a community based training center, and was starting to provide these kinds of services.

The Council signed a contract with that association, and Father Shane was able to report to the members how pleased he was with their work.

"These people came in and we agreed on a trial basis for a month. After the first two weeks, I was sold on them. About seven or eight people arrive on Monday mornings. The supervisor assigns three to do the housekeeping in the rectory, and the remainder clean the church inside, and do what needs to be done outside. They've planted flowers, trimmed the bushes, and the place looks great. I do my own cooking, and I pick up daily, so it's no great problem for me. It's a good arrangement, and the price is reasonable. Best of all, we are helping these people to become independent."

"Any complaints so far?" Peg asked.

"Nary a single one. In fact, I talked with Al Burns, and he's interested both for the Lutheran church and as a placement for his Tommy when he gets a bit older."

❧ ❧ ❧

"I can hardly wait for school to let out," Rita said, "so we can take off for a week at Fenwick Island in Delaware. We love the ocean and walk the sands looking for pretty shells."

Peg said, "I'm for the garden. I love to get out and smell the earth, weed the garden, mow the grass, and even the odor of cow manure is invigorating. It's a welcome change from inhaling medicines."

Alex needed no prompting. "Well, slaves, do your own thing. I'm free to drop the lines, hoist the sails and let the winds take us where they may."

Previously, Alex had taken Rita, Joe, and Father Tom out and they were amazed at how well he and Donna handled the boat. Donna was quite proficient in her tasks, and the guests had nothing to do but sit and relax. It was good for them to see how well these two people coordinated their movements.

Early Saturday, Joe and Donna Edwards sat in the kitchen having breakfast. She had made coffee and toasted English muffins. Mabel was still asleep in bed.

"Daddy, Alex is coming over about ten o'clock to pick me up, and we're off in his boat for the day. I've packed our lunch, and after dinner tonight at his place, we'll go to Mike's

Place for our regular performance. That place is getting quite popular, and I do enjoy playing. Will you be all right?"

"Sure. I'll be fine. You go and enjoy."

"Clara is coming later this morning. There are a few things I want her to finish up. She's bright, and will make a wonderful worker with the visually handicapped. This is good experience for her."

As they cleared the cove, a northwesterly breeze filled the sail, and they glided down the Potomac on a beautiful day, with clear skies and a slight chop on the waves.

"We'll head on down past St. Clement's Island and just beyond St. George's Island, we'll turn north and tie up for a bit at St. Inigoes. Maybe, we'll have lunch there, OK?"

'You're the skipper and I'm the devoted deck hand."

"Still making lots of money? How is Clara coming along?"

"Not loads, but the cash is flowing in steadily, and the bank account is getting fatter. Clara's a wonderful girl and we get along great. She's holding the fort today and can relieve Daddy in case he wants to go out. She and Mother get along very well, and I'm happy to have her with me."

"Speaking of the ol' bat, how . . ."

"Now, Alex, be kind to her. I know how you feel, and I understand Mother. She's doing all right, but she could do much better. It's her mental outlook that's impeding her physical progress. She tends to get lazy, too, and I find myself fighting her to do more things for herself."

"Done any more thinking about when we get married?"

"You know I have, dear. I can't wait for that day to come. I think perhaps in the fall. Maybe she'll be in a better frame of mind."

"Good girl. We'll just have to pray and hope she sees the light."

They sat in the cockpit, Alex keeping an eye on the sails and the jib, one arm around Donna, both silent and content.

In a little while he said, "It's such a warm day, do you want to go forward on top of the cabin, strip off, and get more sun on your already healthy body?"

She looked at him with a faint smile. "That's a good idea. I do need more sun, and there's no one around but you."

"I'm harmless now."

"Yes, and do I ever know it! No more love making. Oh, for those carefree days when we made such great love!"

"I'm being real good these days—saving myself."

"Well, Mr. Goody Two Shoes, I am, too. I have to, but I sure do have wicked thoughts. Someday I'll catch up with you."

Alex let forth a deep belly laugh. "Oh no! Not the two of us pure and clean. One is bad enough! Now, go forward and . . ."

"I know, so you can peek and admire my tan, all over."

He thought of the times they had made love on the boat, and at his house, but he was being a good Catholic and abiding by all the rules. Every Sunday he was at Mass, received Holy Communion from Father Shane, and derived deep satisfaction from his newly found spiritual life. Donna frequently attended Mass with him, and was getting to know when to kneel and to stand. He never inquired about her feelings, but was ready to respond if she raised questions about becoming a member of his church.

She was stretched out on a blanket on top of the cabin, and he could see her breasts a shade lighter than the tan on her arms and shoulders. He was deeply in love. "Damn that woman! Hurry up the fall!"

They tied up the boat at St. Inigoes, had lunch, then a nap, and began the return trip. Alex wanted to get back by five o'clock, so he could shower, cook dinner, and get ready for the evening.

"Y'know, Donna, I'm still amazed at what happened down

at the old Fielding place in April. It doesn't surprise me that Pat Bolton was involved in illegal abortions, but on a fifteen-year-old child! He was sick! Then he got into the drug business. He wanted fast bucks, and in the end, he got a fast ride."

"Some people just never learn. He should have known better."

"I've been curious about that property, so the other evening, I drove down there, and found the house all boarded up. I stayed in the car, and looked around as much as I could. It is a wreck!"

"I can see those wheels of yours turning around, and hear the clash of metal. What's up, genius?"

"Recently Rita met Amy Bolton who was in the hospital to see one of her clients. It turns out that Mrs. Salter and Amy had lunch during which Mrs. S said she plans to sell the house and property, as soon as it clears the court action on Dave's estate and will. This might take some time, but I've been doing some thinking."

"That involves the possibility of buying it?"

"You got it! It would make a dream spot for us. Look, the dock is there, a perfect view of the river, plenty of bedrooms . . ."

"Right now, the place is a mess, mostly charred ashes. From what I hear, there was extensive damage."

"Not to the bedrooms and the living room. I'd love to get inside and check it out. Even with the damage, this would be a good time to renovate and fix up to our own specifications."

"My love, this would take money, plenty of moola, but I'm with you."

"Between us, I'll bet we could make it. You could set up your message center there, and use it for tax purposes. I could sell my house and use some of my stocks. With a good down payment and a thirty-year mortgage, we could swing it."

"You make it sound so easy. Let's think about it some more."

In mid-afternoon, as they neared Colter's Point, he noticed a shift in the wind, and said, "Donna, we'll have to tack here. Take this line and prepare to come about."

He loosened the port line, and as Donna stood to shift position and receive the starboard line, the wind suddenly caught the mainsail boom and it swung, striking her on the side of the head. She was knocked clear off her feet, dark glasses flying into the water, and she landed head and shoulders over the gunnel, her body almost in the water.

Alex saw it and immediately dropped his line and made a grab for her before she fell overboard. There was a cut on her head, blood oozing forth in the water. With the mainsail flapping, he hauled her down to the floor of the cockpit, secured the lines and headed into the wind to stop the forward motion of the boat. He bent over her still body, took her pulse, and noted her irregular breathing. Then he scrambled into the cabin, took a pillow and blankets to make her comfortable, and examined her body for other injuries. She was out, quite unconscious, and he could feel no broken bones. She still had that nasty gash on her head, which he covered with a soaked towel.

Alex was scared, but it did not show. He knew what he had to do, and went about it methodically. He secured the wheel, and turned on the motor so that they would make the best possible time. He moved forward, and quickly lowered the jib, and secured it on the bow. Then he moved himself back to the mast, dropped the main, secured it, but not in a very seamanshiplike manner. Throughout all these maneuvers, he kept glancing at Donna, hoping that she would rise up suddenly and ask, "So, what's up, doc?" But, no, she remained motionless.

With the sails down, he crept back to the stern and revved up the motor so he could maintain speed, although a good wind might have driven him faster. He couldn't risk that.

Strange, he thought, that there were so few boats on the river. Usually on a Saturday, the place would be filled with white sails, but today the river was clear. He desperately needed someone with a two-way radio. Interspersed with his thoughts he remembered to say some prayers.

"Lord, just give me a hand on this one. Send a hero, but quick!"

Alex looked at his watch. It was 3:30 and he was still about forty-five minutes away from the dock. He knew he had enough gasoline to make it, but he checked the gauge and supply anyway.

Fifteen minutes later, he noticed a cabin cruiser heading toward him, off the port bow. As it drew nearer, he waved frantically and blew his horn to signal distress. He breathed a sigh of relief as the cruiser slowed and came close to him.

"Ahoy, cruiser, I need help!"

"What's up, mate?" a cheery voice called back.

He could see a man about thirty, tall blondish, well tanned, slowly approaching. An older man, well up in years sat motionless on a chair in the cockpit.

"We've had an accident. My friend was hit by a swinging boom, and lies unconscious on the floor of the cockpit. Do you have a two-way radio?"

"Sorry about the accident, ol' boy. Let me come closer and tie up alongside. Do you have bumpers? Toss them over the side, so we rub gently. Catch the line when I toss it." Soon the boats were snugged and the young man came aboard.

As he came over the side, he almost turned white when he saw the girl lying on the deck, and even more so when he noticed that Alex was on his knees moving back and forth.

He couldn't get over it and rubbed his head in amazement, and said quietly, "She sure is unconscious, and you without use of your legs? A paraplegic? How in the name of heaven did you ever handle this boat?"

"We're both good sailors. Donna here has a visual problem and could not see the boom as it caught her on the head. Do you have a radio?"

"Yes, but first let me see her. I've had some medical training. Um. A bad gash on the head, blood coagulating, no broken bones," he said as he quickly ran his hands over her body. He took her pulse and checked for other vital signs. He stood up and made for the side. Alex stopped him with, "Put in a call for the La Plata Rescue Squad, and have them meet me at Randolph Keyes dock. He's dean at the college and they know him. Tell them I'm due in just about 4:45, and have them alert Powell Hospital. The fellows know me, Alex Snyder, and they'll come rushing."

Still shaking his head at what he had seen and the condition of the two handicapped people, he returned to his cruiser, and soon was in touch with the rescue squad.

In a few minutes, he returned to tell Alex, "All set. I've passed the messages, and the squad will be at the dock to meet you."

"Thanks. I don't know what I'd have done if you hadn't come here."

"Well, I'm glad I was able to be of some help. I'm Braxton Hall, of D.C. and a medical student at Georgetown University." He stuck out a hand to shake with Alex. "Sorry I can't stay, but I think you have things under control here. Let me take another look at your friend Donna. I want to be sure I didn't miss anything." He went down on hands and knees to give Donna a closer examination, felt all over her body, and said, "Other than being unconscious, she has suffered damage only to her head. The blood has coagulated, and that's a good sign."

"Thanks, Mr. Hall, I appreciate all that you've done."

"Call me Braxton, and give me your telephone number. I'll wait for just a bit and confirm the call I made just to be sure you'll be met. I'll call you later and see how your friend makes out. I wish I could do more for you, but my father in the cabin there is quite old and ill. I'm taking him to St. Inigoes, otherwise I'd follow you back to the dock.

"Keep her comfortable, but don't waste time getting into port, and admit her to the hospital as soon as you can. Good luck!"

Alex pulled in his bumpers, and released the lines to Braxton's cruiser, and waved as the boat pulled away. He noticed that it moved slowly, and Braxton waved, and stayed close as though ready to come back if needed. Alex knelt down by Donna, to whisper, "You're going to be all right, baby. Just hang in there 'till we get to the dock, then to the hospital." He bent down to kiss her cheek, and as he did so, a tear fell on her face.

He turned on the motor, and as he fled up stream, he saw Braxton waving to him in the distance. Alex looked skyward, called out, "Thank you, God," and looked down at his love, motionless on the deck. The throttle was thrust as far as it could go, and the boat sliced the waves as it sped homeward.

As the boat cleared the river and entered the cove, his watch said 4:40 p.m., and there was Joe Alerdyce with Ben Murdoc, waiting and waving on the dock next to his wheelchair.

"Am I ever glad to see you guys," he said as he tossed lines for them to secure his boat. They scrambled down the ladder with the stretcher, and helped Alex to place Donna on it carefully.

Joe was a medic, and took a quick look at her. "Nothing serious we need to do at the moment, Alex. She's unconscious, a gash on the head, slight abrasions. Powell knows we're meeting you, and the resident said he'd be waiting for us."

"I know him, John White, a good man. Get Donna in the ambulance, and take off. I can handle this now. Tell them I'll be right along."

The flashing lights and siren attracted Randolph Keyes, and he came running down to the dock. "Hi, Alex, What's the trouble?"

"It's Donna, got hit by a boom, and is unconscious. The boys are taking her to Powell."

"What can I do to help?"

"I'd appreciate it if you could give me a hand to get up and into my chair, so I can follow the ambulance. Then if you and one of the boys could secure the boat and stow my gear in the boathouse, that would be a great help. Many thanks."

As he helped Alex up, he inquired, "What happened that Donna got hit? She's been pretty good on board, and so far no mishaps."

"She was doing OK until we had to tack, and when she rose to change position, the wind caught the boom, which swung around and clipped her on the side of the head. It was so sudden, and I wasn't watching her."

"Does the wound look bad? Has she been out for long?"

"It's pretty nasty, but the blood has stopped flowing. A med student came by on a cruiser and helped us. I think she'll be all right once she gets to the hospital."

"There you are," the dean said as Alex settled into his chair. "Shove off and let me know how we can be of assistance. We'll take care of your gear here."

As he drove along, he could see the ambulance way down the road, and he increased his speed. Once he knew she was in the hospital, he relaxed, but he still hurried to get into the emergency room to explain to John what had taken place.

"Alex, we've got to run some tests on her, and do a complete examination, then we'll put her in ICU. Why don't you call her family, then go home to freshen up, grab a bite, and come back. By that time, we should have some definite information on her condition."

Alex wheeled himself to his office and called the Edwards house. Clara answered the telephone. "Hi! You're back earlier than expected. How was the day?"

"It was fine, and the wind was just right for us. We got in just a little bit ago. Is Mr. Edwards around?"

"No, he went out about fifteen minutes ago, and said he'd return as soon as he ran some errands. Tell Donna I've cleared up all the things she asked me to."

"Good. Will do. I'm at home now, and when Mr. Edwards returns ask him to give me a call. Many thanks." Purposely he didn't mention he was at the hospital, for that would have raised questions he did not want to answer at that time.

If Joe called him by the time he left home after he showered, and had a bite, he'd call Joe from the hospital.

At home he had freshened up and had a mouthful of a sandwich and milk when the phone rang. "Alex, Joe Edwards, you left a call for me."

Quickly Alex told Joe that his daughter had been hit by a flying boom, and she was now in Powell Hospital. "She was unconscious when I left, and I'm getting ready to go back there now."

"How serious, Alex?"

"We don't know yet. Dr. White was examining her when I left. I'll see you over there."

"I haven't fed Mabel yet, but perhaps Clara can do that for us."

"Ask her to stand by, and if she has a date, maybe the boyfriend can come to the house and wait there for us."

When he came to Alex's office, he said that Clara was wonderful when he told her what had happened. She took over, would feed Mabel and not tell her what had happened to Donna. She'd hold the line open for any calls that might come from the hospital.

When Dr. White came to Alex's office about seven o'clock, he acknowledged Joe and said, "Donna is resting comfortably. You did everything possible on the boat, especially stopping the flow of blood. There are no broken bones, and all vital signs are functioning properly. We won't know the extent of brain damage until tomorrow when we'll run more tests. She may snap out of this quickly, maybe during the night. Anyway, we have her in ICU."

"As you can appreciate, Dr. White, I'm most anxious for my daughter, and it appears that you've done all you can at this moment. Is there anything I can or should do?"

"Nothing, except to pray that she recovers quickly."

"As you may know, my wife . . ."

"Yes, now I know. The name is familiar. I've seen your wife here for treatment. You may need to break the news to her gently. Her progress from the stroke is not going as well as I had hoped."

"May we see Donna now?"

"Certainly. Alex, you know where . . ."

"Thanks, John. I'll be in touch. You on duty tomorrow? Good. I'll come around here after church in the morning."

Her breathing was regular, her face a bit flushed and her body under the sheets was still. The two men watched quietly, Joe taking her hand in his, pressing it and hoping for a response. None. After fifteen minutes, he stood and said, "Alex, there's not much I can do here. I'd better get home to Mabel and break the news to her."

"Good night, Joe. I'll stay here for an hour or so."

Chapter XXXVIII

"I'm pleased to announce that this, our June meeting will be the last for several months. Many of you have told me that with school out, and plans for the summer taking shape, we should hold our next meeting in October. If any of our subcommittees desire to meet, you are at liberty to do so. I'll announce the date, time, and place for the fall meeting later."

Jule then turned to the business at hand. "Since we postponed the May meeting, this is the first opportunity we've had to talk about the tragic happenings in April. None of us can forget the pictures in the *Star* of the devastation in the house on the old Fielding property in which two prominent physicians were killed by the blast of a bomb, and the presence of a fifteen-year-old girl who had received an illegal abortion by one of the doctors."

Dr. Sargent was sitting next to Rita and murmured to her, "Good riddance to them. Pat Bolton was a disgrace to the profession, and Dave Salter was a sneak and unreliable. Had I known what they had been up to, I'd have pressed charges and run them out of the medical society."

Rita said quietly, "Thank God, Judy Ashton is alive and well. She had a rough time of it, and I hope this teaches her a lesson. Her parents are something else. I couldn't get to first base with her mother."

Jule resumed, "At least one good thing came out of the

disaster, and that is the drug scene seems to have abated here. Sergeant Garrity do you have a comment?"

Mike rose to his feet. "Yes, Mrs. Rohm. I'm glad you used the term, 'abated,' but I'm not optimistic that we have wiped out the scourge of drugs in our area. These drugs are insidious, and I'd not be surprised to learn they will be resurfacing.

"Luigi Falk is in the hands of the federal authorities, but the boss in New York has disappeared, no doubt tipped off before he could be arrested. I'm sure another mobster will become the boss and carry on the business. So, we must be vigilant. If two doctors can get caught, other prominent men might fall for the lure of easy money. In the event 'pushers' show up in the fall near the high school, we'd better catch them early, and eliminate further heartaches."

Sydney and Lettie Rogers stood up. Lettie was recognized. "We were able to get our Code of Behavior approved by the student council and the faculty. One of the items is that anyone who signs off on it will refrain from drugs and alcohol, and will also report the presence of any 'pusher' seen near the school. There are many other items on the code, and we've given copies to you for distribution."

Sydney then spoke. "We had a more difficult time at the college, for the code was seen by some as an invasion of their rights as individuals. The council finally approved it, and copies are available for any student who wants one. At least we tried, and most of the council and students approve of what we've done. Now, let's see how well it works."

Jule recognized Dr. Sargent. "Since we are the only hospital around, we accept all persons coming to us for service. We have watched closely the young people in our clinics, and particularly the young unmarried teenagers who arrive in our OB-GYN clinics.

"The fluctuating stream of these adolescents rose in the

first three months, then dropped in April, leveled off in May, and hopefully June will show a decrease. Perhaps our work here is bearing fruit, and I'll believe it when we continue to show a steady decline in numbers. These girls are from both white and black families, with the latter having a greater number."

Ted Queen stood to say, "We've held meetings with some of our black parishioners, and talks by a nurse may be responsible for some of the lower numbers you mentioned."

"Are we doing anything with the parents of our youth, the young men who are partially responsible for these impregnations?" the doctor asked. It takes two to consummate a conception, and there's no point in directing our efforts at the girls, when the boys are also involved, and we don't bear down on them."

Meredith March rose, "That's part of our Code of Behavior. We're trying to get all our students to sign off on it, boys as well as girls."

Al Burns raised his hand. "In our young people's groups, we are trying to get across the same message: Have respect for yourself and the other person, and especially as it pertains to activities between the sexes. We have discussed bodily functions, the use of 'dirty' words, what is appropriate when out on a date, and the dangers of going all the way. At first it was embarrassing for some, but as we talked, the kids relaxed and now these matters are openly discussed."

Mrs. Cameron Price shifted her conservative bulk and rumbled, "Certainly we can be proud of our students in their efforts to promote a Code of Behavior for their peers, and I applaud Reverend Burns' young people for their down to earth talks, but what about the adolescents who don't sign off on the Code, or don't attend church groups? How do they get the messages we are hoping to spread about sex activity, drinking, and using drugs? Who instructs them and what are the messages?"

Tim Borders replied, "I know I'm sticking my neck way out, but I still feel this is a job the schools must tackle. Few parents talk with their kids on this, and more power to those who do. The great majority leave it alone and hope the kids get the information elsewhere."

Mrs. Price asked, "Tim, are you suggesting that our public schools include a health service clinic which will provide pills and condoms as well as explicit sex information classes?"

"If that is the price we have to pay to keep our children from having babies, so be it."

"I can assure you, Mr. Borders, that the school board will pass this only over my dead body!"

There was a flurry of murmurs at this exchange.

Jule quieted things down by saying, "Do we have statistics as to where these adolescents come from, any area of the city where this predominates?"

Rita answered, "Yes, mostly from the eastern part, and a few from the central part."

Mrs. Beatrice Jackson, a black parent said, "That means a black population, and a few scattered white families. If we are to concentrate on the family as a source of such information, this means the mothers will have to be helped, for they are the ones who carry the load. I'd like to suggest that we work with mothers groups in the affected areas, help them with information for their daughters and sons. I know this will scare many of them, but it's worth a try."

Rita turned to her and said, "We'll be happy to assist, and we'll get pamphlets as a guide for them."

Ken Patrick stood to say, "The articles in the *Star* will be available for any such meetings, and I think some of us might talk at these meetings to let the mothers know how serious is the business we've been discussing."

When the group adjourned at 12:30 Rita and Jule had

lunch at the Howard Johnson Motel. Jule said, "I'm glad our sessions are over for the summer. We accomplished quite a lot, and I'm impressed with our student members and their code and the handouts."

"We sure got the community involved, with the mayor, state troopers, the school board, the media, parents, etc. It has been good for all of us," Rita said.

"Let's talk about some important things, Jule. What's new with you?"

"Not much. I enjoy the job, but I still want to get into private practice, the girls are thriving and I'm happy here."

Jule confided to her friend that she and the girls attend St. Agnes Church regularly, and feel at home in the church and with Don. "He has been to our house often for dinner. The girls are drawn to this gentle soul and he enjoys being with them. Don is such a fine person and would make a devoted husband and father to Alma and Ruth."

"Would there be problem with his church if you decided to marry? Do the Episcopalians frown on divorce, and especially for a priest to marry a divorcee?"

"I'll leave that up to Don to explore. What's with you these days?"

"The only concern I have now is with Alex Snyder. He's so distraught worrying about Donna. She's the light of his life, and she's still in a coma. Our neurologist recommended that she be transferred to Johns Hopkins in Baltimore where they are doing research on head injuries. She's been there for a week now, and Alex has been spending all his spare time at her bedside."

"Who's taking care of her message center activities?"

"The student I sent there to learn about working with the visually handicapped, Clara Pucci, has stepped in and is doing all the work now. She is a wonderful girl, and gets along great with Mabel, and this has really helped Joe. Clara is on summer vacation, so she's there full time, and Joe has offered to pay her. It is working out well for everyone."

✄ ✄ ✄

Trinity Sunday was a bright, clear, warm day, and as the parishioners filed out from St. Dunstan's Church, Rita, Joe and the family moved over to the parking lot, where they could see Father Shane talking with Alex. "Padre, please remember Donna and me in your prayers."

"I know, Alex, I always do. How is she doing at Johns Hopkins?"

"Thank God, she's still alive, and it's been three weeks since she went into the coma, and she hasn't moved a muscle since. Her father and I are going to visit her today."

The Evans family joined them for a brief chat, and as they were leaving, Rita invited Alex to bring Joe Edwards back to their house on their return from Baltimore. "You come, too, Father."

Father Tom arrived at the Evans house at five o'clock, and twenty minutes later, Alex and Joe drove into the car port.

Rita looked at Joe Edwards without saying a word.

He responded to her unspoken question. "Donna is still in a coma, and resting. There's been no change in her condition. I've given permission for the doctors to perform an operation on Tuesday which they think might help her. We'll have to wait and see."

Alex had lost much of his pep, but managed to say to Father Tom, "Padre, haul out some of your best prayers for the success of the operation on Tuesday. This has gotta be good. I'm just about strung out waiting."

The operation took over three hours on Tuesday, and afterward, Dr. Jonas O'Hearne talked with Joe and Alex. "The procedure should restore her to consciousness, and we hope to remove the bandages on Thursday. All we can do now is hope and pray."

On Friday morning Dr. O'Hearne came to Donna's room to remove the bandages. He noted on her chart that the night nurse wrote that the patient had stirred, moved her arms and hands, shifted her body, then drifted off to sleep. While the doctor was reading the chart, Donna awoke and called out "Alex! Did you get the sheet on the starboard side? Oh, my head! It hurts! Where am I?"

"Don't be afraid, Miss Edwards. You've had an accident, and you're in good hands. Your friend Alex is out in the waiting room with your father. Also, you're in a Baltimore hospital. Can you hear me?"

"Yes, but faintly. Who are you? I'm in a hospital?"

"I'm Doctor O'Hearne, on the staff here at Johns Hopkins Hospital."

Donna was quiet for a minute, then said, "What happened?"

"When you were in the sailboat, the boom hit you on the side of your head and sent you almost over the side. Alex grabbed you and held on. That was several weeks ago, and you've been out ever since. The other day we operated on you, and it looks as though you've come through in fine shape."

" My head, it's covered with bandages . . ."

"Yes and this is the day we remove the bandages from your head and eyes."

"Yes, but you know I can't see . . ."

"I'm aware that you've had a visual impairment, but I still want to look at your eyes and your head to see how it's healing."

Gently, the doctor removed the head bandage first, then the ones over her eyes. When she complained that her eyes

hurt, he replied that he was not touching her. Then she asked
that he turn off the lights, and he replied that it was daylight.

"Nurse, lower the shades, and Donna, close your eye
lids, then when I tell you, slowly open one eye, and then
the other. We may have something here."

Fifteen minutes later, Joe and Alex were in the bedroom
to see a joyous Donna, half crying, tears streaming down her
face.

"Daddy, I think I can see you!" she cried out, raising her
arms for him to come to her.

He ran to the bed, watching her eyes which were open
and clear, her blonde hair shaved at the point of the operation,
with a small bandage on the scars. Joe's tears mingled with
hers as they embraced, cried, and smothered one another
with kisses. "I can't believe this is happening to you," he
said, reaching for a handkerchief to dry his eyes and blow
his nose.

The nurse handed a Kleenex to Donna so she could do
the same.

"Daddy, I'm so happy, I could cry," and the tears flowed
again.

It took both a few minutes to regain control, then Donna
said, "I can see shapes more clearly now, and the more I look,
you're coming into focus. It's so good to be able to see my
dear father."

Joe kissed her again, then said to her, "Can you see who
is also here?"

Alex inched closer to the bed, as Joe backed away.

"Who is this wonderful man, whose voice I'd know
anywhere? Alex, is that you behind the dark beard I can barely
see? Come closer." Alex had his handkerchief out, wiping
tears from his eyes as he leaned over to touch her hand. "You
can see my beard and face? Thank God you're back, twice
over, from the coma, and now with some vision. I don't know

what to say, Donna, just that it's good to hear your voice again."

There was a quiet celebration and more tears of joy at Donna's return from the darkness. Finally, Dr. O'Hearne told the men that he wanted his patients to rest, and he had some medications to administer.

"Now she needs rest, and when you come back tomorrow, she'll be much better."

Back in the corridor, the two men embraced, shook hands, and wept a little more. "It's so good to have her back to life, Alex. I was afraid for a while that she was a goner."

"All I can say is that the power of prayer is unending."

When Alex left Joe off at his house, Marion opened the door, saw the beam on his face, and said, "How did it go?"

"You'd never believe it. The operation was a success and she's out of the coma, and looks wonderful!"

"I'm so happy for you, Mr. Edwards. You must be relieved to have that over and done with."

"Wait till you hear this. Donna's vision is almost completely restored! The doctor told me he's not quite sure how it happened, but when he removed the bandages from her eyes, she could see. He was as excited as we all were."

When Marion heard this she gave Joe a hug of joy, as Clara came out of the message center and heard the last words.

"Donna can see? She's out of the coma and now can see? I'm so pleased and happy for you," she said and gave him a hug and a kiss.

"Now, I must go in and tell Donna's mother the good news."

Mabel was in her wheelchair when he came up from behind and kissed her on the forehead, then told her the news of Donna's recovery and the return of her sight. At this, her eyes lit up, she managed a smile, then reached for a

Kleenex to wipe her eyes. She scratched on her pad, "When she home?"

"We don't know yet. The doctor has some work to do with her, but I'm sure it will be as soon as possible."

In the kitchen with the two girls, Joe said, "I feel the need to celebrate. Care to join me in a drink?"

Marion said, "You deserve one, a big fat one or two. Yes, I'll be happy to join you in celebration. Make mine white wine, and a Coke for Clara."

"I certainly appreciate what you girls have done for all of us. It's a relief to know the house and center are in good hands while I've been at work or in the hospital. Clara has been such a help. We'd be lost without her here, taking care of Mrs. Edwards and running the center all by herself."

"I like being here, Mr. Edwards, and working with Donna has been good for me. I've learned quite a lot about the visually handicapped."

She returned to the message center, taking her Coke, while Marion and Joe sat in the kitchen talking about their good news.

"As soon as we knew about Donna's accident, I notified Mother Benedicta at the Carmelite Convent, and I'm sure she had the nuns on their knees praying for her speedy recovery. Wait until I tell her that Donna has most of her vision back, and she can see."

"I should ask for a dose of prayer therapy for Mrs. Edwards, but I'm afraid she doesn't care for Catholics, and this is another reason she and Alex don't get along. It wasn't easy before, but when he became a 'born again' Catholic, that was just too much."

"Too bad, for he's such a great guy. They make a nice team."

When Alex got back to his house, the first thing he did was to call the rectory.

"Father Tom? Alex here. We've just returned from Baltimore and I have great news. Donna is out of the coma, and the operation has restored much of her vision. She now has partial sight, and this will improve as time goes on."

"Thank God! That is wonderful news. I'll be happy to say a Mass for her and for you."

The next call was to the Evans, and when Rita answered, he passed on the good news. She was elated and thanked him for calling.

On the day of Donna's discharge from Johns Hopkins, Alex had too many appointments to break, so Joe went alone to bring her back. Dr. O'Hearne told her before she left the room, "Take these drops twice a day in each eye. They will help to relieve the pressure, and gradually improve your vision. I'd like to see you back here in a month, to see what progress has been made. You're a brave girl. Good luck!"

It was a joyous reunion when Alex went to her house after work, and accepted an invitation to stay for dinner.

"Wow! Don't you look ravishing, all in red, my favorite color," he told her.

She leaned down to kiss him, and gave him a hug. "You're like a cuddly bear with that beard, and I love it. Now that I can see you better, I'm going to love you all the more."

Joe came over to ask, "You need some sustenance? Scotch?"

"Yes and make it a double."

He rolled over to be in front, and adjacent to Mabel in her chair, took her hand in his and looking in her eyes said, "It's so wonderful to have Donna back home again with us."

Mabel smiled weakly, nodded her head and withdrew her hand. These antagonists tossed inward, silent barbs to one another. The mother carefully guarding her daughter, while the suitor fought to keep and hold her love. They would never change their positions.

Clara came in dressed to leave. She waved to Mabel and Alex saying, "Got a date tonight, and must get ready for him." She planted a kiss and gave Donna a hug. "I'll be in tomorrow and tell you all about what's been going on in the center. We're up to date at this point. 'Night."

Donna wanted to help prepare dinner, but she became tired and stretched out on a sofa until dinner was ready. Alex took his drink out to the kitchen and talked with Joe while he made the dinner.

Alex called her every day for a brief chat while she convalesced. Soon she began to realize that he was changing. He was cheerful, but there was a certain restraint in his voice, quite unlike the Alex she knew.

When he had missed a day in calling her, she called him to inquire, "Alex, it's getting warm, even hot these June days. Are you going to invite me sailing?"

"I'd like to Donna, but I wasn't sure you'd want to return to the scene of the accident."

"I'm dying to go out again. You couldn't keep me away. Now I want to see everything, the boat, river, bay, everything possible."

"You sure about that?"

"Would I be calling if I wasn't sincere about sailing with you?"

"Great. Are you free this Saturday? I'll get the drinks, and you do the food. I'll pick you up about eleven o'clock."

Now that Donna could see the boat house and the dock, she marveled at this new world she could view. She got a big kick out of the rig he used to lower himself down to the deck, and the basket to place provisions on board. Once they were in the cockpit, she turned to him and said, "First, captain, a hug and a kiss for good luck," and with that she leaned over him, a low cut shirt exposing her bra and full breasts to give him a warm loving embrace.

"Now to get underway," and she went forward to cast off the lines.

Soon they were on the river, Alex with one hand on the wheel, the other wrapped around a beer, while she sat in the stern next to him, humming a tune from *Camelot*. She suspected that something was troubling him, but said nothing, and let him make the first move. It came when he said quietly, "I think, Donna, we'd better ease off a bit . . ."

"What do you mean, ease off?"

"Things have changed somewhat and now that you can see better . . ."

She broke in, "Are you telling me that our love, this relationship has diminished because I've regained some vision? That you don't want to be my eyes anymore?"

"It's different now. You can be independent, and go anywhere."

"Not for a long time, Alex. The doctor says I've made remarkable progress, but I'm still fuzzy and will need help for some time."

"OK. But now you have good travel vision and can do so many things unaided. Give yourself a break and don't get tied to a wheelchair." Alex was angry and upset as he said this to her. And more angry with himself that he had to reveal what was in his mind.

Donna looked out over the river and remained silent for five minutes. She was hurt, and the joy of being out on the boat again with him was roughly taken away. Then she asked, "Suppose it was the other way around, and suddenly you regained the use of your legs. How would you feel if I said 'Let's cool it but remain good friends?' Well?"

"That's different, Donna."

"No it isn't. It's the very same thing, only in reverse. If you hadn't come along, I'd be a stodgy, prim maid going back and forth to D.C. daily and having no fun. Now, I'm alive, and have you to thank for so many things."

"Including getting conked on the head, which almost killed you."

"As a result of which, I now have more sight than before, and can do more things with and for you. It will even get better!"

The arguments raged back and forth, neither one ready to give an inch on his or her position. Donna surprised herself and Alex with the way she fought to hold him. At one point he said, "Your mother would love this repartee, and think it's the only way . . . "

"Mother is a selfish woman. The only way we can handle this is a simple question which I'll put to you right now. Alex Snyder, will you marry me, quickly, without fanfare?"

"God, Donna, you're putting it right up to me!"

"You're damn tootin'—to take a slice of your own language. Well?"

"OK. Yes. I surrender! I should have known better than to even try to let go of you. We'll follow through on our plans for a wedding later this year, but let's ride this out a bit."

"That's better. Kiss me and we'll make up." She made sure he was aware of her passionate nature, and managed to expose as much of her bra and breasts as possible. She murmured in his ear, "I'll let you off the hook this time, but watch out. Anymore of this chatter, and I'll rape you, then you'll have to marry me."

That broke the spell, he roared with laughter and she joined him. "Get up forward, woman, and get me a cold beer. I need to quench a fire within me."

The remainder of the sail was pleasant, and she enjoyed seeing the places along the shore as he pointed them out. When they came back up the river, Donna said, "Isn't this about the place where the doctors kept their boat? And the house is close by?"

"Yes. Their cove is just over there. Shall we go in and look around?"

"Foolish question! By all means we'll look."

The dock was empty, for Dave's boat had been sold. They could look up toward the house, and the front looked as though there was little damage."

"It's all around back. I drove down there recently, but couldn't get in. The back is severely burned out, the garage and rooms above appear to be a total wreck."

They talked about the extent of the damage, how much it would take to get it liveable once more, how could they get a key to go inside and look around, etc.

As they drove home, they talked about the possibilities of the house and what it would take to put it in order. When they arrived, Joe was taking it easy for a change, and he invited them to have a round of drinks while they exchanged ideas. Joe said, "It sounds good, but I'd like to see the place in its burned out state before I make any judgements. Can we see it tomorrow?"

"Sure, right after I go to church and get a bite to eat."

By noontime they were on the road in Alex's car to see the house and property. When they arrived, Alex parked at the entrance to the driveway so they could get a view of the burned out rear, with the windows all boarded up. Donna got out, and walked around to the front. Alex hauled out his wheelchair, and went as far as he could.

Donna was gay, smiling, and excited about the prospects, Joe was noncommittal, while Alex stewed in his chair. He was concerned about many things, especially the financing, and could he swing the deal, how to maintain the place if he bought it. It was a warm day, but the perspiration came not so much from the heat as from the energy he expended in thinking, and also some effort on his part to get his chair as close to the side door as possible.

Around front, Donna peered into the living room. "Daddy, look here and see that big hole over there by the kitchen. It goes right down into the basement. It looks awful!"

"On the other hand, dear, that's good. If Alex buys the place, he can put an elevator there from the ground level up to the kitchen, and he's got it made!"

They walked along the deck, and Joe remarked, "These guys sure knew what they were doing when they placed this house here. Look at that view of the river. This deck, what a place to just laze in the sun and relax! I could fall in love with this spot—and the house—except I know the rear end is a shell."

Donna walked along the front, peeking into the bedroom windows. "See, there's no damage at all in any of these rooms. Everything is in place. Let's go back and tell Alex what we've seen out here."

They gathered by Alex's chair and told him the results of their view of the front. Donna was thrilled and bubbled over with her description of the rooms. Joe was excited when he told about the hole in the kitchen where an elevator could be placed for Alex.

Alex raised the question to Joe, "Care to assess the damage? And what it would take to renovate?"

"I'm no engineer or carpenter, but it looks worse than it actually is. I'd guess that about 55,000 dollars would put it back in reasonable shape. That's a ball park figure. Essentially the house is pretty solid, and the property is valuable."

"Thanks, Joe. I need to do some thinking and scribbling."

The next week, Alex called Mrs. Salter, identified himself, and indicated that they had met when she visited the hospital recently. He explained the purpose of his call to inquire into the possibility of entering the house her late husband had built with the idea he might like to purchase it. She told him that Mrs. Bolton was her agent, and that she had keys to the place. "I'll call her and tell her you would like to see the inside."

Events moved along swiftly from that point. While Alex sat in his chair studying the outside, Amy and Donna went through the entire house, capturing every room with an instant picture camera. Later they laid them out on the dash board and front seat, examining each one, as the women explained the damage. "You can almost follow the path of the blast, emanating from the recreation room, through the garage, totaling the cars there. It blew a hole up through the ceiling into the kitchen, wrecked that place, and moved into the dining room. The bomb in the clinic wrecked it, forced a hole in the ceiling, then blasted the wall into the living room. Fire and water damage was extensive as you might expect, and here we see the soggy mess. It still smells awful in there."

Donna said, "My father was right. The house is well built and sturdy. The damage is great, but not as bad as it looks."

Alex asked Amy, "Could you see everything in all the rooms?"

"Yes. The bedrooms and bathrooms are intact, some slight water and smoke damage. The other rooms are as we described them. I feel the house is repairable."

Joe was pleased to see all the pictures, and they pored over them at great length. Before she left, Donna said, "Mrs. Salter wants to unload the house as soon as possible and she's asking 125,000 dollars for the whole kit and kaboodle, but for cash, she'd come down a bit."

There was more discussion about the need for an elevator, flattening thresholds and removal of thick rugs so the wheelchair would have access to the rooms.

Fired up with enthusiasm, Donna and Alex began to make plans for the renovations, assuming they would be the purchasers. They would have to wait, also, for the estate to pass through the probate court, but Amy felt that this would be completed in the near future. She encouraged them to proceed with their plans for an estimation of the cost so they'd have firm figures when they met with Mrs. Salter for her decision.

Alex called Martin MacIntyre, a local contractor for an expert evaluation of the cost to renovate. "I did a lot of work counseling his son when he got in trouble. I think he owes me one."

"Hello, Mac? Alex Snyder calling. I need some information and figures." He proceeded to ask for an estimate of the damages to the house.

In three days, the contractor called back. "That's a mighty fine place there, Alex, with sturdy walls and good workmanship evident throughout. To renovate the damaged areas, replace the kitchen equipment, and install an elevator would run about $50,000."

"As you can imagine, I'm interested in buying the house and property from the widow, just as soon as her husband's will is probated. If I can meet her price, are you available to take on this job?"

"Depends on the timing. I'd need about a month's lead time, but sure, I can do it. No problem."

Chapter XXXIX

"Rita? When you wrap up for the day, may I come in and chew the rag?"

"Sure, Alex. Make it at 4:15."

He wheeled in, lit a cigarette, and announced, "I need to bounce some things off your head, and since I respect your judgement, I want you to be honest with me."

"Let it ride . . ."

"First, it's about Donna. I'm very much in love with that girl, but now that she has greatly improved vision with chances that it will get better, I don't want her to be tied to me and this condition."

"How does she feel about your attitude? Have you talked this over with her?"

"Yes, and she gave me a tongue lashing you wouldn't believe. She'll have none of my nonsense—even threatened to rape me so I couldn't escape. What a girl!"

"My friend, she is one lovely girl, and has a good head on her shoulders. You should know that true love transcends the physical attributes, and will out last all adversities. So what if one partner has an impediment, it should not destroy the partnership. You both were doing well before she regained her sight, why should this be a hindrance. Go for it, or you'll be the loser."

"The other thing is the house that Pat Bolton and Dave

Salter had bombed out from under them. I'd like to buy it, once it is available."

"Think you could swing it?"

"I've asked Mrs. Salter for first crack and she is encouraging."

"What about the damage, repairs, and the financing? Can you handle all that?"

"You remember Marvin MacIntyre, whose son we helped, and we got him settled? Well, he checked the damage and gave me an estimate of fifty thousand to put it together again. Amy Bolton tells me that Mrs. Salter will be asking 125,000 dollars, but will take less for cash when it goes on the market. I'll need about $165,000 to lock up the deal."

"That's a lot of cabbage, Alex. Got a money print shop at home?"

"No, but I have some resources in my house, stocks and bonds, my disability pension, and my salary. With a hefty down payment, I could take out a thirty-year mortgage and swing it."

"Apparently you've been doing some figuring, and can handle it. If Donna is there . . ."

"Yeah, she could move in her message center and we'd get a tax break for using the house for business purposes."

"You could rent out dock space and add this to your payments. What about maintenance outside?"

"I've thought of talking to the group that does maintenance for Father Tom at St. Dunstan's. Inside, Donna would want to do her own housework."

"You rascal, you're going to marry her after all! Good man. Does she know yet?"

"Well, yes. I need to talk to her father and get his thoughts on all this. Then, I'll let her keep the engagement ring."

A twinkle came to Rita's eyes. "Really, Alex, why don't you let her rape you? It would be fun to see her conquer that bold masculine front you thrust out. Seriously, I'm happy for you, and believe you've done some positive thinking about your lives together. Congratulations!" With that, she came from around her desk to his chair, leaned down and gave him a warm hug and a kiss.

When Alex talked with Joe two nights later, he received the same encouragement and a strong handshake from the man he admired.

"Donna wants a fall wedding, and having made these decisions, I think we should go inside and break the news to her mother."

Donna had been in the center office typing, and came to join them. She knew of her father's conversation with Alex, but was a bit nervous as the trio entered Mabel's bedroom.

"Mabel," Joe said, "Donna and Alex have an announcement to make," he said as he laid a comforting hand on her shoulder. He was aware of how she'd take the news, and he was hoping it wouldn't upset her too much.

Mabel had been sitting quietly in her chair watching TV and turned as the three entered. She looked up, a bit surprised, as they came right in front of her. Alex sat, immobile, his right hand in Donna's as she reached out to place her left hand on her mother's arm. "Mother, Alex and I are very much in love, and we are going to set plans for our wedding."

Mabel jerked her hand away from her daughter, looked her in the eyes, and tears sprang up, and rolled down her cheeks. She grabbed for a handkerchief, to dab at her eyes and stiffened up in her chair, as though affronted by a verbal attack.

Donna looked at her father, and continued. "I know how you feel about this man, but please, for my sake, accept him. He is a fine person, one who has made me happy, and I feel alive again."

Mabel stiffened even more in her chair, her eyes flashed

defiance, and every muscle in her body fought her daughter's words. She looked first at Donna, then at her husband who shook his head as if to say, be kind and willing to our child, give her this chance; then to Alex and the fierceness of her glance told him that she wasn't about to surrender her daughter to a man in a wheelchair. "No!" she screamed from every portion of her body, especially from her face.

Donna continued, "We've talked with Father Shane, and he will marry us in St. Dunstan's church. That may displease you, for I know your attitude about the Catholic Church, but I am resolved to marry him and bring up our children in the Catholic faith. Could we please, please Mother, have your blessing on our marriage? I beg you!"

Joe was standing by her side, with one hand on her shoulder, and as his daughter pleaded her cause, he put pressure on his hand to indicate that she should nod assent, or give some indication that she'd approve of the union. He leaned down to whisper in her ear, "Let go of her! Let her be free to start her own life with the man she loves. Your bitterness will destroy us all. If you love Donna, you'll want her to be happy. You know how I feel about these two, and I've given them my blessings for their marriage."

Alex sat silent. There were so many things he wanted to say, but felt this was between the family members, and he'd better keep his mouth closed, but he was boiling inside.

Mabel looked again at her daughter wordlessly, then at Alex and she went right through him. Finally at Joe, giving him a signal that she wanted to return to her bedroom, moving her hand on the wheel as if to get out as quickly as possible. Joe pushed the chair out of the room, and said not a word.

Donna fell on her knees before Alex, who took her in his arms. "Don't cry, my love. Your mother is not herself." Donna, crying bitterly, kissed her man, clasped her arms around his neck, but her fists were clenched in a rage. "Why, why does she do this to me?" she wailed.

Joe came back to the living room, and Donna rose, to embrace him, and sob loudly. "Don't cry, dear. I think the stroke has affected her mind. Don't pay attention to her. I know she wanted the best for you. Look ahead now and start your planning with Alex. We'll get through this all right. Don't worry. You'll always have me at your side. We both love you in our own ways. Be strong and don't worry."

❧ ❧ ❧

On a stifling hot day in mid July, Mabel did not wake up. She seemed to regress after her rejection of Donna's plans to marry, and became morose, unwilling to communicate with anyone. On this morning, after Joe had gone to work, Donna listened for the bell Mabel usually tinkled when she wanted to get up. By 9:30, Donna opened her door and called softly, "Mother, are you ready?" When there was no answer, she went to the bed, and found her mother still. She felt the face, and there was no sign of life. Her skin was cold.

"Oh my God! Mother's dead!" Donna fell to her knees, and buried her head in the soft summer blanket covering her mother. She cried bitterly, and wondered if she was the cause of her mother's death. After a few minutes, she raised the sheet over her mother's face, now calm and peaceful looking, and ran to the telephone to call her father.

Joe was home in an hour, shaken and weary. Donna met him at the door, and they embraced, cried, and hung on to one another. "She was a good woman, Donna, and we had many a good time together."

"I know, Daddy. She was good to me in her own way. Now she's gone and I'll miss her."

When he heard the news, Alex told Rita, then left for the

Edwards house to comfort Donna and help in whatever way he could.

Randall's Funeral Parlor was filled with friends of the family, a few relatives of Mabel's, and Joe's sisters. Father Shane in his black suit and Roman collar read from the Old and New Testaments, and accompanied the procession to the cemetery where he gave the final prayers before internment.

"Thank you Father Shane for being with us at this time. I appreciate all that you've done for her and for us," Joe said afterward. "We've not been churchgoers, maybe we've missed something. Thanks for your help."

Mabel was adamant to the end and beyond. She had made her own will, and Joe was horrified to read, "If my daughter continues to see and marry that man, she will not be the beneficiary of any of my possessions, in which case, fifty percent shall go to charity, as noted herein."

Donna was heartbroken when she read these words, but then consoled herself with the knowledge that soon she'd be married to an exceptional man, and they were happy making plans for their new life. She told her father, "I'll always love you, Daddy, and Alex won't have to worry about an antagonistic mother-in-law."

💥 💥 💥

Alex's parents were on an extended vacation out West, and planned to visit their son Clinton, the navy flier, and his family in San Diego. Grace, his sister, was the only member of his family able to attend Mabel's funeral. Alex had written to his parents of his plans to marry, but it wasn't until late in August that he and Donna drove to Havre de Grave in Maryland to see them and talk about the wedding.

Donna and Alex's mother embraced warmly, and liked

one another immediately. "We are so proud of our son," she said, "and now we'll have a beautiful daughter-in-law in the family. Welcome, my dear."

Amos Snyder was a tall, good-looking man, stately and always well dressed. He was warm in his greetings to Donna, gave her a kiss on the cheek and a hug. "I must say, Alex knows how to pick a pretty girl. You are most welcome to the Snyder family, my dear."

"Why, I'll be honored and happy to be your best man, son," he replied when Alex asked him to stand up for him. "I think this calls for a drink to celebrate the event."

After they toasted one another in champagne, Donna and her new "mom" talked about dresses, colors, and wedding plans. Alex and his father went out to the porch, where Alex told him about his plans to buy the burned out house, renovate it, and make a home for his new bride. He was delighted, and provided some legal and fatherly tips on the sale of his house, contracts for the renovation, and the purchase of the property. Father and son had a genuine warmth for each other and were not afraid to share deep feeling and love.

Amos rose and excused himself to return to the house. He was back shortly with Mom and Donna.

"Alex, your mother and I want to give you and Donna a wedding present. Since we didn't know just what you'd need because you'd both bring furniture from your houses, we felt that this would be of some help as you cement the partnership between our families. Accept this with our great love and affection."

Donna was sitting next to Alex when he opened the envelope looked and gasped, she looked and cried out in surprise. Alex couldn't believe his eyes. "Great Lord above! Look at this!" He waved a check for 25,300 dollars. "Donna, we're rich! I'm stunned!"

Donna took it, read the numbers and said, "I'm speechless!"

"Enjoy it, son," his Mother said. "We live modestly, and have no need for a great deal of money. Your father won a big case recently, and we decided you two should enjoy the spoils. You're just starting out, and can put it to greater advantage than we would. We know you'll use it wisely."

All four hugged one another, and that called for a round of drinks to celebrate once more.

The following weeks were hectic for all concerned. Amy Bolton handled the settlement transferring Mrs. Salter's house to Alex, and told him, "Since I really didn't do too much, I'm not charging a fee for services. This is my wedding present to you and Donna. I think it's wonderful that you are getting married. The best to you both."

The contractor, Marvin MacIntyre, was jubilant with the contract. "I'll order the materials right away. We can start in a week, and hope to be all finished and out by the latter part of September."

Alex told him, "As soon as you clear out the garage and install the elevator, I want to use it and poke around on the first floor. If there are any changes to be made, I'll let you know."

❧ ❧ ❧

"Alex, we gotta throw us a party for our piano girl, now that she's managed to hog-tie you," Mike told him. "You tell us the Saturday you want it, and we'll roll out the barrels!" In addition, Mike knew many of Donna's clients at the message center, and made sure to pass the word about her wedding. He was not bashful in proposing that they all chip in and get her something nice, adding facetiously "like a keg of beer?"

Donna had asked Rita to help her choose a dress, so the

two went into Washington to shop and spend money wildly.

Marion and Clara planned a shower for the bride-to-be at their house, and when Donna arrived, she was pleasantly surprised to find so many friends and women clients from her center among the shower of presents.

The two Joe's got their heads together to arrange for the quantity and quality of the liquid refreshments to be served, while Rita and Marion helped Donna with the menu for the wedding feast.

Ken Patrick's *Star* had run a feature on Donna when she regained her sight at Johns Hopkins Hospital, and now he was preparing a spread for the wedding "of two of our city's prominent people."

These days, Alex ate dinner with Donna and Joe, after which they pored over samples, colors, which furniture to take to the new house, equipment in what room, how the message center would be set up, etc.

Clara found herself running the center when Donna was out of the office. She enlisted Kyle to pick up and deliver work, when he was not on duty at the library.

Occasionally they sailed, but most of the time was spent in planning, and visiting the house on weekends to do more planning.

"Alex, are all these rooms barrier free? Can you get the chair in and out of the doors. You'll want no rugs or firm ones so you can get over them readily." Between them, they thought of everything. What pleased them both was the elevator, a noiseless one which, as soon as it was installed, they used going from the garage to the kitchen.

"It's a boom market," Amy said to Alex, as she called him to say that she sold his house for 42,500 dollars. He put this money in the bank until he could transfer it as part of the down payment on the new house.

Gifts began to pile up in her house, and Donna began to

realize how many friends she and Alex had. Clara said, "It looks as though everyone in the city knows about the wedding, and we get loads of congratulatory messages in the center. Alex told me he's swamped with mail at his house."

A week before the wedding, Mac called Alex to tell him, "The house is completed, and you can move in anytime. Good luck!"

Alex hired a truck, Kyle rounded up some friends and moved their possessions from La Plata down to the Snyder property. Donna was on hand to supervise and place furniture where she indicated. "Alex, I can hardly wait to get in here and make this our home."

On the last Saturday of September, over one hundred family and friends gathered at two o'clock in St. Dunstan's church as a radiant Donna, in a light blue dress and matching hat, walked down the aisle on the arm of her father preceded by Rita, her attendant. Alex, in a light grey suit, white shirt, and striped tie waited at the altar, beaming as his bride came down the aisle.

Amos, who was at his side, wore a broad smile, and nodded to his wife in one of the front pews.

Father Tom emerged from the sacristy in white vestments, and in a loud voice performed the ceremony. In his homily, he spoke of the sacredness of marriage, and touched on the courage of the bride and groom in overcoming many obstacles. "Alex and Donna, you have met the challenge successfully, and today we rejoice in witnessing your marriage, and pray that only the best of happiness and joy enter your lives."

From the pulpit, he could see the smiling faces of Don Leyton, Jule and her daughters, Al Burns and his family, Phil and Alyce Mason, Ted Queen, Dr. Sargent, hospital staff members, and many others.

When the new bride kissed her husband, Father Tom leaned over and said, "Me, too," and kissed her on the cheek, then he gave Alex a warm handshake.

As the organ pealed forth, the congregation smiled happily and clapped as the bride wheeled her husband down the aisle and out to a waiting limousine.

The Edwards house was adorned with flowers and balloons, the lawn neatly clipped and the garden alive with more flowers. The hired bartender kept the drinks flowing, and the maids made sure that there was plenty of food on the table for the guests who flowed into and out of the house, onto the patio, and throughout the garden. It was a beautiful celebration.

When Donna turned her back to toss her bridal bouquet away, it landed in the hands of Jule, at which her daughters screamed in delight; she blushed, and Don Leyton laughed heartily. "I hear a message!"

Later Father Tom came up to Don to say, "Ol' buddy, if they give you a hard time, I'll do the job up at my discount rate!"

Alex was supremely happy and greeted all the ladies with a kiss, and the men with a firm handshake. "I'm the luckiest man in the world!"

For Donna, it was a joy to see clearly all the people who before were only voices, and she greeted them with warm embraces. "I'm too happy for words. This is the finest day of my life. I've married a dear man."

By nightfall, the party was over, and the guests departed, everyone declaring that it had been a festive and joyous occasion.

Alex and Donna spent the first night in their new house, and stayed there for a few days to settle in. They then filled the boat with gas and provisions and sailed to St. Michael's Island for an overnight stay. They continued their honeymoon by taking a casual cruise down the Chesapeake Bay.

A new life had begun for two courageous people.

❧ ❧ ❧

After the wedding that evening, snuggled under a lightweight blanket, Joe Evans enveloped Rita in his arms and said, "You're such a dear one. Remember the day we were married, and our first night together? I have wonderful memories of that and all the years since. Now I have a surprise."

"Yes, Joe?"

"We'll be moving. I've received advance notice of a big promotion and reassignment to Santa Clara, California."

"I'm so happy for you dear. I have a surprise for you, too."

"Yes dear. I'm ready for anything."

"How would you like to be a father again? I think I'm pregnant!"

THE END